# MEET HIM
## *At the Altar*

### E.L. KOSLO

# Copyright

Proofing: Nikki @naughtynookpr

Cover Design by @elkoslo_writes

Depositphotos: @ VSart, @ nelliromanov, @ JDBHADLA, @ phatthanit, @ Deebs, @ kateja

# Dedication

This book is dedicated to the mistakes of youth and finding your worth. Learning to accept the hard parts of life without losing yourself is one of the most valuable lessons you can ever learn.

# Chapter One:
## The Wedding
### PRESENT DAY

"Are you ready to put the dress on?" Stefanie asked me as she put her hands on my shoulders.

"Auntie Kenna is gonna look so pretty, momma," the small voice of her daughter, Nathalie, chimed in as she stood at her mother's side, looking adorable in her little lace flower girl dress. Her long blonde locks were braided on the back of her head with a few loose curls around her face. She looked so excited that we'd included her in today's festivities.

"She is, sweetheart. But I think she's freaking out a little." Stefanie's voice was more amused than anything as she made eye contact with me in the mirror. "Why don't you go find Uncle Camden?"

My future niece giggled, and I turned as she swept through the doorway, little blonde braids flying behind her.

"I'm not freaking out," I assured her. I was nervous, but I was okay. It'd just taken so long to get to this moment.

"You're sweating, Kendall."

"I'm just a little nervous," I admitted as I shook out my clammy hands.

"You're not gonna pull a runner, are you?" Stef laughed as her smile widened.

"No. This wedding is happening. It's just...a lot." We'd been through so much to get to this day; I was still expecting something to come in and tear it all apart.

"I think he's just as nervous as you are." She would know, being his older sister, but I didn't see him being anything more than a little excited.

"He never gets nervous," I laughed.

"Well, he is today," she nodded. "Cam said he was worried you'd call it off. Is there something you two aren't telling us?"

"No... No, it's nothing," I insisted. I hoped he didn't doubt me because of what'd happened earlier in the week.

"Sounds like something." Stef pinned me down with an expectant look. She never let me, or her brother, hide anything from her.

"HE called me last week. Heard about the wedding from a mutual friend," I confessed. She would find out anyway, so there was no point in hiding it.

Her gasp was quiet, but she was no less surprised. It was a poorly kept secret with my fiancé's siblings that I'd been engaged before.

"What did he want?" The venom in her voice was clear. He'd been friends with her first. All the rest of us had met the first week of university.

"He wanted to meet up to talk."

I watched as her face twisted in disgust.

"I told him no," I hurried out, shaking my head. I had no desire to revisit that part of my past. It was a dark time for all of us.

"Good. That bastard doesn't deserve a minute of your time."

"And what did my brother say?" she asked quietly, searching my eyes. All our pasts were tied together. He was affected by it all as much as I was.

I paused as I recalled the look on his face when my ex's number scrolled across my phone screen. "He wanted to kill him."

"Good," she snarked. "That'd be going easy on him for what he did to you all."

"He sent me an email last night."

"What did it say?" Her mouth was wide open in a comical display of surprise, and I laughed a little in response.

"I don't know. I didn't open it." I didn't want to see it after all this time. He'd made his decision, and I was left to deal with the consequences of his hasty actions.

"Good. Don't," she insisted. He'd cut ties with her as well. She no longer held any friendly feelings towards him she'd once had. I felt terrible at how many people he'd boxed out, but I knew it was in self-preservation.

I nodded as I thought of the unread message sitting at the top of my inbox. Part of me wanted closure... The other part of me wished he'd disappear like he did before.

"Do you want me to read it?"

The shake of my head was subtle, but she understood the intent. HE was the past. I wouldn't let him ruin my future.

"Let's get you in the dress. I'm sure my brother is getting antsy. You've only got a half-hour until showtime."

I stood from the stool I'd been sitting on and blew out a heavy breath. Stefanie was right. Thinking about the past wouldn't affect my future. It'd taken us all a long time to get to where we were.

The ghosts of the past needed to stay there.

"Oh, sweetheart. You look amazing," my dad, Gary, breathed out as he held my shoulders and looked me over.

I felt tears pool in the corners of my eyes as I looked up at my dad. He'd never been the most affectionate parent, but I knew he was having a hard time with me getting married. He'd seen how hurt I'd been when my last expected trip down the aisle fell apart with weeks to go.

"You sure he's the one?"

I knew what he was asking. Everyone assumed that we'd gotten together due to what happened two years ago. They didn't know that we'd dated before. Or that I'd met them both at the same time. We hadn't bothered to clarify any of it to people, either. It didn't matter what they thought they knew about us. We were solid.

I'd honestly never been happier. He wasn't who I'd initially imagined marrying, but I was thrilled we'd finally pulled our heads out of the sand.

"Yeah, Dad. I'm sure. I think he's always been the one," I told him in a tight voice as I dabbed at the corner of my eye.

His dark blue eyes met mine, and he scanned my face before he nodded. His weathered hands cupped my cheeks, and he leaned forward to place a gentle kiss on my forehead. "Your mother and I have only ever wanted you to be happy."

"I know, Daddy. Thank you."

He turned towards the closed doors of the room I'd been given to get myself ready in. My bridesmaids had come and gone, all waiting at the entrance to the church for things to get started.

"You guys ready to go? Everything is in place," Stefanie asked as she nodded towards the part of the building that held the sanctuary.

I nodded, and my dad turned to me, holding out his arm. My hands cupped his bicep, and I gently turned towards the door. The lace of my train made a soft swoosh as we stepped towards the open door.

My future sister, who'd been one of my closest friends for years, sniffled as I walked past her. "You're not going to make me cry," she whispered under her breath as she touched a fingertip to the corner of her eye.

"Don't you start now," I laughed as I watched her face pinch up.

"We've all got money on who cries first," Stef laughed.

"I've got twenty on Cam," my dad announced proudly. My future brother-in-law was crazy, but he was a bit of a sap.

"Kendall is the only one who bet on the groom," Stefanie winked, and I felt my face flush.

"I bet on Uncle Cam." We all chuckled as Nat came running down the hallway and grabbed her mother's hand. "Daddy said it's time to go. He asked me why all women were late. I told him I didn't know 'cause I wasn't a woman yet."

"It's a mystery, Natty bug. No man will ever understand," my dad told her seriously.

"We'll see you down there," she said with a loaded look and let her daughter tug her down the hallway.

"You think he'll cry?" My dad asked curiously as he offered me his arm.

"I know it. You all think he's some tough sarcastic ass, but he's a marshmallow." My groom was a hard nut to crack sometimes, but he was such an amazing person.

"Guess you'll be taking more of my money by the end of the day then," he laughed as we strolled down the hallway and turned the corner towards the foyer where all the bridesmaids were gathered.

My sister, my new one, my dear friend Alison, and my niece were all lined up behind the heavy maple doors. The music from inside the church was muted, but I recognized the gentle melody from the harp that signaled the doors to open.

"See you soon, Auntie Kenna," Nat whispered before she disappeared through the open doors. My father and I lined up just out of sight of the guests and waited for the signal from the wedding planner.

The song changed again, and the petite blonde waved us forward. It was time.

As my cream silk heels crossed the threshold of the sanctuary, the last several years of my life flashed through my mind. I never envisioned the face of the man standing at the end of the aisle being my future, but as his glistening eyes connected with mine...

I knew that he'd been the one all along.

# Chapter Two:
## Freshman Year

### EARLY AUGUST

"This is bullshit. You're my roommate. How can we be in different groups?" I was panicking a little as Alison relayed the information she'd gathered after she checked the rosters for the freshman orientation groups.

"Don't shoot the messenger. I just checked the lists." She held her hands up with a shit-eating grin on her face. I envied her confidence and effortless style. She always looked put together and had flowing light brown hair and wide-set, deep brown eyes. My mousey color of golden-brown lay stick straight down my back.

"I hate meeting strangers," I whined. I was friendly enough, but my anxiety got the best of me in awkward situations. Meeting new people was always a worrying event for me.

"Then it's going to be a long few months for you," she laughed. "That's all the beginning of college is, lots of peopling with strangers."

"Ugh. Don't remind me. Can't I just hide in here for freshman orientation?"

"Afraid not, my friend. The paperwork said if you don't take part, they call your parents." I wasn't sure how she was so relaxed about this. What if my group was full of idiots? Even worse, what if my group was full of vain idiots?

"Fuckers..." I muttered, and she started laughing again.

"It can't be that bad. The groups are coed. You might meet some cute guys," she shrugged.

"That's the last thing I need." I was just trying to survive going to college, adding romantic entanglements to that was a lot.

"Nothing wrong with finding a first-week hookup," she winked as she did a little hip thrust.

"Yeah, that'd be a no," I shook my head as I cringed. "Hard pass."

"You're not a..." she gasped.

My cheeks turned pink as she looked me over.

"Oh, my god. You are!" she practically shouted, and my cheeks went nuclear.

"Shut up!" It was embarrassing enough to be one of the last virgins in my graduating class. I didn't need my roommate teasing me as well. It just wasn't something I was interested in or had been allowed to explore. All my friends were guys I'd known my whole life. I didn't see most of them like that.

"Hey, there's nothing wrong with it. Just don't hold on to that v-card too tightly. You might miss out on enjoying yourself."

"I'm good. But thanks," I laughed nervously.

"If you need me to help pick out a guy..." she trailed off with a wink. I did not need my roommate to be my pimp.

I picked up my pillow and chucked it at her head while she laughed at my expense.

"Shut up, you whore," I laughed as she caught the pillow before it hit her.

"You're just jealous, " she laughed even harder as she threw it back at me.

"Moving on," I sighed as I tucked it under my chin. "Is your group leader male or female?"

"Mine is female. Stefanie, something. She's a junior."

"Nice last name," I giggled.

"I wasn't paying attention. I just found my group number, and yours, then got out of there," Allie shrugged. "Yours is named Kale."

"Like the salad?" I frowned. What kind of person named their kid after a type of lettuce?

"You should totally use that to as fodder to tease him," she giggled.

"Ugh. I hope he isn't a douche." If I had to spend a week with him in charge, I hoped he was at least halfway normal.

"Just relax. This week is supposed to be fun. You gotta lighten up a little."

"Easy for you to say," I rolled my eyes. "You could make friends with a cardboard box."

"Fake it till you make it, baby. You think I like not knowing anyone?" she made a nervous face. "It's awkward as fuck. But I still do it. You'll never get to know anyone if you don't put yourself out there."

I contemplated what she was telling me. I could fake being social for a week... right?

I could do this... maybe. Probably.

My phone pinged with a text message, and I smiled as I looked down at it.

*Dylan: You get settled into the dorm alright?*

> Kendall: Yes... my roommate is actually pretty awesome. You?

> Dylan: Mine is a doofus, but I'm pretty sure everyone here is a geek or a nerd, so I'll have to make do.

> Kendall: Yup... every single person there... which camp do you fall into?

A hand waved in front of my face, and I looked up from texting.

"Maybe you don't need my help," Alison smirked as she nodded at my phone.

"What?"

"Who has that smile plastered on your face?" she asked, as her grin grew broader.

"What are you talking about?" I frowned, not realizing I'd been smiling. It was just Dylan.

"Who are you texting?"

"Dylan," I shrugged.

"You didn't tell me you had a boyfriend," she teased.

"What? No... No, no, no. He's not my boyfriend. I mean, he's a boy, and he's my friend, but no. Nothing romantic going on here," I denied.

"Do you have a picture of this 'friend'?"

I pulled up his Instagram and flashed her a pic I'd taken of him for my senior year photography assignment. It was black and white and showed his curly, dark hair falling slightly over one eye. His light blue eyes were in direct focus and popped against the blurry background of the photo. A smattering of freckles was visible along the bridge of his nose and softly dusting his cheeks until they met his angled jawline.

"He's cute," she nodded. "You sure there aren't any feelings there?"

There had been once. Dylan was on the receiving end of a substantial unrequited crush in middle school. But I'd never told him how I felt. Those feelings had since faded. But I had to admit the boyish good looks he'd always had developed into something quite attractive.

"No," I shook my head. "He's my best friend."

"Bullshit."

"Not you too," I groaned as I sat back dramatically.

"So, other people think you two are into each other?"

"We're not talking about this. This subject is closed. Done. Finished," I insisted. There had been rumors last year, but Dylan was not into me—not even a little. I would have known.

"Fine. Fine. I'll let it go," Allie grinned as she tried to peek at my phone screen. "For now."

She climbed up into her loft bed and propped her feet onto a pillow, pulling out a bottle of nail polish. "You don't mind, do you? The smell drove my dad nuts. I always had to go out on the back porch."

"No, it's fine. Got any other colors?"

She nodded towards a case on her desk, and I grabbed a bottle of pale pink, shaking it against my palm a few times.

"Nope," she shook her head at me. "No boring shit. Get the bright purple out."

"Geez. Are you always this demanding?"

"Yes," she laughed as she meticulously painted her toes. "Now, do what I say."

Not wanting to piss off my new friend this early into the relationship, I obeyed and settled into my plush folding chair with my feet perched on the edge.

"So, do I get to meet this Dylan guy sometime this week?" she asked as she continued to look at the progress she was making on her toes.

I shook my head. "No. He goes to a private engineering school a few hours away. He's got football camp this week."

"Wait? So that hottie is a jock, too?"

I'd never really thought of him that way. He'd been in my friend group that was comprised of the funny, smart kids in our high school. He'd never been friends with the actual jocks.

"Kinda. I guess. He's a running back. But his school is small, and for, like, geniuses, so I guess the pickings for a football team are slim."

"Still, you better watch it. It sounds like he will be popular if that school is full of dorks. Cute and athletic might be scarce. I bet he has a girlfriend within the week."

I felt a tightness in my chest at her words, not quite ready to lose my friend to a new romantic entanglement. It was hard enough to do the long-distance friend thing. Being so far away from him seemed foreign to me.

*Dylan: You ignoring me already?*

Shit.

I screwed the lid back on the polish and texted him back.

> **Kendall:** *Sorry... girly roommate bonding. Toenail painting going on.*

**Dylan:** *Just send pics if there's topless pillow fighting.*

My face flamed. He'd always been one to make suggestive comments to be funny, but it felt different now.

> **Kendall:** *You wish.*

**Dylan:** *...*

**Dylan:** *I do...*

> **Kendall:** *You coming home for fall break?*

**Dylan:** *We'll see. I might have practice.*

**Dylan:** *Definitely Thanksgiving.*

> **Kendall:** *Same.*

**Dylan:** *You play sports now?*

> **Kendall:** *No, smartass. Same for Thanksgiving.*

"Stop smiling," Alison teased, "or I might think you like him."

I glared at her and set my phone down. She was right. I needed to focus on where I was and who I was with. Dylan was still my friend, but we'd both have to get used to being apart.

"Why did I agree to let you pick out my clothes?" I whined as I tried to pull down the denim, barely covering my thighs.

"Because you love me, and you're my new life-sized Barbie."

"These shorts show butt cheek." Turning as I looked in the mirror, my eyes widened as I saw how much of my flesh they left exposed.

"Hey, you told me I had to pick something from your clothes. These were in your clothes. Don't blame me because you only bought half the shorts."

"I hate you." I tried to look intimidating as I narrowed my eyes at her, but she only shrugged, an amused smile on her face.

"No, you don't."

"Why aren't you wearing shorts that go up to your ass?" Pointing towards her much more appropriate length shorts, I felt a surge of jealousy.

"Because I have no problem flirting with strangers," she shrugged.

"Ugh. Not this again. I don't think these are sending the right message."

"Just go with it. Remember. Our goal this week is to have fun and meet new people," she insisted.

I sighed and twisted in the mirror. The shorts were short, but they weren't indecent. And I guess I had an excellent package to show off. "Fine. Whatever. Let's do this."

"That's the spirit," she cheered as she smacked me on the exposed skin of my thigh.

"Hey! You're going to leave a handprint," I laughed as I swatted at her while she danced backward toward the door, out of my reach.

"Some guys would think that's hot."

"Oh my god, you're obsessed," I rolled my eyes.

She flipped me off over her shoulder and strutted down the hallway toward the staircase. Thankfully, we lived on the fourth floor, so it wouldn't be too horrible to take the stairs during the year. The elevators were always packed, since some people were still moving in.

"Alright, my group is meeting in the field between the dorms. You're supposed to be near the trees on the backside of the dorm."

"Group three?" I asked, verifying the intel she'd given me earlier.

"Yup. Have fun," she sing-songed. "Don't do anything I wouldn't do."

"Pretty sure that will not be a problem," I muttered under my breath. Heading down the front steps, I turned onto the sidewalk that led toward the back of the dorm. There were benches underneath a small group of trees where I could see some people already waiting.

The closer I got; I noticed an obvious upperclassman sitting on a bench with a large poster board emblazoned with the number three leaning against the front of it. He looked up just as I stepped off the concrete path and onto the grass.

"Whoa," I breathed out as I looked over at him. He had light green eyes framed by dark lashes and high cheekbones, a golden hue to his skin from being out in the sun. Sandy-blondish brown hair sat in gentle waves, neatly combed against the sides of his head. He had a strong jawline and defined shoulders, a polo shirt hugging the lean muscle underneath. I smiled at his beat-up converse that seemed in direct contrast to his khaki shorts.

He pushed a single finger up against the bridge of his glasses and shot a tentative smile in my direction as I approached. My pulse picked up as I stepped closer, and I caught his eyes lingering on the hem of my shorts. I fought the urge to pull them down as I returned his smile and headed in his direction.

# Chapter Three:
## Freshman Year
### EARLY AUGUST

"Incoming!" A loud shout came from over my shoulder as something collided with my back, and then a muffled curse as the slap of tennis shoes against concrete sounded out behind me.

"Are you alright?" The older guy on the bench closed his book and dropped it on the weathered wood as he headed in my direction. He glared at the person behind me, and then his eyes flashed back to mine.

A soccer ball rolled to a stop a few feet away, and I watched as a blonde guy with stubble leaned down to pick it up as a hand closed on my shoulder.

"I'm so sorry. Shit. Are you alright?" Looking backward, I was met by a solid sweaty chest with a speckling of auburn hair that led down into a pair of athletic shorts.

"Talk about shitty aim, Cor... or were you trying to get the attention of the hottest girl in our group?" the blonde laughed as he walked over towards us.

"What? No. Fuck..." the shirtless one cursed, the last word muttered under his breath. He crouched down slightly so he could make eye contact with me. He was tall. Very, very tall. "I didn't hurt you, did I?"

"No. Uh, it just startled me. I'm fine," I assured.

He blew out a breath and smiled at me, a dimple forming on his cheek. I had to admit. He'd stunned me, but not with the soccer ball to the back. He had close-cropped brownish auburn hair with a little cowlick at the front that made it stick up. His deep blue eyes were framed with auburn-tipped lashes that highlighted the almond shape of his eyes. His face, neck, and chest were covered with freckles, interspersed with smooth pale skin.

"Rory, put your shirt back on and quit acting like a jackass," the older guy scolded him with an eye roll.

"Yeah, Rory. No one wants to be blinded by your pale whiteness," the shorter blonde one teased.

"Fuck off, Joel. You're just jealous," Rory scoffed as he flipped off his friend.

"Of what? Your inability to aim your kicks?" Joel taunted with a grin.

"Guys. Knock it off and take it somewhere else," the older one sighed, looking annoyed with both.

They both stepped back and started pushing at each other. The taller one, Rory, pulled a shirt out of the back waistband of his dark athletic shorts and snapped it towards his friend.

"You sure you're okay?" Turning back towards the older guy, I shook my head and focused on his face.

"Yeah, sorry. That was..."

"Two immature idiots living up to their reputation?" he rolled his eyes.

Nervous laughter bubbled up as he smiled at me.

He wasn't pretty boy handsome like the other two, but he had a definite boy next door thing going on with the glasses and the messy hair.

"Are you in my group?" he asked curiously.

"You're lettuce guy?"

Fuck. Oh, God. Seriously?

"Yup. Heard that one before," he nodded. "Please, God, just don't make jokes about putting me in your mouth and spitting me out. That one is a little much."

My eyes widened as my cheeks heated.

"Sorry, that was probably inappropriate," Kale quickly apologized.

"Uh..." I was at a loss for words.

"So, what's your name? I'm guessing Kendall or Gretchen."

"Cause that's not creepy," I frowned. "Did they send pictures of us or something?"

"No," he shook his head with an amused smile, "there are two girls with names that start with K, and I noticed your necklace."

I looked down at the initial necklace sitting just above the neckline of my tank top. "Nice observational skills."

"Hazard of the trade," he shrugged. "I'm studying psychology. I'm supposed to read people."

"Noted," I told him with a nod.

"Soo..."

"Yes?" I asked, as he looked at me expectantly.

"Which one?" he questioned.

A loud shout drew my attention to the two guys roughhousing with the soccer ball.

"What? Uh. I guess the taller one."

He laughed and turned back toward me. "Your name. Which one are you? Kendall or Gretchen?"

"Oh, right..." I trailed off. I was all over the place today. "Kendall. I'm Kendall Grant."

"Nice to meet you," he smiled. "I'm Kale Roberts. Junior. Resident Advisor in the men's tower, fifth floor. Psychology major."

"Freshman, obviously," I returned his smile nervously. "Fourth-floor women's tower. Fine Arts major."

"We're still waiting for a few more people. So, you can hang out around here till we're ready to do our first team-building exercise."

I glanced around and saw a small group of girls sitting up against a tree, and then the two guys in the field that were still kicking the soccer ball around.

"I'd just stay away from those two. They're going to be a handful," he nodded toward the guys, and I watched as the taller one pulled the blonde one's shirt over his face and smacked his stomach.

"Seems like it," I nodded.

"You can join me on the bench if you'd like," he offered. "I promise I don't bite."

"Uh." I glanced over at the three girls with their heads drawn together. One of them looked over at me and rolled her eyes before she turned back to the other two. It looked like that clique wasn't seeking any new members. "Yeah, thanks."

He walked back to the bench and sat on one end while I awkwardly pulled my shorts down and sat on the opposite side. Kale retrieved his forgotten book and cracked it open, glancing at me out of the corner of his eye before he resumed reading. Feeling more than a little awkward, I pulled out my phone and began scrolling through my texts, seeing one from my new roommate and one from Dylan.

*Alison: My group leader is so awesome! She's RA on 8.*

*Kendall: Mine might be as dull as the lettuce he's named after.*

Alison sent back a string of emojis, including fire, a head of lettuce, and several laughing emojis.

*Alison: But is he hot?*

I glanced at him out of the corner of my eye.

*Kendall: Yes... ugh.*

*Alison: Send me a pic.*

*Kendall: Nope.*

*Alison: You're no fun.*

*Kendall: So I've been told.*

The text from Dylan was a gif of a monkey on a skateboard. He must've been bored. Opening a game, I played a few levels before I noticed that more people had joined us, and Kale was missing from the other side of the bench.

"Alright, group three. It's time to pair up and get to know each other. Pick someone you don't already know and come get a sheet of questions to answer," Kale announced.

We all looked awkwardly around the group, but I felt myself blushing when Rory winked at me from across the group. He took two steps toward me before I felt a nudge at my elbow.

"Do you need a partner?" I looked over at the guy next to me. He was taller than I was, probably around six feet tall. He had short, neatly combed flame-red hair and fair skin.

"Sure, I'm Kendall," I nodded. Looking back across the group, I saw a petite blonde, with shorts even shorter than mine, laughing at Rory with her hand on his chest. He met my eyes over her shoulder and shrugged before he turned his attention back to her.

"Tyler." My new partner introduced himself with his hand outstretched. "Biology major. You?"

"Fine Arts." I smiled as I shook his warm hand and looked up into dark hazel eyes. He had long, pretty eyelashes. Why did the guys always get fantastic eyelashes?

"Nice," he grinned with a nod. "I can't draw a straight line."

"I'll let you in on a little secret," I told him as I leaned in with my voice lowered. He flashed me a conspiratorial smile. "Neither can I."

His smile brightened, revealing bright white teeth, but then very seriously looked down at our list. "Reason why you're here..."

"Uh, my parents made me," he shrugged. "I technically already have enough credits to have finished my first semester, but they said I needed to enjoy my college experience."

"Sounds pretty reasonable. I just wanted to get settled in early and maybe make some friends. My roommate was going to be here, so..." I hated answering all these lame questions too, but I guess that's why we were here.

"What part of the college experience are you looking forward to?" he read off. "You want to go first with this one?"

A shriek from across the field drew our attention, and we saw the two guys from earlier, both with giggling girls clinging to their backs, running across the field.

"Looks like someone else has decided these questions are lame," he chuckled as we took in the display.

"They kind of are," I shrugged. I understood the need to do the getting-to-know-you activities, but they were still lame.

"Okay. Real talk. My classes this semester are all my electives. My dad thought that way I'd have less chance of fucking up while I got used to college," he said in a low voice as he leaned in my direction. "I'm also being pressured into joining his old fraternity because I'm a legacy."

"I'm not even sure what I'm going to do after graduation. My dad said my major was a joke."

"I bet some people in this group won't even make it to graduation..." He nodded over to where the tall guy was trying to bench press his partner. I'd dodged a bullet with that one.

We talked for a few more minutes about which classes we were enrolled in, surprisingly sharing one Intro to Art History lecture. Tyler seemed nice; although he was a little too serious, he was easy to talk to.

"Alright, guys," Kale said as he walked around to stand in front of the group. "Let's walk towards the Hall of Music. There's a presentation to kick off this week for all the different attending orientation groups."

Tyler stood and held his hand out to me, helping me up from the ground. His hand was warm, and I studied his face as his fingers lingered on mine after I was upright.

"Thanks."

"No problem," he responded as he stuffed his hands into his pockets and lingered next to me while the group followed Kale.

Our group got split into two rows once we were inside, but with the angle of the seats, I had a hard time seeing the stage around the head of the very tall person who was right in front of me.

"Do you want to switch seats?" Tyler whispered as he leaned in toward me.

I watched as the bizarre mating ritual that'd started in the field continued. The petite blonde girl was whispering into his ear as he slung his arm along the back of her chair.

"No. I'm okay. I'm sure it'll be fine." I shook my head.

"Seriously, I don't mind," he insisted.

"It's fine, Tyler."

"Yeah, Tyler, it's fine," Rory said in a mocking voice. "Maybe she enjoys staring at the back of my head." He'd turned around in his seat and caught me staring, arching an eyebrow in my direction.

"Well. It is pretty large," I responded in a sarcastic voice. "Kind of hard to miss."

"Apparently, you've been checking out other things." The cocky jerk had the nerve to wink at me.

"Um, no..." I blushed as the girl next to him tittered and pulled him to face her.

"He's an ass," Tyler growled in a disgusted voice to my side.

"Tyler, she doesn't need to know you've been staring at my ass," Rory smirked back toward us before he faced forward and hunched down in his seat.

"Just ignore him," Tyler whispered as he slumped down in his seat a little. "Guys like him are all talk."

The lights overhead dimmed, and I tried to focus on the stage to watch the presentation on the large screen. It was the typical 'here is what our school has to offer' video that'd graced the websites of all the universities that I'd applied to. I found my mind drifting to wondering what else this week would have in store for us all. It wasn't as bad as I thought it'd be so far.

Thank God my roommate had been as cool in person as she'd been in the emails and texts we'd sent back and forth. It didn't look like I'd be making many female friends in my group; they all seemed to be attached to the tiny blonde who was shooting me dirty looks over Stretch Armstrong's arm. I didn't need or want friends like that anyway.

# Chapter Four:
## Freshman Year

### Early August

"So, your entire group is full of hot guys, and mine has two engineering dorks, an international student who spends all his time on his phone, and a guy I'm not sure finished puberty," Alison sighed loudly.

"Well, yeah, they're cute, but two of them are jerks," I scoffed, recalling Rory and Joel's antics with the bitch brigade the last few days. Given, they had done nothing to me, but they were still obnoxious.

"Did you guys decide what you're doing for the lip sync skit?" she asked, with a mischievous glint in her eye.

"I won't spoil it and tell you. You are the competition," I refused.

She laughed as she threw a kernel of popcorn at the side of my head. We'd finished with day four and been given the evening off to relax. The week had been full of group activities, campus tours, lectures on services the university provided to students, and I was happy about the reprieve.

Little blonde bimbo had turned out to be Gretchen, and she was not a fan of me. I wasn't sure why because we'd never actually talked to each other directly, but I could say the feeling was mutual. She'd been insistent on trying to get the attention of every male in our group and maintain dominance over every female. I'd gone to high school with girls like her and wasn't buying into her popularity game.

Tyler had been the only one immune to her charms, so we'd spent most of our time together joking about how lame some of the activities were.

"At least they're giving us the weekend free before classes start. I don't think I could take any more group activities," I sighed, ready to relax. "We just have to make it through tomorrow."

"Easy for you to say. Your team might have a chance of winning something tomorrow."

"You've got some smart people; you guys might do alright on the academic trivia," I offered hopefully.

"Oh, joy. The contest that shows how dorky my team is. Sounds great." She made a disgusted face and fell backward dramatically.

"You'll be fine. No one will remember any of this week after classes start, anyway. We'll be too busy," I reminded Allie.

The last day of orientation had several competitions of different sorts. There was a team relay race, an academic competition, an engineering challenge, and a team lip-sync battle.

My team seemed evenly matched in every subject, so seeing how we did against the other groups from our dorm should be fun. I was looking forward to it, but obviously, my roommate was not. As the week went on, she'd spent mealtimes with my group and had gotten to know almost everyone well.

"You sure you guys can't adopt me for tomorrow?" she begged.

"Sorry. I don't think your leader would go for it. If you're the only normal one, she might need the company."

"Maybe I'll just tie you up in the closet and take your place tomorrow," she wiggled her eyebrows and nodded over at our small, shared closet space.

"That sounds like the perfect plan. No one will ever notice the difference," I agreed sarcastically.

"Alright, guys," Kale addressed the group as we waited at the start of the team relay activities. "This challenge has to involve the whole team. I'm glad you all paid attention when I told you to wear athletic gear."

"What do you think they're going to make us do?" Tyler's whisper over my shoulder and accompanied hand against my lower back distracted me from the question.

"What?" I asked as I glanced in his direction.

"Do you know what they've got planned for this?"

My eyes scanned his chest and neck, up into his vibrant brown eyes. It made me realize that this whole week I'd never seen him look this casual. He was always wearing some sort of collared shirt, but I had to admit, the compression tank he was wearing did him all kinds of favors.

"I think it's an obstacle course. But don't take my word for it. That's just the rumor on the street," I whispered back.

"Excuse me, Kale." Gretchen's nasally voice interrupted. "You might need to repeat what you just said; I don't think everyone was paying attention."

"I said that this is another team-building activity. To see how well you all can cooperate as a team."

Well, that sounded like fun.

"We need to designate a team captain. They have to complete all the activities first and then coach their teammates through it, making sure we all stay together as a unit," he explained.

"Well. I'm thinking since I have experience with leading a cheer team that I'm a natural choice," Gretchen interjected before anyone else could speak.

Of course she does.

"Somehow, being a tiny, peppy dictator qualifies you for leadership now?" Tyler asked in a worried voice.

The snort that followed his inaudible whisper couldn't be helped. Gretchen turned those icy blue eyes in my direction, and I froze.

"You think you could do better? What leadership experience do you have?" she questioned, with one perfectly manicured hand propped on her hip.

"Uh..." My experience with being president of the art club and VP of the National Honor Society wouldn't help with this one. I looked across the group for help from Kale, but it seemed like he was enjoying this interaction. My eyes narrowed at him, and he shrugged. Coward.

"Well, I'm waiting," she tapped her foot impatiently. God, she was annoying. "Who do you think should be in charge?"

Kale interjected, "It's not about being in charge, Gretchen. It's about having someone physically capable of doing the challenges and then helping the rest of the team through it. This challenge is about teamwork. Not hierarchy."

My eyes scanned the group and stopped on Rory. He was athletic, well-spoken, and despite being kind of a jerk, he seemed to possess a certain charm that made people want to follow him.

"I think Rory would make a good team captain," I nodded.

His eyes flashed to mine, the curiosity in them apparent. "I'm cool with that."

"What?" Gretchen asked, clearly not in agreement. "But, babe. We both know that I have more..."

"I agree," Joel interrupted her from Rory's other side.

"What the hell, me too," Tyler agreed from behind me.

"Alright," Kale clapped, satisfied with my nomination. "Sounds like a third of the group thinks you should be in charge, Mr. Chandler. Any objections?"

A low murmur filled the group, but no one disagreed.

"Nope. I think his height might benefit us." I smiled at Rory across the group, and I felt Tyler take a step closer to me from behind.

A huff from the tiny plastic spitfire at his side drew my eyes down.

"But..." Gretchen whined and crossed her arms over her chest.

"No offense, Gretchen," I shrugged when she narrowed her eyes at me. Her loud scoff was almost comical as she glared at me. "But we don't know what all the challenges are; we need every advantage we can get."

"Sounds like we're at a consensus. Let's get into position," Kale directed.

Our group of ten moved over towards the first challenge, which appeared to be some kind of target practice. The head of the dorm Resident Advisors (RA) introduced himself and talked about how it took teamwork and social interaction to succeed as adults.

"Are you sure you guys don't want me to lead? I mean, I'm sure Rory is more than capable, but I'm tougher than I look." Gretchen was still trying to sell herself, hard. Most of the rest of the group was already assembled around Rory. She didn't like the attention being drawn away from her.

"Gretchen, let it go," Kale sighed. "It's for one day. I'm sure you can find some minions to take over the university tomorrow. I hear rush will start soon."

"Fine, whatever. It's your loss." She told everyone with her nose in the air. Even Rory was ignoring her little last-ditch attempt at gaining control.

The head RA came over the speakers again and counted down while all the team captains lined up. I saw Alison lined up at her own team's starting line a few teams over. Rory stretched his arms across his chest and shook them out. Tyler and I stood side by side towards the group's back and watched as the bullhorn sounded. Rory shot off like a rocket towards the other side of the field.

Some upperclassmen handed him a bucket and a blindfold. He lined himself up in front of a tarp with a circular target and placed the bucket in the grass. We all watched as he pulled the blindfold down and tossed bean bags towards the center of the target meticulously.

Somehow, he managed to get all but one of his four into the center target. He ripped off the blindfold and sprinted towards the group, in the lead with only a few team captains hot on his heels.

"Alright. This game is just like bean bag toss. I get to talk to each of you through four tosses. Who's up first?" Rory asked.

Gretchen bounded into action and took off across the field, grabbing a beanbag from the bucket and pulling the blindfold down over her eyes. Her first shot went over the center target and into the outer ring. Rory caught up with her and talked her through the next three shots. She hit two in the center and two inside the farthest circle.

One by one, he talked our teammates through it until I was the only one left. "Let's go, Special K."

He had built up a light sweat from running back and forth, but his enthusiasm was infectious.

"Let's do this," I nodded.

"That's the spirit. Let's finish strong. Think you can manage four in the center?" He was jogging backward as we headed towards the other side of the field.

"I can try. It's pretty much like corn hole, right?"

"You play corn hole?" he asked with an amused smile.

"Normal people can play corn hole too, not just beer toting frat bros," I rolled my eyes.

"I'm not in a frat," he laughed.

"Yet," I clarified with an eyebrow raised.

"You think you've got me all figured out, don't you?" The smirk on his face was kind of adorable, but he was still a jerk... mostly.

"Am I wrong?" I asked. He had fraternity bro written all over him.

"Put on the blindfold, Kendall." He passed me the piece of black fabric, and I settled it onto my forehead, looking back at him.

"I bet you say that to all the girls."

That damn dimple appeared as he smirked at me again. I pulled the fabric over my eyes and felt him guide a bean bag into my outstretched hand.

"Usually, women like to see what I'm doing..." he whispered in my ear as he squared my shoulders to the tarp. My breath caught, and my pulse picked up as I felt the hair on the back of my neck stand up.

"Just like corn hole, visualize the target and smooth release," he coached as he released me. I nodded and followed his instructions, hearing a dull thud as the bag hit the tarp.

"Nice. Just like that." He placed another bag in my hand, and I repeated the motion again and again. "Alright, last one."

"Thanks," I told him quietly.

As my last toss hit and I pulled up the blindfold, I heard our team cheer from behind me. Somehow, I'd managed to toss all four bean bags dead center. We took off running towards the rest of our team while our points were counted.

"Nicely done, Kendall. I think only a few people nailed all four," Kale praised as he held his hand up for a high five.

"My dad loves to play. It's kind of second nature for me," I shrugged.

"Well, you'll be popular at tailgate parties," Joel laughed as he elbowed Rory. Gretchen was still pouting with her arms drawn across her chest. Her two little minions were flanking her as she glared at the guys.

The head RA came over the loudspeaker again and announced that our team was tied for second out of twelve teams. Our team managed to keep our points high over the next few group exercises.

"Alright, next is the three-legged relay race," Kale announced. "We'll have five pairs that need to make it down and back to the pole on the other side of the field."

"Ooh! I'm good at these," Gretchen clapped. "You gonna be my partner, Rory?"

"I'm pretty sure her perfume must be called *Desperation*," Tyler whispered in my ear. I tried not to laugh, but he was right; she was desperate for his attention. Tyler stepped forward, and I could feel his chest press up against my back as his hand settled on the outside of my hip.

"Or maybe it's called *He's Just Not That into You*," I responded quietly, hoping no one overheard us.

"You'll probably want to pair up with someone who is a similar height to you. Trust me; it'll make things easier," Kale suggested.

We all scanned the group, literally sizing up our teammates. Rory and Tyler were by far the two tallest. Most of the other girls were short, Gretchen being stuck with one of her giggly friends. Joel was the shortest male, only an inch or two taller than I was. Judging by the grin on his face when the other four guys paired up with each other, he wasn't upset he got stuck with me.

"Looks like you're with me, Kendall," he smiled as he appeared at my side.

"Hope you can keep up," I teased.

He laughed as he grabbed a set of ties from the pile near Kale's feet and stepped up next to me. "You want to tie us up, or should I?"

"Normally, I make the guy buy me dinner before I let him tie me up," I smirked.

He placed the ties into my outstretched hand before he stepped up beside me and lined his leg up with mine.

"My treat in the dining hall tonight if we win this thing," he offered.

"Pretty sure we all have meal plans." He smiled at my snarky remark, but it didn't seem to faze him.

"I might spring for the up charge and get you a Rice Krispie treat."

"Big spender. How do the girls resist you?" I said in a mocking voice.

"Just tie us together, smart aleck," he winked.

Luckily, my long legs paid off for once. Our knees were almost exactly at the same height as each other. That'd make this so much easier. I quickly tied us together at the thigh, knee, and mid-calf. Gretchen whined the ties were cutting into her skin while the rest of us lined up.

"Alright, Ty and I are gonna take the lead, then the two sets of girls, next up are Adam and Ken. Kendall and Joel can anchor," Rory instructed, as he and Tyler lined up at the starting point.

"Sounds good, man." Joel reached over for a fist bump, and I shifted as his body leaned.

"Why are we the anchor?" I asked after he straightened back up.

"All state for track and field," he announced proudly, puffing his chest up a bit.

"So, you're not a soccer player?" I asked, recalling the first day of orientation.

"That too, but four hundred meters was where all my ribbons came from," he responded. It sounded like Joel was quite the high school athlete.

"Impressive," I nodded.

He smiled as we stood at the back of the group.

The RA started us again, blowing a whistle to start the race. Rory and Tyler stumbled a little, but locked arms and powered their way to the other end of the field. Their long legs gave them a definite advantage over the other groups. Gretchen and her partner yelled at each other the whole time but made it back without face planting. By the time Joel and I were up, only one other group had sent their last pair across the field.

"Alright, hold on tight and let's do this," he coached.

It was a weird sensation to feel his leg flex against mine as we hobbled our way along at a steady speed. The hair on his leg tickled mine, but we managed to stay in the lead around the pole.

"Shit. They're speeding up." I could see the other pair a few teams over, trying to take the lead.

"Just keep going," he insisted. "Pick up the speed a little and don't let them pull your focus."

Nodding, I tightened the link my arm had on his and looked towards where the rest of our teammates were cheering us on.

"We got this, just a little faster," he urged. My legs were burning by the time we made it back to smack Kale's hand. I didn't look toward the other team, but I think we managed to win from the cheers surrounding us.

"Good job, partner," Joel smirked as he leaned down to release the ties on our legs.

"You weren't half bad either."

"Next time I have to get tied to someone, I'm finding you," he laughed.

"Because that happens all the time," I laughed back. Joel shrugged and smiled, holding his hand up for a high five.

"Nice job, guys. The bonus points for first should throw us into the lead. Only one activity left," Rory cheered in front of the group.

The last activity was a scavenger hunt in the engineering quad. Gretchen was surprisingly helpful with her knowledge of the university history, and we breezed through it, finishing second behind Alison's team.

The RA director got up in front of the group after we'd finished and started reading off the team totals. By the time he got to the top three, our number still hadn't been called.

"Looks like you guys might have pulled this one off," Kale speculated, looking back at us with a smile.

"Number three... number three... number three," Rory started a low chant as the RA called the second-place team. When he announced we'd won, it was a full shout from the members of our group as we jumped up and down. They released the groups back to the dorm after we'd been given our faux gold medals with the university logo on them.

"Who's coming to the fountain with us?" Rory called out as our group stood off to the side of the bigger group.

"Just keep it clean, Rory," Kale told him. "You can still get arrested for nudity."

"Oh, come on, my brother runs through the fountain naked once, and I'm being lectured because he's an idiot," Rory rolled his eyes. It sounded like he came from an unusual gene pool.

"I'm just saying, campus police will take you in if you do something dumb," Kale shrugged.

Tyler stepped in beside me, bumping his shoulder against mine. "What do you think they're talking about?"

"God, you two are clueless," Gretchen rolled her eyes at the two of us. "It's like a university tradition to stand over the jets in the engineering fountain on the last day of orientation."

"And Rory's brother did it naked?"

"Yes, he's a legend," she smiled. "Ten push-ups totally naked over a jet before campus security hauled him off. I heard it was quite a sight."

"Wouldn't that be kind of painful?" Tyler shifted and pulled at the hem of his shorts.

"The jets hit his chest, not his junk. He's not a total moron. My older sister was a freshman when he was," she told us.

"Who's in?" Rory asked again. Gretchen, of course, clung to his side as half of our group headed back to the dorms with Kale.

"Are you coming, Special K?" Rory asked, glancing at me.

Tyler looked down at me and smiled. "I'll do it if you do."

"Fine, yes, whatever," I agreed. "Let's do it."

Gretchen and her friends ran through first, screaming at the top of their lungs as they got blasted with the cold water.

Joel showed off by holding a plank over a jet for the whole time it was on. Tyler got down and did ten push-ups over the central jet, his hair a slicked-back mess.

"Is it freezing?" I asked as he stepped in front of me, water dripping from his hair and clothes.

"Let's go find out," he laughed as he reached down and grabbed behind my knees, hoisting me over his shoulder.

"Don't you dare drop me," I laughed as he walked into the center of the fountain just as the jets turned on.

"Put me down. Put me down," I shrieked as the spray shot me in the face.

"Sorry," he apologized, laughing as I slid down his chest. His hands lingered on my waist as I looked up at him. As the spray calmed and the water dropped back down, he used a finger to push my wet hair out of my face.

"No, you're not," I teased him.

"You're right. I'm not." He stepped in closer and looked down at my lips as my heart raced. "I want to..."

"Ahhh!!!" I laughed as the water shot back up and soaked both of us. He shook his head and grabbed my hand, pulling me back to the small group sitting along one of the concrete benches.

"No push-ups, Kendall? I'm kind of disappointed. I thought you were a badass," Rory teased.

"None of the other girls did them." I pointed over to the group attempting to ring out their hair.

"But you're not like them, are you?" he said in a low tone as he shot a look at Gretchen and her friends.

"God, I hope not," I shuddered.

The guys all laughed, and Rory pointed towards the center jet of the fountain. "Go on now..."

"You're so bossy," I rolled my eyes and pretended to be annoyed with him bossing me around.

"Maybe you're just all talk. Guess Special K isn't so special, after all."

I looked back at Tyler. He shrugged his shoulders at me.

"Fine. Ten push-ups," I agreed.

"Do the proper kind too, no girly push-ups," Rory told me. I narrowed my eyes at him and pulled off my soaked tank top, handing it to Tyler before I walked back towards the fountain in my sports bra. Timing the jet as soon as it died down, I got into position and started doing push-ups, the guys counting from behind me. The water shot up, my arms stalling on four as I tried to keep it from spraying in my eyes.

"Damn, girl," Joel called out.

"Shit, that's hot," I heard Tyler say from my other side.

"Trying to prove a point, Kendall?" Rory yelled.

They all stood a few feet away as I finished the tenth rep, and the water pressure eased off. Tyler was standing next to me, holding out a hand to pull me up as I stood.

"Alright. You proved me wrong," Rory conceded. "No girly push-ups coming out of you, Grant."

"Happy now? Anything else you'd like me to do to prove I'm worthy of your approval?" I asked in a snarky voice.

"Nope. You've more than got it," Rory laughed as I rang out my tank and pulled it back over my head.

"Now I believe someone owes me a Rice Krispie treat. Let's go, boys," I yelled over my shoulder as I headed back toward the dorms.

# Chapter Five:
## Freshman Year

### NOVEMBER

"Quit pulling at your skirt," Alison laughed as I stood in front of the mirror on the closet door, twisting to make sure it went down far enough. She'd let me choose my outfit for tonight but had vetoed my idea of wearing leggings under my denim mini skirt.

"I'm going to freeze," I whined.

"You're going to be in a barn most of the time," she rolled her eyes dramatically.

"We're sleeping in a tent tonight," I told her as I looked back over at her.

"Why? Aren't there people bringing their cars?"

"Have you seen his car?" I asked, referring to Tyler's tiny compact. "I don't think he could even lie down in the back seat, much less fit both of us in there."

She wiggled her eyebrows before she made a crude motion with her hands. "Don't need to take up a lot of space if you use him as a mattress."

"Sounds romantic." She laughed at my exaggerated eye roll.

"Because a two-person tent in a field that smells like manure screams romance," she said in a mocking, high-pitched voice.

"It's a produce farm, not livestock."

"Fertilizer... duh," she rolled her eyes.

I heard my phone beep with an alert from across the room.

"Looks like lover boy is getting anxious," she teased.

I held my hand out toward her. "Pass me the phone."

She reached over to my desk, picking up my phone and looking at the screen before she extended it toward me with a smirk on her face. "It's your other boy toy."

"He's not my boy toy. Dylan has a girlfriend."

"Called that one." She did. It didn't even take him a week into school to get tagged in pictures with a blonde girl. She seemed kind enough, but I was missing my friend. We still texted and sent each other stupid memes, but his phone calls were few and far between.

"It doesn't matter, and she seems nice," I told her as I gave up adjusting the denim skirt.

"That's code for she's not that cute," Alison laughed as she gave me a pointed look.

"She's pretty..." I trailed off. She wasn't a plastic Barbie doll like Gretchen, but she wasn't unattractive.

"Whatever. What did he want?"

I glanced down at the text.

> *Dylan: Will be home Tuesday before Thanksgiving. Want to catch a movie?*

"He's trying to make plans for over break."

"Did you tell Ty about Dylan?" she asked curiously.

"Yeah, why wouldn't I?"

"I don't know," she shrugged. "Sometimes guys get weird about girls having other guys as friends."

I laughed as I tied the tails of my plaid shirt low across my stomach, then rolled up the sleeves. "It's fine. Tyler knows D and I are just friends. And most of my friends this semester are guys, so..."

"Hey, I'm your friend," she frowned.

"I said most. Not all."

"Did you pack the 'essentials'?" she asked teasingly. I averted my eyes when I looked towards my small overnight bag by the door. Tyler and I had been dating since orientation pretty much; he asked me on an actual date the night before classes started. Most days, we ate breakfast together and walked to campus.

He'd been on the same floor as Rory, and coincidentally they had rushed the same fraternity, both as legacies. We didn't hang out with him much, but I saw him occasionally in the hallway when I went to see Tyler. They were supposed to be sharing a room in the frat house next year with Joel and another pledge.

"It might not even happen tonight."

"This is the first time you guys are sleeping alone somewhere without a roommate. It's the perfect opportunity," she told me.

"We'll see. We've only been together for three months," I shrugged. It still made me nervous thinking about having actual sex.

"You are building this up to be a bigger thing than it should be," she sighed.

"Agree to disagree."

"You love him, don't you?" She phrased it like a question, but I could tell she already knew my answer.

"I think so," I nodded.

"And you trust him?"

"Of course," I replied honestly.

"Then just stop worrying about it and stay in the moment."

"That's easier said than done," I sighed as I made a few last-minute adjustments to my braids.

Tyler picked me up from the dorm, clad in a pair of faded overalls with a tight green henley shirt underneath that showed off his arms. He'd been hitting the gym and the climbing wall in the student center lately.

"You're going to be cold," he told me after he climbed into the driver's seat of his car, his warm palm settled on my knee.

"That's what I told Allie."

"I mean, I'm not complaining. You look... like a naughty farmer's daughter," he teased as he tugged on a braid.

"You gonna sneak me off into a hayloft, mister farmhand?" I teased back.

"I don't think there's a loft in the barn, but I can zip the sleeping bags I brought together." Not knowing how to respond, I shifted in my seat awkwardly. Not that I didn't want to take things further with him; I was just unbelievably nervous. "Hey. That wasn't implying anything. You know I won't push this further without your consent."

We'd had the responsibility discussion. I'd gotten on the pill at the student health center shortly after we started dating, but we had been taking our time. Both of us living in the dorms and having roommates provided little privacy, so we'd not gotten that far with physical intimacy. Don't get me wrong... there was a lot of kissing and grinding going on with the stolen moments we had, but full nudity hadn't come into play. I loved that he didn't pressure me into something, and he wasn't that experienced either.

"I know, and you're amazing for that. It's not off the table, but let's just see how the dance goes without pinning any expectations to it," I told him.

"The tent is already up. Chad let a bunch of us come over earlier and get our gear set up before we needed to haul things out of the barn."

"Are there many people staying?"

"Some. Most of the pledges. We're on clean-up duty in the morning. Some people also booked hotel rooms because their dates refused to sleep in a tent," he whispered. I laughed as I thought about some of the girls I knew his frat brothers were dating. Some of them were high maintenance.

"You mean the princess squad is actually stepping foot inside of a real barn? It's just totally crossing the line to expect them to sleep in a tent overnight?"

"Pretty much," he nodded.

There were cars lined up in a field across from a two-story white farmhouse when we pulled into the gravel drive. A large red barn across the field had the doors wide open, and I could already hear music drifting out. Tents were interspersed about ten feet apart under an outcropping of tall trees.

"Doesn't look like we'll have a lot of privacy after all," I mused, a little disappointed.

"Don't worry. I got here first, so we're far in the back corner. It's as good as we're going to get." Part of me knew Alison was right. As long as I loved and trusted Tyler, the when and the how didn't matter. "Let's put your bag in the tent and then head over. I've got some rum we can sneak into our thermos."

"Are you trying to corrupt me, Mr. Kain?" I smiled over at him.

"Never, Miss Grant," he teased as he leaned across the center console, cupped the back of my neck, and drew me towards his supple lips. The same warmth I felt every time he kissed me surged through me. "Mmmm. We might need to sneak off early. I'm not sure if I can keep my hands to myself with you wearing that skirt."

"I have to admit you're pulling off the overall look." My voice was low as I ran my hand over his defined shoulder and into the hair at the nape of his neck.

"You haven't seen the hat yet."

I laughed before I gave him another slow kiss, lazily pressing my tongue against his. "Well, now you've piqued my interest. I need the full visual."

He wiggled his eyebrows and leaned back after planting one last kiss on my cheek. Reaching over the seat, he grabbed a cowboy hat from the back seat and climbed out of the car. I wasn't expecting to start a relationship right at the beginning of college, but I had to admit that Tyler had set the bar pretty high. He opened doors; he was polite; he always made me feel like my opinion mattered. When he opened my door and helped guide me out of the car, looking handsome with that hat pulled low over his forehead, I decided I was going to relax and let things happen naturally tonight.

"Oh, come on, you brought a ringer. That's hardly fair," Joel whined as he looked over at me, his gaze lingering on the exposed skin on my legs.

"He's right, Big T. Using Kendall as your partner is like cheating. Especially since she's not even drunk," Rory agreed.

"So now it's my fault that your dates are alcoholics?" Tyler laughed as he pulled me tighter against his side.

"Hey! Hey... hey... hey... I resemble that comment." Gretchen dissolved into giggles as she clung to Joel's arm. Her romantic entanglement with Rory had been short-lived, and it hadn't taken her long before she moved on to his best friend.

"I'm not an alcoholic. Don't lump me in with that one," Bridgette, Rory's new girlfriend, insisted as she cringed, looking over at an intoxicated Gretchen.

"Sorry, Bridge, you're right," Tyler agreed as he gave her an apologetic smile. "You and Kendall are the exceptions."

"Don't pretend you're not drunk," Rory laughed as he looked over at his girlfriend. "I saw you taking shots with Gretchen earlier."

"I never said I wasn't drunk..." she shrugged, a light blush staining her cheek. I couldn't tell if it was from embarrassment or the alcohol she'd consumed. "I said I wasn't an alcoholic."

"Semantics." Rory laughed as he stepped in behind the tall blonde and wrapped his arms around her tiny waist. I wanted to dislike his new girlfriend because I was afraid she was another Gretchen, but she was nice. They'd met about a month into school in a study group and had been inseparable ever since. She spent quite a bit of time in his dorm room, so we often passed in the hallway, but unlike Gretchen, she'd never been unfriendly toward me.

"Okay, enough talking, Rory," Joel rolled his eyes as he untangled himself from Gretchen. "Let go of the girl and let's do this."

Rory leaned down and laid a scorching kiss on the side of Bridgette's neck while she giggled. Tyler tightened his hold on my hips as we waited for Rory and Joel to get lined up on the other side of the table.

"I feel like we should make Kendall do shots for every time she makes one," Joel laughed, giving me a cheeky wink.

"Whatever, sore loser. We both know I'm going to be as sober at the end of this game as I am now."

Since they needed every advantage they could get, we let Rory shoot first, his ping-pong ball hitting the lip of the head cup and bouncing off.

"Ahhh! The great Chandler missed a shot! Maybe we should have your girl-friend shoot for you," Tyler teased as Rory's face pinched in disgust. He hated losing and was fiercely competitive. I could relate, but his attitude still sometimes left an unpleasant taste in my mouth. There had to be more substance to him behind all that bravado, but he rarely let his walls down around me.

"Whatever. Just take your shot," Rory muttered, taking a sip from his beer can.

Tyler carefully lined himself up in the center of the table before he smoothly sunk a shot into the center cup.

"Nice!" I cheered as he straightened up and gave me a bright smile. The two of us worked back and forth, meticulously clearing the field. By the time only two of their cups were left on their side of the long table, they had only managed to sink two of ours.

"Damn," Joel sighed, his voice taking on a bit of a slur. "Either we're really this bad, or they're really that good."

"You're that bad," Gretchen hiccupped as she wobbled next to their side of the table with a red cup in her hand. Joel was going to have his hands full with drunken Gretchen this evening.

"You're up, Special K. Let's see how good that aim is," Rory taunted as he flicked a ping-pong ball in my direction.

Knowing that it wouldn't matter because we were so far ahead, I carefully lined up a shot that bounced in front of the lead cup and sunk with a satisfying splash in the back one. Usually, that move would've gotten us two, but we were on the home stretch.

"Show off," Joel rolled his eyes.

I shrugged and laughed as Tyler stepped up beside me, placing a wet smacking kiss on my cheek before he shot towards the last cup standing. It spun around the rim a few times before it dropped in, and the drunk girls around the table cheered as Rory and Joel both downed the last of their beer.

"Rematch?" Joel slurred as he braced both hands against the edge of the table.

"Nope," Tyler shook his head. "I'm gonna go celebrate with my girl."

He picked me up and threw me over his shoulder before he strode out of the barn with a chorus of catcalls following us out.

"Put me down," I giggled as I swatted at Tyler's back.

"Calm down... I'm working on it." His long legs carried us across the field, and I laughed at his determination. Neither of us was all that intoxicated. He'd had a few swigs of the rum he'd snuck in, and the one cup we'd each been forced to drink.

"Here we are. Home sweet home. At least for tonight." My nerves picked up as he gently settled me on my feet and held open the tent flap.

"It's bigger than I thought it'd be," I told him as I peeked inside.

He stifled a laugh, and I joined in when I thought about what I'd just said.

"I didn't want you to feel crammed in here with me. I know it's not a hotel room... but hold on." He dipped inside the tent and dug around in his bag. One by one, he flicked on battery-operated tea lights and placed them in the corners of the tent, and a soft glow illuminated the space. Tyler had put up a queen-sized air mattress which filled up most of the area, a dark green sleeping bag open on top.

"Come sit with me?" He asked with a shy smile on his face as he perched himself on the edge of the mattress. As I took his hand and sat next to him, my nod was shaky. His large palm felt searing on my knee as he scooted closer to me, softly rubbing the exposed skin below the hem of my skirt.

"I meant to ask you something a while ago, but it just never seemed like the right time." It was more for curiosity's sake than anything.

"Sure..." he nodded, "you know I'll tell you anything."

"Why do they call you Big T?" He shot me a panicked look, and I could see a faint pink glow spread across his pale cheeks."Nevermind. You don't have to tell me."

He laughed as his free hand scratched the back of his neck.

"No. It's fine. They're jerks anyway, but..." He paused as he scanned my face. "It stands for Big Tuna."

"What?" I laughed as he looked embarrassed. I wasn't sure if his friends were fans of a particular TV show, but that was an oddly specific nickname.

"Why?" There were pink spots high on his cheekbones, stained with a blush as I looked up at him. "Why would they name you after a fish?"

"Uh, it's more of a size reference than anything else. Not necessarily the fish."

"You guys are weird." I shook my head. Many guys in the house had ridiculous nicknames, but I still wasn't getting it. "I'm not following. Why would they call you tuna because you're tall?"

He coughed, and his fingers squeezed my knee. "The size isn't referring to my height."

"Oh..." I thought about it for a moment before I looked at his nervous face. "Oh!"

"Yeah..." The flush on his face was full blown, and he wasn't making eye contact with me.

"How would they even...?" I trailed off as I realized he was referring to something of a delicate subject.

"We share a communal bathroom," he shrugged as he looked anywhere but at me.

"Right..." How was I supposed to respond to that? I'd never actually felt it outside of his clothes, and it wasn't like I had any experience to compare sizes.

"Listen. I know it's not that big of a deal, but they won't stop calling me that, and I'm sorry if it makes you uncomfortable. We don't even have to do anything if you don't want to..." His nervous rambling endeared him to me even more, so I didn't even have to think as I leaned in and captured his lips with mine.

"Fuck..." He breathed out as he broke the kiss and laid his forehead against my shoulder.

"Sorry. I just couldn't help myself." I never wanted him to feel self-conscious around me.

"No, it's not that. It's just..." he sighed as he trailed off.

"Talk to me."

He lifted his head and cupped my jaw, gently stroking his thumbs over my cheekbones. "I know I'm not the most talkative guy, but I want you to know how I feel about you."

My heart was hammering in my chest as he swallowed heavily and took a deep breath. "I'm pretty sure I'm in love with you."

"Me too..." His eyes lit up at my whisper and nod. He didn't even hesitate as he pulled my face towards him, passionately stealing my breath and setting me on fire. Hands and lips roamed as we eventually settled underneath the warm sleeping bags.

"We don't have to do anything," he panted as he kissed along the side of my neck, and his fingers unbuttoned my plaid shirt.

"I want to. I want this. Just relax," I murmured as I unhooked the clasps on his overalls.

Nervous anticipation filled me as we both shimmied out of our clothing until the only thing separating us was my denim skirt. Tyler's chest was firm, lean muscles on display as he propped himself above me, stroking back the loose hairs that'd fallen out of my braids.

"I do love you, Kendall. I can't believe you're real sometimes." I felt moisture pool in the corners of my eyes as he gazed at me with pure adoration.

"How do we...?" I trailed off and cleared my throat.

"I... uh... I should get a..." He leaned back, and I watched the muscles in his pale shoulders move as he dug into his bag. When he rejoined me, he laid down, facing me, and stroked his fingers along my cheek. They trailed down my neck and to my shoulder as he pressed the little packet into my hand. He kissed me deeply as I fumbled to cover him. Rolling to his back, he helped me get on top.

"Oh..." I gasped as he helped guide me, his face a mask of nervous concentration. It wasn't perfect, and neither of us knew what to expect, but as he kissed and touched me, I'd never felt more wanted.

"Sorry if that wasn't what you expected," he apologized shyly as he gathered me into his arms, and I settled my head onto his chest once we were done  It had felt good after the initial burning sensation died down, but it had been over quickly. I wasn't expecting much; I knew Alison said sometimes guys had a hard time holding back the first few times.

"It was amazing..." I sighed as I looked up toward him.

"You don't have to soothe my ego," he laughed. Okay... it wasn't perfect, but I don't think it is for anyone. The important thing was that he showed me how much he cared for me the entire time.

"They say it only gets better with practice, right?"

His smile filled his entire face as he kissed my forehead and held me tightly. "I'm definitely in for getting as much practice time as possible with you."

My eyes drifted shut as I listened to the steady timbre of his heart. He fell asleep quickly, but I struggled with the noises filtering through the tent. The dance was still in full swing; the music showing no signs of stopping.

Carefully slipping out of the sleeping bag, I redressed and headed towards the farmhouse. Chad's parents had a bathroom they'd given all the students permission to use. The house was quiet as I slipped inside and locked the door behind me. My cheeks were flushed, and my braids were a mess as I glanced at myself in the large mirror.

It didn't take me long to clean myself up with a warm washcloth, throwing it in the hamper in the corner. Hopefully, Tyler was still asleep when I returned; I didn't want him to think I snuck out on him after what had just happened.

"Oh!" My hand flew to my chest as the door swung open, and I noticed Joel leaning up against the wall directly across from where I was standing.

"Sorry... didn't mean to scare you." His voice was low and smooth as he stepped forward... he smelled faintly of something fruity, his bare chest glistening in the low lights. The muscles on his lean, athletic body stood out as he moved. I'd not expected him to be quite so chiseled.

"Why are you half-naked?" After Tyler and I snuck away, the party got much more interesting, apparently.

"Gretchen..." he sighed as he looked down at his chest.

"Uh. Nevermind. None of my business," I stuttered nervously as I planned my exit strategy.

"Not like that," he laughed as he reached forward and fingered the end of one of my braids. "She spilled her drink on me. I came in here to get cleaned up. Did you and Tyler enjoy your little celebration?"

"Uh..."

"That awkward, huh?" He was holding back laughter, and I was suddenly embarrassed that he could tell something had happened between us. I wondered if we'd be the talk of the pledged tomorrow.

"No... it was..." I trailed off as I felt a blush stain my cheeks, quickly averting my eyes away from him.

"I gotta admit, I admire his determination. I wasn't sure if he could capture the attention of a beautiful, smart girl like you," Joel mused, nodding in my direction as he gave my body an appraising look. "But here we are..."

"Isn't he your friend?" Tyler had never indicated that there had been any problems between himself and any of the other pledges.

He took another step towards me, his warm skin brushing against mine. "That doesn't mean I can't be jealous."

Nervous laughter bubbled up. Joel had always been friendly with me, but he'd never shown a genuine interest. Not like this. "Well. Yeah, can you let me through?"

"Just know you've always got more options than you think." He took a step to the side and held his hand out to the side. "Don't settle for comfortable."

"I'm going to pretend this conversation never happened, since I know you're drunk. But being with Tyler isn't settling for anything." Joel's attitude towards our relationship was making me angry. Tyler and I respected each other and cared about each other; I didn't appreciate him indicating otherwise.

"If that's what you've gotta tell yourself."

I felt my irritation build up as I walked away from him, the screen door of the farmhouse snapping closed loudly as I rushed outside. My feet carried me across the field and to our tent quickly. Luckily, I had no more awkward encounters on the way.

Tyler was asleep, turned on his side as I slipped underneath the covers with him, and tried to calm down. I hoped Joel didn't remember what he'd said to me tomorrow. I know I was willing myself to forget the way he'd looked at me.

# Chapter Six:
## Freshman Year

### MAY

"I can't believe we only have a few nights left in this place." This was the first time I'd seen Alison semi-emotional about anything. She was usually easygoing, and I couldn't imagine her being anything but that. I was going to miss her terribly over the summer.

"It seems a little surreal that we've almost finished a whole year. I'm going to miss this place," I agreed.

"You're going to miss our tiny dorm room that smells faintly of mildew and communal bathrooms?" There was the roommate that I knew and loved.

"Okay, no. I will not miss that part. But I am going to miss you and Tyler. And all the friends we've made."

"July cannot come fast enough. My summer is going to be so boring. Same small-minded people I grew up with, in the same small town." I wasn't sure about what this summer held. Tyler was going to be busy most of the summer.

"There aren't any friends you're excited to see?" Since spring break, I hadn't seen Dylan, and I was excited to catch up.

"Not really. I've known them all since we were in diapers. The smart ones won't come home, and the others never left."

"You can come to visit earlier if you want to. It'll just be me hanging out with Dylan, alternated with me teaching classes at the community center."

She shuddered. "I don't know how you can stand to teach children."

I laughed at the look of outright disgust on her face. She'd thought for a hot minute that she wanted to teach, but after a few underwhelming teacher observations, she'd quickly changed her mind.

"It's art. Everyone has fun." I'd helped some with classes at the community center when I was in high school, but I got to teach some beginner courses this summer. Another nice perk would be unlimited studio access and a discount on supplies.

"Unless you're horrible at it and your life drawing teacher encourages you to find a major that doesn't involve your piss poor illustration skills." She had enrolled in one of my intro drawing courses, thinking since it covered her fine arts core requirement it'd be easy.

"I told you it'd be harder than it looked." Everyone thought that drawing people would be easy, but there was so much contouring and light balance involved, it was quite tricky.

"At least your drawings resembled people." I burst out laughing as I recalled the reaction of the first life model to her illustration. She hadn't known how to handle drawing shadow and contouring, so it looked vaguely like abstract line art. Then, there was the suspicious blank area in the middle of the paper where she outright refused to draw his uncovered lap.

"You didn't need to worry about hurting his feelings. He's used to people looking at him naked." The model hadn't even cared that the classroom was full of tittering freshman females; he just proudly disrobed and let it all hang out.

"I know. But let's hope the poor guy is a grow-er and not a show-er, because I was underwhelmed." She tried to hold a straight face, but we both dissolved into laughter.

"Speaking of growers." Her arched eyebrow sobered me quickly.

I'd confessed to her one night how awkward my sex life was. It wasn't bad, but it wasn't good either. Tyler always made me feel cared for and took care of me, but he also had little in the way of stamina.

"Let's not go there." She'd assured me that losing my v-card would be worth it, but sex was still a point of frustration for me.

"Oh, come on, isn't this supposed to be what you talk to your girlfriends about?" Alison loved any bit of gossip, so she was dying to dissect Tyler's performance.

"I love him. He's a nice guy."

"I know he is, but have you tried talking to him again?"

With a red face and shaking hands, I'd tried to talk to him without insulting him, but it hadn't gone well. Things hadn't been the same since then. No guy wants to hear that they are disappointingly quick in bed.

"No. It is what it is," I shook my head. "I don't want to have that conversation again."

She shrugged as she gave me a sympathetic look. "Maybe it's time to cut your losses."

"What the hell, Allie?" Was her solution to difficult situations always to bail? "You're saying I should break up with him because he cums too fast?"

"Well, maybe you're just not physically compatible. Do you see yourself ending up with Tyler if he's a two-pump chump?"

"I can't with you."

Seriously.

"Just trying to give you some friendly advice. If the physical chemistry isn't there, he's probably not the one," she said cautiously. "If you're with the right person, it should just come naturally."

I understood what she was saying, but we were compatible in other ways. Tyler was my best friend. We could talk for hours. I felt closer to him than I had any guy before, even Dylan.

My phone chimed with a few text messages, and I pulled it out of my pocket.

*Dylan: Freedom, sweet freedom... done with my last final.*

*Dylan: When are you heading home?*

*Kendall: I have two more. I'll be home on Saturday.*

*Dylan: Can't wait to see you.*

I smiled at his message and then opened the other one that came through.

*Tyler: Meet me after your last final Friday? I've got some news.*

We'd planned to go out to breakfast before my parents came to pick me up, but I wasn't arguing with more time together. It would be hard to be a few hours away from each other all summer.

*Kendall: Sure. How's studying going?*

*Tyler: It's going. I have to get back to it.*

"Quit ignoring me," Alison pouted. "Let's finish packing up this shit so we can watch a movie."

"Such a drill sergeant." She'd been on me all week to stay on top of packing and studying, so we weren't doing everything last minute.

"I still need to study for my final in the morning."

"Okay, okay. I'm folding." I pulled down a stack of hangers and started folding my clothes into the duffel bags I'd be taking back home in a few days.

"I can't wait to have a bigger closet next year." Her eyes got this dreamy look whenever she talked about our apartment together next year.

"Don't forget your own bathroom, too." That was my favorite part—no more communal bathrooms.

"Yes! No more flip-flops in the shower."

"I'm just happy we found a decent place within walking distance." Neither of us had been interested in rushing when it'd happened earlier in the semester. I had no interest in playing nice with the Gretchens of the world. We'd rented a two-bedroom apartment close to campus for next year, but hopefully, it was a place we could stay in the long term.

"Not that I don't love you, but I'm looking forward to having the privacy of my own room."

"Same girl," I nodded thoughtfully. "Same."

"Hey, come on in." Tyler's dorm room looked like mine now did, a pile of bags near the door and a virtual blank canvas.

"Where's Joel?"

He took my hand and pulled me down next to him to sit on the edge of his twin bed. "He's out with friends getting pizza."

"You mean we've got some alone time?" I grinned as I leaned forward to kiss him on the cheek. He grabbed my hand as he sat there stiffly, running his long fingers over my own.

"So, what's this news?" I asked curiously; he wasn't acting like his usual affectionate self.

"I found something out this week about next year." His voice sounded worried. I wondered if he was second-guessing being in the frat next year. He said he enjoyed it, but he hated all the required time that cut into studying.

"Is it something about the house? I thought they'd already given out your room assignments?"

"Well, it affects that too, but this is something we talked about a few months ago."

"Just tell me already. You're being all cryptic." He was making me a little nervous.

"They had some spaces open up in the study abroad program for next semester."

"Okay..." I trailed off. He'd talked about it a little, but he said he didn't even know if he wanted to go if spaces opened up because it was a big commitment and disrupted his plans here.

"I'll be going to London, at least for the first semester, in early August."

"Wow, you got in. That's amazing." He'd been wait-listed for a study abroad program working with a global health initiative based in London.

"I'm pretty excited, but..." He shook his head and blew out a heavy breath.

"What's wrong?" I shifted sideways to face him and watched as his posture deflated.

"I'm not even sure how to say this." His voice was low and nervous, cracking towards the end.

"Just talk to me." I ran my fingers through his hair, and he flinched away from me.

"This isn't fair to you." *Wait... what?*

"What are you talking about?" When we had talked about it, we agreed that long-distance was still a possibility.

"I've got that internship this summer, and I know I was supposed to visit you for a week, but now, with me leaving in August..." he trailed off as he leaned away from me.

"Oh." He was blowing me off.

His face was a contrite mask of regret. "Kendall, I'm sorry."

"You're breaking up with me," I whispered as I looked at him in disbelief. We'd been together for the whole school year—almost ten months—and he just wanted to throw it all away.

"I don't think I can do the long-distance thing for that long. If the fall goes well, I might stay the whole year, and..."

"Just stop," I put my hand up, shaking as I processed that he was doing this right before we went home. I guess at least he had the decency to wait until all my finals were over.

"I..."

"Stop!" He pulled his hand away from me and sat there, looking chastised. "Would you let me talk?"

"Okay," he replied with his head lowered.

"Don't you think I should get a say in this? I'm okay with long distances. We're both busy now, but we've made it work. We could do Skype or something. It may even make us more productive without the distraction of..."

He started shaking his head, and my voice trailed off. "No."

"Oh. Oh..." I took a long look at his profile, finally understanding what he was saying. "YOU don't want this anymore. You don't want me."

"It's not that I don't want you. I just think it's a lot of pressure put on both of us to maintain something that might not be worth it."

"Wow. Really?" I stood up and turned to him, the venom in my voice clear. "Don't worry. Never mind, I get it now. You don't think I'm worth it."

"Kendall..."

"No." I threw up my hand. "Nope. Don't *Kendall* me. I'm going to leave. And you're going to lose my number. I can't believe I wasted this whole year on you if this is how you're going to end it."

"I didn't mean to hurt you," he sighed, looking as if he was going to cry. My first reaction had been sadness, but now I was rolling right into anger.

"You just told me I'm not worth the effort of a discussion about a long-distance relationship. How you feel about me is abundantly clear," I hissed as a tear leaked out of the corner of my eye. I wasn't sure whether it was from anger or sadness, but I needed to leave. Now. "Goodbye, Tyler."

I turned towards his door before the first tears fell, slamming the door behind me as I headed for the elevators. My vision was blurry as I rushed around the corner, and I didn't notice him until a large hand had closed around my wrist.

"Kendall?" I looked up, and Rory stood there with a concerned look on his face. I hadn't seen him since before finals, his hair was chaotic, but he looked relaxed. He must be done with his exams as well.

"Let go of me," I croaked out as the tears ran down my cheeks, the dam finally breaking.

"Hey, what's wrong? Why are you crying?"

"Just leave me alone," I begged as I tried to tug my arm out of his warm hand. I didn't need a witness to my breakdown, especially knowing that he'd be Tyler's roommate next year.

"What happened? Did Tyler do something? Do I need to go kick his ass?"

"No. Just let go of me and leave me alone. And tell your stupid frat brother to forget he ever met me." I hoped I never saw Tyler again. He could keep his two pumps to himself and find another girl to keep unsatisfied.

"Did you guys break up?" A loud sob tore out of me, and he gently pulled me into his chest, cradling the back of my head. "I'm gonna take that as a yes."

I drew in uneven breaths as I felt the soft cotton of his shirt become wet with my tears. I couldn't believe how naïve I'd been.

"He's an idiot. I guess he told you."

My head pulled back, and I looked him in the eyes as his hands settled on my shoulders. "You knew?"

"He had to clear it with the house to keep his membership," he shrugged. "And they had to shift another guy into our room to keep numbers up."

"How long have you known?" Tyler acted strangely before finals, but I chalked it up to him needing to study. Now, all the pieces were making sense. He'd been actively hiding this from me.

"Since Monday, why?" My jaw clenched, and his eyes widened. "He just now told you? He's known they were trying to open a space for him for weeks."

"Just stop. It doesn't matter. I need..." Stepping back, his hands fell. I swiped at the wetness on my cheeks with the backs of my hand as I sniffled.

"Do you wanna go to the dining hall? Talk for a bit?" His blue eyes were filled with concern as he looked down at me. I appreciated the concern, but he was too close to all of this.

"No."

"Alright. You've got my number if you need anything," Rory nodded as he stuffed his hands into the pockets of his shorts.

"I just need space. Tell him not to contact me."

He nodded and rocked back on his heels, still giving me a wary look. "I'll pass along the message."

"Thanks. Uh, sorry." I waved my hand at the large wet spot in the center of his shirt.

"No problem," he smiled. "Take care, Kendall."

"You, too. Have a good summer." I tried to smile, but I'm sure I probably looked like a disaster. At least I hadn't worn any makeup this morning.

He nodded, and I turned, escaping into the elevators. My parents couldn't get here fast enough. I needed to get away from this place.

# Chapter Seven:
## Two Weeks Before the Wedding
### (ALMOST) PRESENT DAY

"Oh, my God. Seriously, Allie?" Stef was shaking her head as she looked over at Alison. We were currently sitting in the car, parked in front of one of the few male revues in town. I'd never been, but Alison insisted I needed this experience before I walked down the aisle.

"Oh, come on!" Allie scoffed. You don't think they're looking at half-naked girls right now?"

"No. I really don't," Stef insisted. "I just got a text from Cam with a pic of them all in a cigar and whiskey bar."

"Well, I'm going to see some almost naked men tonight, with or without you guys."

Watching my Maid of Honor face off with one of my bridesmaids had to be one of the funniest things I'd seen in a while.

"This just seems like too much of a cliché," Stef sighed as she looked towards the neon sign mounted above the innocuous-looking building. Inside, dozens of thirsty women were just waiting to see random oiled-up men in their underwear.

"That baby daddy of yours must not be getting the job done," Allie taunted. "You're awfully uptight."

"Oh, you just had to go there. Didn't you?" Stef growled as her eyes narrowed at Alison.

"You'd think for someone who used to be fun; you'd be down for watching your closest friends and your new sister getting humped by greased-up strangers."

"Now you're just making it sound creepy," Stef laughed. She wasn't wrong.

"Hey, this is a classy place," Alison argued as she crossed her arms over her chest.

"Oh, my God. I can't with you," I giggled as they both turned to where I was seated in the back.

"Why don't we let the bride tell us what she wants tonight," Stef suggested.

Alison turned in her seat and gave me an imploring look. "She wants hunky men to gyrate on her lap, right?"

"She already has a hunky man she can ask to gyrate on her lap..." Stef trailed off as she made a face.

"What the...? Ew. Did you just...?" Allie asked as she looked at Stef like she'd lost her mind. "About your own brother?"

"Yeah. That may have been a little too far," Stefanie agreed with distaste.

"Ya think?" Allie's whole body shuddered, and she made a gagging sound. "Alright. Now we have to go so I can get the mental image of that out of my head."

"Sounds like a pretty pleasant mental image to me." The two of them turned and looked at me, shaking their heads.

"Well, you're the one marrying the guy. Of course, you'd think it'd be hot," she scoffed. "Seeing him almost naked is something that'll be burned into my mind for the rest of my life. I don't need any reminders."

"We thought you were out of town!"

Alison would never let us live that down. We have one encounter outside of my bedroom, and suddenly it's the end of the world. "Well, I came back early. And now I can't look at our kitchen counter the same way ever again."

"You're moving next month anyway," I shrugged. It was the end of an era.

"Not the point."

"You're losing focus here, Allie..." Stef tried to redirect our excited friend back to this evening's events. It was two weeks before the wedding, and we'd decided to have our respective bachelor and bachelorette events now, just in case anyone overdid it.

"Right! Naked men. Let's go," Allie hopped out of the passenger seat and opened the rear door, extending her hand inside the car to yank me out onto the sidewalk.

"Here. Put these on." A white paper bag was thrust into my hands, and my eyes widened as I looked inside.

"No." I shook my head as I took in the plastic monstrosity my best friend expected me to wear—nope—not going to happen.

"Oh, come on! You people are no fun. You're young. You only get married once," she insisted with a pout. "Well. We hope, anyway."

"She's only getting married once." I laughed as Stefanie shot me a stern look.

"Only once," I nodded. This one was sticking. He was my future, and our feet were toasty warm. I had faith; it wasn't all going to fall apart this time.

Alison smiled at me. "Right. You only get married once, so you better enjoy your last night of freedom."

"The wedding is in two weeks." I pointed out.

"Well, fine. Thirteenth from the last night of freedom." I could tell that my friend was just trying to create a fun night for me, and I'd do the same for her, but I didn't need crazy accessories to do it.

"Fine. Whatever. I'll go see the half-naked hunks for you," I conceded. "But I'm not wearing the penis bobble crown."

"Seriously?!?! That's the best part." Allie exclaimed. *Good. Then she wouldn't mind if I saved it to force her to wear it.*

"The sash is more than enough." I would not be one of those obnoxious brides covered in penises.

"Wait till you see what it says," Allie laughed as she pulled out a white sash from the bag.

"Same Penis Forever," Stef said in a flat voice, rolling her eyes. "How romantic."

"Wait till you see yours," Allie clapped as she started digging through the bag in her hands.

"Oh, God. You're nuts, Allie." I giggled. She had gotten way too into this. The last time she hadn't gone to this much trouble planning things. At least I didn't think she did. We hadn't gotten this far the first time.

Allie pulled out a handful of hot pink sashes, and I started reading the rhinestone messages emblazoned on them. "Pecker Inspector...really?"

"That better not be mine," Stef told her with an edge of warning in her voice.

"Don't worry. It's not." She thrust the other into Stef's hand.

"Hot Mama, that one's not so bad," I shrugged as I looked at it. At least hers didn't have a rhinestone penis on it.

I heard a chime, and Allie pulled her phone out of the pocket of her dress. "Alright. The others are already in there. The show is about to start and they're having trouble keeping people out of our seats."

"Fine, whatever. I guess we're doing this. Just don't tag me in any photos on social media. The parents would have a field day with this one." Stef had gone back to work this year teaching after Nat started preschool.

"Me either," I agreed. "I don't need the university seeing me wearing a sash with a rhinestone penis on it."

"You guys are no fun." She pouted.

"Promise me no embarrassing pictures, Alison." We were here to have an enjoyable night out, not make mistakes we couldn't take back, or have crazy pictures posted on the internet.

"But..."

"Promise me. Or Stef and I will go find the guys," I warned. They wouldn't mind if we crashed their party.

"Ugh. Fine." I knew we were raining on Alison's fun, but we were old enough to know better. It was one thing to be reckless at twenty; I hoped those days were in the past now that we were grown adults with jobs and kids.

"I might go find the guys anyway," Stef teased. I knew she wouldn't leave me, but she enjoyed getting our friend wound up.

"No! Kendall needs to have at least one night of fun before she's an old, boring married lady."

"Like me." Stef often referred to herself as an old, boring married lady, so it was appropriate. I thought she was still fun, but obviously, our prior ties had changed over the last several years.

"Because my fiancé is known for being a party pooper," I laughed. He'd been quite the troublemaker a few years ago.

"You know what I mean. You spend every night with him. It's my turn to have fun with you." She was right. This was the end of an era. We'd been roommates for a long time. I owed it to her to at least pretend to have fun at my bachelorette party.

"Alright. I'll wear the sash and let you take pictures, but you can't tag me in anything."

"Deal. I've gotta have some photographic evidence to show your kids you were fun once," Allie giggled.

"Somehow, I don't think my future children are going to want to see pictures of me getting a lap dance at a male revue. There isn't enough counseling in the world to make that visual trauma go away."

"Fine. Then I'm using it as blackmail," Allie laughed as she put her hand on her hip.

"You're forgetting who I'm marrying. He'll think it's funny." He would. Then he'd probably offer to give me my own private lap dance. Maybe I should find the guys.

"Whatever. Less talking and more banana hammock stuffing. I've got a purse full of ones, and I know where to spend them." She pulled open her little rhinestone clutch to reveal a stack of dollar bills. She was prepared for this one.

"Lead the way." I gestured towards the door. Might as well get in there.

An hour later, glitter and confetti covered my hair, I'd had clothing thrown at me, and I was more than a little drunk.

"I told you this would be fun!" Allie yelled over the pulsing music as we waited for them to clear the stage for the next performer. Alison had reserved us front-row seats, and I had to admit, it'd been a fun show to watch.

"So fun," I giggled as Stefanie pushed another cocktail into my hand.

"There isn't enough alcohol to erase this experience from my brain," she whispered directly into my ear as Alison bounced in her seat.

"Nope." I bit my lip and shook my head. This was going to be embedded in my memory for quite a while.

"Alright, ladies and gentlemen. Now comes my favorite part of the evening." The MC came over the microphone, and the crowd went wild, cheering.

"Surprisingly, we only have one special guest tonight, she's getting married in two weeks..." My eyes went wide, and I looked over at Alison.

"Love you." She blew me a kiss and shrugged as the crowd cheered again.

"Let's put our hands together and get Kendall up on stage for her own special performance."

Stefanie started laughing as I downed the rest of my drink and started shaking my head.

"Oh, Kendall. Where are you? We've got a special package ready for delivery," the MC called, and the crowd went wild again with laughter and cheers.

"Don't you dare," I growled as Alison stood up and started cheering as she pointed at me. She was dead.

"She's right here!"

"I hate you," I growled as I tried to slump down in my seat. It wouldn't work, though. There was nowhere to hide when you were in the front row—damned sneaky Alison.

"Go get her, boys." The MC laughed as two scantily clad waiters appeared in front of me. They lifted me, chair and all, and started carrying me to the stage while the crowd went wild. Bright lights prevented me from seeing the audience clearly, but I just knew that Alison had to be up front filming this. I was going to have to steal her phone later.

"Kendall here just graduated with her master's degree. What do you say we take her back to school tonight?!" The crowd went wild again, and I saw several of the performers line up in the wings of the stage. Most of them were wearing suits or dress shirts; one, in particular, was wearing a tweed jacket with elbow patches.

A familiar old Van Halen song pumped through the speakers, and I laughed from my seat at center stage. The men gyrated to the beat, creating a loose formation around my chair. When they got to the chorus; I could hear the audience sing along.

"I think these ladies are *Hot for Teacher*!" The MC called out, and the men simultaneously ripped off their shirts and jackets. I laughed as I watched them work their way towards the edge of the stage, grinding and continuing to strip off their clothes. It was quite a sight to see up close. I was almost enjoying the show... until the one with the tweed jacket turned and headed toward me.

"Oh, shit," I muttered under my breath as he strutted his way across the stage, shedding clothes along the way until the last thing left covering him was a tiny piece of cloth.

He stopped in front of my chair and reached forward to grab the back, leaning toward me as his hips pulsed to the beat. My knuckles gripped the sides of the chair tightly as I watched him move inches from my face. He seemed to enjoy my reaction as he placed a foot on the chair between my legs and thrusted his hips practically in my face. I was sure my face was bright red as he continued his dance, luckily, not touching me.

"Let's give our bride-to-be a round of applause!" The crowd cheered again as the guys all waved and cleared the stage, stopping one by one to kiss me on the cheek. They led me off the side of the stage and back to my seat that'd been replaced in a daze.

"That was awesome!" Alison bounced in her seat, and I quickly downed the drink I'd been handed when I sat back down. The rest of the night was a blur of alcohol and half-naked bodies as we sat through the rest of the show.

My friends and bridesmaids were drunk off their butts, except for Stef. We got them into Ubers, and then she drove us back to my apartment. I helped a drunken Allie from the car and supported her weight as I struggled to unlock the door and go inside. Depositing her into her bed, I grabbed a bottle of water from the fridge.

"Drink this, Alki..." I insisted as I helped prop her head up with a pillow.

"Mmm. That was fun," she giggled as she hiccupped and then rolled over. I was going to miss seeing her every day.

The apartment was quiet as I retreated to my bedroom. Not bothering to turn on the lights, I stripped off my sash and dress and slipped into the shower in my en suite bathroom. It felt good to rinse the sweat and glitter off my skin. Wrapped in a towel, I headed for bed, smiling when I saw the familiar head of messy hair on the pillow next to mine.

"You didn't tell me you were coming over after you guys were done," I whispered as I stood next to the bed.

"I left a little early. Cam didn't want to go home yet, so I caught a ride back here," his voice was rough from sleep, but he looked wide awake now. "Should I leave?"

He smiled as he rolled towards me and tugged at the top of my towel.

"Hey! Hands to yourself, Mister," I laughed as I tried to dance away from his reach. A large hand clamped down on my hip and held me in place.

"Is that what you want?" His voice was low as he slowly parted the towel and ran a fingertip across my collarbone while the soft cotton pooled around my waist.

"Maybe..." I sighed as he traced my skin and propped himself up so he could touch me.

"Liar." His gruff laugh sent a shiver through me as he leaned forward and captured a nipple between his soft lips. He pulled me into the warm bed and guided me to lie back on the pillows, his body covering mine. Then, he proceeded to thoroughly remind me why I was so looking forward to walking down the aisle to him.

# Chapter Eight:
## (Before) Sophomore Year

### JULY

"You'd better not be thinking of standing me up again." I looked up from my perch on the edge of my stool to where Dylan was leaning against the doorway to the ceramics classroom.

"Shh... don't break my concentration. I've been trying to throw this bowl for an hour, and I keep messing up the lip."

"Maybe you should just try again tomorrow," he shrugged, a wry grin on my face. He knew me. Until this bowl was on a drying rack, he knew I wasn't going anywhere.

"Shhh... let me work."

He sat down on the stool at the throwing wheel beside me, quietly leaning forward with his forearms resting on his thighs as he watched my hands manipulate the mound of clay. My hands gently smoothed the round mound in front of me, the wet slip of the clay against my fingers slowly helping the cylinder shape form. It was a little unnerving to have an audience, but he was quiet.

I slowly worked the cylinder upward until it was the height I needed, using subtle pressure. This part typically wasn't the problem. My problem was staying balanced as I moved my fingers to put pressure in the center and slowly create the center of the bowl. The rim flared out as I opened the center, and I held my breath as I pulled my hands away to grab my tools. First came cleaning up the inside of the shape, thinning out the excess clay.

My fingers were slimy as I dipped my sponge into the little water bucket to my side. The first pull of my fingers against the outside of the shape, and it looked like what I was going for. The second pull, and my bowl had finally taken the form I'd been trying to accomplish. Third pull, and I was satisfied with how it looked.

I glanced over at Dylan and smiled as I dropped the sponge into the bucket. His eyes were tracking my movements intently, and a thrill rushed through me when his eyes met mine. "That was amaz—"

"Shh. I'm not done yet. Don't jinx it." Slowing the wheel's spin, I grabbed my needle and methodically thinned out the base. Then, I carefully evened out the lip and pulled my hands away.

"Kendall..."

"Shh..." I picked up my sponge again and ran it up the outside of the bowl, carefully smoothing it out. Then, I squeezed the excess moisture back into my bucket and soaked up the water in the center of my bowl.

"Are you d—"

Pulling my hands free for a moment, I looked over at him in irritation. He was always trying to rush things. "Would you just be patient for once?"

The smirk he gave me as he held his hands up in defense brought a smile to my face. "Trust me; I've been patient."

He had. This summer had started rough. After Tyler dumped me the day before I came home, the funk I was in lingered. I knew I was better off without someone who didn't respect me, but it still hurt. I'd shown and given him parts of myself that were special. Knowing that it hadn't meant the same thing to him cut deeply. Losing Tyler, himself, didn't hurt anymore. Losing trust was still a gaping wound I didn't know how to close.

"Let me pull this off and get it covered to dry." I grabbed my wire and wet it before I carefully slipped it underneath the bowl—the clay released from the surface of the wheel with little resistance. Retrieving my drying board from behind me, I transferred the piece and then covered it with damp paper towels. I'd trim it tomorrow when I came back after my morning class.

Dylan followed me to the cabinet where I stored my supplies and stood silently as I put everything away. "Am I allowed to speak now?"

"You're the one who showed up earlier than I told you to." I glanced at my watch and saw that our agreed meeting time was still five minutes from now.

"I got off early and didn't want to go home." His hair was matted around the sides; he'd been on site all day, wearing a hard hat. The big black steel-toed boots he wore had dried mud around the edges and a thick layer of dirt and grime coated on the laces.

"You could have at least showered and changed your boots."

"I wanted to see you," he shrugged as he turned a boyish grin on me.

"We've seen each other every day for the last two months."

"And I only have thirteen days left with you before football camp starts," he murmured as he looked away and ran his fingers through the messy, dark curls at the back of his neck. I wasn't sure how to respond to that. It was going to be hard for me, too. We'd spent so much time together lately; I don't know how I survived most of last year away from him.

"We still going to the drive-in tonight?" They'd completely restored an old drive-in movie theater a few miles outside town. They showed family movies most of the time, but occasionally they'd pick up one of the summer release action movies. I'd teased Dylan relentlessly over his continued obsession with Marvel comic book characters, but I secretly enjoyed ogling the actors who portrayed them.

"Yeah. I managed to get my dad to switch cars, so I folded down the seats of the SUV." His car was tiny, so we usually ended up stretched out on a blanket in front of the vehicle, but the last time we'd gone, it'd rained. We ended up soaked and covered in mud by the time we got everything picked up and in the car.

"So, you switched cars but couldn't manage to shower?" My eyes rolled at the shrug that followed. "Who said I want to sit in a confined space with you when I know you've been hot and sweaty all day?"

"You think I'm hot?" he laughed as he arched an eyebrow at me.

"Temperature-wise... not looks-wise, oh arrogant one. You don't need anyone inflating your ego." He had enough girls at school doing that for him. Alison was right; he was a hot commodity on campus.

"That wasn't a no..."

"Are we fishing for compliments now, Dylan?"

He pursed his lips and quirked an eyebrow at me. "Just curious."

I closed my cabinet and wiped my hands on a towel before grabbing my dirty supplies and heading for the sinks. I'd found out the hard way that waiting to clean your tools was a bad idea.

"Why do you care, anyway? Is your fan club not fulfilling their duties?"

He frowned as he looked over at me. "Fan club?"

"Those girls who like to tag you in pictures on Facebook and Instagram. They seem to think quite highly of you." His feed was full of pictures with girls hanging all over him. He never seemed starved for female attention.

"Is that jealousy I detect? Worried someone might take your place?"

I scoffed as I turned back to the sink, using a brush to scrub underneath my short fingernails. "Hardly. They wouldn't follow you around so much if they knew how annoying you are."

"Doesn't seem to stop you."

Dylan had also come home for the summer unattached. The girl he'd been dating had transferred to another school starting in the fall term, and neither one of them had thought it'd be workable for them to keep dating.

"Oh... wow. Ego much? You think I'm the one following you?" I laughed with an eye roll. "Who showed up early because they missed me?"

He cleared his throat and shifted, averting his eyes from me. "Anyway. I wanted to see if you had any requests for snacks. I was going to stop by the store."

"You know what I like," I shrugged.

He looked over at me, shaking his head. "I do, but I'm trying to be a gentle-man."

"What has gotten into you? You're weird today."

He turned away from me and grabbed a clean towel from a hook, gently pressing it into my hands when I turned off the water. "I'm weird every day."

"You said it..."

"Alright. I get it. You don't want me around. I'll pick you up at six. If it makes you happy, I'll even go home and shower first."

"Thank you." Blowing a kiss over my shoulder, I watched as he looked at me one last time before turning towards the door and heading out.

His long legs took large strides, the denim on them tightly conforming to his skin. The skin on his arms and neck was deeply tanned from the hours he spent outside every day. He had an internship with a local civil engineering firm. I'd never tell him, but the muscles that'd popped up in his arms and chest since last year were pretty hot. Football training and hard labor had transformed him from the teen I'd grown up with into a man.

*Dylan: Running behind. Are you alright with walking over?*

I'd just finished drying my hair and threw it up into a ponytail.

*Kendall: Fine with me. You always take forever.*

*Dylan: You're the one who called me stinky.*

Kendall: You WERE stinky.

*Dylan: I prefer manly.*

Of course, you do.

Kendall: If that's what you have to tell yourself.

*Dylan: See you in a few.*

Quickly throwing my cell phone and house keys into my small purse, I checked myself over in the mirror again before leaving. Dylan's house was only a few streets over, so I cut through a few backyards at a brisk walk and knocked on his door within minutes. I could hear the loud clomp of his feet on the stairs before he pulled open the front door, and my mouth went dry.

"Damn, that was fast. Did you run here?" Dylan asked as he ran a towel over his hair. The curls were wilder than usual, curled tightly against his head. If I thought the muscles in his arms were impressive, the ones on his bare chest put those to shame. I didn't remember him being this ripped last summer, but I hadn't been paying attention then.

"No, just took the shortcut. Were you... uh, planning on wearing a shirt to the movies?"

I tried my best not to look at his bare chest, but I couldn't help it.

"Well, that was originally the plan... but with how much this seems to bother you..." he trailed off with a smirk, reaching forward to run the back of his finger down my flushed cheek. A burst of warmth traveled up my neck, and his smirk deepened at my sharp intake of breath.

"It's..." My voice cracked. "It's not bothering me."

"Alright." He stepped forward and pulled the door closed behind him. "The car is packed. Let's go then."

The bare skin of his chest brushed against my arm as he joined me on the top step. I looked over at him with wide eyes as he pulled the door shut.

"Seriously? Get a shirt."

"It's already in the car, too, Drama Queen." The heat in my cheeks was uncomfortable as I fruitlessly tried not to look, but it was right there, and he smelled so good now that he'd finally taken a shower.

"You're a jerk."

"Pretty much," he laughed as he jumped to the step below, pinching my side as he quickly took off towards the open back of his dad's SUV. Pulling a black T-shirt over his head, he covered all the exposed skin that'd been making it hard for me to concentrate. The old feelings of attraction I'd denied for Dylan roared back to life as I watched him open the passenger door and gesture for me to climb in.

"Let's go already. Always making us late, Ken."

"Yeah, cause I'm the one that takes forever to do my hair."

He ran a hand through his damp, messy curls and shrugged. "It's not my fault I was cursed with this mess."

The door closed with a soft click after I climbed in, and I fidgeted with my hands as he got in and started the engine. "They're doing a double feature. Civil War and then the new Infinity War."

"You'll be in superhero heaven all night," I laughed.

"Don't pretend you don't like these as much as I do." He glanced over with his usual smirk. Was his jawline always this defined?

"I don't obsess about them like you do."

"But you probably know just as much as I do about comic book movie lore." That was true, but I'd never tell him that.

"Hardly."

"What character do those annoying twins from the nineties sister play?" he asked as he tapped his fingers on the steering wheel.

"Scarlett Witch." I hated that he was testing me to prove a point. He knew I wouldn't lie and wanted to make sure I knew he was right about this.

"What other Marvel character has Chris Evans played?"

"What are you trying to prove?"

"Just answer the question," he glanced at me again quickly as he pulled the car to a stop at the last stoplight before we headed out of town.

"Jonny Storm." His smile was radiant as I narrowed my eyes at him.

"Otherwise known as...?"

"The Human Torch." He knew I had a weakness for Chris Evans. I mean, just look at him.

"Who was the actress who played his sister?" He fired off, not letting me get out of this.

"Jessica Alba."

"One more. What other actor played the same Fantastic Four character and a character in a newer marvel film?" This would typically trip people up, but I'd watched all these movies with him multiple times, even the bad ones.

"Would you quit?"

"You also said he had a nice ass," he laughed. Of course, that ass would remember I said that.

"Oh, my God. You're a jerk."

The SUV slowed down, and I knew he'd keep hounding me for an answer all night. "And the answer is?"

"Michael B Jordan."

Dylan looked over at me with a self-satisfied grin. He was so smug. "Who is the Marvel dork in this relationship?"

"You are."

He shook his head as he pulled the car into the parking lot of the movie theater. He found an open space near the side and maneuvered the vehicle to face the back end toward the screen. "You want some popcorn?"

"I thought you said you knew me," I teased. Of course, I wanted popcorn; that was a given.

"Just get out of the car, smartass."

I climbed out and met him at the back of the car. He pulled open the tailgate, and I gasped as I took in what he'd done. A futon mattress propped up inside the space, a cooler sitting on top of it.

"Hold on." He jogged to the side door and pulled the lever to lie down in the middle row of seats, the futon mattress reclining back. "Grab the speaker."

I pulled the metal speaker from the stand we'd parked next to and laid it just inside of the back of the car.

"Here." He pressed a paper sack filled with warm popcorn into my hand and held his hand out to me.

"You were busy this afternoon." He usually didn't even bother cleaning the fast-food trash out of his car when we were going somewhere.

"Now, do you see why I hadn't showered yet?"

"I guess," I sighed. "I could have helped you."

"Shower?" The cheeky grin on his face was teasing, but thinking about him in the shower was a dangerous topic.

"Shut up..."

"I didn't want you to. This is to make up for getting soaked the last time we were here."

"It was kinda fun," I laughed. We'd spent the whole ride home laughing and joking despite all the shaking as we sat in our cold, wet clothes.

"Until I fell in the mud trying to put stuff into the trunk."

"It wasn't all bad. At least it slowed down enough we could still watch the movie through the windshield."

"You're right. It wasn't all bad." He stepped closer and sat on the open tailgate next to me, his fingers brushing against mine.

"You wore that little strappy white tank top." What did my see-through tank top have to do with... Oh. My cheeks turned pink as I glanced sideways at him. The look he was giving me was one I wasn't used to having aimed at me.

"So, uh, what other snacks do you have in here?" I leaned back and looked inside the cooler; a reusable grocery bag tucked inside. My fingers closed on a package of peanut butter M&M's, ripping it open and popping a few in my mouth. I didn't trust myself to speak right now.

His pinky continued to lightly stroke mine as he watched me with a faint smile on his face. Somehow, he'd managed to change our dynamic in a matter of hours. Or had it been changing all summer, and I hadn't noticed?

The month of May had been spent with me avoiding talking about school and the spectacularly horrible last day. I cried myself to bed every night for a week before I decided Tyler wasn't worth my tears.

"Let's get situated before the previews are done."

I nodded and pulled myself up onto the mattress, grabbing a pillow and turning around to face the tailgate. Laying down on my stomach, I clutched the pillow under my chin and continued to pop the candy into my mouth.

Now that I saw it... I was nervous. What exactly did Dylan want from me?

"You warm enough? I've got a blanket." A soft plush blanket was neatly folded on the other side of him.

"It's eighty degrees, and we're in an open vehicle." And sharing a blanket just seemed a little too intimate.

"Right." He nodded as he kicked off his boots and pulled himself up onto the mattress next to me, sitting awkwardly. "Need any other snacks? Water? I've got soda..."

"Dylan, chill. Just lay down." Maybe I wasn't the only one that was nervous.

He settled next to me, not quite touching me, but I could feel the heat of his body close to mine. "I heard the new one was intense."

"You mean you didn't look up spoilers this time?" I scoffed; he couldn't help himself. I always waited to look up articles on the movies until after we'd seen it, but he was the impatient one.

"I have some self-control."

I turned my head to look sideways at him, and he mirrored my actions, his curly hair falling over the edge of his pillow. The cut of his jaw had become more defined than I remembered it being, a light scruff covering it.

"Do you? Do you really?"

He reached a single finger hesitantly to brush a strand of hair out of my eyes, the contact sending goosebumps down my arm.

"You have no idea." His voice was low as he shifted incrementally closer and cupped the side of my face with his palm.

"Dylan..." I murmured as he shifted again, his chest brushing against my arm.

He didn't speak as his hand slipped to the back of my neck. His tongue peeked out to wet his lips, and my eyes tracked the movement. When they connected with his, my breath caught at the fire burning within.

"What...?" My voice was breathy as he leaned forward and brushed his lips against mine softly.

He pulled back slightly, his eyes flashing to mine before he increased the pressure of his hand on my neck and pulled me towards him. His tongue slipped between my lips as my hands gripped the soft fabric of his shirt. I needed something to anchor myself as his kisses made me lightheaded.

This changed everything, and we had less than two weeks left to figure it out before we returned to separate schools.

# Chapter Nine:
## Sophomore Year

### SEPTEMBER

The weather was still surprisingly warm for late September; the sweat beading along my hairline in the eighty-five-degree heat. My feet hit the pavement with a gentle thump as I rounded the corner of my apartment building at a light jog. I'd taken up running after my last class a few days a week.

The treadmills at the student health center were usually busy this late in the afternoon. I tried to avoid going there as much as possible. It only took one awkward run-in with Tyler's pledge brothers to keep me out of there. They were friendly, but a few of them took seeing me as a free pass to hit on me before Joel told them to leave me alone. We lived close to campus but were still far enough away; I wasn't worried about running into people near my apartment.

As I slowed my pace, my hands on my hips as I tried to catch my breath, I didn't notice the tall figure leaning against the side of my building. "Hey."

I pulled my remaining earbud out and looked up at Dylan with a faint smile on my face. "Hey. What are you doing here?"

"Finished up with classes early, and we don't have a game this week." He stepped forward and placed his hands on my waist, his fingers brushing underneath the hem of my tank top.

"Why didn't you call me?"

"Am I interrupting something?" The smirk on his face warmed me. He damn well knew that I had planned to drive down to see him tomorrow.

"No. I'm just surprised and sweaty," I laughed as I gestured to my sweat-covered tank top.

"I don't mind you sweaty." My breath caught as he pulled me flush with him and skimmed his nose down my temple.

"Ugh. I probably smell. It's so hot."

Laughing, he backed away and grabbed my hand, punching the passcode into the door of the building. This wasn't the first time he'd visited me at school since it began. We hadn't defined our relationship, but I knew I didn't intend to see anyone else. The long-distance thing was awkward sometimes, but we tried to text and call each other as much as our studies and schedules allowed.

"I wasn't sure when I'd get the chance to come up here next, so I took the gamble that you wouldn't mind some privacy." He was living in the house of the fraternity he'd joined last year, crammed in a tiny room with a roommate.

"How ever will Brady survive the weekend without you?"

"I'm sure he'll live. Jen had already shown up when I was packing to leave." His roommate's girlfriend attended a state school about ten minutes from their campus. She practically lived in their room at the frat. Dylan had confessed that he'd invested his birthday money in a pair of noise-canceling headphones so he could avoid having to listen to sex noises coming from the other side of their loft.

"And how is his lovely girlfriend?"

"As verbose as ever." She never talked... like ever. It was a little unsettling, but I could respect her for not needing to fill every second of silence with meaningless chatter. "Is Allie home?"

"I don't know if she's back from class yet today. But I know she's supposed to be around this weekend," I told Dylan quietly.

"Hmm, too bad," he teased as he looped his arm around my waist.

"Her room is on the other side of the apartment. I don't think you have to worry about her not being quiet."

"I wasn't worried about her being quiet." He followed me closely up to the second-floor apartment, kissing the back of my neck as I unlocked the door. We hadn't slept together yet, but we had done other things. It turns out Dylan's hands weren't only good for catching footballs.

"Down, boy. I need to shower," I laughed as I pretended to push him off.

"That seems to be a recurring theme with us. One of us is always stinky."

"It's you." I nodded thoughtfully as I turned my face and snuck a kiss to his jaw.

"Then you must be the dirty one," he growled and nipped at my neck as the door swung open, and he pushed me inside.

The apartment was quiet as we walked down the hallway to my room. I did not miss the dorms at all this year. Alison's only complaint was that we weren't old enough to go to the bars yet. Didn't stop her from convincing her orientation leader last year to buy us booze.

Joel had tried to invite us both to the house for parties, but I'd always declined. It'd be weird since they were all friends with Tyler, and I didn't want to make Dylan uncomfortable with me hitting up frat parties.

I grabbed a tank top and a pair of shorts out of my closet and watched as Dylan stretched himself out across my futon bed.

"Comfortable?" I laughed as he pulled a pillow out and propped it behind his head.

"I'd be more comfortable if my hot girlfriend was cuddled up with me."

"Well, you better go find her," I teased. He'd never called me that before. It simultaneously scared me and thrilled me. I wasn't sure if I was ready to be called someone's girlfriend again.

This already had the potential to be devastating if we screwed this up. Letting my attraction to my best friend cloud my judgment could change both of our futures. I couldn't go back to being just his friend, and I wasn't prepared to lose him from my life.

"Would the label be so bad?" he asked as he sat up and watched me closely.

"No, but..." My quiet voice trailed off as I toed off my running shoes.

"I think it's time we had this conversation, Kendall." I knew it was, I'd deflected before, but I was terrified. If we made this real, then it had the potential to break me. I hated feeling that vulnerable.

"We will, but..."

He nodded his head toward the bathroom. "Go shower. We don't have to have it right now."

"Thank you." I rushed into the bathroom, dropping my sweaty clothes into the hamper in the corner.

As the water beat down on my hair, I closed my eyes and tried to gather my thoughts. I had very strong feelings for Dylan that went way beyond friendship, but I'd already had one relationship crash and burn. It felt like I was setting myself up for an even bigger heartbreak if I let things go further, but things couldn't return to what they were before he kissed me.

The soft click of the door was barely audible against the noise of the spray, but my heart sped up as I felt the cool air rush into the shower as the curtain parted from the wall.

"What are you doing?" I was almost breathless as his finger traced the water droplets across my shoulder.

"Please don't push me away." He knew I was trying to keep him at arms-length.

"I'm trying not to." I nodded; it was hard to let another man in, even Dylan.

His large hands traced down the outside of my arms as he interlaced the fingers on our hands and pressed his warm, bare chest to my back. "You can't tell me you don't feel this."

I shook my head as his lips connected with the back of my shoulder.

"You're going to hyperventilate if you don't calm down," he whispered.

My breath had picked up as he kissed across my skin and sucked lightly at the side of my neck. I was shaking against him as he drew our joined hands to rest on my stomach.

"I can't help it. I'm nervous." And shaken by my developing feelings for him.

His lips caressed the shell of my ear, and I melted back against him. "You know me. I just want to make you feel good."

His warm hands left mine and traveled further south, driving me into a frenzy before I broke in a wave of intense sensation. The moans echoing in the small bathroom just seemed to spur him on as he pressed himself against my back.

"I want to call you mine. Please," Dylan pleaded with a moan as my hand reached behind me and closed around him. It didn't take long for him to follow me into bliss, and I was in a daze as he grabbed a washcloth and cleaned us both up. "I know you're scared, but I can't explain what you mean to me."

"Dylan, I..."

"I'm not asking you to confess your undying love for me. I just want to be your boyfriend." In theory, it sounded like the perfect next step, but my heart feared letting him have the power to break me.

"Okay," I nodded as I let out a shaky breath.

"Okay?" His voice was a little louder as he processed that I would give this a try.

"Yes." After my nod of acceptance, he turned me toward him and cupped my jaw as he took possession of my lips, stealing my breath and making me dizzy.

"About time you came up for air," Alison teased from behind me.

"Shit!" I yelped when I hit my head on the freezer door as my roommate snuck up behind me.

"Not sorry," she smirked. "I thought we were going to hang out tonight."

Dylan and I had spent most of the weekend in my room talking—and do-ing—other things. He'd left about an hour ago, knowing if he didn't leave now, he'd have to go at four a.m. to make his morning classes.

"We can still hang out," I assured her.

"It's, like, almost ten," she sighed, clearly annoyed with me. I felt terrible for spacing on our plans, but it hadn't been intentional. Dylan had a way of making me lose track of time.

"Since when do you go to bed early?" I teased. She never went to bed before midnight.

"I don't, but it's not the point. I don't get to see you that often during the week. Sunday nights are girl time." She was right. Our schedules didn't coincide, so we spent a lot of time just missing each other between classes.

"I'm sorry. Dylan showed up here and…"

"And you two acted like bunnies all weekend." I bit my lip at her exaggerated eye roll.

"Not quite." We still hadn't taken that step yet, but it was only a matter of time.

"Not what it sounded like to me," she shrugged, pinning me down with a knowing look. A few times, I knew we'd gotten a little loud, but he was just so excited I'd finally agreed to label this.

I couldn't hide the blush creeping up my cheeks.

"That's what I thought," she nodded.

"We didn't." I shook my head.

Her laughter rang out, and my face was red by the time she turned on the ques-tions. "Why not? He's hot. And he's gotta be better than Two-Second-Tyler."

"I don't want to rush things," I sighed. Giving Dylan that part of me was a big deal. With him, it would mean more.

"It's not like you just met him. He's been your friend for how long?" Alison didn't understand the emotional attachment I still placed on sex. It wasn't just about feeling good to me; it was intimate and personal.

"Since the sixth grade." We'd just clicked, and somehow, all these years later, we still did.

"You've gotta quit living life stuck in your head. Just grab it by the horns and ride it like there's no tomorrow," she snickered.

"Why does it sound super dirty every time you try to give me advice?"

"It's a talent. It took years to hone this skill," Allie nodded seriously. "Speaking of grabbing things and riding them."

"Oh, my God. Stop," I giggled as I scooped another bite of ice cream onto my spoon.

She narrowed her eyes and tilted her head as she looked at me. "Does he like to have his hair pulled?"

"I don't know!" I laughed loudly.

"Well, you should find out!" She nodded eagerly.

Hair pulling aside. Maybe it was better just to let my head catch up on this one and go with my heart.

# Chapter Ten:
## Sophomore Year
### FEBRUARY

"I can't believe you're abandoning me on the most depressing holiday of the year," Alison pouted, with her bottom lip pushed out.

"I'm sure you'll be fine. Didn't 'what's his face' invite you to that singles party thing?"

"Yes. But seriously? I get that they're trying to be ironic with all the other houses throwing sweetheart dances, but I don't feel like getting hit on all night," she sighed loudly.

"So, don't go," I shrugged.

"But he's kinda cute," she whined as she dramatically threw herself backward.

"Then go."

"But I don't want to look desperate. I don't think Benji invited me as a date," Allie cringed. "I don't want to be like that girl in the movie where the guy isn't into her, and she thinks she's his girlfriend."

"Then flirt with all his brothers and see if he makes a move," I laughed. Alison was a flirtatious person by nature; it wasn't like it'd take much effort.

"What if he doesn't?" Allie looked concerned about what this guy thought about her. She must be interested in him for real.

"Then find some other guy to ride like a bull. Isn't that the advice you gave me?"

She gave me a dirty look, sticking her tongue out at me. "And how is our curly locked stallion?"

"He's good," I smiled. "Busy. I can't even imagine all the homework he has with his engineering courses."

"Did you get your studio work done?" She knew I spent additional time in the lab trying to get projects ahead to take extra time with him for Valentine's.

"Yes, Mom," I sighed. "I turned in my ceramics project and my sculpture sketches before I left the art building today."

"Did you submit that painting and the pastel drawing to the art show?" Every year, the university had an undergraduate art show held at the President's house. My drawing professor had encouraged me to enter one of my projects from last semester into the show this year.

"Yeah," I nodded. "I should hear next week if anything got in. It's a long shot, though. They don't pick a lot of underclassmen to be in the exhibit."

"You'll get in." Her voice sounded so sure. I wasn't as confident in my work as she was.

"Quit changing the subject. You need to go to that party. I think you'll have fun."

"Aren't I usually the one encouraging you to do things?" she laughed.

"Kind of annoying to be on the receiving end, huh?" It was fun for me; usually, I was the one whining about overthinking things.

"Don't get used to it," she told me as she narrowed her eyes.

"I'll be back Sunday afternoon." Despite it being a holiday weekend, I had recently tried not to bail on our girl time. Our schedules weren't the opposite this semester, but we decided quality time together was good for the apartment morale.

"You better be. I'd hate to change the Netflix password for tardiness," she teased.

"You're just mean today," I scoffed. That was just playing dirty.

She laughed as she stuck her tongue out at me. "You still love me, anyway."

"Either that or I'm scared of you," I shrugged, trying not to laugh.

"Works for me."

Having a car on campus made my life so much easier because now I could see Dylan whenever my schedule allowed. It wasn't ideal to be dating someone two hours away, but we made it work. We only had three more months of school to get through until summer break, and then we'd get to see each other every day. Late summer and early fall also brought both of our birthdays. It was weird to think we'd be turning twenty-one sooner rather than later.

It felt like I existed in two separate worlds lately. I spent all week getting in as much studio time as possible, so I didn't have to go in on the weekends. And I spent my weekends mostly driving down to see Dylan.

He'd made two more trips to see me since we'd officially started dating, and we'd spent the majority of Christmas break together. There had only been a few weekends we couldn't see each other.

> Dylan: Text me when you get here. I'll come to carry your stuff.

My phone pinged with a text as I parked my car in the lot behind the fraternity house.

> Kendall: Too late.

Before he responded, I was out of my car and through the back door.

> Dylan: You never let me show off my gentlemanly skills.

> Kendall: Since when have you had those?

As I turned the corner to the back staircase, I heard the slap of bare feet on concrete and saw a mop of messy dark hair over the top of the partial wall at the top of the stairs.

"Hey, you." His smile was bright as he looked down at me; I loved the way he still looked at me.

"Hey," I responded, my smile equally obnoxious.

He quickly descended the rest of the stairs and grabbed my bag, tossing it to the floor before he cupped my face and kissed me softly.

"Hmmm... someone started without me," I laughed at the faint taste of alcohol on his tongue.

"Just a little pre-gaming with Brady," he shrugged.

"Is he going to the formal tomorrow?"

"Yeah. Jen seemed excited. She's got a few friends from her sorority that were invited too," he nodded. "You could always see if they'd let you get ready with them tomorrow. I'm sure they wouldn't mind."

"I think I'd just rather get ready at the hotel." Jen and I still weren't all that friendly, and I didn't know any of her friends.

"She's not that bad. You might have fun," he coaxed, but I shook my head.

"I just get the feeling she doesn't like it when I'm around." No one had that persistent of a resting bitch face.

"I don't think she likes it when I'm around either," he laughed as he grabbed my bag, heading back up the stairs with me following behind.

As I reached the top of the stairs, he intertwined our fingers and pulled me close as we walked down the hallway to his room. A few of the guys were lounging in their bedrooms as we passed by, and they all called out their hellos. Pretty much everyone in the house knew who I was at that point.

"Kendall! Finally. This dude has been moping all week. I think he needs to get laid!" Dylan's loud, but friendly roommate was born without a filter. I learned quickly not to get offended by what he said to me.

"I'll get right on that, Brad," I laughed from the open doorway. Dylan chuckled and pulled me into his side, kissing my cheek and along the side of my neck.

"Sounds good to me." His voice was low in my ear, sending shivers down my spine.

"Ahem." An annoyed feminine cough drew my attention, and Brady started laughing as his girlfriend stood from the couch on the other side of the room.

"Oh, chill out, babe. You know I was joking," he rolled his eyes.

"I wasn't," I laughed. As soon as we were alone, I had no problem with the plan to reconnect with Dylan. I'd missed him this week.

Brady held his hand up for a high five and I smacked it, the other occupant of the couch coming into view. A dark-haired girl was seated next to Jen on the couch with her arms crossed tightly across her chest and an annoying smirk on her face.

"Oh, hi. Sorry, I didn't realize anyone else was in here," I apologized quickly. "I'm Kendall."

"I know who you are." The glare on her face didn't budge as she sized me up.

"Nice to meet you?" I'd meant it as a statement, but my inflection caused it to sound like a question. Something about this girl unsettled me. She raised an eyebrow and didn't respond, just sitting there staring.

"Anyway. I'm starving. Want to put my bag in the loft, and we can go get food?" I asked Dylan as I nodded at my bag still in his hand.

"Can you bring me back dinner?" Brady pouted. "I'm too lazy to go down to the kitchen."

"Dude. There are tons of leftovers down there," Dylan sighed.

"You know he doesn't cook," Jen rolled her eyes, and her mouth twitched almost into the shape of a smile.

"Microwaving is pretty foolproof these days," I laughed as I looked over at the still pouting Brady.

"Tell that to the char marks on the one in here because he left foil on something," Dylan laughed. Sure enough, there were some faint brown marks outside the door on their white countertop microwave.

"I didn't think it'd light on fire." Brady held up his hands in self-defense.

"Wow. Your mother must be proud," Dylan rolled his eyes at his goofy friend.

"Fuck you, dude. I still aced that biochem final last week." Brady was the definition of book smart, but it didn't extend to the rest of his life.

Dylan laughed and threw something at Brady's lap. "Dumbest smart kid I know."

"Aw, it's okay, Brady," I assured. "We don't want you to starve. Of course, we'll bring you back food."

Brady's face lit up. "Awesome! You're the best."

"Do you want apple slices or yogurt in your Happy Meal?" I teased, but I wasn't joking.

Jen huffed, and her silently sulking friend continued to stare.

"Hmm. That is a hard decision," he scratched the scruff on his chin as a look of concentration passed over his face.

"Really, Brady?" Jen sighed loudly, obviously not amused by his antics.

"What? I like nuggets. Kendall gets me," he shrugged.

"Alright. We're going to leave," Jen said as she stood from the couch and nodded at her sour-faced friend. "Make sure you're on time to pick us up tomorrow."

"Of course I will be, babe. I set the alarm on my phone and everything," he smiled proudly.

"Thanks, baby." She walked over to where he was sitting at his desk with his feet propped up and kissed him on the cheek.

"Come on, Lise," she gestured to her friend that was staring at Dylan with a curious look on her face.

I stepped to the side, blocking her view of him. "Nice to meet you, Lise."

"It's Lisa... with an A. Only my friends call me Lise," she told me with disdain in her voice, rolling her cold blue eyes.

"Okay, then." I nodded, not impressed with her bitchy attitude.

"Bye, Dylan. I'll see you around." She gave him a lingering look and followed Jen out the door.

"Well, she was a ray of sunshine," I grumbled as the two of them disappeared down the hallway.

"It's cause she wants to ride... Ow! Shit, dude!" Dylan smacked Brady on the back of the head.

"Knock it off, Brady."

"Fine, fine. Subject dropped." He assured as he rubbed the spot where Dylan had smacked him.

"I feel like I missed something there," I frowned. It wasn't like Dylan to be so defensive.

"It's nothing. Let me go stow your stuff," Dylan told me as he walked towards his side of the room.

Brady awkwardly stared at me with a calculating look on his face while Dylan climbed up the wooden ladder. "You guys the real deal?"

"Me and Dylan?" I asked, curious why he was asking.

"Yeah," he nodded.

"I guess so," I smiled as I looked towards where my boyfriend had disappeared.

"Cool, cool." He nodded and then changed the subject. "I bought Jen a lavalier."

"I'm sure she'll love that," I smiled.

"Dylan was pissed when he found out you can't lavalier a non-Greek."

Oh...

"It's alright. I don't have time for being so involved with something like a sorority, so I don't mind," I shrugged. I spent long hours in class and in the studio. I wasn't sure where I would even fit anything else in coming to see Dylan.

"That's cool. This lifestyle isn't for everyone."

I nodded as he tapped a pencil on his knee. This was the first time I felt like he'd tried to have a serious conversation with me, and I wasn't sure how to react to what he was saying.

"You ready?" Dylan climbed back down and crossed to where I was standing, grabbing my hand.

"Yeah. Let's go," I nodded.

"Don't forget my nuggets," Brady reminded as he continued to look at me curiously.

"We won't," I assured. "See you later."

"Good talk, Kendall."

"Uh, yeah." If you could call it that.

I was quiet as Dylan led me down the back staircase and to his car in the parking lot. He opened the door for me and held it open, closing it softly when I was seated. "What were you and Brady talking about?"

"Just the lavalier he bought Jen," I responded. He didn't need to know about the other stuff. I wasn't even sure what Brady was questioning me for.

"Oh, cool. There's some ceremony her sorority has to do before he can give it to her."

"Sounds complicated." I didn't understand so many things about the traditions involved in that lifestyle.

"It's tradition," he explained. "Kind of a rite of passage if they're going to get engaged next year."

"And that's the plan?" I couldn't think of anyone our age making that big of a commitment.

"Yeah," he smiled as he looked over at me.

I nodded and stared out the window. This whole Greek tradition thing was foreign to me. I always felt a little out of the loop.

"Do you ever think about that?"

"About getting engaged?" I asked, looking at him out of the corner of my eye.

"Yeah." He glanced over as his hand left the stick shift to cover mine softly.

"Sometimes. But it's a little soon, right?" We were still young.

"Why do you say that?" His voice sounded a little disappointed.

"Isn't that something we're supposed to think about after graduation? We're only twenty."

"I guess you're right," he agreed, but his voice still sounded off.

"What's wrong?" He hadn't been acting like himself since he climbed back down the ladder in his room.

"Nothing," he shook his head and gave me a small smile. "I just miss you sometimes."

"I miss you, too, but we've got it mostly figured out."

"I know," he sighed. "But Brady is moving out next year to live with Jen off-campus. We're never going to have that option."

"Maybe we will after we graduate," I offered quietly. Long-distance was hard and different, but we were solid.

"That just seems like a long time from now," he sighed.

"Does it bother you that I don't go to school here?"

He shook his head slightly, but he didn't answer.

When we got to the restaurant, he seemed nervous, but we still managed to have a good time. He seemed to perk up talking about the stupid things that happened at the house.

"Wait. So, a pledge got locked out of the house naked?" I laughed as he told me a story from earlier in the semester.

"Yeah. It was hilarious. He got picked up by campus security."

"Did he get arrested?" You'd think he'd get ticketed, at least.

"Nah. They felt sorry for him. Poor dude had his clothes stolen by his ex's sorority sisters because he hooked up with some new girl."

"Why did he have his clothes off outside, anyway?" I laughed.

"Dare," Dylan shrugged with a smile. "He lost a card game. His big brother locked the side door. Didn't think he'd wander off when he couldn't get in."

"And nobody got in trouble?"

"No, the university doesn't like to call the county cops for things. They don't want to risk the bad press."

"His ass would've been in jail if he did that on my campus, accident or not," I chuckled. I knew at least two people who'd been thrown in the drunk tank for public intoxication while wearing clothes. Naked would add public indecency to the charges.

"You also have, like, twenty times as many students on campus. And your own campus police."

"True." I nodded.

"You ready to get out of here?" he asked as he tucked his card back in his wallet and stood from the table. He held out his hand and gave me an amused grin.

"Yeah. Let's go," I smiled as I took his hand and stood, tucking myself into his side. "Don't want to keep Brady from his Happy Meal toy for too long."

Strong arms closed around my waist as I finished clasping my necklace and straightened it out along my chest.

"You look gorgeous." The way he looked at me in the mirror still awed me. Never in a million years did I believe that my middle school crush would end up being my great college romance.

"You don't look too bad yourself, handsome. You look hot in a bow tie."

And he did. He'd rented a tux for the formal with a vest that matched my dress. It all felt very fancy. Another traditional experience for him that I felt a little on the outside of. Most of his fraternity brothers brought girls from other sororities on campus or the state school, like Brady and Jen.

"You ready to go down?" They'd reserved a small ballroom at a local hotel and were serving a sit-down meal before the dance started.

"Yeah. I'm ready." I was so not ready. I knew he was excited about tonight, but I always felt a little left out. I knew these people, but I was only around a few days a month. They had all kinds of little inside jokes I didn't understand. When it was just Dylan and me, our relationship felt solid. But when we interacted with the people in my life or his, there always seemed to be a lag with fitting in.

"Thank you for being here tonight, Ken. You know I love you, right?" he sighed as he kissed the exposed skin on my shoulder.

"I love you, too, Dylan." He turned me around to face him, slowly kissing along my jaw and to my ear, licking along the shell while I clutched his arms.

"I was going to wait, but I got you something." My heart sped up at the thought of him getting me a gift.

"You didn't have to buy me anything." He didn't need to buy my affection; I was already his.

"I know. But I wanted to do this. It's Valentine's Day, and I wanted to show you how much you meant to me."

"Dylan..." I whispered as I looked back at him, feeling a little emotional.

"Just. Here, sit down." He guided me to the end of the bed and helped me take a seat.

Walking to the closet, he knelt and grabbed something from his overnight bag. He held a little gray jewelry box in his hand when he returned.

"Dylan, what?" My eyes widened as I looked up at him.

"It's not what you think it is." He slowly opened the box and turned it towards me. Nestled inside was a delicate silver ring. It had a small solitaire diamond in the center with a vine filigree wrapping around the band.

"It looks like a ring." My heart beat faster when my eyes looked between the contents of the box and his nervous smile.

"Well, it is. But it's not an engagement ring or anything."

"So, it's my Valentine's Day present?" I asked quietly.

"No, it's..." he laughed and scratched the back of his neck. "I know it's prob-ably cheesy, but it's a promise ring."

"Oh..."

"I know. But even you agreed we were young. I just want to show you I'm committed." His smile faltered a little as I stared directly at the delicate little ring.

Wow. A promise ring. That was...

"I don't doubt your commitment, Dylan."

"I know you don't. But I like the idea of you wearing my ring," he smiled. He looked so sure of everything. I felt terrible for feeling like I didn't fit into his life, but this was a serious step for him.

"Okay." I nodded as I took the tiny ring out of the box, watching it sparkle in the light.

He took it from me and slid it onto my ring finger. It was a perfect fit. "Do you like it?"

I held my hand out and imagined it a few years from now, holding an entirely different set of rings. "I love it. Thank you, Dylan."

"At least it fits," he laughed. "I may have tied a string around your finger while you were sleeping."

"Oh, my God, you goof," I giggled as I looked down at the ring on my hand. It was light, but heavy with intent.

"Clearly, it worked." He looked proud of his problem-solving skills. "I love you, Ken."

I cupped his face and kissed his lips softly. "I love you, too."

And I really did.

# Chapter Eleven:
## Sophomore Year
### MAY

"Tell me again why he isn't here?" Alison stood in the doorway to my room, giving me a hard time as I tried to put on my makeup.

"Would you just stop?"

"It's kinda shady," she scoffed as she rolled her eyes.

"It is not shady. Dylan has a final in his statistics class in the morning. I can't ask him to drive up here just to drive right back." It wasn't Dylan's fault he had school commitments.

"You got a flipping award from the university," she insisted.

"It's not that big of a deal," I sighed. I mean, it was, but I was fine with him not being here. I understood, at least.

"Oh, so they just give them out to everyone?" she smirked as she pinned me down with a knowing look.

"Well, no. Just one for each year," I admitted. When the selection committee notified me I'd been selected, I thought I was getting punked by one of the other art students. Never in a million years did I think that I'd win.

"Then it's a big deal!"

"There were only four sophomores in the show," I pointed out. Many of my classmates that I knew had submitted pieces, but they had selected only four of us. "I had a twenty-five percent chance of getting it."

"And how many students submitted work for the show?" Damn her for being so smart.

"Probably a few hundred," I shrugged.

"And how many of them had pieces accepted?" She arched her eyebrow at me as she leaned back into the door frame.

"Like, fifty."

She stood there with a raised eyebrow. I got it. I did. Getting an emerging artist award from the Dean of the university's wife was kind of a big deal within the Fine Arts department. She hand chose the pieces they showed and awarded four students with small scholarships at each grade level.

Alison was pissed that Dylan wasn't here. He was originally planning to drive up for the reception, but his professor had scheduled a 7:00 a.m. final for the following morning. I wouldn't jeopardize one of his grades for this.

"I'm just saying I don't like it," she told me, for like the twentieth time since I told her he wasn't coming.

"I know. I was disappointed, too." The timing wasn't ideal, but life didn't always happen how you wanted it to. Sometimes people couldn't get out of obligations.

"You realize he's been in our apartment, like, six times," she pointed out.

"Okay...?"

"You are always the one having to drive down there," she said with exasperation.

"I get out of class early on Fridays, and my first lab isn't until ten-thirty on Monday," I explained for the thousandth time. "It's just easier if I'm the one going there."

"For who?" She still looked unimpressed.

"Where are you going with this?" Tonight was supposed to be about me, and I felt like she was attacking me for things I couldn't control.

"You never prioritize YOU in that relationship."

"Long-distance is complicated. Someone has to make concessions to make it work," I shrugged.

"And it's always you," she sighed.

Dylan had more going on than I did. He had an internship, football, the fraternity. I only had one professional artist's society, and we met on campus during the week, so it was never a problem.

"Stop making up excuses in your head and think about what's really going on in your life. I'd hate to see you throw away parts of your life for some guy." She gave me a sympathetic look, and I shook my head.

"He's not just some guy."

She tilted her head to the side and gave me a sad smile. "I know that. Trust me. I know that. But you've isolated yourself from your friends here. When was the last time you went out with any of us?"

"You know I don't like to spend time with Tyler's brothers." It was all kinds of awkward. I felt even more on the outside with them than with Dylan's.

"You know they'd pick you if they had to choose," she pointed out. It wasn't like we hadn't all met at the same time.

"Well, it's not an issue," I insisted.

"So, you're alright with me being your only friend?" she asked curiously.

"I've got..."

"But do you?" she asked again, and I came up blank. *Was she right?*

"I need to get ready. Let's just let this go for now," I begged, not wanting to think about this.

"Please, just think about it."

I nodded, lying to my friend. "I will."

Alison had abandoned me about three minutes after the reception started, to flirt with a waiter who was in one of her classes. My parents had gotten stuck in traffic, so they ran a little late. Luckily, the awards part of the reception wasn't for another half hour.

"It's lovely." I was startled at the voice behind me. I'd been standing there staring aimlessly at my drawing. I hadn't even realized anyone was standing behind me.

"Oh, uh, thank you," I sputtered nervously as I took in the tall brunette standing at my side.

"So, you're Kendall," she smiled softly.

"Yes," I frowned. "I'm sorry. Do I know you?"

She didn't seem offended at my inquiry. Her hand extended towards me, and I placed mine in hers, giving it a firm shake. "Deidre Powell. I'm Dean Powell's wife. I curated the show."

"Oh, wow. I'm sorry." My nervous laughter caused her smile to grow.

"It's fine," she reassured. "I know people don't recognize me when I'm not standing next to my husband."

"You must think I'm an idiot," I laughed nervously.

"On the contrary, dear. I admire your eye. And your honesty. Few people admit when they don't know someone. I'm glad you didn't pretend to know who I was."

She leaned in close and put her hand next to her mouth. "To be honest, I'm not impressed with the ass kissers."

"So, I shouldn't tell you I love your necklace?" I grinned.

Her laughter rang out, and a few people turned in our direction but quickly returned to their conversations. "I like you."

"Oh, thank you," I told her, a little disarmed by how friendly she was. Sometimes academics could be a little stuffy.

"Congratulations on your sale." She nodded at my piece mounted to the wall.

"Excuse me?"

"The illustration." She pointed at the sticker in the bottom right corner. "It sold."

Students could price their pieces as a part of the show. I'd priced my framed illustration at four hundred dollars, not expecting it to sell.

"You didn't know?"

I shook my head as I looked at the little nameplate mounted underneath the frame. I'd barely noticed the little red star sticker before she pointed it out.

"I was disappointed it sold so fast. I was trying to convince Preston to purchase this one as well." My eyes widened. "I don't suppose you take commissions, do you?"

"I haven't before, but..." I trailed off. The president of the university's wife wanted to buy my work. I was clearly in an alternate universe.

"Take my card. I'd like you to use this same technique to illustrate one of my jewelry pieces." She fingered her necklace, and I realized she must also be an artist.

"Are any of your pieces on display?" I asked curiously. Her necklace was unique, combining blown glass beads and delicate gold filigree work.

"Oh, no," she shook her head with a smile. "But I sell them at a gallery downtown. This show is just for the students."

"I'd love to see your work sometime," I told her honestly. I probably couldn't afford it, but I was curious about what the rest of her work looked like.

"When we get that commissioned piece arranged, you can come to my studio."

Fighting the urge to fangirl, I smiled widely at her as I nodded. "That would be amazing. Thank you! I haven't taken a jewelry-making class yet, but I'd love to next year."

"Let me know if you do," she nodded. "I'm teaching one section of the studio classes for Fine Arts majors next year."

"I definitely will. Thanks so much!"

"Well, I'm being summoned, but it was nice to meet you." She glanced over my shoulder and waved to a couple, who were motioning for her attention.

"You too!"

When I came to the reception, I was expecting just to wander around and then have the Dean of Fine Arts hand me an envelope in front of the rest of the artists invited. I was not expecting the Dean of the university's wife to talk to me, much less try to commission a piece from me.

A chime came from my pocket, and I quickly pulled it out, expecting it to be from my parents.

> Dylan: I love you. I'm sorry I couldn't make it up. Take pictures for me, and I'll drive up once my final is done.

Smiling, I replied to him, walking along the exhibit pieces.

> Kendall: I miss you. I'll have my mom take pics once the reception starts.

My mind was so distracted with Dylan that I wasn't paying attention to where I was going.

"Hello, Kendall." I looked up at the person standing in front of me and smiled widely.

"Oh, my God, Kale! I haven't seen you since last year."

"I saw your pieces," he told me as he nodded in the direction where they displayed my work.

"Oh..." I wasn't expecting to see him here, and that he'd found my work was even more unexpected.

"The use of color in that illustration was very interesting. I'd love to pick your brain about color and reactions to moods sometime." Leave it to Kale to be interested in analyzing a drawing.

"All work today, huh?" I laughed. Even at an art exhibit, he seemed to be all business.

"No." He looked down and scratched the back of his head. "I mean, I am here because the Dean of Fine Arts invited me, but I can enjoy the work."

"She invited you? I thought you were a psychology major," I frowned, not seeing the tie-in.

"Very good. I'm impressed you remember." The grin that lit up his face warmed me in a way I wasn't expecting. He'd always been kind of aloof last year.

I'd not seen him at all since the end of orientation. "Did you pick a Fine Arts specialty?"

"I'm not a hundred percent sure yet. I'm torn between sculpture and fiber arts."

"Not drawing?" he asked, curiosity clear in his voice.

I shook my head. "No, I enjoy it. But I don't feel a particular passion for it. I enjoy creating tangible things that I can pick up with my hands."

His eyes locked with mine, and he nodded slowly. "Passion is important. Especially if you're going to commit to something."

"Exactly," I smiled. "I couldn't commit to drawing because it doesn't hold my heart."

"Hmm..." he hummed as he squinted at me.

"What?"

He stepped closer and brushed my hair behind my shoulder, his hand lightly touching my bare shoulder. "What holds your heart, Kendall?"

I wasn't sure how to answer that question. Dylan had a large part of my heart occupied, but even Allie saw that our relationship wasn't ideal.

"I'm not sure," I answered honestly. I was far from having everything figured out.

"Well, I hope you find it. You deserve to have whatever you desire." His intense demeanor both unsettled and intrigued me. Normally, I would have perceived a guy who said something like that to be flirting with me, but I had a hard time reading him.

"Spinach! Hey!" Alison threw her arms around my neck and hugged me as Kale watched with amusement. "Whatcha doing here? Hot date?"

"Not quite," he gave her a small smile. "This is more of a professional engagement."

"It's so good to see you, right, Kendall?" she said suggestively.

"Yeah, it's been nice chatting." I nodded as I rolled my eyes at my friend.

"And what were you two chatting about?"

He looked at me for a moment, pausing before he spoke. "Passion."

"Oh, really..." she trailed off in a mischievous tone.

"Isn't that what art is? An expression of passion?" he asked her.

"Among other things, but I'd have to agree with that," she nodded. "Well, I don't want to interrupt, but I saw your parents walk in a few minutes ago."

"Oh. I should go find them," I looked over her shoulder and through the crowd.

"Let me," she insisted. "You finish up your 'chat' with Romaine."

"You know that Kale technically is not considered lettuce, right?" he told her.

Allie started laughing as she turned away from us and called out over her shoulder. "Don't care, Arugula!"

"Sorry about her," I apologized once she was out of earshot.

"Don't worry about it," he shook his head. "I'm used to the jokes."

"It was nice to see you," I told him honestly. Alison was right. I needed to pay attention to the friends I'd made on campus, try to find a balance with my life.

"You as well," he smiled as he reached forward and brushed my hand with his finger.

"I should go." My feet didn't move as he nodded.

"Maybe I'll see you around next fall," he told me softly as he took a step back.

"I thought you were graduating?"

"I am," Kale nodded. "Next weekend."

"Then how will I see you?" I smiled. He was so cryptic sometimes.

"I'll be in your building quite a lot, actually. I was assigned an Art Therapy course as a part of my graduate Teaching Assistant work," he told me. "We should grab a coffee sometime so we can have that color discussion."

The involuntary blush that flooded my cheeks couldn't be helped. "I don't think so."

He tilted his head to the side slightly, studying me. "May I ask why?"

"I have a boyfriend."

He pursed his lips and nodded. "I wasn't aware sharing a beverage with an acquaintance was out of bounds for a healthy relationship, but whatever you think is best."

His hand came forward to squeeze my arm before he moved past me. "It was nice to see you, regardless."

"Likewise." I smiled and watched him walk away.

# Chapter Twelve:
## Summary After Sophomore Year
### LATE JUNE

"Hey there, birthday boy," I called as I stepped next to Dylan's bed at his parent's house.

"It's not my birthday yet," he grumped as he pulled the covers up over his head and burrowed into his pillow. I'd spent the night last night but had left this morning to go pick up breakfast for him. His parents didn't care if I stayed over. The perks of them knowing you since you were twelve.

"Well. You won't be here for the actual day, so today is your pseudo birthday."

"Shouldn't I be able to sleep in on my pseudo birthday?" he mumbled as I ran my hand through the tuft of hair that stuck out the top of the covers.

"Your grandparents will be here in two hours," I reminded him.

"Ugh," he grumbled as he pushed his head into my touch.

Even though I'd been in a weird place at the end of the school year, the summer had been good for our relationship. We saw each other almost every day and had reconnected in a way that wasn't possible being two hours apart.

I also had to admit that the sex had been mind-blowing. Dylan's parents loved me, so we spent a lot of nights together. My parents begrudgingly let my curfew lapse as long as I kept in contact. They knew and trusted Dylan. They just didn't want it happening under their roof. My dad liked to pretend I was still his innocent little girl.

"Come on, sleepyhead. Take a shower with me. I brought donuts."

"Hmm. Maybe I should dirty you a bit before we get clean..." His face peeked out from under the covers, and I laughed as his hands reached for my hips.

"How dirty are we talking?" I chuckled.

"Very." He pulled on my hips, and I fell backward against the pillows, giggling as he climbed on top of me.

"Mmm. You're warm." His skin was warm from lying underneath the blankets as he covered my body with his partially clothed one. His hips pressed into my shorts, and I could feel how excited he was already. "And hard."

"Fuck," he moaned as he shifted his hardness into me, grinding slowly as his hands slipped up the back of my tank top.

"Mmm, yes."

His pupils dilated at my soft moan, and he pushed my tank up over my torso, pulling up the cups of my bra. His warm wet tongue covered my chest, and I lost myself in the dual sensation of his soft lips and scratchy stubble. "I wish I could continue to wake up like this every day."

"Me too. But we've got two weeks until you leave," I sighed as he leaned back with a sad smile.

"So little time, so many things I want to do with you." He yanked off the rest of the clothes covering me and showed me a few of the things he wanted to do to me until we were both breathlessly panting against the dark sheets. I knew being apart for another year would be challenging, but I was sure we could get through it.

"Grandma, you remember Kendall," Dylan said as he stood next to where she was glaring at half the people in the room.

"Of course, dear, I remember your little friend from Christmas." Grandma Constance gave me an unimpressed smirk.

"She's my girlfriend, Grandma," he sighed as he rubbed his face and then glanced over at me.

She zeroed in on the way he nervously played with my promise ring, squinting at my finger. "I don't understand why you young people are always in a rush to run down the aisle."

"Didn't you get married to Grandpa at nineteen?" he asked as his hand tightened on mine.

"And we were in the middle of a war. I had to give him some kind of incentive to come back." His grandfather had been in the Korean War. He'd experienced some hearing loss, so it always felt like everyone in Dylan's family was yelling when his grandparents visited. I secretly hypothesized that his grandpa used his 'hearing loss' as an excuse not to listen to his grandma.

"Well, I hope you both give it serious thought before you do anything foolish like getting married before you graduate," she sighed.

"Don't worry, Grandma." He glanced over at me and squeezed my hand, rubbing my ring again. "I've given Kendall's place in my future quite a bit of thought."

Goosebumps covered my arms as he tugged me closer. The look of devotion in his eyes was palpable.

"Don't make the mistake your cousin did," she warned. His cousin had gotten pregnant in her junior year of school and dropped out. His grandmother had threatened to write her out of the will.

"We won't," he assured her.

"I won't have any more illegitimate great-grandchildren. You need to be responsible," she scolded. Well, this was embarrassing.

"Mom, leave them alone. They're both responsible young adults," Dylan's mom, Annette, told her mother as she approached us.

"At least they go to separate schools so they can't shack up. I don't understand living together before you get married, either."

*Man, Grandma Constance was a ray of sunshine tonight.*

"Mom. Let it go. Dylan can manage his own love life," Annette sighed.

"I know he's a smart young man, but you never know what dumb decisions the youth of today are going to make in the name of love," she rolled her eyes.

I wasn't sure, but I was pretty sure she was calling him dating me dumb.

"Grandma, I love Kendall. She's been my best friend for years. We'll be fine."

Dylan's mom dragged Grandma Constance into the kitchen, and I turned to him with wide eyes. "What the hell was that?"

"You've met her before, more than once," he frowned as he shook his head at her antics.

"But still."

*Seriously?*

"You know she's batshit crazy." She was, but she was rude, and he just acted annoyed instead of standing up for himself or me.

"We haven't even sat down for dinner yet." Tonight was going to drag on if this was how it started.

"It'll be fine." He tugged me in closer and kissed me softly, his hands pressing into the small of my back. I lost myself in him for a few moments until an obnoxiously loud laugh from the kitchen broke the spell.

It was going to be a long night.

"So, I'm not sure if Dylan ever told me, what are you studying, Kristal?" she asked as soon as we were all seated at the dining room table.

"Grandma..." Dylan sighed, and she gave him a faux look of innocence.

"It's fine," I told him quietly.

"What? Did I ask something I shouldn't?" She asked, not looking apologetic at all.

"No, it's nothing. I'm a Fine Arts major."

She raised an eyebrow and looked at me, then Dylan, and then to his mother, who smiled at me and nodded her head. "And what are your career plans for when you graduate?"

"Grandma..." He squeezed my knee beneath the table, and I covered his hand with my own.

"I haven't decided yet. I'll probably try to teach somewhere and produce my own pieces for some of the local galleries."

"So, you're planning to return here locally?" She narrowed her eyes at me when I shrugged.

"It depends." I wasn't sure where we would end up.

"On what exactly?" she asked with an edge to her voice.

I glanced over at Dylan and saw his pinched face. He was irritated. "Grandma, just let it go."

"And what if my grandson gets a job somewhere else?" she asked as her voice rose a little.

"We'll figure it out when the time comes. There are community art classes and galleries everywhere. My plans can be flexible," I shrugged.

"And you think selling your 'art' is a viable career? You'd be able to support yourself without my grandson?"

"Mom. Really?" Annette scolded her mother, shaking her head.

"What? It's a question. I thought modern women were liberated." Evil grandma shrugged as she looked at her daughter.

"It's rude, Mom. And frankly, none of your business."

"Kristal can answer me if she wants to," Grandma Constance challenged, eyeing her daughter.

"Constance, I don't have concrete plans because I have two years of school left until I get my degree. Right now, it's not an issue," I explained. "If you're concerned about me taking advantage of Dylan, don't be. We'll decide about our future together."

She made an unimpressed noise in the back of her throat.

"What, Grandma?" he sighed.

"Nothing," she shook her head and pursed her lips. "It's been clarified that my opinion doesn't matter."

"Quit being so dramatic," he rolled his eyes.

Grandma Constance scoffed as she stared across the table at us. "So, my concern for you makes me some kind of drama queen."

Grandpa Lewis snorted, and everyone looked in his direction. I knew I liked that man. He pretended he'd not been paying attention.

"I don't understand where this is coming from," Dylan sighed again.

"You're going to be making a nice salary with your engineering degree from a very prestigious college when you graduate. I'd hate for someone to capitalize on that by taking advantage of your generosity."

"Alright, Mom. That's enough," Annette said firmly from beside her mother. "We've known Kendall and her family for a long time. She's a nice girl, and she would never take advantage of Dylan."

"Intentionally," Constance said dismissively.

Dylan's hand tightened on my knee, and I flinched in surprise.

"Sorry." His apologetic eyes looked down into mine.

"Well. I think I'm going to head home now," I announced as I gently pried his hand off my knee and placed it back on his leg. "I'll see you tomorrow, Dylan. Happy early birthday."

"Ken, wait." He threw his napkin on the table and followed me to the living room, where I retrieved my bag.

"What?" I would not sit through more of that uncomfortable interrogation. I knew where I wasn't wanted.

"You're just going to leave?" I could tell by his tone that he was hurt, and tonight was about him, but it was better if I left.

"She doesn't want me here," I pointed towards the dining room.

"She doesn't..."

I put my hand up and kept talking. "I'm going to let you finish your evening with your family in peace before I say something I'm going to regret."

"She doesn't mean it," he insisted.

I shook my head and walked around him towards the door. "As I said, I'll talk to you tomorrow."

"It's supposed to be my birthday dinner. Don't I get a say in who is here?"

"I love you, but I won't sit through any more of that tonight. Call me when they leave tomorrow," I apologized.

He stepped forward and kissed my cheek, slowly drawing me towards him with his hands on my waist. "I'm sorry."

I shook my head and placed my hand on his clean-shaven cheek. Another concession to keep Grandma happy. "This isn't your fault. Please don't apologize for other people."

"I don't know what's gotten into her," he shook his head and covered my hand with his own.

"I do. She's decided she doesn't like me, and nothing I say is going to change that tonight." Grandma Constance had always been cold, but tonight she was just downright rude, and I didn't deserve it.

"So, leaving is the answer?" He sighed, and I ran my other hand through the hair on the side of his head.

"It'll be fine. Spend time with your grandparents."

"I'm coming over the second they leave the driveway," he insisted.

"That works for me," I gave him a sad smile and nodded. I'd probably be waiting for him as well.

"I need to pick up your birthday present tomorrow, and I want you to go with me," he told me. "And no, I'm not telling you where we're going."

"Alright," I smiled. "I won't bother your surprise."

"I love you," he whispered as he leaned in towards me.

"I know. I love you, too." I nodded as I leaned up on my tiptoes and kissed him softly.

I'd spent the evening lying in my bed and listening to music to distract myself.

Eventually falling into a restless sleep, I was awoken by my phone buzzing on the pillow next to me.

*Dylan: They're packing the car.*

*Dylan: I'm coming over in an hour.*

I crawled out of bed and took a scalding hot shower. The heat shock always made it easier for me to clear my head. By the time I'd dried my hair and thrown on a lightweight cotton dress, Dylan was sitting on my bed waiting for me.

"You look nice today," he smiled.

I looked over his khaki shorts and a short-sleeved button-up shirt. It was different from the jeans and t-shirts he wore to school and on the worksite. "Thank you. Looks like you cleaned up a little as well. You should wear a collared shirt more often."

"Well, let's not go crazy," he grinned. "I have the rest of adulthood to worry about dress clothes."

"You're going to be a very handsome young professional someday," I assured him.

He sat back with his hands braced against the mattress and watched as I put my earrings on and slipped my feet into some strappy sandals.

"You ready?"

Dylan made a humming sound as he stood and crossed the room to where I stood. My heart beat faster as he placed his hands on my hips and pulled me into him. His heart was hammering as I rested my hands on his chest, watching his Adam's apple bob with a heavy swallow. "Let's go before we don't leave this room all day."

"Hmm. That sounds like a pretty good birthday present to me," I told him suggestively. Naked presents were fun, too.

"Tease," he grinned as he smiled down at me.

"I'm only a tease if I don't intend to follow through. You should know better by now."

He pressed his hips into mine, and I could feel the effect my words were having on him. Before I could plan another teasing remark, he leaned down and captured my lips in an almost bruising kiss. He stole my breath as he tilted his head and pressed his hot tongue into my mouth.

"Shit," he panted after he broke the kiss as he gently laid his forehead on mine.

"Well, that was unexpected," I sighed, trying to recover.

He laughed as he shifted his hips, readjusting himself. "Let's go. I don't trust myself in here, and we have an appointment."

He took my hand and led me outside to his car, tucking me into the passenger seat with a soft kiss on the cheek. I watched the landscape of suburban houses go by as he drove us to our mystery destination. When he pulled into the parking lot of a jewelry store, I looked over at him and was met with a smirk.

"Come on. Let's go."

When we got inside, he led me over to a marked counter for cleaning and pickups.

"What did you do?" I asked him as he stepped up to the counter and pressed a call button.

His answering grin was suspiciously innocent. "What?"

"You didn't need to buy me jewelry again," I scolded.

"I wanted to," he smiled. "Chill out. It's for your birthday. Let me spoil you a bit."

"It better not have been expensive," I worried. He didn't need to be confirming his grandmother's suspicions that I was taking advantage.

"It wasn't. Don't worry about that. I've got some money saved up. I wanted to get you something nice."

"Can I help you two?" A sales associate crossed over to where we were waiting, and Dylan handed her a slip of paper.

"I've got a pickup."

"I'll be right back. Let me go pull that from the back." She wandered through a doorway in the back corner of the shop.

Dylan took my hand, tugging me along after him as he aimlessly looked at the cases that surrounded us. He paused in front of a case full of rings, contemplating the contents inside.

"Here we are, Mister Collins."

He took the small bag—decorated with the jewelry store's logo on the side—from her hands.

"My name is Ginger. Is there anything else you and your girlfriend would like to look at? We have a special on these if you'd like to go over pricing." She gestured at the case, pulling out a brochure that said 'engagement rings' on it.

"Oh... no... we're good." I shook my head as I stepped back.

"But..." Dylan nudged me and cut me off.

"Sure. We'd like to look at that one." He pointed to a white gold setting with two bands of diamond chips that extended down the sides. It had a modestly sized round solitaire in the center. It was a beautiful ring.

"Of course," Ginger smiled as she unlocked the case and pulled out a velvet board, placing the ring into a slot and pushing it across the counter towards Dylan. "Would the lady like to try it on?"

"What?" My eyes widened, and my pulse quickened as Dylan picked up the ring and took my hand. He slowly slipped it into place and then looked up at me.

"Dylan…" I whispered as he pulled my hand closer and gently turned it so he could look at it better.

"It seems to fit." He nodded as he smiled up at me and then over at Ginger.

"Most of our display rings are a six and a half," she told him.

He turned his head and smiled at her. "Then that's perfect."

I was still speechless as he started talking to the salesclerk about cut and clarity, karat size, and types of gold. My eyes couldn't stop looking at the ring on my finger.

There was an engagement ring on my finger.

"Kendall?" Dylan asked, his voice sounding amused.

"Hmm?" I snapped out of my daze and looked up at Dylan.

"She asked if it feels like it sits well on your finger. Is the size right?"

"What?"

"Does it fit?" he asked again.

"Oh, uh. Yes." I nodded.

"Do you like this one?" he questioned with a bright smile.

"Wait, why? You're not impulse buying an engagement ring, are you?" I asked with wide eyes.

The sales associate giggled as her head moved back and forth between us as we talked.

"And what if I was?" he asked curiously, the smile never leaving his face.

"Seriously?" He was crazy. This was crazy.

"If you like it, it's yours." He nodded as he squeezed my hand.

"You can't be serious. You're proposing right now?" My voice rose several octaves as I stared at my crazy boyfriend.

"No," he laughed as he slid the ring off and placed it back on the velvet pad. My finger felt a little naked without it. I ran my thumb over the back of the other ring Dylan had given me that I wore on my right hand.

"Do we need to discuss financing options?" Ginger asked him.

"Dylan?" My eyes widened as he nodded at her.

"I'm not proposing right now. Calm down," he told me in a quiet voice. Easier said than done.

He turned to the sales associate. "Can you place that on hold? I can come to fill out the paperwork tomorrow."

"Of course, Mr. Collins." She placed the ring inside a small velvet pouch and pulled a plastic tray from under the counter. She took Dylan's contact information and walked to the back with the tray.

"What just happened?" I whispered as he pulled me to his side.

"We picked out your engagement ring," he told me in an amused voice.

"Was this why you brought me here?"

He laughed as he picked up the jewelry bag and pulled a little gray box from it. "No... your birthday present was the real reason, but it saved me a trip."

"You're going to buy it?" I asked with wide eyes.

"Stop acting so shocked. I didn't propose to you yet. You'll have to be patient for that part," he laughed. "Now, open your present."

He pushed the box toward me, and I picked it up. Nestled inside was a heart-shaped pendant with my birthstone, a sapphire, in the middle for September.

"It's gorgeous. Thank you," I sighed as I pulled the delicate chain from its place.

He fastened it around my neck, softly caressing the skin of my collarbone with his fingertip. "Happy early birthday, baby."

We left the shop hand in hand, my mind racing at the thought that I might be engaged soon.

# Chapter Thirteen:
## Two Days Before the Wedding
### (Almost) Present Day

I spent the morning doing what I did most mornings for the last two months.

*Groom: How does it look?*

*Kendall: Like it did yesterday.*

*Groom: I meant the color, smartass. Did they show up yesterday?*

*Kendall: It's definitely blue.*

*Groom: You're the one who picked out the color.*

I laughed, as I imagined the exasperated inflection in his voice. He liked to remind me of what I picked out as if he thought I didn't like them.

I snapped a picture and attached it to a new text.

*Kendall: And I did a damn good job of it.*

He sent back a nervous emoji.

*Groom: Tease.*

*Kendall: You were worried, weren't you?*

*Groom: no.*

*Groom: ...*

*Groom: Maybe a little. Painters are expensive.*

> *Kendall: Don't worry. I love it. It looks amazing.*

*Groom: I hope they finish it on time.*

> *Kendall: They are cutting it close.*

*Groom: I wanted to carry you across the threshold on our wedding night.*

Aww... my heart warmed when he made these sweet little confessions to me. There was more to him than met the eye. I couldn't have found a better partner to start my life with. I sometimes still couldn't believe that I could have missed out on this wonderful man if life had gone differently for us.

> *Kendall: You still can.*

*Groom: There isn't any furniture.*

> *Kendall: Never stopped us before.*

*Groom: ...*

> *Kendall: Sorry. I know you're busy at work. I shouldn't tease you.*

*Groom: ...*

He kept typing things and erasing them, my mind racing as I tried to anticipate his response.

*Groom: My apartment - 30 minutes.*

> *Kendall: What?*

My pulse jumped when I thought about the implications of his command. With shaky fingers, I sent him a shocked emoji.

*Groom: You can read.*

*Kendall: Seriously? I haven't even gone in the house yet to check progress.*

*Groom: The house will be there later.*

The smirking emoji he sent next made me laugh. That might as well be his mascot emoji, he'd perfected the arrogant smirk.

*Kendall: You've got work.*

*Groom: I have more pressing issues to handle right now.*

*Kendall: I love it when you talk dirty.*

*Groom: If you're late, I'm spanking you.*

*Kendall: Yes, please.*

I couldn't help following it up with a crying laughing emoji.

*Groom: That wasn't a joke.*

My skin prickled as an open hand emoji and a peach came through next.

I smiled as I looked at my watch and then back at the house. I wanted to see the progress on the kitchen yesterday, and I needed to check-in at the office. With the semester starting soon, I needed to work on some curriculum, but I still had time. It could wait.

"Fuck. Not enough time," I sighed as I looked toward the freshly painted front door. Over the last several months, it'd been my responsibility to check in with the contractor. He gave me regular progress updates and was amazing at letting me pick options in real-time. The builder's designer was notorious for not responding to emails.

*Groom: 27 minutes.*

When he got bossy like this, the sex between us was truly explosive. Something about him knowing what I liked and being completely confident in his effect on me turned me on. He had his moments when he could be gentle and tender, showing me with his body how much I meant to him. But when he fucked me without being apologetic about his attraction to me, I'd never felt anything like it.

His car wasn't in the parking lot when I pulled into my guest parking space, the lot was empty for a Thursday morning. Most people were at work. That just meant I could be loud. He loved it when I was loud. It was part of the reason he'd gotten his own apartment after graduation. He was tired of having to tiptoe around roommates.

### *Groom: 3 minutes.*

"So bossy," I laughed as I walked up to the apartment door and punched in the code to unlock the deadbolt.

"I heard that." The low voice from behind me scared the shit out of me, and I jumped as the door swung open.

"Holy shit, you scared me," I laughed nervously as I turned towards him.

"Get inside." He braced his hands on the handrails in the stairwell, and his shoulders flexed in a way that made his dress shirt pull snug against his chest.

"How did you get here so fast?" I asked him with a smile. He was probably speeding again.

"The office is only twenty minutes away," he shrugged.

"You must have run out of there like a bat out of hell," I laughed.

"I don't have any appointments until after lunch." He told me with a smile. His schedule had been sporadic as he filled in his coworkers on projects they needed him to handle while we were on our honeymoon.

"Won't your boss wonder why you're gone?" I laughed. He was a cool guy, but we were going to be gone for two weeks. Now was not the time to be slacking off.

"I put an off-site meeting into my calendar," he winked. Of course, he'd probably been planning this all morning, and I just fell into his trap.

"Is that what this is?" I rolled my eyes and put my hands on my hips. He thought he was so clever.

"Why are you still standing in the doorway talking to me? Get your ass inside." He nodded his head and pointed toward the open door.

"I'm sticking to my bossy assessment from earlier." I tilted my head at him and gave him an unamused look.

"I'll show you bossy," he growled as he quickly ascended the remaining few steps and scooped me up in his arms.

"Show off," I laughed as I put my arms around his neck.

He kissed my cheek and carried me inside, kicking the door shut and carrying me into the kitchen. He deposited me onto the counter and immediately started his mission to get me naked.

"We have a bed here," I giggled as he unbuttoned my blouse, his lips blazing a trail down as he exposed more skin.

"Less talking." He grunted. Apparently, he'd reverted to a caveman.

"More fucking?" I laughed as he yanked on my open blouse and peeled it down my shoulders.

"You may not have been late, but I'll still spank you," he taunted.

"You say that like it's a bad thing." My fingers unclasped his belt and pulled it open, quickly unbuttoning his slacks and using my feet to inch down his pants.

"Someone is eager," he chuckled. Like he was protesting. Please.

I plunged my hand inside his boxer briefs and took hold of him. He throbbed in my hand, and I got a thrill from the way he threw his head back and groaned as I worked him over.

"Someone doesn't seem to be complaining," I giggled as I increased the pressure of my fist.

"Fuck," he grunted as his hips flexed into the motion of my hand. "Oh, God. Why are you so good at this?"

"Are you complaining?" I teased, leaning forward and kissing along his firm jaw, briefly stopping to suck at his pulse point.

His large hands pulled the cups of my bra down, and he firmly flicked his thumbs over my nipples, causing me to moan into the skin of his neck.

"No, not at all," he groaned as he threw his head back. "I keep waiting for this to fizzle out, and it just gets hotter."

A loud moan tore out of him as my other hand slipped lower and rubbed the skin behind his sac firmly. His hips jerked, and I felt him swell in my hand.

"We're getting married in two days, and you're waiting for this to get less hot?"

"Oh God. Ignore me. Sense has obviously left my brain right now." He buried his nose into my hair, his panting breaths warming the side of my face. "Keep going... fuck... fuck... right there..."

He squeezed my breasts one last time before he gripped the waistband of my leggings in his fingers and lifted me from the counter to pull them down my legs.

"Oh God, it's cold," I shrieked as my bare cheeks hit the granite countertop. But the firm thrust of one long finger into me made me forget my name, much less that my ass was cold.

"Are you cold now?" he whispered into my ear as his thumb found the source of my pleasure and applied firm pressure.

"Nooo. Oh... Oh God..." I arched backward, and his hot lips burned a path down my neck, and he spent several minutes biting and licking my nipples as he drove me closer to orgasm.

"Fuck, you're so hot," he growled as he unclasped my bra and pulled it off, throwing it behind him.

I laughed as it landed on a cabinet knob. "Oh, my God..."

"Stop laughing. Do you really find this funny?" His fingers curled, and I let go of him, gripping the counter on either side of my hips as he worked me into a frenzy.

"Nooo. Fuck. Oh, oh." My head dropped back as I pushed my hips into the motion of his hand. Those long fingers drove me to distraction regularly.

"That's what I thought." He was so cocky sometimes.

"Why is your shirt still on?" I panted as he looked up and made eye contact with me.

"Really?" He shook his head as I nodded, pulling back and unbuttoning his cuffs before he rolled his shoulders, and his shirt slowly revealed his toned arms. He dropped it to the floor and pushed down his boxers, reaching down to pull off his shoes.

"Leave it," I shook my head.

"What?" He laughed again as I hopped off the counter and bent myself over the edge, my breasts pressing into the cool, smooth surface.

"Don't worry about the rest. Just fuck me."

He blew out a loud breath and grasped my hips, tilting them up as he squatted down a little and lined himself up.

"Oh God... Yes." My voice was breathy as he pushed inside in one smooth motion and pressed his warm chest into my back.

"Is this how you like it?" His low voice sent a shiver down my spine, and I moaned as he pulled his hips back and then snapped them forward repeatedly, working himself into a rhythm that was driving me closer and closer to the edge. "Do you like it when I'm so desperate to get inside you that I leave work early and race home to bend you over the kitchen counter?"

"More." I tried to find something to grab hold of on the slick counters as he pulled me roughly into him, his strong thighs hitting the backs of mine with each powerful movement. He reached around with one hand and pressed it into where we were joined, keeping me anchored to him with his other. The erotic push and pull of him manipulating my body for our mutual pleasure was maddering.

Before I could even try to stop it, I was crying out and spasming against him, convulsing as he kept going, harder than before. His hips pistoned forward, pressing me into the front of the cabinets as his cock swelled inside of me.

"Fuck..." He moaned as his fingers dug into my hips, and he released inside of me a few moments later. His warm lips connected with my shoulder, and he whispered devotions into my skin as we both came back to earth. "Mmm. I love you."

"I love you, too. Even when you're a bossy dick who constantly wants me on yours when we should be pretending to be productive adults." He laughed, and my heart swelled at the sound and the way he held me tightly with no signs of letting go despite real life calling us beyond the four walls of his apartment.

Soon, we'd be defiling a whole new kitchen.

And in a few days, I'd be meeting him at the altar.

# Chapter Fourteen:
## Junior Year
### SEPTEMBER

"I can't believe you turn twenty-one before me," Allie pouted as she looked up at me from the couch in our living room.

"You only have a few more months," I rolled my eyes at her dramatic display.

She groaned as she leaned back into the corner of the couch, draping her forearm across her face. "Months. I have months."

"You'll be fine. I'm sure that we'll have lots of fun when you're old enough to go next semester," I insisted. I knew Allie would be dragging me out to the campus bars with her as soon as it was legal.

"I hate you," she pouted. "Why do you have to be the older one? You're practically an old married lady, and you won't even go properly enjoy your twenty-first birthday."

"I'm going out to dinner with you, aren't I?" I pointed out. She'd insisted, and I knew I owed her that much for how much of an amazing roommate she'd been over the last few years.

"I can't even have a drink with you. It's not fair," Allie frowned.

"It'll be here before you know it."

"Ugh," she moaned. "You just don't get it. I've been waiting for years to be old enough to go to the campus bars, and you get to go first."

"I'm not even sure if I'm going anywhere on campus," I shrugged, but that just made her frown deepen. She thought I was wasting my opportunity. "It's not like I have all that many people to go out with."

"Wait. What?" she asked as she sat up and looked over at me. "I thought Dylan was coming up this weekend to take you out?"

"He was," I gave her a sad smile, hoping she didn't go off about his lack of attention again.

"Why are you saying it like that? In the past tense..."

I cringed as I shook my head. I hadn't meant to open this wound again. "He's not sure if he can come up. There is some kind of mandatory pledge event, and he is supposed to be there to get assigned to his little brother for the year."

"Are you fucking kidding me? This again?" she growled.

"Let it go, Allie. He'll come up next weekend if he can't come now," I insisted. He'd already cleared his schedule. "It's not like it matters. He's already given me my present."

I fingered the pendant around my neck, remembering that day in the jewelry store. He still hadn't proposed, but I knew he had the ring. I thought it might happen around my birthday, but not if he changed plans.

I was trying not to dwell on it.

"I thought you guys were doing better?" she sighed as she gave me a sympathetic smile.

"We are," I insisted. We had been, at least. At home for the summer, we'd built a solid foundation. But as soon as we started school again, we were being dragged in opposite directions again.

"Doesn't look like it if he's canceling your birthday plans," she raised her eyebrow at me with a smirk.

"I wasn't with him for his birthday," I shrugged.

"I thought he was at that football team group retreat." Of course, she'd remember that.

"He was."

She narrowed her eyes at me and crossed her arms over her chest. "Not the same."

"Just let it go, please," I begged. I hated feeling all this tension. I was disappointed that we both had commitments that kept us apart, but the extra stress of others judging from the outside was almost too much sometimes.

"Fine. But I still think you need to go out this weekend," she insisted, a calculating look appearing in her eyes.

"By myself? No thanks." I shook my head. I was not being that loser.

"Joel is twenty-one already," she shrugged as she pinned me down with a knowing stare.

"No," I shook my head. I knew plenty of Tyler's brothers had turned twenty-one over the summer, but I was not going out with them. It was still too awkward.

"Oh, come on, he's cute." She bounced a little in her seat.

"And I'm taken," I reminded her.

"Kale is twenty-four," she pointed out.

"Good for him," I rolled my eyes.

"Don't you see him on campus?" she asked, implications of something creeping into her voice.

"I have a few times, yes." I nodded. I wasn't giving any of her ideas merit.

"Come on! You're killing me! You're so lame!" she exclaimed as she threw her arms up in the air.

"Nice to know how you really feel about me," I laughed as I threw a cotton ball at her. She insisted on giving me a pedicure since I wouldn't make an appointment for my birthday.

"Why are you always throwing things at me?" she laughed as she dodged the tiny flying fluff.

"Why are you always saying things that make me want to throw stuff at you?" I growled. She was always starting shit.

"You know you love it..." she laughed as she finished painting my toes.

I gave her a cheesy smile and tilted my head to the side. "I can honestly say that you're my favorite roommate."

"I'm your only roommate." She arched an eyebrow.

"That's why you're the favorite," I shrugged, and then she was throwing cotton balls at me.

"Happy Birthday, baby." I sighed at the defeated sound of Dylan's voice on the other end of the phone. He wasn't coming.

"Thank you," I responded softly.

He sighed into his end of the line, sounding tired. "I'm sorry."

Afraid that my disappointment would flood my voice, I remained quiet.

"I promise I'll be up there next weekend. I tried to get out of this, but they wouldn't let me," he did sound disappointed, but I was just hurt at this point. I acted like it wasn't a big deal to Allie, but it felt like I was being pushed aside for the fraternity again.

"It's fine."

"It's clearly not fine," he insisted, his voice rising a little. "I feel like an asshole."

"I'm not sure what I'm supposed to say here," I responded quietly. If I were honest with him, it wouldn't change anything.

I heard loud yelling in the background, followed by Brady's laugh. He must have been at the house. "They're calling us down to dinner. I have to go. I love you."

"Me too."

"Happy birthday," he said sadly, and I felt my eyes tearing up.

The call disconnected, and I blew out a breath, trying to keep from crying. Alison was right. I pushed everyone away after Tyler, and I broke up and spent all my time with Dylan. I wasn't sure what to do.

On the one hand, I had an amazing boyfriend who I'd known half my life that had already bought an engagement ring. On the other hand, I had one real friend and spent my entire week working my ass off to keep myself functionally isolated from my own college experience.

"Knock, knock!" Alison peeked her head around the door and saw me sitting on the edge of my futon, probably looking dejected. "He's not coming."

"He's not coming," I sniffled as I wiped a single tear from my cheek with the back of my hand.

"No, no, no, no, no. No crying on your birthday," she insisted as she pointed at me from the doorway.

"I'm sorry."

"Stop it," she insisted. "You get yourself together. We're going out."

"What? Where?"

She ignored me and moved to my closet, angrily yanking the hangers apart and sorting through the contents.

"No, not Kendall Barbie again," I whined.

"Nope. You be quiet. And stop crying. Go put some eyeliner on," she ordered as she pointed toward my open bathroom door.

"Why do I need eyeliner?"

"Because you're going to be hot tonight," she told me, her voice not leaving any room for negotiation. "We're going to a club. You're going to drink legally, and I'm going to post pictures on your social media to show that douche canoe that you have a life without him."

"I do?"

"Put this on." She threw a short black dress at my head and disappeared into my bathroom. I sat there in shock for a few minutes and tried to process what was going on. "Get up, take off those sweatpants, and put on that dress."

"Why are you being mean to me on my birthday?"

"Because you're hot, and you don't deserve to be neglected on your twenty-first birthday," she told me, shaking her head as I opened my mouth to protest. "We are going to this club, you are going to get drunk, and you are going to have fun."

I nodded as she moved toward my doorway.

"Now!" She walked out, and I stared after her for a few moments before I stripped off my oversized sweats and pulled on the dress. It wasn't as bad as I thought it would be.

"Eyeliner!" she yelled down the hallway again, and I headed to the bathroom.

Wetting a washcloth, I wiped my face and then put on makeup. I heard my phone pinging as I got myself ready. It felt good to look at myself in the mirror as I carefully applied some shadow, a thick smudge of eyeliner, and mascara. Not bothering to look at the phone, I pulled out my curling iron and put loose waves in, spraying the ends before I tossed them.

"Yaaassss! You look hot!" Alison had also put on a skintight dress and some heavier makeup. "Let me do a few shots, and then our ride should be here."

"Shouldn't I be doing the shots?" I laughed, feeling a bit better.

"Psh, it's legal for you. I'm pre-gaming because I know they'll ID me." I followed her out to the kitchen and watched as she shot back three consecutive shots of rum.

"Woo," she hissed as she plunked the glass down on the countertop. A text scrolled across her phone screen. "Let's go. Our ride awaits."

She thrust my purse into my hands, and I followed her down the stairs to the back parking lot. A black four-door sedan with tinted windows was waiting near the door.

"Are you kidnapping me?" I laughed as I stopped walking a few steps behind her.

"Hardly. I just scrounged us up a ride, so we didn't have to walk across campus in the dark," she laughed.

"Like, a taxi?"

"Just a friend who owes me a favor," she shrugged as she leaned back and grabbed my arm, tugging me toward the car. We climbed into the backseat, and I vaguely recognized the girl sitting in the passenger seat.

"'Bout time you called in that favor. I was beginning to think you were waiting for me to name my kid after you," her friend laughed. She had long red hair, glasses, and freckles dotted across the bridge of her nose.

"Now that I think about it, maybe I should have," Allie laughed at her friend.

"Nope, too late now." The woman turned towards me and waved. "You must be Kendall. Happy birthday."

"Oh, thanks," I smiled awkwardly.

"Kendall, this is Stevie. She's an old friend from the dorm," Allie introduced as the woman smiled at me.

"Thanks for giving us a ride."

"Of course," she nodded. "When I heard it was your birthday, and you got ditched, I was happy to help this one pull off at least a good celebration."

Giving Allie a pointed look first, I forced a smile toward Stevie. Allie shrugged, and I tried to pretend it didn't bother me that she told people my boyfriend ditched me on my birthday.

"Hey. It's fine. Men are stupid," Stevie laughed.

"Hey!" The driver, a man with shoulder-length, dark, curly hair, looked over at her with a scowl.

"Oh, get over yourself." She pushed her hand into his shoulder, and I spied the enormous engagement ring and wedding band on her finger.

"I see you're both still in the honeymoon phase," Alison laughed, and I saw the driver smile and laugh to himself.

"Sorry. This is my husband, Porter. We both graduated last spring and got married about six weeks ago," Stevie explained as the man gave me a smile in the rearview mirror. He had striking, light blue eyes.

"Oh, congratulations," I told them.

"Thanks. Anyway, so, you're twenty-one?" she asked as she looked over the back of the seat at me.

"Yes." I hated awkward small talk, but she seemed like a nice person.

"That's always a fun birthday to recover from. Remember to drink lots of water before you pass out," she advised.

"You've already got this mom thing down," Alison laughed.

"Pretty sure an infant doesn't need to hydrate after binge drinking," Stevie told her in a flat voice, but Alison just rolled her eyes at her friend.

"Details..."

The car stopped in front of a club that let people in, starting at age eighteen. So, this was how she planned to join me tonight while getting me drunk.

"Try not to get too wasted. And tell those jackasses to behave themselves," Stevie told Alison as she scooted over toward the door.

"Yes, Mom."

"Call me if you want a ride home," Stevie insisted.

Allie saluted her friend before she hopped out of the car.

"Thank you," I smiled at her as I scooted toward the open door. Allie was standing on the curb with an impatient look on her face.

"It was nice to put a face to a name. Have fun," Stevie smiled before I climbed out and closed the door softly.

Allie was already talking to the guy at the front door as I walked up the sidewalk.

"ID, please," a burly looking bouncer requested with his hand outstretched. I pulled out my license and handed it to him. He looked at it with a small colored light and then returned it. He strapped on a green wristband, stamping my hand and nodding towards the door. "Happy Birthday."

"Thanks!" I smiled at him, feeling a little nervous. I hadn't been out much on campus. This was all new to me.

The music was thumping as Alison pulled open the glass door and tugged me inside.

"Come on. They're already here," she shouted as she pulled me towards some tables at the side of the large dance floor already half full of intoxicated coeds.

"Who are they?" I yelled over the music, and she smiled over her shoulder at me.

"You'll see."

My nerves kicked in as she waved at a table of people in the corner. As they came into view, I saw several familiar faces and a few new ones.

"Special K!" Rory stood up from the table and waved as we approached. It was obvious he was already a few drinks in. Bridgette, the same girl he'd brought to the barn dance freshman year, was practically sitting on his lap. She smiled and waved at me.

"Hey, Bridge!" I hollered in her direction.

"Oh, I see how it is. Don't say hi to me," Rory laughed as he held his hand over his heart.

"Hello, Rory." I rolled my eyes, and his girlfriend giggled.

"He's needy when he's drunk. Just ignore him," she laughed as she pushed him back into his seat.

"I was going to do that anyway," I told her with a laugh.

His mouth dropped open, and the entire table laughed.

"She's right, dude. You are pretty high maintenance," Joel laughed at his friend from the other side of the table.

"This from the guy who dated the biggest attention whore on campus," Rory rolled his eyes before he threw a wadded-up straw wrapper at his friend across the table.

"I never dated you, dude," Joel laughed as he dodged the tiny flying object.

They started pushing each other, and the few other girls at the table rolled their eyes before introducing themselves.

I turned to Allie, and my mouth dropped open as I noticed a guy wrapped around her back, kissing her neck.

"Stop, Benji," she giggled, and he looked up at me, resting his chin on her shoulder.

"So, is this the guy?" I asked in surprise as I finally came face to face with the mystery man that Alison had been hiding from me.

"The guy, huh? She was talking about me?" He asked me with an amused look on his face.

"Maybe a little," Alison teased as she turned her face toward him. "Or maybe there's some other guy."

"Happy Birthday, Kendall. It's nice to meet you finally. I'm Benji," he greeted as he held out a hand around his giggling girlfriend.

"Same," I smiled. "I was beginning to think she made you up."

"How would you know? You're never home on the weekends," she teased as she stuck her tongue out at me.

"Fair enough," I nodded.

"Alright. Enough small talk. Time for shots, and then I'm going to dance. Who's in?" Joel asked as he downed the cup's contents at the table.

"Dude, your vagina is showing," Rory laughed loudly.

"You're just jealous. I actually know how to move my hips," Joel shot back, and Rory's face sobered a little.

"Oh, my God. Bahaha..." Rory's girlfriend broke into hysterical laughter. He looked like he was about to say something, but then sighed and took a drink of his beer.

Joel looked straight at me and raised his eyebrow. "How 'bout it, birthday girl? I'll buy your first shot."

"I don't kn..."

Allie grabbed my arm and pushed me in his direction. "She'd love to."

He rounded the end of the table and hooked his arm around my waist. "I feel like I haven't seen you in forever. How've you been?"

Joel steered me towards the bar on the far wall and signaled to the bartender.

"I'm okay. Just been busy." I nodded. I'd spent so long avoiding them all. It felt a little awkward to be seeing the group again.

"I feel you on that one. School has been kicking my ass this year," he agreed and smiled at me.

A female bartender stopped right in front of us and pulled two plastic mugs from under the counter, placing them in front of us. "Tap or well drinks?"

"I'll take a bud light. She'll have an amaretto sour," Joel told her confidently.

"Wrist bands?"

Joel held up his arm, showing off his green band. I followed suit, and she nodded, filling up our drinks and pushing them across the counter. "Anything else?"

"Two blow jobs." I felt my face heat when he glanced over at me and winked.

She quickly took out two shot glasses and proceeded to layer them with several types of alcohol, topping them off with a flourish of whipped cream. I reached for the shot, and Joel grabbed my wrist.

"Ah, ah, ah. Not so fast." He halted my hand and nodded at the shot glasses.

"What?" I frowned. I thought he was buying me a shot.

"No hands," he laughed at my shocked face and pulled the shot glasses to the edge of the counter. "Come on. Show me whatcha got."

Taking a deep breath, I nodded and turned towards the bar. I looked at him out of the corner of my eye as we both leaned forward and wrapped our lips around the edge of our shot glasses. He straightened and flicked his head back, swallowing the contents of his glass before he pulled it out of his mouth. His tongue licked the edge of his lip, clearing the remnants of the whipped cream.

I swallowed back my shot and licked the glass before his fingers closed over mine and pulled it away. "Tastes good, right?"

"Mmmhmm..." I hummed as he reached toward me and rubbed his thumb across my bottom lip.

"Come on. Let's get out there." He nodded towards the dance floor, and I shook my head.

"Yes. Let's go drop our drinks off at the table." He grabbed my hand and pulled me back through the crowd.

Allie glanced down at our joined hands as we stopped at the table and raised an eyebrow. I shook my hand free and took a substantial gulp of my drink before Joel grabbed hold of me again and tugged me onto the dance floor.

He turned me to face him with his hands loosely gripping my hips, and I awkwardly placed my hands on his shoulders. His hands guided my hips into a fast swivel that matched the song. After the tempo changed to a more sensual beat, he pulled me closer and pushed his leg between mine.

"Relax." His breath was hot against the side of my face as he leaned in towards me.

"I'm not good at this," I laughed, and his hands drifted to the small of my back, pulling my chest flush with his.

"You just need to let your guard down and move with me. Don't force it." His hips pressed forward, and he led me into a slow grind, losing himself in the beat. He watched my face closely as we danced, his thumbs caressing me. The feeling of his fingers searing me through the thin material of my dress.

The next song started, and he gripped my hips again, turning me to face away from him in a fluid motion that took away my breath. He pressed himself in closer and rotated his hips, lightly grinding into me from behind.

Joel's lips grazed my shoulder, and I looked over my shoulder at him, taking in the naked look of desire in his eyes. He drew one of my arms up and placed my hand on his cheek while he ran his palms down my side, gripping my hips more firmly.

"You're gorgeous," he whispered in my ear, and I felt my breath catch. I shouldn't be doing this. I had a boyfriend. I pulled away from him and turned around, taking a step back.

"What's wrong?" he asked as he looked at me with concern. I could tell he didn't know what had happened, but I felt like I was skirting the line of my commitment to Dylan.

"I'm thirsty. I'm heading back," I shouted so Joel could hear me over the music, and I took off towards the table.

Allie and Benji were sitting on a stool making out while two of the girls who'd been there before were giggling at something on their phones. I picked up my mug and took several long drinks before placing it back on the table with a dull thud. My best friend detached herself from her new boyfriend long enough to notice I was standing there. "Hey. What's wrong?"

"I think we should go."

"Seriously? We've been here less than an hour," she whined.

"Hey..." Joel stepped up next to me and placed his hand on the middle of my back. I cringed, and he dropped his hand. "Did I do something? I thought we were having fun."

"You two looked hot out there," Alison giggled as she looked between the two of us.

"You were attached at the lips to Benji. You weren't even watching," I laughed as she shrugged.

Turning to face Joel, I picked up my drink and took another long pull until my mug was empty.

"Slow down there," he laughed as he took the empty mug from my hands and placed it on the table.

"I'm fine."

"What's going on?" he asked, obviously sensing the change in my mood.

I blurted out the first excuse I could think of to explain my behavior. "I have a boyfriend."

He nodded. "Alright."

"I shouldn't be here," I shouted as he stood there with an amused smile.

"Because you have a boyfriend?"

"Yes." I nodded.

He laughed as he took a drink from his mug. "You realize we were just dancing, right? "

"But..." I felt my face flame as I recalled the sensations that ran through me at the feeling of Joel's hands manipulating my body to sway to the beat.

"Nothing we did was out of line," he insisted as he reached up and pushed a strand of hair from my sweaty cheek. "I'm not looking for a commitment from you. I just wanted a dance partner for the night."

"She's socially deprived. You'll have to excuse her inability to have fun," Alison laughed, obviously eavesdropping on our conversation.

I frowned at her, and she winked at me. "I can have fun."

"Can you?" she challenged.

"Yes!" I yelled back, narrowing my eyes at her.

"Then let's do another round of shots, and you can show me how fun you are," Joel laughed as he placed a hand on my back. I managed not to flinch this time, but the heat was still there.

Allie flagged down a waitress, and two shots of tequila later, I was feeling much lighter. I hadn't had the urge to check my phone yet, and drunk Kendall was having too much fun to bother. As the night went on, I relaxed and enjoyed myself, knowing that Joel didn't have an agenda, and I needed to stop being so codependent on Dylan.

A buzzing sound from the floor startled me awake, and I scrubbed my hand over my face. My mouth was dry, and my temples throbbed as I tried to remember what happened last night.

"Ugh," I groaned and shifted, a heavy weight pinning down my hips.

Pressing my face into the pillow, I peeked one eye open and was met with a riot of blonde hair next to me.

"Oh, my God," I whispered, suddenly wide awake.

"Shhh... too loud." A masculine voice groaned as the owner of the messy hair raised his head, and tired blue eyes met mine. "Hey."

"What...?" My voice was simultaneously high-pitched and gruff at the same time.

Joel smiled and pushed a strand of my hair away from my face. "Calm down. It's not what it looks like."

"Oh shit," I groaned and closed my eyes.

"Kendall, chill," he laughed, his voice lower than I remembered it being.

"I'm in bed with another man," I whispered. "I'm a horrible girlfriend."

My head shot up from the pillow beneath me. "Oh, my God! What did I do?"

He started laughing and rolled away from me, sitting up. I looked at the wall behind him and realized I wasn't even in my bed. How drunk was I last night? "Kendall. Calm the fuck down. My head hurts."

I started shaking my head, and he was still looking at me with an amused smile. "Nothing happened."

"But..." I squeaked.

"Am I naked?" My eyes drifted down to his wrinkled shirt and jeans. He was still fully clothed and lying on top of the covers. A throw blanket was pooled around his thighs.

"No, but..."

"Are you naked?" I lifted the sheets and saw my thoroughly wrinkled dress.

"No..."

"Does it feel like we...?" He trailed off, and I averted my eyes and shook my head. "Then will you calm down and quit shrieking? You're going to wake up my roommates."

My phone kept vibrating, and he leaned over me to grab it from the floor. "You might want to check that."

I pressed the button to wake the screen and saw several missed text messages.

*Dylan: Just checking in. You're not answering your phone.*
*Miss you.*

My guilt flared as Joel sat watching me quietly.

There was a missed message from one of Dylan's friends. She was always someone I enjoyed hanging out with, and I wondered if she was texting to send me a happy birthday message. I clicked on her name and almost choked on my tongue as a picture pulled up.

**Chelsea: Thought you deserved to see this.**

"I need to go." I swung my legs over the end of the bed and looked down to find my missing shoes.

"What's wrong?"

They were under the desk across the room, so I stood on wobbly legs and grabbed them before I scooped up my purse and headed for the door. "I need to go. Where am I?"

"Our study room," Joel said quietly, his face concerned.

"Shit. I need to get home."

He frowned as he climbed off the bed and carefully placed his palms on my shoulders.

"Is Allie here?" I asked, watching him.

"Yeah, she's probably with Benji," he nodded. "What's wrong, Kendall?"

I took a deep breath and tried to stop the tears I could feel building.

"Hey." He placed a finger under my chin and pushed it up, looking into my eyes. "Talk to me."

"No. I need to go." I shook my head as I leaned away from him.

"What was on your phone, Kendall?" His voice was low and quiet. I could tell he was trying to calm me down.

"I... I need..." I was minutes from freaking the fuck out and needed to get home.

"Take a deep breath," he encouraged as his large hands on my shoulders held me still. "That's it... In... Out...."

A sob caught in my throat, and he pulled me into his chest as he pried my phone out of my hand. He held my head to his chest as he looked down at the picture Chelsea had sent me.

"Fuck." He cursed as he looked down at the image.

Tears rolled down my cheeks as I broke down and sobbed into his chest.

"Hey. Hey, breathe, Kendall." I hiccupped against him, and he dropped my phone to the floor, the screen momentarily flashing with the picture.

There it was, that bitch Lisa, sitting on Dylan's lap with her lips on his neck. As if that wasn't bad enough, the comment underneath the Instagram post just pounded the nail into the coffin.

*Love lazy Saturdays with my boy, D. #lovehim #finallyofficial #couplegoals*

# Chapter Fifteen:
## Junior Year
### SEPTEMBER

"What do you need from me?" Joel asked quietly as he slowly pulled me away from where I'd been snot sobbing against his shirt.

I wiped my eyes and pushed my hair from my face. I was sure I looked like a total mess. "I need to go back to my apartment."

"Are you going to confront him?" he asked quietly. "That's pretty fucked up."

"After I get myself together, I think I've got to drive down there," I sighed. This wasn't something I could deal with on the phone, and it certainly couldn't wait another week to be dealt with.

"I can drive you. I mean, if you want. Be there for moral support." I took a good look at Joel and saw that he was being sincere. He may have been immature at times, but he was a decent guy.

"No." I shook my head and smiled at him sadly. "I need to do this by myself. I can't let other people clean up my messes."

"I can beat the shit out of him if you want me to," he offered, his voice sounded like it was joking, but the look in his eyes told me otherwise.

A tired laugh burst out of me, and I placed a hand on his scruffy cheek. "That's sweet. But, no."

"I hope she gives him an STD."

"Oh, my God, stop," I laughed, shaking my head at him.

"You know what we call girls like her that hang around here?" he asked with a mischievous grin pulled across his lips.

"I don't think I want to know," I giggled. I could just imagine all the wild things frat boys said when girls weren't around. I know I'd heard my fair share of nasty stuff from the guys in Dylan's house.

"A Huffy... she's got ten speeds and lets anybody take a ride."

"That's horrible." I shook my head, but he'd gotten me to smile.

"There's another one I like, too," he grinned as he looked over at me.

"Don't tell me." I shook my head, but I knew he would tell me, anyway.

"You mean I shouldn't tell you we call them ATMs?" he laughed. "They like to take your money, and anyone with a debit card can make a deposit."

"Ouch," I cringed. "You guys are brutal."

He gave me an amused smile, reaching forward and squeezing my hand. "Those aren't even the worst of them."

"Charming." His smile widened as I rolled my eyes at him.

"Hey, it's a house full of guys in their early twenties. We're not exactly the most charming male specimens," he admitted with a shrug.

"So, you're the exception to the rule?"

He turned sideways to face me. My face tingled as he ran his fingertips across my cheek and pushed my hair away from my face. "I'm not perfect, but I also like to think I try to respect women."

"By flirting with girls in relationships?" I asked quietly. Remembering how he'd looked at me last night.

"Only when they don't see their value because they're in a relationship with a douche."

I remembered what he'd said to me in the hallway at the barn dance. That he was jealous of Tyler. Oh God, Tyler... was I about to look like I was doing a walk of shame with him watching?

"What?" he asked, obviously sensing my abrupt change in demeanor.

I narrowed my eyes at him in askance.

"You looked panicked there for a second."

"Tyler isn't here, is he?" I asked quietly, looking toward the door to the rest of the house.

"Nah," he shook his head. "He's still in London. Extended the study abroad thing."

Thank God.

"You deserve better than both of them."

I appreciated the concern, but I still didn't know what was going on. "You don't even know Dylan."

"Do you?" He studied my face as I stood there quietly.

I wasn't sure if I did anymore. I never thought he'd be the type to cheat. But apparently, it's hard to know what people are capable of until things hit the fan.

"Maybe I don't," I admitted quietly. That was the hardest thing to realize, that my best friend could just stab me in the back like that.

"I know you're a big girl and can handle yourself, but don't let him try to weasel his way out of this. You were sent that picture for a reason."

"I don't even know if it was real," I shook my head. "It was on her personal Instagram page. He doesn't have one."

"That you know of," he told me with an eyebrow raised. He was right; if this had been going on under my nose, then who knew what else Dylan might have been hiding.

"Why don't we look it up," he suggested as he looked around on the floor.

"What? No." Wasn't that an invasion of privacy?

He grabbed my phone and pulled up the photo, using his own to pull up her Instagram account.

"Gotta give her something, bitch isn't totally stupid." He showed me the screen. She'd set her account to private. "Should I request her?"

I shook my head and opened my account, hesitating for a moment before I logged out and then logged back in with Alison's.

"Sneaky," he grinned as he smiled at me.

I submitted the request, and I put my phone down. "Well, I guess we'll have to wait to see if she responds."

"She already did." The screen loaded, and hundreds of pictures popped up as her account became visible. Morbid curiosity came over me, and I began scrolling through the posts. The one from the photo was gone, but I saw Dylan in more pictures than I was comfortable with. Lisa, with an A, spent more time in my boyfriend's room than I did.

"That's him, right?" Joel nodded at Dylan's smiling face.

"Yeah..." I stopped on one particular photo from the week he was at training camp. It showed him in a pair of swim trunks, with Lisa thrown over his shoulder in a bikini. He was grinning for the camera with a smile I rarely saw, and I felt my stomach twist.

Lisa: *'Taking a break from camp to cool off' #campushottie #footballbfs'*

"Can you take me back now?" I asked quietly as I locked the screen on my phone. I didn't need to see anything else.

"You sure you don't want me to come?"

I shook my head, trying to fight the urge to cry again. "No. I need to do this by myself."

My palms were sweating as I pulled into the parking space I'd considered my own and turned off the engine. Luckily, no one was outside because I didn't want anyone to let him know I was here.

The back door had been left unlocked, but I could hear the telltale sounds of video games and guys trash talking as I moved quickly toward the back staircase. My heart started hammering as I hesitated at the door to his room. It was cracked open, but I could hear voices inside.

Dylan was sitting shirtless in his desk chair, feet propped up on the desk and his laptop open. It sounded like he was watching a movie.

Moving into the doorway, I stood there for a few moments before he turned his head and saw me. Panic flickered across his face before a wide smile formed on his lips, and he abruptly sat up.

"Hey!" he stood up quickly and made his way toward me. "You didn't tell me you were coming."

"Should I have?" he stopped moving at my curt remark and looked at me curiously.

"I would've taken a shower first. I'm sure I'm gross. I know how you feel about me being stinky," he laughed, but I didn't find it all that amusing.

"Need to wash something off?" I accused, the irritation clear.

"You okay?" he asked as he looked over at me, and his brows pinched together.

I shook my head and sat down gingerly on the end of the couch. I didn't know what had happened on it. "No. To be honest, I'm not."

"Are you still mad at me for not being able to come up last night? I'm sorry... but..."

"No." I shook my head as I looked over at him.

"I'm glad you're here. Maybe I can take you out tonight." I couldn't believe that I would have to pry this out of him. I guess at least I was spared finding them together.

"I'm not staying that long."

Sitting back down in his chair heavily, he turned towards me and grabbed my hand. I slowly pried it off and shook my head.

"What's wrong?"

"I thought you had the pledge thing this morning," I accused. It was only early afternoon, and he still looked like he'd barely rolled out of bed.

"I did," he nodded, the frown still there. Good.

"Want to tell me why Chelsea sent me this picture?" I asked as I unlocked my phone with shaky hands and turned it in his direction. He tried to take it out of my hand, but I jerked it back and raised an eyebrow at him.

"What?" His eyes widened in a way that would've been comical if this situation didn't involve me. "That's not real."

"The picture or the relationship announcement?" I asked, my previous irritation now morphing into outright anger. "Because it looks like you're wearing the same sweats that you have on right now."

"I can explain," he breathed out, his frantic eyes finding mine.

"Please do. I'm sure this will be riveting stuff."

He blew out a breath and tried to smile at me. I didn't return it. "She's got a crush on me."

"Really? Because this looks like more than a crush," I pointed at the picture as I got angrier and angrier at the fact that my boyfriend was dismissing a girl sitting on his lap and kissing his neck.

"Not for me," he shook his head. Great. So, not only was he cheating, but it meant nothing to him.

"Really? Because I could see her faking one picture, which she's now taken down, but this isn't the only one with you in it." I pulled open the Instagram app, which was still logged into Alison's account, and started scrolling. His eyes widened when he saw his face all over her account.

"She's a friend."

"Who has a crush on you and implies in more than one post that you're her boyfriend and not mine," I stopped and pointed out her cutesy little hashtags that implied their relationship was more than friendly.

"I am." He nodded.

"Excuse me?"

"I am yours," he insisted in a strained voice. "We've been together for over a year. You're my best friend, Kendall. I..."

"Do you have any idea how this made me feel? Getting a text from your friend showing me that?" Especially on my birthday, at least I hadn't seen it at the club. I would have rather not seen it at all.

"I'm sorry." He leaned forward and tugged at his hair, making it stand up at the ends.

"If Chelsea is sending me this, she obviously sees a problem with what is going on," I told him, my voice cracking a little. This had blown a gigantic hole in my trust for him. Had I been missing the signs of this for months?

"I promise I've never kissed her," he whispered as he looked up at me with regret.

"Oh, great. That makes me feel better," I growled at him. "But you let her sit on your lap and kiss you and carry her around shirtless while she's wearing a bikini." My voice increased in volume as I worked myself up, and he looked like a chastised puppy. "But glad to know that you've never kissed her!"

"I can tell her we can't be friends anymore," he offered quietly, refusing to look back up at me.

"And what happens when she shows up around here, anyway?" She was friends with people in the house. Her own best friend was Dylan's former roommate's girlfriend. Lisa was always going to be around, and I couldn't do a damn thing about it.

He sat there quietly, not even trying to offer another lame excuse.

"The damage has already been done here," I sighed.

"What?" His head shot up, and he looked at me with his eyes wide.

"I don't know if I can trust you," I told him honestly. I couldn't. He may have claimed it wasn't cheating, but he didn't discourage her behavior.

"I didn't cheat on you," he insisted.

"Maybe not physically, yet. But I can see you have more than just friendly feelings for this girl. If you didn't—on some level—enjoy the attention, she never would have gotten that close to you for any of those pictures to exist. This isn't just some platonic friendship for her, and I..."

He sat there quietly, looking at my face and then closing his eyes.

"If I can't trust you, then maybe we shouldn't be thinking about marriage," I continued as my voice broke and tears filled my eyes.

His eyes snapped open, and he reached for my hand again. "Ken..."

"I don't know how I didn't see it before. This was always going to be a dead-end," I whispered as I looked over at him.

"What are you talking about?"

"You can't even defend me to your grandma," I told him, hating that he made me into this insecure version of myself.

"Not this again," he sighed, and I pulled away from him.

"No. Not this again," I insisted as I shook my head. "I'm done."

"You don't mean that," he said lowly, shaking his head at me and trying to get closer. I put my hand up and pushed him back.

"I'm pretty sure that I do," I nodded. "I don't like who I am with you. This isn't who I am. I'm not some desperate girl who begs a guy who doesn't respect her to pay attention to her."

"Ken, I love you," he pleaded, watching me sadly.

"No," I shook my head and took a deep breath. "I think if you really look at our relationship, I don't think you do. You love the idea of me. And for a while there, it was great..."

"It is great. What are you talking about? What we have works. I know I'm busy, but you..."

"Really?" I interrupted. "Because I saw the look of panic on your face when I walked in here. That isn't how you should respond to seeing someone you're supposedly in love with."

"You're just going to throw all this away because of a misunderstanding?" he whispered.

I shook my head and stood up, wiping my eyes and looking down at him. "You threw this away the second you allowed someone else into our relationship. This isn't on me. This is on you, Dylan. And I'm not letting my relationship with you dictate my life anymore."

"But..."

"No, Dylan. Please," I shook my head again as a tear leaked out. "I can't put myself last anymore. I need to live for myself and not in your shadow."

I'd wasted over a year of my life making compromises for someone who claimed to love me. It was time I'd started loving myself enough to know when enough was enough.

# *Chapter Sixteen:*
## *Junior Year*
### LATE OCTOBER

"**Y**ou sure you don't want to come to the house with me?" Alison asked as she leaned into my doorway. I knew she was still worried about me, but I was finally coming out of the funk I'd been in for the last month.

"No, I'm good. I'm trying to make friends. Most of the people at this party will be from the art department." I'd been spending time during the week on campus with one of the girls I had a few classes with, who I'd previously blown off because of Dylan. Now that I didn't have the blinders on, I'd gotten to know quite a few people who I saw on an almost daily basis.

"Not gonna lie, I'm disappointed," Allie pouted. "But I'm glad you're not hiding away anymore. It's good for you to get out and attempt to meet new people."

"Don't worry, Hermit Kendall is gone," I assured her. I hadn't realized how many people I'd alienated before.

"I know you said you're swearing off relationships, but it doesn't hurt to get some harmless practice." Alison gave me a knowing smile, and I shook my head at her.

"No. No random hookups. I'm over the drama."

"Has he tried to contact you again?" I shook my head and glanced at my phone. I knew she was asking about Dylan. It'd been hard for me to walk away, but I knew it'd just keep getting worse if I didn't make a clean break.

"No." I was done. I refused to respond, even if he did.

"Want to talk about it?" she offered with a sympathetic smile. I appreciated the offer, but...

"Fuck no."

She laughed as she typed in the code to unlock her phone. "She hasn't posted anything else since she took that post down."

"Don't care." And I didn't. He may not have physically cheated, but he knew that what he had allowed was not respecting our relationship with how guilty he'd acted.

"Maybe she was crazy," she mused as she looked over at me with a guilty smile.

"Besides the point. I thought you didn't like me with him, anyway."

"I don't," she confirmed. "But I also don't like you turning into a zombie for a month."

"I'm fine." I insisted. When I'd left the house that day, he'd quietly walked me to my car, and I hadn't spoken to him since. His silence spoke volumes to me, and I had finally started realizing that I'd made the right decision.

"Don't lie." Alison frowned as she looked over at me. She knew I was still sad about what happened quite a bit, but I was trying not to dwell on things I couldn't change.

"I'm over it," I shrugged.

"Really?" She pointed to the necklace that was still around my neck. I had shoved his promise ring into the bottom of my desk drawer. My fingers touched the stone for a moment before I reached back and unclasped the chain. I deposited it into Allie's palm and turned back into my room without another word.

"What am I supposed to do with this?" she called after me.

"Don't care."

"Are you allowed to list jewelry in the student classifieds?" she laughed, but I think she was serious.

"Guess you'll have to find out," I told her with an amused smile. Holding onto the things he'd given me would just be keeping the wound open. It'd probably be healthier for me to put them away and move on.

My costume was hanging on the hook over the door to my closet. I'd bought it before Dylan and I had broken up, but now I was wearing it for different reasons.

I didn't need a Bruce Banner. Black Widow could take care of herself.

Pulling on the skin-tight black faux leather suit, I fastened the belt and headed to the bathroom. Heavy eyeliner and mascara completed the look once I'd put loose curls in my long hair.

> **Joel: You coming to the house tonight?**

> **Kendall: Nope.**

Joel sent back a crying emoji.

> **Kendall: Sorry, not sorry.**

*Joel: Hot date?*

*Kendall: Fishing for information?*

He sent me a gif of Robert Downey Junior saying 'Maybe' and pulling a funny face.

*Kendall: Don't bring iron man into this.*

*Joel: I am Iron Man.*

He sent me a picture of himself in an iron man costume. That must be what he was wearing to their costume party tonight. He pulled it off well.

I slipped on my costume and sent him a photo back.

*Joel: Hot.*

My heart sped at his comment. We'd had flirty text conversations, but I was not getting into another emotional relationship any time soon. I'd jumped from Tyler to Dylan, and those had both crashed and burned.

*Kendall: Gotta go.*

*Joel: Please come to the house.*

He sent me a pic of him making a pouty face with the mask of his costume pulled up on top of his head. As much as I was tempted to give in and let things progress between us, my heart just wouldn't be in it. I'd rather have him as a friend than nothing. Dylan's absence had left a gaping hole. I missed his friendship more than anything. Making the same mistake twice was not on the agenda.

*Kendall: Have fun tonight.*

*Joel: Ouch.*

Grabbing the fake plastic gun for my costume, I strapped it into the holster on my hip and headed out.

"Have fun tonight!" Alison called out to me as I stepped into the hallway.

"You too! Don't get too wasted," I laughed. Poor Benji would end up taking care of her all night.

"Benji likes it when I'm a little tipsy," she laughed. Tipsy, yes, falling down drunk, no.

"I don't want to know about your freaky sex stuff," I laughed, and she started giggling.

"Don't knock it till you try it!" she laughed harder as I pulled out my IDs and tucked them into my zipper pocket.

The weather on campus had cooled down as I headed toward the house a few blocks away, where the party was held. Angie, the girl who'd invited me, was in several of my classes this semester. She lived with a few other fine arts majors in a duplex.

As I turned the corner, I could hear the bass of the music thumping. I hadn't gone out all that much other than the occasional frat party with Tyler or Dylan. I felt like the wild oats most people sowed as freshmen hadn't happened for me.

"Kendall! You made it!" Ange exclaimed as I walked through the doorway. I didn't have to worry about finding the one truly familiar face because she was already sitting on a couch by the front door.

"Yeah. Thanks for inviting me, Ange..."

She was wearing a pair of round brown ears on a headband and appeared to have a tail sticking out the back of her brown leotard and tights.

"Are you a monkey?"

"Yeah. I finally talked my boyfriend into a couple's costume, and this is what he picked," she rolled her eyes, but I thought she looked cute.

"Is he a banana or something?"

"Not quite." She nodded her head towards the other side of the room, and I saw a guy dressed head to toe in a yellow suit, tie, and tall hat.

"Aw, Curious George. That's adorable."

"At least I get to be a sexy monkey, if that's a thing," she laughed.

I looked back towards the 'boyfriend in the yellow hat,' and my eyes widened. He was deep in conversation with a guy I hadn't seen in a few months, but I easily recognized, nonetheless.

"Oh. That's one of the grad students who live on the other side of the duplex," she nodded as she looked over towards her boyfriend. "Crap. I forgot his name."

"Kale."

"Isn't that a lettuce?" she frowned as we both continued looking over at the two men.

"Cruciferous vegetable," I answered automatically, feeling a little dorky that I'd remembered that information. I guess Kale had made an impression on me.

"Wow, okay. You need to get yourself a drink," she laughed as she gave me a funny look. "You are way too sober if you're now a produce expert."

"It's only because he—you know what—never mind. A drink sounds good right now." I laughed nervously.

She led me into the kitchen, past Kale, who was still engrossed in conversation with the boyfriend in the yellow hat. I wasn't sure if I should say hi to him or wait for him to notice me.

Our last interaction had been a little strange. I wasn't quite sure how to read him. I had seen him in the art building a few times in passing, but he'd been busy, and I never knew how to handle awkward conversations with acquaintances. I knew him, but I didn't know him.

"You doing shots, beer, or a mixed drink?"

Being here relatively by myself, I was not doing shots. That was how I ended up in Joel's bed on my birthday. Even though it was innocent, I would not risk repeating that. I still don't remember how we even got back to the frat house.

"I guess just a rum and Coke, easy on the rum," I told her. She knew I didn't go out much.

"As long as you don't start talking about vegetables again because then you're doing shots with me," she told me seriously as she started pouring my drink into a plastic cup.

"How do you know talking about them won't happen more if I'm drunk?"

"Wow. Take this. You need to catch up." She poured me a shot glass of the rum and shoved it into my hand. It burned slightly on the way down, but I relaxed as I felt the pleasant sensation make its way through my body.

She was right. I just needed to relax.

"So, how do you know Kale?" she asked curiously as she nodded toward the doorway.

"He was my freshman orientation leader. And he also TAs a class on art therapy now," I told her as I sipped my drink.

"Have you taken it? Is it worth checking out?" she asked curiously. I knew many art majors were signing up for the class because it could satisfy their psychology requirement and still had something to do with our field.

"I've got it on my schedule for next semester. It's a completely new course load. I'm hoping the school adopts it as a major," I nodded. It was a growing field, and I was intrigued.

"Have you declared your Fine Arts specialty?"

"Sculpture," I shrugged, "but I still feel like I need something else. Not sure how to translate that to the real world."

"I feel you on that one. My parents were not thrilled with my Fine Arts concentration choice until I declared illustration. I think my dad didn't want me selling pieces out of a van at art fairs for the rest of my life," she laughed.

"I mean, it might be a total waste of time, but the subject intrigued me," I admitted. "I've read all kinds of studies on how the creation of art can impact the recovery of patients and reduce stress levels in children."

"Okay, enough about school. We're here to have fun. I need to float, but let me know if you need me," she told me as she squeezed my arm and stepped around me to head back into the party.

"Thanks, Ange."

She took off back toward the living room, and I was left to lean against the counter in the kitchen awkwardly. Without Alison, I'd forgotten how to socialize with strangers. Not that it had ever been a skill of mine.

People filtered in and out, talking and laughing. I was almost content to people-watch, always more comfortable on the outside.

"I never would have pegged you for the femme fatale type." A deep familiar voice pulled me from my thoughts, and I turned toward Kale with a smile.

"Excuse me?"

Kale nodded at my costume while he leaned against the door frame with a bottle of beer loosely dangling from his fingertips. "I don't know... maybe Pepper Potts, but I didn't think Black Widow would appeal to someone like you."

"And what kind of someone would that be?" I asked curiously. He had a picture of who I was figured out already.

"Smart, but thoughtful. Careful about her actions. Likes to be an observer," he shrugged as he pinned me down with an expectant look.

"Are you saying I'm not capable of kicking ass like Natasha?" I teased.

"Oh, I'm sure you could. I just don't think you would. You'd probably try to use your wit before your fists," Kale grinned and stepped a little closer.

"Are you psychoanalyzing me, Kent?" He was dressed as Clark Kent, wearing a pair of dark-rimmed glasses that made his eyes pop. Underneath his unbuttoned white shirt was a tight-fitting Superman costume. I had to admit that I had not imagined his chest looking as defined as it did underneath that costume.

"That's not usually one of my party tricks," he smiled, and it was a genuine smile for once. I hadn't seen very many of those out of Kale.

"And what is? Donning the ingenious disguise that is your glasses? Because no one would ever discover your real identity that way," I teased.

He smirked as he took a few steps toward me, placing his bottle down on the counter. With his glasses on, I'd never really appreciated how blue his eyes were. If he weren't slightly condescending, he'd be quite handsome.

"As a chronic observer of the human condition, I can honestly say that people often overlook what is right in front of them."

"Or their creator can perpetuate a lie by writing in a few well-placed props that most people will ultimately see through," I challenged.

"It's always easier to see things from the outside, isn't it?" he asked curiously. "It amazes me how the human mind can rationalize certain behaviors because a person is too close to the source."

Chills ran down my spine, and I shook my head slightly. That line of thought hit a little too close to home. I'd been blind to a lot of things over the last year. Kale was right. It was always easier to see the flaws as an observer.

"You okay?" he asked quietly as he watched me closely.

"Yeah... just... I think you might be right," I sighed.

"It's why they teach the psych majors to be impartial observers. Feelings make things too complicated. Assessing a situation is easier if you remove the bias."

"I thought you were all about passion and understanding emotions?" The smirk that crossed his face at my question was a little cocky, and I found myself captivated by his facial expressions.

"I said passion expressed emotions," he clarified. "Which is good for people like you. Artists manifest emotion in physical form."

"Sometimes art is just art," I shrugged. I'd created plenty of projects for classes that were technical demonstrations of skills, not filled with hidden emotion.

"You know you don't believe that." He smirked.

"I don't?" I asked defensively, crossing my arms over my chest and tilting my head.

"The creator may not be consciously doing it, but even the most mundane art expresses some sort of emotion. Through the color, form, medium..." He trailed off and stepped toward me, leaning his hand against the countertop next to my drink. "You never came to find me so we could have that conversation about color."

"Was that an actual offer?" I knew it had been, but I'd been so wrapped up in Dylan that I couldn't let myself be around anyone else.

"I asked you, didn't I?" He lifted an eyebrow. "But wait, that's right. You have a boyfriend. I forgot that conversations over coffee are automatically dates."

"Had."

"Hmm?" he asked as he leaned in fractionally closer to me. I could smell his aftershave, and it was doing things to me. The rum was more potent than I'd expected, or maybe it was the man.

"I had a boyfriend. Past tense," I corrected, and a slow smile spread across his lips.

"I'm sorry to hear that," he said genuinely.

"I'm not." I shook my head as I tried to push down the twinge of pain I got when I thought of how everything fell apart with Dylan.

"Not an amicable split?" he asked curiously, still analyzing me. He really couldn't help himself.

I shook my head once. "I guess at least it saved me a messy divorce down the road. Sometimes people aren't who you think they are."

"Or maybe they're exactly who they've always been, and you didn't see it," he speculated.

"Maybe. I might not be as good of a judge of character as I thought I was," I sighed.

"When people only show you the best parts of themselves, it's hard to know someone," he responded quietly.

"That's a bleak outlook," I frowned. Maybe I was fooled in my past by sweet declarations and thoughtful actions, but I hated to think that I never really knew who he was in the first place. I couldn't have been blind for years. That'd just be depressing.

"It might be, but it's a realistic one. You have to let your guard down and be vulnerable if you want to connect," he explained.

"Easier said than done."

"That's true," he agreed with a nod, "but if you want to have a meaningful relationship and share true passion, you have to let someone see the ugly and accept you, anyway."

"Is that what experience has taught you? Because all it's taught me is that I have questionable taste in men and friends," I told him bitterly.

"Maybe you're looking for the wrong things. Even pretty apples hanging on a tree can be rotten inside. Have you ever tried to get to know someone past the superficial?"

I shrugged and shook my head. "I thought I had."

"Put the hormones and physical attraction aside. They just cloud your judgment and create a false connection between people," he advised.

"How is that even possible?" I laughed as I took another sip of my drink. Kale's assessments made sense, but would that even progress past friendship if I weren't attracted to someone?

His fingers crept forward and flipped my hand over, gently tracing down my palm. "Physical attraction and the body's responses trigger hormone release, making you feel a connection with someone."

He stepped forward again and ran a fingertip along my jaw. "Physical touch can do the same thing, create intense feelings of euphoria."

My breath caught as he stepped closer, staring at my lips. My heart was pounding as I tried to maintain eye contact with him. "Kissing can do it on a larger scale."

I swallowed, and his smile grew as he tracked the movement.

"You want to know how to tell if a man is attracted to you?" he asked quietly, and I nodded without even knowing I was consciously doing it.

"H..." I cleared my throat. "How?"

"The vein along the side of his neck may pulse with increased blood flow. His eyes will dilate." I studied his pupils.

"He'll find excuses to touch you." The skin on my jaw he'd grazed still tingled, and his hand lingered on the countertop near mine.

"He'll look at your mouth, maybe bite his lip." His eyes slowly flicked down again, and I felt a blush rise in my cheeks.

"He'll lean in toward you. Sometimes under the guise of hearing you better, but it's really because it makes him look larger and more inviting." He smiled as he watched my reactions to him. He was studying me.

"The most important one is that he'll initiate a conversation with you."

I frowned as I watched him. "Why is that important?"

"Because if a man doesn't seek you out, he'll lose interest. Men who are truly attracted to a woman will be the pursuer." He quietly watched me process the information, biting his bottom lip as he studied me. My eyes tracked the movement, and he smiled.

"So, how do you separate all of that to get to know who someone is?" If the attraction part were so overwhelming, it'd be hard just to ignore altogether.

"You embrace the attraction and push past it. Have conversations about real things, talk about your families, try to let your guard down, and they'll follow suit," he explained. "You have to want to build a relationship."

"Hmm, well, then that's where my problem lies. I'm not looking for a relationship," I told him seriously. Relationships so far have only caused heartbreak and extra stress. I needed to start focusing on school and my future, not some man.

"That's too bad," he smiled sadly.

"Why do you even care?" I narrowed my eyes. Had this entire conversation just been some seduction routine for him?

"Because everyone deserves to find true intimacy."

"Isn't that the last thing most college guys are looking for?" I asked sarcastically.

"Maybe, but it's just because they don't understand that a quick fuck only leaves you satisfied in the short term." My mouth went dry at hearing him say the word fuck. It seemed almost scandalous coming out of his mouth.

"I don't think they care," I laughed, and he tilted his head.

"You'd be surprised how many people use their bodies to distract themselves from connection because they're frightened, not horny," he said plainly.

"Well. More power to them. I'm just fine being by myself for now."

He nodded and ran the tip of his finger over one of my knuckles. "You'll be ready someday..."

The question was... who would be there when I was ready?

# Chapter Seventeen:
## Junior Year
### JANUARY

"K endall!"

"What?" I shouted through the door as I ran my towel through my damp hair.

"Put on some clothes and get out here!" Alison yelled back. She pounded on the door, and I grabbed my robe, wrapping it around myself before I stepped into a pair of panties.

"What's wrong?"

She was pacing across my room with her phone in her hand.

"I need to get ready for class. You're freaking me out." The lock on her face was downright hostile, and I didn't know what was getting her so worked up.

"Sit down," I encouraged as I nodded at my futon.

"Ugh. I seriously want to murder this bitch," she growled as she gripped her phone tightly.

"What are you talking about?"

She thrust her phone in my hand before she leaned back on my futon, pulling a pillow into her lap. "Hit play on the story."

I pressed play, and a boomerang showed a feminine hand pushing a gray ring box across a glass counter.

> Lisa: *Out with the old...*

The next story started, and it showed a close-up of a necklace made up of Greek letters and then a picture of Lisa kissing Dylan's cheek.

> Lisa: *In with the new...*

I handed her the phone and turned, walking to my dresser.

"That's it? Nothing to say?" she asked loudly, obviously expecting a reaction out of me.

What was I supposed to say?

"No."

"Are you kidding me? It's only been three months," she shouted, and I shook my head, wishing that I could just forget all about Dylan and Lisa with an A.

"It's none of my business."

Her mouth dropped open as she looked over at me. "How can you not be upset right now?"

"Oh, I'm upset, but we broke up. He can have that crazy bitch if he wants her," I shrugged. I was more disappointed that I'd been right about his cheating in the first place. If he was buying her a lavalier three months after I broke up with him, then it was serious.

"I know I haven't been the most supportive friend with him, but I know he meant a lot to you," she said sadly. Meant, in the past tense, was the keyword. He had meant a lot to me, but now he didn't anymore. He'd ensured that.

"You were just trying to protect me. I obviously couldn't see the warning signs in my relationship." I pulled on my jeans and stepped into my boots, leaning down to zip up the sides. "Please, just let it go."

"But..."

I shook my head as I stood back up. "I can't keep picking the scab on this."

"Alright." She nodded as she put her phone in her lap.

"I need to go to class." I finished getting ready on autopilot and took off for my walk across campus. I couldn't dwell on this, or I'd fall back into the depression I'd been in after my birthday.

The lecture hall was only about half full as I sat about ten rows back in the middle. I pulled out my laptop and started checking my email. I felt the seat next to mine shift as a body occupied it, and I continued to focus on deleting my junk mail as they got their supplies out for class.

This was one of the non-arts classes I was looking forward to. Behavioral Psychology and Human Interaction. Kale's involvement in the new Art Therapy courses had sparked an interest. I was also slated to have him as the TA for my class later in the week.

A pencil tapped on the lid of the closed laptop beside me, and I glanced over, doing a double-take.

"Took you long enough." Rory Chandler was sitting in the seat next to me, leaning his cheek on his propped-up hand, an amused smile on his face.

"Oh, I'm sorry," I smirked as I looked over at his face. It'd only been a few months since I'd seen him last, but he looked different. "Was I supposed to drop everything and fangirl over your presence?"

"Well, that would be nice, but a simple hello would suffice," he laughed as he smiled at me.

"Hello, Rory."

He sat back in his seat, swiveling it as he clasped his palms on the back of his head. "Hello, Kendall. I thought you were an art major."

"I am," I nodded.

"And you just happen to be a fan of modern psychology?" He mused, with a cocky smirk on his face. I honestly admired his confidence. He never seemed to feel or look out of place anywhere.

"Would that be a problem?" I raised an eyebrow at him, and his grin widened.

"No, but personally, I'd be taking the Psychology of Attraction course if I was filling an elective." I tried to hold in the laughter at his comment. A campus legend taught that class. She was a very liberated woman who ran a sexual chemistry lab in the 1970s.

"It's not an elective. I'm contemplating a double major."

He looked at me expectantly. "In?"

"Fine arts and art therapy."

He pursed his lips and sat upright. "I didn't realize they had a major available in that."

"So, you're an expert on the course catalog now?" I teased. It just came naturally to act like me with him. He appreciated that I was sarcastic and didn't sugarcoat things.

"No, but my brother did his undergrad in psychology." He shrugged. Interesting. His brother was not only a nudist but also a psychologist, which seemed fitting.

"It's new."

"Actually..." I trailed off as another familiar face picked up Rory's bag and tossed it on the floor behind his chair.

"Well, look at that. I'm late for class, and I've been replaced," Joel laughed as he smiled over at me. It'd been a little while since I saw him in person as well. He looked good. His hair was a little shorter and styled in a way that made the mess look orderly. Both looked like they'd been working out often. Circumstances had pushed my running to the back burner over the last year.

"Now, don't go underestimating your value," Rory teased as he looked over his shoulder at his friend. "Sidekicks are just as important as the main character."

"Wow. Really?" I laughed, and Rory shrugged his shoulders.

"Are you sure you're the superhero? I'm thinking more about the narcissistic well-meaning character who is jaded by tragedy and becomes the antihero," I smirked as I watched his eyes flare with something akin to irritation and appreciation. "After all, I've got it on good authority that Joel is Iron Man."

"Seriously, not you too?" Rory groaned as he made a face at me.

"What?"

Joel was trying to hold in repressed laughter as he smiled at me. "He's still jealous I won the house costume contest."

"I'm not jealous," Rory pouted as he crossed his arms. He did look rather jealous.

"He dressed up as the green lantern and expected people to know who he was," Joel laughed.

"Dude," I shook my head as I looked over at Rory. "You gotta go Marvel if you're in it to win it. People only know who the main Justice League characters are. They can't be throwing in characters who have only had minimal screen time because some wannabe A-list actor needed to be a superhero."

"Hey, he got a wife out of the deal," Rory argued, and I rolled my eyes.

"Yeah, still not seeing the appeal," I countered with a laugh. "Why throw away the Black Widow for a downgrade?"

Rory was staring at me with his mouth hanging open.

"What?" I didn't think I had something on my face.

Joel smirked as he nudged his friend. "I told you."

"What? What does that mean?" Had they been talking about me?

"Who are you?" Rory's voice sounded weird. I'd never seen him look shocked at anything.

"What does that mean?" I laughed nervously. They were acting strangely, and I didn't know how to read the looks they were giving each other.

"Okay, don't take this the wrong way, but that shithead ex of yours better not expect to get you back because we're keeping you," Rory laughed as he bumped his arm against mine.

"Dude, you're scaring her," Joel rolled his eyes as he settled into his seat and smiled at me around Rory.

The professor interrupted our little game of back and forth with starting class, both guys quieting down and dropping the subject.

"What were you going to say before Joel showed up?" Rory whispered after a few minutes.

I stopped typing and averted my eyes. "What?"

He leaned in further, and his breath hit softly on my cheek with his whisper. "You said 'actually.' Actually, what?"

Before we got sidetracked with comic book characters, I scanned back and remembered we were talking about my major.

"Kale is one of my TAs."

His eyes widened at my low whisper. "No shit?"

I nodded and smiled at him. "Yup. Should be interesting."

His low laugh set goosebumps off across my skin. "Are we talking about the same Kale here?"

"Be nice," I hissed as I tried to pay attention to the professor, explaining how he set up the grading system for the course.

"I'm just saying. He's a little stale," he shrugged as he swiveled in his chair.

"He's a nice guy," I whispered as I continued to listen to the professor.

"Oh, I get it," he mused as he sat back a little and flashed me an amused smile. "What?"

"You like him," he told me, the smirk firmly in place again. Kale was handsome, and something about him intrigued me, but did I like him? He was going to be my TA. Wasn't that violating some rule?

"No."

"No?" he asked as he tried to keep in his amused laughter.

"No." I shook my head again.

"You're going to break Joel's heart," he whispered as he leaned in toward me again.

"I'm trying to concentrate here," I told him as I leaned away from him.

"My boy over there likes you," he said lowly, nodding back to Joel. He was writing something in his notebook, only occasionally glancing over at Rory and giving me a questioning look.

"Pay attention."

He laughed again and leaned in. I could feel his warm breath on my neck. "Syllabus... blah, blah, blah... mandatory attendance... blah, blah, blah."

"Quit." I pushed against his shoulder, and he laughed as he sat upright.

"Quit what? Distracting you from being bored to death? The first week is always administrative bullshit," he mumbled, but obviously, others heard him as a girl in the row ahead of us turned around and glared.

"See. You're distracting other people, too." I nodded.

"I'm a very distracting person," he said with a cocky air. I'd give him that. Between the snark and that damn jawline, he had the power to stop people in their tracks.

"Go distract someone else," I hissed, and the smile that lit up his face made me roll my eyes.

"But your reactions are so much fun," he teased.

"Shhh." I kicked the back of his shoe, and he looked over at me in surprise.

"Geez. The abuse."

My eyes rolled as I turned myself away from him and stopped responding. I could already tell by his body language that I amused him. I wasn't giving him any more attention. Maybe if I ignored him, he'd leave me alone. Next class, I'd insist on sitting next to Joel. He didn't behave like an overgrown child.

"It's okay, I won't tell." I side-eyed him, and he winked. "I won't tell anyone that you're hot for your teacher."

"Who's got a hot teacher? Definitely can't be this guy." Joel made a cringing face when he looked toward our professor at the front of the lecture hall. He was an average-looking man... average height, average weight, average looks.

"The elbow patches on his tweed sport coat complete that sexy look," Rory nodded and tried to keep a straight face.

I bit my lip to hold in the laughter that wanted to break free.

"Oh, we better be quiet, Joel," Rory told his friend as he turned in his direction. "We're distracting Kendall from this riveting explanation of how to turn in assignments digitally. We wouldn't want to interrupt her learning any of the information that he's reading directly out of the syllabus he emailed out."

"You're a dick," I said under my breath, but I knew he heard me.

"Why, thank you. I prefer the title asshole." Rory laughed.

"He's perfected his craft over many years of practice," Joel nodded. I made eye contact with him and shook my head.

"Don't encourage him."

"He'll act this way regardless of what either of us does," Joel shrugged.

"Sad, but true," Rory nodded with an unaffected smile.

"You be quiet." They both smiled at me and quieted down while the professor talked about our first assignments, including a small group project.

"Dibs," Joel whispered as he leaned back and tossed a piece of paper at me behind Rory's back.

"It's groups of three or four. Who do you want to work with?" I whispered back.

"We could find another girl if it'd make you more comfortable," he offered.

"She doesn't need to find another girl, dude. She's got you," Rory laughed, and Joel rolled his eyes.

"Yeah, cause I'm the girly one. Mister 'I use multiple hair products.'"

"I like to take care of myself," Rory defended, and I tried not to laugh.

Joel leaned around Rory and put his hand up next to his mouth. "I saw a pastel pink hairdryer in his drawer."

"Dude. That's Bridgette's."

Joel leaned back again. "He uses it every morning."

I couldn't hold in my laughter as I watched the pale skin on Rory's cheekbones turn pink.

"Aw. It's okay if your favorite color is pink," I teased as I put my hand on Rory's forearm. He looked down at it and back at me with a startled look on his face. I pulled it back and awkwardly put it in my lap.

"He owns a hot pink polo shirt," Joel confirmed.

"Dude. Have you been borrowing my clothes again?" Rory accused.

"Uh, no. Your shirts would be a tent on me," Joel shook his head.

"Are you calling me fat?" Rory's mouth dropped open, and I may have snorted a little.

"Well, they do call it the *big* and tall," Joel laughed.

"You're just mad because I'm big all over." He raised his eyebrows at Joel, and I watched as Joel's entire face deflated.

"Dude." Joel hissed, his eyes shifting over to me nervously.

"Sorry. That was too far," Rory apologized.

"What?" I asked as I looked between the two of them. The casual joking had gotten serious, and I didn't know what they were talking about.

"Nothing. Don't worry about it. Rory is just being a jerk again," Joel sighed.

"Okay then…" I nodded and tried to focus back on my laptop. Taking notes was a lost cause at this point.

"Is it easier just to meet at the house?" Joel asked quietly, turning the subject back to our project. Normally I'd be fine with that, but I was not going over there if Tyler was back. Some people were better left in the past.

"Or we can come over to your place," Rory offered. I must have paused a beat too long.

"I don't mind the house. It's just that..." I trailed off. It'd been two years, but I still didn't want to run into Tyler.

"Ah. Big T is out. Since he stayed on his study abroad, his seniority was dropped for room selection, and by the time we knew he was coming back, we were full. He lives off campus," Rory explained, somehow knowing that was my hesitation.

I nodded and then started packing up my bag. Our professor was long gone, and I needed to get some lunch.

"Alright, well, just text me the plan. I gotta get to my next class." Rory pulled his bag over one shoulder and saluted Joel and me before bounding down the steps to the door at the front of the lecture hall.

"So..." I wasn't sure how to be alone with Joel anymore. We'd talked pretty frequently for the last few months, but we were still in a weird place when we were by ourselves. While my heart had healed, I didn't know how to move forward. I wasn't sure I had it in me to carry a full course load and put in the effort to date.

"When's your next class?" He asked softly as he scooted over into Rory's abandoned seat.

I glanced at my watch. "Two and a half hours."

"Would you..." he trailed off as he cleared his throat. He seemed nervous. Maybe Rory was right, and he did really like me.

"Hmm?"

"Would you wanna go get some lunch with me?" he asked quietly as he looked down at the desk. "I mean, if you're hungry. You don't have to, but I..."

"Yeah. That'd be nice," I agreed, smiling as he stopped rambling.

He exhaled and nodded, wiping one of his hands on his pant leg. "The Union, or do you want to walk somewhere off campus?"

"Union is fine," I agreed. We both grabbed our bags, and he followed close behind as I headed toward the door at the back of the room. He reached forward and opened it, holding it open for me.

Point for manners.

"What's up next on your agenda?" he asked as we started walking side by side.

"Statistics," I made a disgusted face. I was not looking forward to more math.

"Why the hell would an art major be taking stat?" I frequently asked myself the same question. But It'd been the only math course that fit into my schedule.

"Required core. It was either stat or calculus."

"That's rough. Do you have ANY fun classes this semester?" he asked curiously.

"Advanced ceramics," I shrugged. I'd gotten in a lot of practice last summer at the community center and was eager to get throwing on the wheel again.

"That's fun?"

"Why? What's your idea of a fun class?" I asked, while he smiled over at me.

"Well, my stat class was last semester." He bumped his shoulder against mine and smirked at me as we walked down the sidewalk and across the quad toward the student union.

"Yeah, it's so riveting," I rolled my eyes.

"I'm taking golf," he admitted, and I looked over at him.

"Like, as an actual class?"

"Yeah, it was either that or the flower arranging," he chuckled.

"*That's* an actual class?" I didn't know these were even in the course catalog.

"Yeah, in the Ag department," he nodded. "It's apparently a good place to pick up chicks."

"On the prowl, are you?" I tried to hold in my laughter, but it slipped out. It seemed a little too much to take a class purely to meet women.

"Not exactly." The shy smile he aimed in my direction made him even more endearing.

"Why not?" I hadn't seen him with anyone for a while. That didn't mean he hadn't been dating, but not anyone Alison knew about.

"I'm just not into the whole serious relationship business," he sighed.

"No?" I asked curiously. I wondered what had turned him off to the prospect of a relationship.

"Can't deny that I enjoy going out on the weekends," he shrugged. He seemed to enjoy the bar scene. "I tried to date someone last year, but I swear she would've put an ankle bracelet on me to track my movements."

"Clingy?"

"She hated it when I talked to anyone but her if we went out to parties. Didn't want me to go to the parties at the house if she couldn't be there." Yeah, that sounded a little desperate.

"Sounds like you were just dating the wrong person."

"Oh, I know she was the wrong person," he laughed with a nod.

"Let me guess. She was hot?" I rolled my eyes. I hated when guys got into these superficial relationships. Kale was right. Most people stayed with the physical because they didn't want to look past it.

"Well, she wasn't unattractive," he laughed as he opened the door for me. We descended the steps into the lower level, and he placed his hand on my back as we navigated through the light lunch crowd. "I think I'm just waiting for the right person to come along."

"Ah, waiting for the perfect match to drop into your lap?" I mused. If only it was that easy. It'd be nice if life were a little less unpredictable.

"No, but if she does, I won't argue," he laughed. "What about you?"

We grabbed trays and made our way through the food lines. Joel stepped around me and swiped his student ID when I put my tray down and laid my salad down on the scale. "I got this."

"Wait. You don't have to..." I argued as I tried to give the cashier my card.

"I figure I owe you one," he smiled as he pulled my hand back. The warm contact of his hand on mine was nice.

"No, you don't but thank you."

"It's the least I could do since Rory stole your Rice Krispie treat back in the day," he smiled. "That bastard is always stealing something from someone."

"He's not that bad. Isn't he your best friend?" I asked curiously.

"Yeah. That's why I can get away with calling him a bastard."

We quietly talked while we ate, him filling me in on what he knew about the mutual friends we'd had freshman year. I was woefully still out of the loop. It was hard to remake friends when people had cemented their friend groups a long time ago. I felt like I was constantly playing catch-up for the mistakes I'd made. The time I'd wasted.

"So, what about you?"

"What about me?" I frowned as I tried to gauge what he was asking.

"You on the prowl?" he teased.

A surprised laugh burst out of me, and I made a clawing motion with my hand. "Rawr."

"You're such a dork," he laughed as he shook his head.

I nodded and took another bite of my salad. "Yeah, pretty much."

"So, yes?" he asked, his face openly curious.

"No. I don't know," I shrugged. "Maybe being open to new possibilities wouldn't be all that bad, but I'm not looking for a husband."

He held up his sports drink bottle, and I clinked it with my bottle of tea. "To new possibilities."

# Chapter Eighteen:
## Junior Year
### FEBRUARY

T he fraternity house was quiet as I snuck up the back staircase of the old Victorian mansion. Joel was still in class, but I needed somewhere quiet to work. I knew he wouldn't mind if I snuck into the study room to get my paper done.

"God. Fuck. Turn it off already," A loud exclamation made me startle and hit my head on the door frame after I clicked on the light switch.

"Off, now!" The gruff voice called out, and I turned it off, plunging the small room into darkness.

"Sorry. I didn't realize anyone was in here," I apologized, squinting into the darkness as I could barely make out the tall form lying at the edge of the double bed pushed up against the wall.

"Well, now you know. Get the fuck out. Joel isn't here," Rory growled, much more hostile than I was used to him being. He'd been an ass in the past, but I thought we were on better terms now.

"Are you okay? God, it stinks in here. Did you murder something in here?" I asked as I got a whiff of something particularly pungent.

"Go away."

I could barely make out his form curled up; blankets now pulled back up over his head.

"Are you sure? If you're sick... I can..."

"GO AWAY!" He bellowed, and my eyes widened.

"Fine. Geez. Sorry for trying to be a good friend." I closed the door softly behind myself and stood there for a moment.

> Kendall: I think your roommate is dying. SOS.

*Joel: He still hasn't showered?*

So obviously, Joel knew something was going on.

*Kendall: It smells like a dead raccoon.*

*Joel: Poor bastard.*

*Joel: Why are you at the house so early?*

*Kendall: Typing a paper and needed quiet. The house was closer than the library.*

*Joel: Benji at yours?*

*Kendall: Yup*

*Joel: I'd steer clear of Rory. He's in mourning.*

*Kendall: What?*

*Joel: She cut him loose.*

*Kendall: His mother finally cut the cord?*

*Joel: lol*

*Joel: Bridge dumped him.*

*Kendall: Oh shit.*

*Joel: For her women's studies TA.*

*Joel: Who's a chick.*

*Joel: As you can see... he's not taking it well. I can deal with him when I get home. Just go to the library.*

I thought about it for a second and decided that while he didn't want me here, he also needed to stop smelling like a petting zoo.

"Get up, jackass," I told him firmly as I reopened the door, bracing myself for the smell.

"I thought I told you to go away," he groaned.

"Get up. You need to shower." My finger flipped the light switch up, and he groaned loudly, throwing his arm over his face.

"I'm fine."

"You're not fine," I insisted as I pulled at the corner of his blanket. "Get up."

"I left you alone after Ty. Why won't you go away?" he whined.

"Because I care about you." Sometimes I wasn't sure why, but he was my friend, and he was in pain.

"Why? She didn't." My heart broke a little at his confession. I knew exactly what it felt like when someone you invested years in threw it all away.

Tyler abused my trust. Dylan carried on a secret relationship with a girl behind my back and then lied about it. Mutual friends had told me that his parents had met her before we were even broken up. Who does that?

"Well, then she's an idiot." She was. I never understood cheaters; end the relationship before starting with someone else.

"No. Apparently, me being busy with school gave her permission to screw around. I just didn't expect this," he sighed.

"Yeah. I can't say that I saw a change in sexual identity coming out overnight, either. I'm sorry. But you know what, you're both probably better off." If she couldn't be faithful now and was questioning who she was, it was better Rory knew sooner rather than later.

"Or she is. God. This is fucked. At least if it were with some guy, I'd just go kick his ass."

"That's probably not the answer, either," I told him quietly, shaking my head.

"But it'd make me feel better," he shrugged, pushing himself up to a seated position.

"I'm sure it would, but if that were the case... I'd go slap the shit out of that bitch, Lisa."

"Fucking assholes," Rory growled as he ran his long fingers through his greasy mess of hair.

"Yeah. People can be that sometimes." I agreed. Mostly when you least expected it.

"How do I even move on from this? I was thinking about asking her to move off campus with me next year."

I sat down heavily on the other side of the bed, and he turned in my direction. His hair was a chaotic mess, sticking up all over the place, darkened by the fact he probably hadn't showered in a few days. He swiped a few tears from his cheek and leaned forward, burying his face in his hands.

He took in a shuddering breath as I tentatively laid a hand on his shoulder. "It's better you found out now."

"My parents loved her," he mumbled.

"But they probably love you more." The collateral damage when people broke up sucked. I'd been close with Dylan's parents for years, but I had no plans to speak to them or their son ever again. I was sure grandma Constance was jumping for joy. She and Lisa would probably love each other.

"Yeah, pretty sure my siblings would disagree," he laughed.

"Siblings are supposed to have a love-hate relationship with you growing up. It'll change," I assured. My relationship with my sister had shifted already since I'd been in college.

"What did your family do about dickhead Dylan and Temu Kendall?" I held in a laugh at his description of Lisa.

"My sister never liked him, and my parents told all their friends he cheated on me. Makes for really fun awkward conversations when I go home for breaks." Dylan's parents weren't talking to mine anymore because they were embarrassed that the whole town knew their son was a cheater.

"Maybe I should just be celibate," he groaned.

"I did seriously consider a nunnery," I agreed. Relationships were so stressful. I was afraid to sign up for that again.

He chuckled and turned towards me, tugging on my hair. "I can't imagine you in a habit."

"No?"

He shook his head. His eyes were tired and red-rimmed. It twisted my heart to see him going through this. It sucked. "No. You curse too much."

"Yeah, because I'm the one with the fucking cursing problem."

"Bitch, I don't know what you're fucking talking about," he almost laughed.

We sat quietly for a few moments until I took a large breath and got a whiff of how foul he was.

"Okay, you gotta do something about that smell. People are going to think there's a dead body in here." I wrinkled up my nose as I looked over at him in disgust.

"Don't be nice to the heartbroken guy or anything," he said sarcastically.

"Really? Going to try to guilt-trip me into being nice to you?"

A small smile appeared on his lips as his tired blue eyes looked over at me. "Is it working?"

"No. Get out of here," I shook my head and pointed to the door. "And burn those sweats."

*Gross.*

He crossed the room to the closet and pulled out some clothes, throwing his towel over his shoulder. As soon as he was out of the room, I was picking up random food wrappers, empty sports drink bottles, and takeout containers and shoving them into the trash can. Normally, they kept this room neat, but it needed a cleaning. Next, the sheets were tucked into a pillowcase and thrown by the door for washing.

"Are you cleaning our room?" Joel was leaning against the doorframe with his arms crossed against his chest.

"Someone needed to," I shrugged.

"The cleaning lady took one look at him in here yesterday and walked back out. She won't clean unless the room is picked up."

"You could've helped your friend, ya know." He laughed, and I held up my hand. "And I don't mean by getting him drunk."

"He didn't need anyone to help him do that," Joel assured. I could only imagine the amount of alcohol Rory had ingested to forget his girlfriend left him for another woman.

"Does she still have stuff here?" I asked quietly as I looked over at the dresser and desk I knew belonged to Rory.

"You gonna help him purge Bridge from our room?" Joel asked with an amused smile.

"If that helps." I nodded. It felt good to get my reminders of Dylan out of my room after our breakup.

He stepped into the room and reached for me, gripping my hip and pulling me towards him. "You're a much better friend than either of us deserves."

"I don't think you give yourself enough credit. You were there when things blew up with Dylan."

He cupped the back of my neck with his hand and leaned forward, gently kissing my temple. His lips lingered over my cheekbone and my heart stuttered, thumping heavily in my chest. Joel had never come quite this close to kissing me.

"Ken, I..." He hesitated, and I turned my head just slightly, my lips grazing his.

Suddenly, I was crushed against his muscular chest, his fingers gripping the side of my face as he tilted my head and pressed his lips fully against mine. My fingers clutched the sides of his shirt as he passionately caressed my lips with his, over and over.

The sound of a thump against the door startled us apart, and I stepped back as Joel sat down in the desk chair and pulled a soccer ball into his lap.

"Real inconspicuous," I hissed while I tried to keep the laughter at bay.

His cheeks turned pink as he looked up at me, the goofy smile on his face matching mine.

Rory pushed the door open, thankfully fully clothed in non-rancid jeans and a T-shirt. The towel partially obscured his face as he vigorously ran it over his hair. He still looked like shit, but at least he was clean. Baby steps.

"Happy now?" he asked as he gestured at his clean attire.

"Well, at least the rest of us can come back in here now," Joel nodded.

"You can thank your girlfriend for that one." Rory nodded at me.

"I don't have..." Joel started nervously as he looked at me out of the corner of his eye.

"God, you two are ridiculous. Joel, just ask her out already. I really can't listen to any more unrequited love moaning from you."

Joel's eyes widened as he looked up at me.

"I'll wait out in the hallway for you," I told him nervously.

My fingers grazed Joel's shoulder before I walked out, frowning at Rory as he stood there watching me with a blank look on his face.

"I'm sorry about him. Being dumped has reverted him to asshole Rory," Joel apologized as he joined me and closed the door behind him.

"It's fine. He doesn't faze me. I'm sure I was a real treat to live with for most of October."

"He was just joking about the love thing." Joel aimed his eyes at the carpet as he scratched the nape of his neck.

"It's fine. That kiss kinda clued me in that you might like me." My fingers lightly grazed his, and he looked up at me, a wary look in his eyes. "I kinda like you, too."

I did. But I was still scared. Dylan's behavior had shaken my foundation. I didn't know if I could fully let anyone in. I wasn't sure if I was ready.

"Do you have any plans for Friday?"

My heart thumped in my chest as I looked at his hopeful expression. "You mean Valentine's Day?"

He gulped, and I shook my head lightly.

"Can I take you out?"

"Not sure if you'll be able to find a reservation somewhere on this short notice, but what were you thinking?" I asked quietly.

"They're showing a movie at the student union. I might already have a few tickets," he admitted shyly.

"That sure of my answer?" I teased.

"No, but I hoped you'd go with me," he told me quietly, taking my hand more firmly in his and stroking my fingers.

"Depends on the movie."

He smiled and turned his hand, enclosing mine inside his larger one. "I've been assured it's an old classic. It came out before we were born. My mom and my sister told me you'd love it."

"You talk to your sister about me?" I asked quietly. I knew he might have feelings for me for a while now, but he talked about me to people who didn't even know me.

"She's very nosy."

"That's kind of adorable," I admitted. "So, when exactly were you planning on inviting me? Four days is cutting it close. What if I had plans?"

"I've been trying to get you alone for weeks," he whispered as he looked down at my mouth again. We'd been together a lot for our project, but Rory was always there.

"You know you have my phone number. You could have texted me."

"I wanted to ask you in person, I might not be the suavest guy, but I wanted to see your face," he smiled softly. "Make sure it wasn't a pity date or something."

"The only person I might pity right now is through that door," I nodded, thinking of his sullen friend.

"Yeah. This has fucked him up bad. They were together for almost three years."

"Anyway..." he changed the subject quickly. "I'll pick you up at six. Dress warmly. I want to take you somewhere after."

The snow gathered softly on my windowsill. It'd been snowing all day. Luckily, it hadn't been bad when I was out for my early ceramics lab.

My phone chimed from the desk before my watch started vibrating.

"What the…" The number flashing across the screen was not one that I was expecting, especially not today.

My heart was pounding, and I felt my palms clam up as I reached to grab it, pressing the green button to connect the call.

"Kendall?"

Holy shit. What did he want?

"Are you there?"

"Hello?"

I paused for a second, closing my eyes. As much as I loathed to admit it, I missed him. Dylan's voice sounded exactly like I remembered, and my heart ached as I held the phone to my ear.

"Hey."

"Hi." He paused for a second and then started talking again, his voice quieter. "How've you been?"

I don't think he wanted the answer to that question.

"Fine," I told him quietly.

"Did I call at a bad time?"

Glancing down at my watch, I noticed I only had a half-hour until Joel would pick me up.

"No." I had enough time for whatever this was. "What do you want, Dylan?"

Bitterness had crept into my voice, and I knew he could hear it, too.

"I wanted to talk to you about something. I felt like I needed to be the one to do it."

"Then talk." I encouraged him when he was quiet for a beat too long.

"I…" His breath sounded shallow over the phone, and it only fueled my annoyance. I hadn't talked to him in months. He hadn't apologized for anything that had happened. He didn't even acknowledge that what he'd done was wrong. The longer he paused. The angrier I got. He'd pursued me. He'd thrown our friendship away and betrayed my trust.

"If you're just going to sit there and breathe into the phone like a stalker, then I need to go. I have plans tonight."

"I proposed."

Whoa.

"Are you there?" His voice sounded unsure and a little worried.

"Is that all?" How dare he call on Valentine's Day and drop this in my lap?

"Kendall..."

"I need to go." I could already feel tears pooling at the corner of my eyes. I wasn't still in love with Dylan, not by a long shot. But this cut deep. I'd been with him for over a year, and he bought a ring for me.

"Kendall, wait. I..."

I pressed the red button to end the call. Staring down at my phone as the first tear slipped down my cheek. He'd been with her for five or six months, and he'd asked her to marry him. He said he didn't cheat on me, but I wasn't sure what the truth was anymore. Of course, the selfish bastard had to call me on Valentine's Day to tell me.

The phone in my hand pinged with a text message.

> *Joel: On my way over.*

> *Joel: Don't forget your gloves.*

The heels of my hands rubbed at my eyes as I tried to get myself back together. Joel didn't deserve to have our date ruined because of my douchebag ex-boyfriend.

"Hey, I'm headed out," Alison told me from the door of my bedroom.

"Joel's on his way over, too," I nodded as I tried to get myself back together.

"You okay?" she asked quietly. I was sure I looked a little stunned. I was a bit shocked.

"I will be." I nodded.

"What's wrong?" she asked as she took a step forward. "Have you been crying?"

"I'll be fine. Just got some upsetting news." I shrugged as I tried to push down the swell of emotions that the phone call had brought up in me.

"Do you need me to cancel on Benji?"

"No. You guys have fun," I smiled as I looked up at her. "I'm not letting this ruin my night. You shouldn't either."

She looked at me skeptically but nodded. "Just text me if you need me."

"I won't. I'm good. I promise."

She nodded before pulling my door closed.

Knowing I didn't have much time, I rushed to the bathroom and touched up my eye makeup. I needed to clear up any signs of crying.

"Fucking asshole."

The more I thought about it, the more irritated I got. Calling me today, of all days, was completely self-serving on his part. How had I never noticed how selfish he was?

As my phone buzzed with the front door intercom alert, I answered and pressed the code to unlock the outside door. A soft knock sounded as I pulled on my coat, and I took a deep breath. I blew it out slowly before I opened the door.

"Where's your coat?"

"Hello to you, too," Joel smiled as he stood in the doorway. "Left it in the car."

"Here..." I murmured as I reached up and smoothed away a few snowflakes from the hair hanging over his forehead.

His hand cupped my side, and I felt myself blush as he leaned in and kissed my cheek.

"You look cute." His other hand tugged on the puff at the top of my winter hat.

"You told me to dress warmly." I could feel the blush rising in my cheeks as he looked down at me fondly.

"I did. I'm glad you listened. Let's get going. It's open seating, so unless you'd like to crane your neck back the entire time, we should go get seats." He grabbed my hand and held it loosely as I grabbed my purse and followed him out the door, locking it behind me.

"No hints about the movie?"

He laughed as we descended the staircase. "You'll find out in like ten minutes. I'm sure you'll survive the suspense."

"Fine," I faux huffed. Joel's eyes met mine, and he winked before we cut down the hallway to the back door. He was double-parked behind my car, the engine still running.

"Risky, someone could have stolen your ride," I teased.

He reached into his pocket and pulled out a key fob, the doors clicking as he hit the unlock button. "Kind of hard without the keys."

He tucked me into the passenger seat and then got into the driver's side. He rubbed his hands together and blew on them before grasping the wheel and putting it in drive.

"You told me to wear gloves. Where are yours?" I scolded.

"In my coat pockets," he smiled widely, obviously amused at my concern for him.

"Men are weird."

"You've just now figured that out?" The humor in his voice was clear.

"Well, no. But I don't understand why half of you never wear coats."

He shrugged and glanced over at me as he pulled out onto the street. "Because we're lazy."

I couldn't argue with that logic.

He parked in the visitor parking across the street from the Union, quickly pulling his coat over the seat before opening his door. I watched as he pulled it on, smiling at me through the window before he made his way to my side.

We'd spent quite a bit of time together in the Union as of late, either working on our group project upstairs in one of the study rooms or the basement eating in the food court.

"I don't think I've ever been to the movie theater here," I told him as we walked down the stone steps.

"The house has rented it out a few times for brotherhood nights. The bowling alley, too."

"Oh God, please say we're not going there," I cringed.

"Maybe another time. Why?" he smiled, looking over at me curiously.

"I'm a terrible bowler," I admitted. Terrible might not even accurately describe how truly bad I was.

"Seriously? You can throw bean bags like a champ, but you can't bowl?"

I shrugged as I followed him down the steps to the lower-level entrance of the old movie theater. "Don't ask me to explain why, but I've never been a good ball handler. The holes are always too small."

He burst into surprised laughter, and I blushed in response when I ran my words back through my mind. "Pervert."

"You're the one who said it," he laughed as he held his hands up. He was right. Sometimes I just said the most unintentionally stupid things.

"Yeah, well, excuse me for not knowing what to do with heavy balls."

He laughed again and pulled me to his side as he handed the two paper tickets to the student posted at the door. The theater was about half full, but he led us toward an empty row near the back.

"Trying to get some privacy?" I teased.

"I just don't enjoy sitting in the middle." He pointed up at the speakers that ran down the center of the ceiling on a metal bar. "It gets too loud with those over your head."

He helped me pull off my coat and put it in the empty seat next to him before shrugging out of his own. He grabbed something out of the pocket and dropped it into my lap before he sat down.

"How did you know I liked these?"

He shrugged. "Alison told me."

I pulled open the tab on the box and then the small plastic bag inside. The red, waxy candy was sweet on my tongue as I took a bite.

Joel was watching me with an amused smile on his face. "Headfirst. Poor fish."

"Really? Would you rather I ate it tail first?"

He opened his box of Reese's pieces and smiled at me as I popped the rest of the Swedish fish into my mouth.

"That's why I like my candy not in the form of an animal."

"Are you saying you don't like gummy bears?" I asked with faux shock. But seriously, who didn't like gummy bears?

"Not really." He shook his head.

"Alright. Hand me my coat. I'm not sure if we can be friends," I joked as I reached across him to pretend to grab my coat.

He caught my hand and tucked it inside his own as he leaned his shoulder towards mine. "Maybe I don't want to be your friend."

The lights dimmed before I could respond, but I could feel his eyes on me. I liked him, but I wasn't sure if I was in the right headspace to take this further with him.

We'd kissed once, and there was obvious chemistry, but my track record wasn't the best.

The opening credits started, and I immediately knew what movie it was. I laughed when I saw Billy Crystal open the car door and sit down next to Meg Ryan and her ridiculous feathered hair.

"I love this movie." His answering smile was enough to help me relax and just enjoy spending time with him.

We quietly sat through the unconventional love story, laughing at the diner scenes, crying—me—through the sad parts. As much as I didn't want to admit it, this helped me process my feelings. Dylan's call had stirred things up inside of me. I wasn't quite healed from the cracks he left in my heart, and it wouldn't be fair to Joel to pretend that I was ready to date, knowing that it could turn into something potentially serious.

Joel walked quietly beside me as we left the theater, his hand nestled at the curve of my back.

"What's up next?"

"Well, we could go sledding with the snow or maybe just take a walk around campus, the colored lights on the fountain glow through the snow." he suggested.

"A walk sounds good." As Joel looped his arm with mine, his gloved hand holding loosely on mine, the air was crisp.

"You're quiet tonight," he whispered, the sound of the snow underneath our shoes the only sounds around campus.

"I'm sorry. I don't mean to be," I apologized. I was having an enjoyable time with him.

"What's on your mind?"

I shook my head. "It's nothing. I've just had a weird day."

Our feet crunched in the packed snow, snowflakes softly dancing in the air around us.

"You know you can talk to me. If something is bothering you, I'm here to listen." His voice was sincere, and his offer was sweet, but I wasn't sure how to open up about this to anyone, much less the guy who may want to date me.

"I don't think you'd want to listen to this," I admitted quietly. "I didn't even really want to listen to it earlier."

He tugged me towards a bench at my humorless laugh and wiped off the seat.

"You're going to make me talk, aren't you?" I sighed as I looked over at him.

"Yup. Resisting me is futile," he nodded.

"Well, I already knew that." I winked. Every time I pulled away, he was there patiently waiting.

"You're avoiding," he accused quietly as he turned so he could look into my eyes. "You always try to use humor to deflect."

"I do not..."

He gave me a speculative look.

"Okay, fine, maybe a little."

"Still stalling," he teased.

My eyes slowly studied the outline left by my boot in the snow.

"Dylan called me earlier." Joel's hand tightened on my own, and his nostrils flared. "I wasn't sure if I should answer, but..."

"Are you getting back together?" My eyes shot up to him.

"No. Hell no. So much no," I shook my head.

"What did he...?" His voice sounded curious, but I could tell he didn't want to push.

"He's engaged." The heavy breath I let out was full of emotion I still couldn't identify. Betrayal, loneliness—jealousy. I wasn't entirely sure.

"Wow. That's fast," he drawled. "To the...?"

"Triangle boobed bitch who he cheated on me with?" The anger from earlier seeped into my voice, and I couldn't hold it back. "Yes. Lisa with an A."

He laughed as he put his arm around my shoulders. His body felt warm against my side. "He's an idiot."

"Yeah, I'd have to agree with you on that one." I nodded. He was an idiot. And I hated that he'd replaced my once caring friend. Time wasn't always kind to people.

"Did Rory tell you he calls her Temu Kendall?" he asked quietly.

"Yeah, he might've said something. How do you guys even know what she looks like?"

He looked down and raised an eyebrow.

"Alison."

"Yup." He nodded and looked a little embarrassed to have taken part in my roommate's snooping on her social media. "She likes to make fun of the stupid shit she posts."

"I guess everyone needs a hobby." I was going to have to log into Alison's account again to unfollow her. I truly didn't want any more intel. The door to that part of my life was firmly closed, locked, and nailed shut.

She meant well. I knew she did, but it would be too soon if I never saw Dylan again.

"Are you alright?" Joel asked quietly as he traced his finger along the side of my covered leg.

"Yes. No. I don't know."

"Are you over him?"

I looked over at his worried eyes and nodded my head. "Yes. So much, yes."

"But..." I turned sideways to face him. He was very handsome. "I'm not sure if I'm ready for another relationship."

"Oh." The disappointment that crossed his face made me feel horrible, but I tried to be fair to him. I was still broken, and he didn't deserve only to get part of me.

"I'm sorry. I know you like me, and I like you too, but..."

"Not like that," he finished as he glanced away.

"No. No, that's not it. I know if I gave it a real chance, I could fall for you." I confessed honestly. The silence stretched out as his fingers caressed my shoulder. "That's what scares me more than anything. My track record isn't the best and losing you too would shatter me."

"You're not going to..." he whispered, but I shook my head.

"We don't know that."

He nodded. "You're not ready."

"No," I admitted quietly. "I'm not."

Part of me wanted to throw caution to the wind and just kiss him, hesitations be damned, but I couldn't do that.

"I can give you space."

"I don't want to push you away, either." Navigating this in-between place was difficult. Joel liked me and wanted to date me, but I couldn't commit myself to him the way he deserved.

"I'm not going anywhere. I meant we could still hang out, but I won't pursue you—romantically."

My eyes closed, and I leaned forward, tears pricking my eyes. "I feel like a bitch right now."

He leaned forward and grazed my cheek with his cold lips, using his gloved hand to push back my hair.

"Hear me out. I'll give you the space you need to figure things out. Date other people, whatever will help you get to the point you want to be at," he insisted.

"I feel like I'm leading you on." That was the last thing I wanted to do.

"I'll date, too. But as soon as you give me the green light..."

The heat in his eyes was intense. I wasn't sure how this would work out without one or both of us getting jealous or it blowing up in our faces.

"Okay." I nodded. I didn't have any other alternatives. I had to trust that he knew what he was getting into.

"Alright." Joel smiled lightly, pulling me a little closer.

"You sure?" If he wanted an out, I would give it to him.

"Positive." I nodded at his answer, and he leaned in, his lips slowly coaxing mine apart. I clung to the lapels of his peacoat, anchoring myself to reality as his tongue met mine.

His cheeks were rosy as he pulled away, leaning back in for one final soft kiss. "Deal?"

"Deal," I breathed out nervously.

"As soon as you give me the green light…" he trailed off, and I blew out a breath and nodded.

# Chapter Nineteen:
## 2 years & 6 weeks Before the Wedding
### APRIL - SENIOR YEAR

"Kendall?" His voice carried through the phone, sounding slightly worried, but I didn't know who else to call.

Alison had already returned home, and I was alone in my apartment.

"Hey, talk to me. I can hear you breathing..." he pleaded as I held the phone to my ear. "Cough once if someone has kidnapped you..."

I sniffled and tried to find my words.

"No?" he mused, still sounding concerned. "Hmmm. Yodel if you slipped in the bathtub and you can't get up."

I huffed a quiet laugh, and I could just hear the smile in his voice. "So, you're not naked? Damn."

"I..." my voice was strained and quiet.

"She has a voice!" his deep voice laughed. "What's up?"

"I..." I hiccupped, and a half-hearted sob ripped through me.

"Kendall? Are you crying?"

"I need you." My raspy voice carried through the line, and I heard a thump as he cursed.

"Ow. Fuck!"

"Please..." I pleaded. I needed him because I felt like I was about to fall to pieces.

"Are you okay? Are you hurt? Where are you?" His voice was panicked. "Ken, answer me."

"I'm... I'm at home..." I sniffled.

"I'll be right there," he assured.

I knew I should get out of bed and at least try to pull myself together, but this morning had completely broken my heart. Once again, I'd misjudged someone and let them get close enough to destroy me.

I heard the front door open and close. Heavy steps sounded down the hallway, and I felt a little breeze as my door swung open. He said nothing as he sat down beside me and pushed the hair away from my face. The same magnetic jolt I'd always felt at his touch caused me to take in a long, shaky breath.

"What happened?" His hand ran underneath my hair and rubbed lightly between my shoulder blades. Warmth spread through me as he tried to comfort me.

"He left me," I whispered as I looked up into his eyes.

"Wait. What?" He looked confused. "Who left you?"

"He called off the wedding."

His eyes widened, and his hand paused on my back. "Are you kidding me?"

"I wish I was." I rolled a little to my side and looked up at him.

"Start from the beginning. What happened?" he insisted. He hadn't seen this coming, either.

"He came over this morning. Told me he needed to talk to me about some things," I whispered and cleared my throat. It was already sore from crying. "I should have known when he wouldn't kiss me."

"Fuck," he groaned as he looked at me in disbelief.

I pushed myself up to sit beside him with my legs crossed. He reached for my hand and held it in his lap, softly running his thumb over my fingers.

"Do I need to go hunt him down?"

"No, he's probably gone by now. His car was packed," I admitted sadly. He hadn't come to have a discussion. His mind had been made up this morning, and I had been completely blindsided.

"Did he say why?"

"He got a late acceptance letter," I explained, that letter burned into my retinas. A piece of paper that set the destruction of my future into motion.

"Where?"

I shook my head, still not quite believing it. "About a thousand miles away from here."

"Are you going with him?" His voice was cautious, but I could see that the possibility of me leaving, too, scared him.

"I can't. It's too late to transfer into an art therapy program at a different school. The closest program is four hours away from him." I had looked after he left, still somehow hoping that I could follow him, and we could make this work.

"He couldn't stay here? He had an offer here, too." My rescuer's voice rose as it sunk in that this was final.

"He didn't want to," I sighed. He didn't want me, either.

"What the fuck?"

"Yeah," I nodded sadly.

"So, he just left?"

My eyes closed, and another few tears slid down my cheeks. He stroked his thumbs across my cheeks and pulled me into his chest.

"How could he do this?" his voice broke as he held me against him. I knew this would hurt him, too.

"I don't know. Things had been strained for the last few months."

He sat back and cupped my jaw in his hands. "Don't make excuses for him. This was a shit thing to do. If he had a pair of balls, he never would have done it like this."

"I guess at least we didn't get married and try long distance only for it to fail," I whispered. That would have been an even bigger disaster. Better for him to leave than be a divorcee in my early twenties.

"He's a coward," he hissed as he looked into my eyes.

"Did you know?" I asked quietly. They were such good friends I couldn't believe he'd leave him behind, too, and without a word.

He paused and shook his head. "He told me he'd applied a few places out of state, but I didn't know he'd been accepted."

"The wedding is—was—in six weeks. What am I supposed to do now?" I felt lost. At least things hadn't gotten this far with Dylan.

"You cancel everything you can and send his parents a bill," he retorted.

"Oh God. Can you imagine the look on his mother's face?" My eyes widened, but then my face fell. "I'm supposed to pick up the dress this week."

Thankfully, it hadn't been terribly expensive.

"We could burn it in the fire pit at the house," he shrugged with a small smile.

"My sister is going to have a shit fit. She was already upset that I got engaged before her." My engagement had put a strain on our relationship, and this might just completely tip her over the edge.

"She's still your sister. I think she'll be more supportive than you think," he insisted. I wasn't so sure.

"What am I supposed to tell everyone?" We had over a hundred guests invited, and the invitations had already gone out.

"The truth," he nodded.

"That he's a jackass?" I tried to force a smile and got a small one in return.

"That he was offered an opportunity for school across the country and didn't want to have a long-distance relationship." Hearing him say it hurt. He'd left because he didn't want me. He said it was for my own good, but it was to protect himself when it came down to it.

"Can I just pretend this never happened and rewind to last year?" I groaned as I leaned my head against his bicep.

"I wish it worked like that." He pulled me towards him, and I crawled sideways into his lap, burying my face into his neck as he held me. "You're going to be okay. I promise."

As the tears started again… I prayed he was right.

# Chapter Twenty:
## Summer Before Senior Year
### JUNE

T he university had been out of session for almost a month, but it didn't seem that much different other than going to classes.

"You ready to go yet? I'm done. Let's get out of here," Kale asked from the door of his office.

I glanced back and rolled my eyes at his impatient stance. "Yeah, just give me a minute. I've got a few more data points to enter."

"They'll still be here tomorrow," he sighed loudly. He was impatient sometimes.

I waved my hand at him and kept entering the information into the computer. "I know, but I want to get this done. It'll make it easier for you guys to analyze data tomorrow."

When I applied for a summer work-study position, I didn't know that Kale would technically be my boss. He'd been friendly but kept a professional distance throughout the semester when he was my TA. Now that he wasn't in charge of my grade, he'd been warmer towards me.

"I'm not worried about it. Right now, I just need a drink. All this computer modeling is making my head hurt," he groaned as he took off his glasses and rubbed the bridge of his nose.

We were a part of the data collection, entry, and analysis team for some of the psychology experiments that the university was running in their labs.

"You going out with friends?" I asked curiously. I knew he had roommates and other grad students he hung out with, but I'd never actually seen him with people.

"I didn't have a concrete plan. Just wanted to grab a cold beer and a burger."

"Come out with us tonight," I blurted before I'd processed what I'd offered.

"Define us." His gaze was skeptical. I could tell he wasn't too keen on hanging out with a group of undergrads.

"Joel, Rory, Alison, and Benji. Joel is heading back home tomorrow, so we're going out for one last hurrah." I shrugged. He'd met most of them before, but I knew he wasn't a huge fan of the guys.

"Is that going to be tough for you?" he asked curiously.

"Is what going to be tough?" I wasn't sure what he was referring to. I went out with them all the time now.

"Doing the long-distance thing again, wasn't your ex long distance, too?"

"Oh, uh..." I looked back at the computer screen as he tilted his head to study my response. I'd noticed he did that a lot. "Joel and I aren't technically dating or anything."

"No? Could have fooled me," Kale smirked as he raised an eyebrow. He was still quite observant, to an almost alarming degree.

While Joel didn't push things romantically, he had picked me up from class a few times. Kale had obviously seen me with him. Our friendship had grown closer, despite dancing around our attraction to each other.

"It's complicated," I shrugged. I was the one making it complicated, and I knew that, but time had made it easier to process my trepidation about entering another romantic relationship.

"So, he's been friend-zoned," Kale nodded.

"No. It's not like that," I insisted. "I'm not ready for a serious relationship."

"So, you've got him on the hook," he smiled, looking a little impressed.

"He suggested we date other people until I'm ready," I shrugged. Joel had gone on a few dates, but he'd been upfront about it. I appreciated the honesty but also secretly hoped they were horrible.

I hadn't yet, but I also spent most of my downtime with Alison hanging out with the guys at the house. I may have been avoiding putting myself out there again.

"That's mature of him," he smirked.

"I thought so," I challenged back. I liked that Joel wasn't forcing things, but I felt guilty for pushing him away. I knew he wouldn't wait forever.

"And naïve of you to think that he's not screwing these girls."

My mouth dropped open at his blatant remark. "Really? Are you that cynical?"

"I'm pragmatic," he shrugged. "Plus, he's a twenty-one-year-old male."

"Not all guys sleep around," I insisted. "Weren't you the one that told me that as well?"

He shrugged and smiled wryly. "Who knows? He might be the exception."

Inputting the last few numbers into the data fields, I spun around in my chair and narrowed my eyes at him.

"Hey." He held his palms out in front of him and backed up a few steps. "I'm just pointing out that the longer you take to 'get ready,' the farther away he may distance himself from you."

"We see each other all the time." I knew it was a weak argument, but I knew that part of what he said was right. I couldn't drag my feet forever.

"That friend zone is a sketchy place to come out of," Kale mused. "By the time you let him in, he may have put you in there.

"So, what am I supposed to do? Go out with the first guy who asks me?" I asked sarcastically.

"Well, that depends."

Oh, I was interested to see what he had to say about this. "On?"

"Are you attracted to him? Do you enjoy his company? Don't just jump on the first dick that offers you a ride."

"Are you referring to..." I waved my hand in the general direction of his junk. "Or just speaking figuratively?"

"All the above. Take your pick." He shifted as he leaned against the counter, widening the stance of his legs. He'd been right. It was easy to spot the signs of attraction if you knew what you were looking for. Kale tried to stay aloof, but if I was reading things right—he was looking for the green light of his own.

"I..." His stomach growled, and I lost my train of thought as we both let out a nervous chuckle. "You coming with?"

I reached under the desk for my bag, and he nodded as he closed his laptop and packed it away, throwing his strap over his shoulder.

"You want a ride?" he offered as we walked down the hallway to the back of the building.

The lab was only a short walk away from my apartment. Most days, I walked or jogged into work. There wasn't a lot of parking on campus that didn't require a special permit.

"How did you score a permit?" I asked curiously. I knew some grad students had difficulty getting off the waiting list.

"Perks of the job," he laughed. "It also helps that I can take a compact spot."

When we stepped outside the back door of the psych building, I'm not sure why I expected a compact car, but his vehicle was not that.

"Seriously?" I felt my pulse pick up as I stared at the only vehicle parked in the few spaces.

"Seriously, what?" he asked, an amused smile on his face. Kale was just full of surprises.

"You drive a motorcycle?"

"Why not? Did you have me pegged for a smart car or something?" he laughed as he took his messenger bag off over his head. He folded down the top and tucked it into a bag mounted to the side of the bike.

"Yeah. Honestly, I did. You don't seem..." I wasn't sure what he seemed like, but driving a motorcycle wasn't it.

"I think you'll find that not everyone fits into the stereotype you make up for them in your head."

"Don't judge a book by the cover?" I laughed as I took a deep breath.

"Something like that," he nodded. "You dig deeper than the surface, and people may surprise you."

He walked closer to the sleek black and blue metallic bike, grabbing a small helmet out of the saddlebag and pressing it into my hands. He pulled out a key and freed his own from a cord lock attached to one wheel.

"Clever," I nodded as he stowed the lock into a small compartment.

"It only works if the weather is nice. I just hate carrying around a helmet."

I clasped the chinstrap on the one he'd given me and tightened it down. He extended his hand towards me, and I grasped it as I swung my leg over the seat, sliding in close behind him.

"Feet on the pegs. We don't need any trips to the emergency room for burns," he said loud enough that I could hear him. Then, he pulled his helmet on and straightened himself up.

Glancing down, I followed his directions and was glad I hadn't worn sandals today.

"Hold on."

I put my hands on his sides and flattened my chest against his back. He grasped my hands and pulled them forward. "Don't be shy. I don't bite."

"At least not with the helmet on," he laughed loudly.

"Haha."

"Where are we going?" I gave him the general directions to a sports bar that was just off-campus. A few guys from the house bartended there to get discounted drinks on weeknights.

The engine purred beneath my seat as he started the bike, navigated out into traffic, and quickly sped up. My fingers were clasped to his firm chest tightly as he wove in and out of the light traffic across campus. A few guys I knew had bikes in high school, but it felt different, clinging to Kale, the wind whipping through my hair.

I felt the phone in my pocket buzz several times and wondered who was so desperate to get a hold of me. Noticing a familiar car parked near the front door as we pulled into the parking lot, I knew I probably had an answer.

"Looks like we've got an audience." Kale nodded toward Joel, who was leaning against the side of the building by the front door, looking down at the phone in his hands.

Another buzz, and I pulled out my phone.

> *Joel: We've got a table when you get here.*

> *Joel: Are you still coming?*

> *Joel: I'll wait out front.*

Uncoupling the buckle on the helmet, I pulled it off and handed it to Kale to stow. He smiled as he pulled off his helmet and watched me shake out my hair.

> Kendall: Look up.

A smile lit up Joel's face, and he scanned the parking lot until he saw me. His brow furrowed as he took in my stance next to the bike, and then his eyes cut to Kale.

"You've been spotted," Kale teased in my ear as he nodded at Joel.

"Be nice," I warned him as I pushed my phone back into my pocket and ran my fingers through my hair.

"I thought you two weren't a thing?" Kale smirked as he stood back up after securing both helmets.

"We aren't." I shook my head and felt slightly guilty as I looked up at Joel. He didn't look upset, but I couldn't get a read on his expression.

"Prove it."

I broke eye contact with Joel and turned towards Kale. "What?"

"Go out with me," he smiled as my eyes widened. "On a date. Isn't that what you're supposed to be doing?"

"Yeah," I confirmed skeptically, "but I'm supposed to be dating people who actually want to date me."

"Did I not just ask you on a date?"

I did a double-take and felt a blush rise in my cheeks. "Wait. For real?"

He tugged on one of the belt loops on my shorts. "Yeah, what do you think?"

I glanced back over my shoulder at Joel. He was patiently waiting by the door. Much like he was patiently waiting for me to make up my damn mind.

"We can talk about it when you give me a ride home," I told him quietly, a little startled by his offer.

"Fair enough. Let's go. I'm hungry." Kale secured his bike, and we quickly joined Joel by the door.

"Hey, didn't know you'd be joining us, man." He reached his hand out to Kale, and they sized each other up because this wasn't awkward.

"Yeah, Kendall suggested I join you guys." Kale shrugged and then smiled back at me.

Joel's smile looked a little confused as he nodded and opened the door.

"He said he needed a beer and a burger. I knew this place would fit the bill."

"Where's your car?" Joel asked quietly.

"At the apartment. I walked to work today."

"I can drive you home later if you want," he offered. Normally I would have taken him up on the offer, but I had already agreed to a ride with Kale.

"Aw, that's cute that you think you'll be sober enough to drive. Is Rory already here?" I teased, hoping to get the focus off my transportation home. It bothered me a little that Joel might think something was going on with Kale and me.

"Yeah, we rode together," he nodded as he placed his hand on my back. "I'm sure he wouldn't mind dropping you off."

"Already covered, man, I'll drop her off," Kale chimed in, and I narrowed my eyes at him.

"Should you be drinking if you're gonna take her home on your bike later?" Joel asked with a bit of a bite to his tone.

"One beer at the beginning of the night doesn't constitute drunk driving." Kale shrugged. I didn't see him as the type to risk himself or his expensive bike on getting drunk.

"I wasn't..." Joel sighed and shook his head.

"Okay!" I said loudly, nodding toward the door. "Anyway. I'm hungry. You two are probably hungry. How about we go sit down and order food before my stomach eats itself?"

The back and forth was getting on my nerves.

"Radicchio!" Alison cheered as she saw him heading toward the table that our other friends had claimed.

"Did you google the different names of salads?" he rolled his eyes, but this was part of their banter. I think they both secretly enjoyed it.

"Yeah, of course I did," she scoffed. "So, that I'd be prepared on the off chance that I ran into you?"

"She might've," Benji laughed.

She looked over at her boyfriend in mock horror. "Whose side are you on?"

"Yours, baby." He kissed her cheek and pulled her into his side. "I'm always on your side."

"Whipped." Rory coughed into his fist, and the table burst into laughter.

He made eye contact across the table and winked as I sat down next to Kale, Joel taking the seat on my other side.

"So..." Joel said slowly as the other occupants of the table all stared over at the three of us.

"Anyway..." Kale said simultaneously, and I closed my eyes briefly, regretting my decision to go out tonight instead of going home.

Rory seemed amused at my predicament as both men tried talking to me simultaneously.

"How's grad school been treating you, Kale?" Thankful for the deflect, the table started talking about their plans for the next school year.

"It's good," he nodded. "I'm already putting out feelers for a Ph.D. program. Not committed to anywhere yet."

"I just want to make it to graduation," Alison sighed.

"Here, here." Benji clinked his bottle against her glass. Neither one of them had plans to continue their education past May yet.

The GRE was looming in my future. If I were serious about pursuing art therapy, I'd need at least a master's degree. Luckily, the program was finally available as a major to continue on the non-thesis master's track. Clinical hours would be required, but I'd rather get hands-on experience than have to defend a paper.

"So, what exactly are you two working on in that lab all day?" Rory asked curiously, watching me.

"It's top secret."

Joel laughed and bumped his shoulder against mine. "Sounds ominous."

"Not so much, but the university makes us sign non-disclosures," Kale told them. It was not that interesting.

"I spend a lot of time putting numbers in spreadsheets. It's not that exciting," I told them with a small shrug.

"But you get paid, which means your cell phone stays turned on, so even though it's boring as fuck, you keep showing up each day," Alison laughed. "No offense, Frisée."

Kale made a show of rolling his eyes at Alison, but I secretly think he liked she paid enough attention to tease him.

"None taken. It's why I know research isn't my calling."

She got a devious grin on her face, and I braced myself for her comment. "Ah. You're more into the mind fucking part."

"Yup. Exactly. I live to shrink people's heads." He held his fingers up in front of his face and closed one eye, pretending to squish her head from across the table.

"Wow. Is that actual humor coming from you?" she gasped as she covered her mouth, eyes comically wide.

"I've got many layers," he admitted with a wink. Once you got past the serious exterior, Kale had a relaxed sense of humor.

"Not even going to touch that one, Endive," Alison laughed.

"Kind of like girls and Joel's penis," Rory joked, before he lifted his beer to his mouth and took a drink.

"Be nice," I scolded him. Sometimes his humor went a little too far.

"Oh, come on. It was a joke," he argued as he looked around the table for someone to laugh.

"Kind of like your ability to keep a girlfriend," Joel shot back and crossed his arms over his chest.

"Not you, too," I frowned as I flicked him in the arm.

"Do they always act like this?" Kale whispered as he watched the two men go back and forth at each other across the table.

"Yes," I sighed. "At least they're not drunk."

"You mean it gets worse?" He chuckled, and a tingle ran through me at his warm breath on my cheek.

"So much worse."

"And I was thinking maybe they'd come a long way since their freshman year," Kale laughed. I remembered their antics during orientation. It seemed like such a long time ago.

"This is them coming a long way."

Kale rolled his eyes and brushed my hair off my shoulder. "I'm sure their families would be proud."

I shrugged. Since we'd all started hanging out again, it'd been the norm for them to tease each other. "You get used to it."

"Do I have to?"

I leaned in closer and whispered in his ear. "I thought you wanted that date."

He sat up a little straighter as I leaned back, nodding. "I guess I can learn to deal."

After he'd finished his beer, I could see Kale watching the dynamic of our group, studying the interactions between each member, and taking mental notes. He'd join in with his dry humor occasionally, but I could tell he was analyzing where he'd fit in.

As Benji tried to convince a slightly intoxicated Alison to go home, I could tell the night was winding down.

"You ready to get out of here?" Kale asked as he placed his hand on my back.

I nodded and reached down to grab my bag.

"You're leaving already?" Joel slurred a little as he pouted at me from my other side.

"Yeah. What time do you leave in the morning?"

He sighed loudly, obviously not looking forward to his trip home. "I'll probably head out before noon."

"Text me when you get home?" I asked, and he gave me a soft smile.

"Yes, Mom." I arched an eyebrow at him. "Sorry. Probably should cut me off now."

His eyes were slightly glazed over, and his breath was heavily tainted with the smell of rum and the sweet soda it'd been mixed with.

"Get some rest. And be safe." I worried about him driving by himself if he was hungover, but he wasn't leaving early.

"I will." He leaned in towards me but then stopped as he looked over my shoulder to where I could feel Kale waiting behind me. "I'll see you next month."

I nodded as he squeezed my hand.

"I'll make sure he gets tucked in, Special K," Rory assured as he joined us.

I groaned as I narrowed my eyes at him. "God, I thought that nickname had finally died."

"Gotta keep you on your toes." The boyish smirk he gave me made it hard to be annoyed him.

He shrugged as I pulled my bag over my shoulder and turned to Kale. He was watching the three of us interact, a curious smile on his face.

"You ready?"

He smiled and held out his hand. "As long as you are."

I nodded, ignoring his hand, and followed him out to the bike. The ride back to my apartment differed from the one to the bar. Something about the night sky and the light wind relaxed me as I clung to Kale's powerful chest.

"Let me walk you up." He helped unclasp the buckle on my chin strap, his fingers grazing my neck.

"Are you trying to be a gentleman?" I teased, trying to break the tension I was feeling between us.

"Maybe." He took off his helmet and hung it on the handlebar.

"I already agreed to go out with you," I rolled my eyes, pretending to be put out.

"Gotta make sure you don't back out."

I laughed nervously as I smirked at him. "Who knew you were this insecure?"

"Shh," he whispered as he leaned in closer. "It can be our little secret."

He lingered as he angled his face down toward me, his warm breath washing over mine. Sensing his hesitation, I straightened up, my nose brushing against his.

"Are you trying to get me to kiss you?" he whispered against my lips.

"Maybe," I breathed as I felt his lips just barely graze mine, the vibrations from his words coursing through me.

"Who knew you were this insecure?" he teased, and I smiled.

"Shut up." The low rumble of his chest as he huffed out a laugh pulled a smile at my lips.

"You first," he murmured as he closed the tiny space between us and captured my top lip between his. I'd expected unbridled passion from him with the way he'd laid it on thick at the party all those months ago.

It was more than that. The careful way he coaxed my lips open. It was just as measured as the rest of his personality. But I couldn't deny the thrill that rushed through me as he tilted his head and deepened the kiss, his fist grasping the back of my shirt as he pulled me against his chest.

"That was unexpected," he murmured as he pulled away from me, still looking down at me with those smoldering eyes.

"Mmhmm," I hummed as I looked up at him, feeling a little lightheaded.

He gently pecked my lips once more before he led me towards the building, leaving me thoroughly confused as I climbed into bed a short while later.

# Chapter Twenty-one:
## Summer Before Senior Year
### LATE JUNE

"Damn, you should get dressed up more often," Alison sighed from my doorway.

One more pass of the straightening brush through my hair, and I was ready. Sort of... "Is this alright? You sure I won't look out of place?"

"Girl, you look hot, but classy. Totally appropriate." She nodded as she took in my outfit.

"Why am I so nervous?" I shook out my hands and tried to calm down.

"Because instead of a normal date, Kale just had to take you to a cocktail reception with half the people from his department, including your bosses."

"Oh yeah." I nodded. "That."

"You'll be fine. People like you, and you're good at small talk despite your hatred of people," she teased.

"We've been over this. I don't hate people," I rolled my eyes.

"Just socializing with new ones," she said knowingly.

"I can cancel. Maybe I should cancel." I paced around my room as she shook her head at me.

"There is a hot guy who is probably wearing a suit, at least a tie, headed to our apartment. I'm not telling him you're refusing to go."

"Ugh. I'm already sweating. Who has an outdoor party in June?" I whined. This was a bad idea.

"Um, half the people who get married in June," she laughed, and I took in another shaky breath, trying to calm myself down. Being this nervous wouldn't make the evening any easier.

A loud knock sounded on the apartment door, and it appeared I was out of time.

"I got it. It might be Benji. Take a deep breath. You'll have them all eating out of the palm of your hands."

"Because I'm so charming," I rolled my eyes.

"Not with that attitude," she laughed as she walked out my door.

Washing any excess makeup off my hands, I carefully dried them and straightened out the front of my dress.

Laughter wafted down the hallway as I closed my door. Kale was perched on the edge of the sofa, talking to Benji. They seemed to get along, and Alison watched the two of them talking with an amused smile on her face.

"Hi..."

"Hey, you look amazing." Crossing the room in a few long strides, he leaned in and kissed me on the cheek, his warm lips lingering for a few moments.

He smelled amazing, and he pulled off the relaxed, professional look well. He had on a pair of charcoal-colored slacks with a lighter gray pinstriped dress shirt. The top button was open and showed off a tiny sliver of chest hair.

"Thank you. You clean up nicely as well."

His fingers gently touched mine as he pulled away. "You ready to go?"

"Yeah," I nodded. "Ready as I'll ever be. Is this okay for the party?"

He trailed his eyes over my dress again as he took a step backward. "It's perfect."

"Be good, kids," Alison teased as she sat down on Benji's lap on the couch.

"I don't think you've made a lettuce joke since I've been here. You feeling alright, Alison?" he teased, and I shook my head at him.

"Eh. I'll give you a pass this time," she said in an unimpressed voice as she waved her hand at him.

"Ran out of types?" he smirked.

"Bitch, please. Go put on your Bibb and get out of here."

Benji looked up at her like she'd lost her mind, and Kale arched an eyebrow at her. "That's it?"

"Shut it, Leaf."

"I'm disappointed in you." He sighed as he looked over at me with a grin.

"Eh. We had a good run." She shrugged and rolled her eyes.

"You two are weird," I smiled, enjoying their mildly entertaining banter. At least they seemed comfortable enough to tease each other.

"Why am I included in this?" Kale asked, sounding a little offended.

"You encouraged her."

He rolled his eyes. "She was going to do it, anyway."

"He's probably right." Alison nodded from her perch on her amused boyfriend.

"Let's go," I nodded toward the door. "I don't want to make you late."

He glanced down at his watch. "We've got plenty of time."

"Don't keep her out too late," Alison teased. "You two have work in the morning."

"Yes, Mom," I smiled over at her.

Allie blew us a kiss from her perch and Benji waved.

Kale slipped his hand into mine and lightly tugged me towards the door. I grabbed my clutch off the counter and pulled the door closed behind us.

"I don't have to ride the bike in this, do I?"

"No," he shook his head. "I've got a car tonight."

"Is it a smart car?"

He laughed as he pushed open the front door of the apartment building. An older model black convertible was parked at the curb with its top down. "Sorry, I guess I should have warned you."

He opened the passenger side door and helped me into my seat.

Rifling through the contents of my tiny purse, I pulled out a ponytail holder and loosely bundled my hair up to keep it from blowing around.

"The drive isn't very long. It was such a pleasant day today, and I thought it'd be nice to have the top down," he apologized.

"I'll live. It's an outdoor party in the middle of the summer. I doubt everyone is going to have perfect hair," I shrugged. He didn't need to know that it'd taken me twenty minutes to style.

"I like that you're practical."

The car started with a low hum. After he shifted the car into drive, he covered my hand with his own and pulled it onto the center console.

"But you're apparently not all that practical. Fancy bike and now a sporty car," I teased.

"The car belongs to one of my roommates," he explained. "He loaned it to me when I said I had a date."

"That was nice of him."

"He's been begging me to ride the bike for months. I figured I'd put him out of his misery so you could be a little more comfortable," he smiled as he squeezed my hand.

"Thank you. I appreciate not having to worry about flashing random people as we drive by."

He glanced over at me with a wry smile. "You can still do that if you'd like. It might be a little harder sitting in the car, but I won't stop you."

The more time I spent with Kale, the more he seemed to open up and joke around. He wasn't quite as uptight as he appeared to be. I contemplated what it'd be like to date him. This was what Joel wanted, after all.

Kale was attractive, clever, and well educated. We seemed to be attracted to each other, but I still hadn't felt that big spark. I knew it was naïve to want something like that, but I did.

"Ha, ha. I think I'll pass," I told him. "I'm good with keeping my clothing intact for the evening."

"That's too bad."

Before I could formulate a response to his forward comment, he turned onto a tree-lined drive and parked behind a line of cars. "How many people are there supposed to be here tonight?"

"I'm not completely sure. It's for almost all the faculty and staff, and people could bring dates," he shrugged. "Maybe a hundred."

"Wow." I hadn't expected that many people.

"It's not some big uptight affair. They usually have a buffet on the patio, and people just sort of mill around and network."

"So, you've come before?"

"Yeah, last summer I attended," he confirmed. "But it should be much more enjoyable this year."

"Why's that?" I smiled.

"Because I've got a date, and I won't be forced to mingle alone."

"Ugh. You're making me mingle?" I groaned, and he shook his head at me.

"Don't worry, I wouldn't have asked you to come with me if it was going to be that bad," he assured. I wasn't so convinced. "There is an open bar, if that makes it any easier."

"Psh, of course, that makes it easier. Why didn't you lead with that?"

"Am I going to have to carry you out of here later?" he teased.

"Eh, probably not. I'm not a huge drinker. A few glasses of wine, and I'll be ready for bed."

"Sounds like fun. Count me in," he said with a wink.

"Oh, you think you're funny now?"

He shrugged as he turned off the engine and pressed the button to put up the roof. "You smiled, didn't you?"

"Touché, Mister Roberts."

He helped me out of the car and kept hold of my hand as we walked the rest of the way up the drive. I expected to head to the front door, but he tugged me around the side of the house. Gentle music wafted through the air, mixed with the sound of laughter. It looked like the party was already in full swing, with groups of people dotted throughout the lush backyard of the large house.

"Hey, look at me," he coaxed as he pulled my hand towards himself, angling his body so he could see my face. "I'll be with you the whole time."

My heart warmed at the smile on his face as he squeezed my hand. "Thank you for doing this. I know it isn't ideal, but I appreciate you coming with me."

"Don't mind me." Nervous laughter bubbled up, and his smile widened. "I'm just a little intimidated."

"You shouldn't be. You're funny and friendly when you want to be," he teased. "This will be a piece of cake."

"You're going to owe me cake when this is over."

"Next time I take you out, I will." He nodded.

"That's presumptuous of you."

"Just wishful thinking." He shrugged.

Before I could respond, a female voice called out behind me, and we both turned towards it.

"Kale! How long have you been here? I was thinking I was going to be the only one here." A modelesque brunette pulled Kale into a half hug, kissing his cheek as I took a step back.

"We just got here, Maddie. This is Kendall."

"Oh! Hello. You're the girl he works with at the lab," she said, holding her hand out toward me. "Undergrad, right?"

"Yeah, it's nice to meet you."

"Same. How's working with this one going?" She tugged on his shirtsleeve, giving Kale an indulgent smile.

"It's been going fine. I can't complain. It's a job, right?"

Leaning in close, she whispered. "We both know it's boring as hell, but everyone has to do it."

"Well, we should probably start circulating," she told Kale. "Second semester TA selections haven't been posted yet, and we know you don't want to get stuck with the art students again."

I couldn't read his face when I looked up at Kale. He never acted like he didn't enjoy working with my class last semester, but it'd been an undesired assignment, according to what she said. She squeezed his free hand and wandered back into the crowd of people.

"What was that?" I asked, glancing at him. Did he think that being involved with the Art Therapy program was less than other assignments? He'd seemed passionate about the subject when he spoke in small group discussions.

"Oh, she's one of the other master's track students," he shrugged as he watched her walk away and then smiled down at me.

"I got that much," I told him flatly. "Was teaching my class that bad?"

"No. Not really." He shook his head, the small smile still stretched across his lips. "I could give a lot of input to the course structure since it was new."

"But she implied..." I trailed off. Starting a fight at a cocktail party was not what I was trying to do, but I was not about to be told my choice of a major was less than.

"It wasn't my first choice," he admitted. "Some people in the department see it as frivolous supplementary support."

"Oh," I sighed, hating that he confirmed it for me. "Then why did you bring me here? What if someone asks my major?"

"Some of the faculty brought their spouses. Not everyone is an academic."

I wasn't sure if I should be insulted by that statement. Going into this blind, I felt like I was setting myself up to be judged. I was excited to take graduate classes eventually, finally feeling like I could take my art and use it to help people.

"You don't have to talk to people if you don't want to," he told me softly, but I still felt like he'd put me in an awkward situation.

"Come on, let's get some food," he suggested quietly a few moments later. After we'd filled up on the light appetizer selection and grabbed a few drinks, Kale started circulating.

There wasn't anyone who was inherently unfriendly. Still, I could tell that spouses and dates were at this event to be an accessory, not necessarily someone to have a conversation with. A few people talked to me, but I could see the flicker in their eyes when my academic track was revealed. Some of them looked at me like I was an experiment, the others like they pitied my choice of major.

I'd never felt more insecure about my future in my life. I was an intelligent woman, and I felt like they didn't respect me because I found my calling in the arts and not the academic track. I would have been miserable being a straight psychology major. Some people, like Kale, found a genuine passion for it, but my heart was just not there.

Observing Kale, though, he was more relaxed than I'd seen him. These were his peers, his colleagues. He fit in here.

"You alright?" he asked as he started the car, placing his palm on my knee.

"Yeah, I'm good." *Just questioning all my life choices.*

The car was quiet on the way home. He'd left the top up, soft music filling the confined space. I hated to let this experience cloud my view of Kale, but this was a part of him. Could I be an accessory at parties, knowing that some of his colleagues looked down on my future profession?

When I added the double major, I thought I'd been choosing a profession that took what I was good at and applied it to a meaningful service. I still thought that, but obviously, Kale was in the house of thought that it was less than the rest of his field.

When we pulled up to my building, I was nervous.

He quickly opened my door and helped me stand, leaning forward to kiss my lips lightly. I didn't return the kiss with the same enthusiasm, and he pulled back, studying my face.

"Thank you," he told me quietly, his hand lingering on the side of my neck. I still felt an attraction to him, but I couldn't get past the fact that I didn't feel like I'd be considered an equal in a relationship with him. It may have all been built up in my head, he seemed to enjoy my company genuinely, but I still felt insecurities creeping in.

"Yeah. No worries. I'll see you in the morning?" I asked quietly, already knowing the answer. We worked in the same lab, so we'd be seeing each other. I hoped my awkward feelings would dissipate overnight.

Nodding, he took my hand and walked me to the front door of the building. He didn't follow me inside, and I didn't invite him. I wasn't sure if there was a point. It seemed like our futures were going different places.

As I got ready for bed, I felt a little disappointed but more prepared to consider a relationship with Joel. Not having much dating experience, I hadn't been on an awkward date. Most of my dating history was with someone I was already dating. The relationship was already established.

"Hey." Alison peeked her head in my room as I brushed out my hair.

I looked up and smiled at her eager face. "Hey. How was your night?"

"Aren't I supposed to be asking you that question?" she teased. "How was your night with stale salad?"

I rolled my eyes and shook my head at her. "You guys have got to stop calling him that."

I sighed loudly as I tried to figure out how to answer her. He was a nice guy, and I was attracted to him. He just wasn't someone I saw having a future with.

"That much fun, huh?"

Opening my mouth a few times to respond, I still couldn't formulate a response. "It was..."

She laughed at the iffy expression on my face. "A little stale?"

"Yeah... definitely won't be going out with him a second time. Once was enough."

# Chapter Twenty-two:
## Summer Before Senior Year
### JULY

Rory: I'm bored.

Kendall: And...?

Rory: Why do you have to work today?

Kendall: Because I have to work every day.

Rory: Sounds tedious.

Kendall: Pull the silver spoon out. Not everyone can have Mommy and Daddy pay all their bills.

The primary reason for staying on campus was to avoid going home for the summer. Partially because of Dylan's wedding, but mostly because my parents decided I needed to be more responsible before I graduated. That meant they told me they would pay for school, my rent, and car insurance. Everything else was on me. When I discovered I could get class credit while getting a paycheck this summer, staying had been a foregone conclusion.

It wasn't an unreasonable expectation, but it also meant that I needed to save up some money this summer, so I didn't have to work so much during the school year.

Rory: They don't pay for everything. I've had a job before.

Kendall: What happens when you have to get a big boy job next year?

Rory: That's what MBAs are for.

Kendall: Are you avoiding the real world?

Rory: Aren't you applying for the master's program?

Kendall: Touché.

Kendall: You sticking around here?

Rory: Maybe. I cast a wide net, but I'd like to stay in the state.

Kendall: You going to be like that old movie where that guy was living in the frat house well into his mid-twenties?

Rory: Van Wilder wasn't in a frat.

Kendall: Of course you'd know that.

Rory: It's a classic.

Kendall: I think you have a crush on Ryan Reynolds.

Rory: What's not to like?

Kendall: ... A lot.

Rory: Aren't you supposed to be at work?

Kendall: I am.

Rory: No, you're talking to me.

Rory: Do I need to tattle on you to stale salad?

Kendall: He won't care.

Rory: The perks of dating the boss.

Kendall: We're not dating.

Rory: You went on a date with him.

Kendall: One date does not equal dating.

Rory: Harsh.

Kendall: Why do you care?

Rory: ...

Kendall: ...

Rory: Have any weekend plans?

Kendall: Not that I know of.

Rory: You do now.

Kendall: Oh really?

Rory: Yup.

Kendall: I don't recall being asked...

Rory: You got a better offer?

Kendall: ...

*Rory: No?*

"Did you upload the data set to the server?" Kale asked from behind me, and I froze. "I can't find it."

"Shit." I dropped my phone into my bag and quickly moved the file I'd been working on into the shared folder on the department server.

"You're distracted today," Kale teased from the doorway to his office. He didn't look mad, thankfully.

"Sorry. It's there now."

"Thanks." He went back into the office, and I leaned back, checking to make sure he couldn't see me as I snuck my phone under my lab table.

*Rory: I promise it'll be fun.*

*Rory: Are you ghosting me now?*

*Rory: I'll come to find you.*

*Rory: That sounded creepier than I intended it to.*

*Rory: Not that I was trying to be creepy.*

*Rory: Put a guy out of his misery.*

Biting my lip to hold in my laughter, I started typing a response.

*Kendall: You're needy.*

I quickly erased the message, squinting at the screen while thinking of my response.

*Rory: I can see you typing.*

*Rory: Shit... creepy again.*

*Kendall: ...*

*Rory: Now you're just being mean...*

Kendall: I'm working.

Rory: This weekend?

Kendall: Right now. You almost got me caught.

Rory: Almost only counts in horseshoes and hand grenades.

Kendall: You're so weird.

Rory: What? It's something my grandma says.

Kendall: Now you take your social cues from an octoge-narian.

Rory: She's in her 70s.

Kendall: That makes it so much better.

Rory: It does, actually.

Rory: She's a cool grandma.

Kendall: Oh? Does she stay up past eight p.m. and play poker instead of bridge?

Rory: She'd like you...

My fingers paused over the keys. I wasn't sure how to respond to a comment like that.

Rory: You're doing it again...

Kendall: ...

Rory: I'm taking silence as a yes.

I typed in my response and hit send... immediately wishing I hadn't.

> *Kendall: Fine. Yes. It's a date.*

*Rory: Who said I was asking you on a date?*

"Shit."

*Rory: I'll pick you up for our 'date' at four tomorrow.*

My heart was pounding as I dropped my phone back in the pocket of my bag. I needed to focus on making it through the rest of the day. Worrying about the implications of tomorrow could happen after work.

> *Kendall: What am I supposed to wear?*

I was sitting at my desk wrapped in my robe, no clue what to wear for whatever this was with Rory.

*Rory: Clothing?*

"Well, that's not helpful," I muttered as I frowned at the text message on my phone. "Allie! I need your help!"

I heard a thump, and then my door swung open, my roommate standing there with a startled look on her face, her messy bun hanging haphazardly off the back of her head. "What's wrong? You okay?"

"No, not really." I shook my head.

"What's going on?"

"I'm pretty sure I'm going out on a date with Rory this afternoon," I blurted out, and her eyes widened.

My phone pinged with another message, and I shook my head as I read it.

*Rory: Or not. Your choice. I can always adjust our plans.*

Alison's mouth dropped open as I looked back up at her. "Are you blushing? Is he sexting you?"

"No..."

"That wasn't very convincing," she laughed. "Okay. Start again. Why do you think this is a date?"

"He kinda implied it might be," I cringed. Or I slipped and said date, and now he was teasing me.

"I'm not following," she frowned.

"He wanted to make weekend plans with me."

"What kind of weekend plans?" she asked curiously as she narrowed her eyes at me.

"I don't know," I shrugged. "He didn't say."

"You didn't ask?"

I shook my head and frowned. "No?"

"What are you supposed to wear?"

"I don't know," I whined. "He won't tell me. That's why I need help."

"Give me your phone." She extended her hand out, and I placed it into her palm. "Damn..."

"What?"

She held up her finger and kept scrolling. "He's super flirty with you. When did this start?"

"He wasn't flirting, was he?" It was hard to tell with him. He was always like this with me. Had things changed, and I didn't notice?

"That's what it looks like to me," she smirked.

"I don't know. This is how we always are."

"Hmm..."

"What's hmm?" I asked her, exasperated with this entire situation. This was not part of the plan.

"I guess I never thought anything of it before," she shrugged.

"What are you talking about?"

She made an amused face, turning her head to the side. "You two kinda flirt all the time."

"No, we don't." I shook my head. I would know if I was flirting, right?

"This back-and-forth banter is like your version of foreplay," she laughed as she looked at my flabbergasted face.

"What? How did I not pick up on this before?"

"I just thought you guys liked to rip on each other. But that no clothing comment was pretty suggestive."

My mind scanned over all the other interactions we'd had over the last several months. Was Rory flirting with me? And for how long?

"Shit," I whined as I looked up at her in terror. Why was this happening now?

"Hey. No, don't freak out. It'll be fine."

"But..." I sputtered.

"Do you like him?" she asked curiously.

"I..."

"Oh, my God, you do." She clapped her hands together before she started pulling open the drawers on my dresser.

"What am I supposed to do?" I was supposed to be dating to be ready to start a relationship with his best friend. This was completely unexpected.

"He asked you out, so go out," she shrugged like it was that easy.

"But what about Joel? And Kale?" I wasn't dating either of them exclusively. But wasn't this stepping on their toes?

"They all know the score. You told both of them you weren't interested in committing to someone yet."

"But aren't they going to think...?"

"Stop it! You don't worry about what they think," she scolded as she turned and pointed at me. "Are you ready to commit to dating Joel?"

I shook my head no.

"Are you committing to dating Kale?"

Another shake.

"So, you're single. Single women can date whoever they want, whenever they want, without having to explain themselves."

"I've never dated two people at one time, much less three." I was going to hyperventilate.

"Stop trying to over-analyze this. Just go today with an open mind and enjoy yourself," she instructed. "For all you know, there could be zero chemistry."

"Easy for you to say," I muttered. Allie didn't freak out about everything or get nervous.

"You need to get out of your head and just let life happen. I know it's scary to open up to people, but you might miss out on something great by being scared." Now my roommate was a relationship guru. This had to be an alternative universe.

"But Rory?"

She bit her lip and shrugged her shoulder. "He is hot."

My mind drifted back to when we first met. I had initially been attracted to him. But he always dated girls like Gretchen and Bridgette.

"Stop thinking and put this on." She tossed a cute floral halter top and a pair of mid-thigh length denim cut-off shorts at me.

"You don't think this is too casual?"

"It's fucking hot out there. Just make sure to put on some sunscreen." She disappeared from my room as quickly as she appeared. A shriek and some feminine and masculine laughter sounded from down the hallway. Benji must have spent the night again.

I missed that part of a relationship. The coupley things. Cuddling... spending downtime together. The sex. I hadn't had sex since before my birthday.

> *Rory: You ready, or are we going with the clothing-optional date?*

> *Kendall: You'd like that. Wouldn't you?*

> *Rory: ...*

> *Rory: I feel like this is a trap.*

Swiping my screen to activate the camera, I flipped the view and held it above my head, taking a selfie of my outfit.

> *Rory: Nice angle.*

> *Rory: I can see down your shirt.*

The surprised laughter that burst out of me was unexpected. He always had a way of disarming me.

> *Kendall: Would you rather I wear a turtleneck?*

> *Rory: Might be a little warm.*

> *Kendall: So, we'll be outside?*

> *Rory: Stop fishing. I'll be there in 5.*

My mind was racing as I waited for Rory to arrive. Alison had pointed out some things I'd either ignored or overlooked.

"He's here." Spinning towards the door, she was standing there with an amused smile on her face. "Nobody is saying you have to marry the guy. Just keep your options open."

Before I could respond, there he was, standing in my doorway just behind her. "Ah, so this is what your room looks like."

"You've been in our apartment before," I rolled my eyes as I looked over at him.

"But I've never been down the hallway," he shrugged as his eyes looked around and then lingered on the exposed skin of my legs.

"And?"

"It's cute." He nodded, and Alison cleared her throat, a smile on her face as she looked between the two of us.

"I'm gonna." She hooked her thumb over her shoulder and ducked under his arm.

"I guess you've never had a reason to be in my bedroom before," I mused quietly.

"And I've got one now?" He took another step forward, and I got a whiff of his cologne as I took a deep breath.

"I don't know. Do you?"

His steps were measured as he approached me, slowly, like I was going to spook if he moved too fast. "Do I?"

"Quit throwing the question back at me. You're the one who insisted I make plans with you."

"You didn't put up too much of a fight." He reached forward and tugged on the hem of my top, his knuckle grazing the bare skin underneath.

"To be honest, I'm not sure what's going on here," I whispered, licking my lips.

His eyes connected with mine, and a slow smile spread across his face. "Neither am I."

We looked at each other for a few moments. The air charged with something different, but still a little exhilarating. "You ready to go?"

"Yeah," I breathed as I tried to get my bearings around him. "I'm ready."

For what, I still wasn't a hundred percent sure, but I was about to find out.

"Oh, my God. No more," I groaned as I shook my head.

"Just a little bit more. You can take it. It's so good," Rory encouraged, his voice low as he looked at my mouth.

"Oooh. I don't think I can." Opening my mouth, he slipped it inside, my mouth watering.

"That's it. See. I told you that you had room for a little more." I laughed as I licked the sugary sweet cinnamon mix from my lips. "Just admit this was a great idea."

I held onto my stomach as I watched him eat the last bite of the sweet fried dough.

"You're going to have to carry me out of here," I groaned.

"So, you're not ready to use the rest of our tickets now?" he teased as he held up the wad of tickets he'd insisted on buying.

"Not unless you're ready for me to puke on you."

Rory's plans had been surprising, but we'd been enjoying ourselves. I'd almost completely forgotten that the county fair was going on this week. "While that sounds super sexy. I don't think we're at that stage in our relationship yet."

"Is that a stage you're expecting?" I laughed. I wasn't aware puking on your date was a thing.

"Well, it has happened before, but I can't say it's a desirable stage. Kind of a mood killer," he made a face, and I couldn't help laughing.

"I think you've been dating the wrong kind of girl if that's normal."

"Yeah. I'm pretty sure that's an understatement," he nodded. He hadn't shown much interest in dating since things ended with Bridgette. I thought he'd jump into another relationship with the same type of girl, but he hadn't.

Picking up the now empty plate, he held his hand out for me as he stood. "Are you ready to have the conversation about our questionable taste in partners?"

He didn't let go as we briefly paused by a trashcan and continued toward the buildings that housed the 4H animals. My eyes lingered on the veins running up the back of his hand, leading to his muscular forearms.

He'd worn a light blue T-shirt that made his eyes look even lighter and a pair of dark board shorts. The summer sun tinted his hair a light auburn color.

"So, no to the exes talk?" He squeezed my hand, and I glanced up. A gentle smile pulled at his full lips, and I blushed under his gaze. Luckily, it was hot enough outside my cheeks were already pink.

"No. I think we have enough information about that to know we both have had lapses in judgment."

"But not all the time." He was uncharacteristically quiet as he shifted his hand and interlaced our fingers.

The smart-aleck response that normally would have flowed out caught in my throat as his warm palm pressed against mine.

"We'll see…"

He was slowly breaking down my barriers, and I wasn't sure what to do about that.

We wandered through the buildings, admiring the gorgeous horses. It was amazing how tall some of the stock horses truly were. "My God, he's huge."

"Why, thank you," he laughed as he pulled me closer to his side and put his arm around my back.

"Oh, shut it, you smartass. I was talking about the horse."

"What? Do you think I'm hung like a horse? That's quite presumptuous, Kendall," he teased in a high-pitched voice. "I don't put out on a first date, you know."

Flattening my palm across his mouth to shut him up, I pinched his side with my other hand. "There are kids in here. Quit being a turd."

His hand covered mine, and he dragged it away from his mouth. "Calm down. No one is paying attention to us."

"Stop talking about your junk." I narrowed my eyes at him, and he winked.

"What? You want to see my junk?"

A surprised laugh burst out of him after I smacked the back of my hand against his stomach. "You wish."

"You're just going to smack me if I respond to that," he laughed as he turned away from my threatening palm.

"Probably."

He leaned down, lips barely grazing my ear. "I probably shouldn't find it sexy when you act all sassy." My eyes closed, and I took in a shaky breath as he lingered, so close to me but not quite touching. "But I do." One of his fingers gently traced down the outside of my arm, and my eyes snapped back open when he grasped my hand. "Let's go spend those tickets. I think you've had enough time to digest."

"I guess you're right." I nodded, swallowing down the nerves that'd been high the entire day with him.

"Just remember that," he replied with a smirk.

"There's always got to be a first time for everything."

He pinched along my side, and I danced away from him. He tugged our joined hands as I tried to escape, and I crashed into his side. "There's no escaping me now."

"Yeah. You're like a fungus."

He growled and started tickling me with his free hand, holding me close to his side.

"Stop! Stop! Okay! You aren't a fungus."

"That's better," he nodded, and I went in for the kill.

"You're more like a parasite."

"Hey! I'll have you know that my organism isn't on the micro side," he teased, unable to resist another joke about his dick.

"It's all about size with you guys, isn't it?"

"Flaunt it if you got it," he laughed as he wiggled his eyebrows and pushed his hips forward.

"Yeah, well, you can keep it in your pants."

"I'm gonna remember you said that," he teased.

"You sure you got enough room in your brain with all that ego?"

"I think you like my big... ego." He leaned down and ran his lips along the back edge of my jaw, slowly ghosting them across my skin as his large palms tugged my hips towards him. "I think you secretly like this back and forth."

My skin erupted into goosebumps as one of my hands rested on his chest. His heart was hammering against my palm, almost faster than my own. "It's a secret?"

His lips grazed the skin of my neck as I melted against his chest, gathering his warm shirt in my fist. Catcalls and loud laughter startled him away from me, and he straightened up, throwing a glare at a group of teenage boys who were walking past us.

"Come on. Let's spend those tickets. You promised me some rides." I said nervously, pulling away from him.

"Oh, I'll most definitely promise you a ride," he teased with a smirk, unaffected by getting interrupted.

"Keep it in your pants, Romeo. This is a family fair."

His fingers poked my ribs again, and I shrieked as he tried to resume tickling me.

Rory excitedly led me from one ride to the next before the sun set and the air-cooled off enough to be comfortable. Only four tickets remained when we finally stopped to get something to eat for dinner.

"Stop eating it like that," he groaned.

I swallowed the bite of the rich cornmeal in my mouth and frowned at where he was staring at me from across the table, his half-eaten burger abandoned.

"Like what?"

"With the pornographic noises," he sighed as he shook his head.

"What?" I mumbled as I licked the remnants of my meal from my lips.

"You keep making these throaty humming noises," he accused, looking uncomfortable.

"I do not." I took another bite and chewed the corn dog quietly.

"Well, you're not doing it now."

"I'm just over here innocently eating my dinner," I smiled.

"No." He pointed a finger at me. "You're over there doing something indecent to that poor corn dog."

"You jealous?" I teased, and his eyes widened.

"Yeah, maybe I am."

"Finish your food so we can ride the Ferris wheel. The lights are finally turned on," I changed the subject from his insistence I was creating real live food porn.

"They're not the only thing," he muttered as he raised an eyebrow in my direction.

My teeth worried my lip, and I threw one of my French fries at him. He picked it up, popping it in his mouth. "Thanks. These are good. I didn't want to assume we'd be sharing food yet."

"We shared an elephant ear earlier, you ding dong."

He held his hands up in front of him, looking chastised. "There's no reason for name-calling."

"You just can't help yourself, can you?" I shook my head.

"No, I can't," he grinned in response.

"Hmm," I smirked and continued to stare at him.

He leaned across the table, stealing another fry and shoving it into his big mouth. "Mmm."

The flashing lights of the midway, paired with the joyful and sometimes terrified shrieks of the riders, heightened the excitement as we approached the line for the Ferris wheel.

"You're not afraid of heights, are you?" he asked as he looked up at the large wheel.

"No. Are you?" I shook my head.

"Pfft. I'm not afraid of anything," he insisted.

"Yeah, okay, tough guy."

We'd crossed into some unspoken territory as Rory stepped in close behind me and loosely looped his long arms around my waist as we waited. Everything seemed natural with him. It was almost too good to be true. I kept waiting to find some fatal character flaw that'd make me question my attraction to him.

By the time we'd gotten to the front of the line, the tension that had been building between us all day had my blood humming. When the empty car stopped in front of us, I didn't hesitate to take his extended hand to climb in close beside him. One of his large hands gripped the metal edge of the car as his arm ran behind me. His other one absently played with my fingers as we jerked forward and started our climb into the sky.

"It cooled down quite a bit." His voice was quiet as he looked down at me with a lazy smile.

"Has it? Still feels pretty warm to me."

"Well, you are pretty hot," he teased with a wink.

"Those lines usually work for you?" I smiled as I shook my head.

"Typically. Not doing it for you?" His eyes followed the movement of my tongue as I wet my lips.

"I'm willing to overlook it," I shrugged.

"Is that so?" he smirked as he scooted in a little closer as the car swung on its ascent to the top.

"Mmhmm."

His fingers traced a maddening pattern along the bare skin of my neck, causing me to shudder. "You cold now? Make up your mind, woman."

"No, not cold," I breathed out as I took in a shuddering breath.

"Hmm, and what are you?"

As I watched his face come toward mine, achingly slowly, the words caught in my throat. His body jolted towards mine as the wheel stopped and the car rocked from its place at the top.

"I'm gonna kiss you," he murmured, his eyes darting between mine, giving me one last chance to back out.

"Then do it," I taunted.

The moment his lips touched mine, my entire body broke out in goosebumps. Neither of us noticed as the cars started moving again, taking the wheel back down and up again. I wasn't sure if the lights that danced beyond my eyelids were from the way his tongue stroked mine or the ride itself. When we finally came to a stop, I was dizzy and breathless, my lips tingling.

"You ready to get out of here?" he asked quietly as we walked away from the rides, both a little unsteady from that intense kiss. I don't think either one of us had expected it.

"Yeah."

His hand grasped mine as he silently tugged me out the exit and towards the parking lot. A tense quiet permeated the car as he drove toward campus, his thumb gently stroking the back of our joined hands on the center console.

The lights were off as the door swung open to my apartment. "Looks like Alison is gone."

That was all the encouragement Rory needed to spin me around, lift me, and have my back pressed to the wall. His foot kicked at the door until it slammed shut, and I laughed against his lips while he pressed himself against me, both hands clutching my ass.

"Stop laughing," he growled as he pressed into me, and I discovered he hadn't been joking about his size.

My skin buzzed as he kissed me until I couldn't breathe, throwing my head back with a thump and gasping for air.

"God dammit," He growled as I felt him shift and reach into his back pocket. Turns out the buzzing wasn't from him. It was his phone. He held it out to the side and looked at the screen, his grip on me loosening. "Shit."

"What? What's wrong?" I panted as I looked over at his face. He looked a little freaked out.

"I've gotta go." He lowered me to my feet and kissed me softly before he shoved his phone back into his pocket.

"What?" Was he just leaving?

"Family emergency. I've gotta go." The urgency in his voice startled me. He was serious.

"Wait, what's wrong?"

"It's my sister."

"Is she okay?" I asked quietly. He wasn't giving me much to go on.

"Yeah, they'll be fine," he nodded, but I could tell he was worried. "But I need to drive home tonight."

"This late?"

"Yeah..."

Thoroughly confused, I grabbed his hand as he tried to pull away from me. "Wait. When are you coming back?"

"I'm not sure. I'll be back before orientation training, but I need to get going," he told me quickly, squeezing my hand. "I'll text you when I get there."

Rory kissed my cheek one last time as he walked out the door, the click echoing in the dark apartment.

# Chapter Twenty-three:
## Summary Before Senior Year
### JULY

As July went on, the weather just kept getting hotter and hotter.

"Fuck, it's like the surface of the sun," I groaned as I pulled open the outer door of the building and was hit with a blast of warm air.

The air conditioning in the old psych building luckily managed to keep up, but I felt like I was melting on my walks home.

Things had been quiet since Rory left town. I wasn't sure how to take his radio silence. He'd texted me in the early hours of the next morning to tell me he'd arrived safely, but I hadn't heard from him since then.

Joel had been texting me often, but he, too, had largely been quiet. Maybe I had left things too long.

Kale had been flirty after work, but I still didn't know where I stood with him. The attraction was there, but I was more confused now than ever.

"Hey there, stranger." I stopped in my tracks as I looked up toward a voice I hadn't expected to hear.

"Joel! Hey." He pushed off the wall he'd been leaning on just outside the door to the psychology building. "Aren't you hot?"

"I don't know. Am I?"

Rolling my eyes at his playful answer, I took in the sweat beaded along his brow. He'd been waiting at least a little while.

"It's like a hundred degrees out here. How long have you been waiting?"

"Not long," he shrugged. "It felt good to stretch my legs after being stuck in the car."

"I thought you weren't coming back for a few more weeks." I wasn't arguing with the pleasant surprise, but I wasn't expecting it today.

"My schedule lightened up, and it wasn't worth waiting around for hours," he shrugged.

"You gonna try to find something part-time until school starts?"

"Maybe. I'm not sure yet," he smiled as he stepped closer to me. His skin had a deep tan that hadn't been there before he left for home. "I just needed out of that house. I forgot how loud it was."

"You live in an actual frat house," I laughed. The guys were loud. There was always something that set them off.

"Still quieter than my younger siblings," Joel smirked.

"But I bet you're never bored," I smiled, remembering how quiet my house had been after my older sister went off to college.

"I also never have privacy," he frowned. "And teenage boys are gross."

I started laughing, and he reached forward, tugging my bag off my shoulder and nodding for me to walk. "You used to be a teenage boy."

We set off along the sidewalk toward my apartment building. It was nice to have the company.

"And I was probably just as disgusting as my little brother." He made a face and shook his head. "Thank God I outgrew that stage."

"Did you?" I teased as I looked over at him.

"I don't think I've had a hot shower in a month," he frowned.

"You share a bathroom with them all?"

"No, but that little pervert took like five showers a day." The disgusted look on his face caused surprised laughter to erupt from my lips, and he scowled at me. "I don't know how the damn thing didn't fall off."

"I'm so glad I only have one uptight sister," I laughed. No worries of teen boys beating off in our shower.

"Oh, I have one of those, too." He smiled. I could see why he wanted away from them. Even in the house, he could go to their study room for privacy.

"So, school is like a vacation for you?"

"I'd rather be living in a house full of rowdy twenty-somethings than at home with the circus," he nodded.

"So, no moving home after graduation?" I teased.

"Nope. Not even close," he told me as he shook his head. "Thankfully, my GRE scores came back."

"How'd you do?"

"Three nineteen combined," he shrugged, but I could tell he was proud of his performance. Those were solid scores.

"So, you're not just a pretty face," I teased as I punched in the code for the front door to my building.

"Well, I am that, too," he laughed as he tried to flutter his eyelashes.

"So modest."

"Have you taken the exam yet?"

I shook my head as he followed me toward the stairs. "I'm scheduled to take it in September. Application deadline for next year is the beginning of December."

"I can give you my prep books," he offered. "Rory should be done with them by now. He was supposed to take the test a few weeks ago."

"Look at us, all acting like responsible adults," I mused nervously, trying not to think about him mentioning Rory.

"Who would've guessed?" Joel laughed, and I smiled at him.

"And Tyler thought you two idiots wouldn't graduate."

"Tyler was wrong about a lot of things," he told me as his face turned serious. "Douche."

"He is ancient history," I laughed as I thought about how ill-matched we'd been. "God, I had horrible taste."

"I dated Gretchen," Joel laughed. He had me beat with those three words.

"After Rory, at that. You win."

We both chuckled as we headed up the stairs to my floor. "Can we blame them on the mistakes of youth?"

"Probably. The more important question is if we learned from our mistakes."

His comment made me pause. Was I still making the same mistakes?

Joel had given me time to figure out my life. I felt more conflicted now than I had on Valentine's Day. I'd dated as he told me to, but now I was less sure of what I wanted. My feelings for Kale were unexplored. Rory fell off the grid after a night I still wasn't convinced was real. Maybe the answer had been right in front of me all this time.

"Jury is still out," I shrugged.

"Anything I can do to speed up the final verdict?" he asked curiously, his hand grazing mine.

"Not play off of stupid legal puns?" I smiled as I looked up at him.

"Fair enough," he laughed as he lingered in the doorway to my bedroom.

"You can come in," I told him, taking in his tense body language.

"I didn't want to assume," he told me quietly. I appreciated that he let me lead, but I felt like neither of us was sure how to act.

"You don't have to tiptoe around me, Joel. I thought we were friends."

"We are."

"But?" I asked curiously. He was still holding back from me. I had screwed this all up.

"I'm not sure how to act around you without pushing you," he admitted, his voice soft.

"Act like yourself. You don't have to walk on eggshells. If you cross the line, I'll tell you."

"The line keeps moving," he said sadly.

"I'm sorry. I know you've been patient with me, which I appreciate more than you know." I nodded absently, suddenly nervous.

"But you're still not ready," he sighed.

"I might be." I shook my head as I looked over at his cautious gaze. "I don't know."

"Maybe I should go. Get settled. We can catch up another time. I know I didn't give you a choice, just showing up as I did," Joel said nervously as he stepped away from me.

"Please don't go." I wasn't ready for him to leave yet. Things had been left unresolved between us for months.

He was quiet as he nodded and sat down beside me on the edge of the futon. "Tell me what to do here."

As I looked up to his patient, honest, boyishly handsome, compassionate face, I realized that to know if I was truly ready, I had to trust him enough to catch me if I stumbled.

"Kiss me."

He still hesitated as he scooted closer, his leg brushing mine as we continued to do the dance of will they or won't they. "Are you sure? I'm not pulling back anymore if we do this."

"Joel..."

Grasping my hand in his, he held it to his chest as he looked down at me. "I'm serious. I know I've been hovering for the last few months, but after being away from you for the last month..."

"I know this is what I want," he told me, his voice full of conviction.

"It's what I want, too," I admitted quietly. The feelings I'd pushed away for him were still there, lingering under the surface, no matter how hard I tried to hide them.

"Please." The pleading quality of my voice didn't escape me, but I think he was just as eager to see where things between us would go.

"Are you...?"

"Stop asking me if I'm sure and kiss me. I'm sure. Please. Just..." His lips cut off my huff with gentle pressure, his tongue coaxing my lips to open achingly slowly as he leaned me back against the futon. My heart was hammering frantically as he hovered over me, kissing me until I couldn't think straight.

"God, you're gorgeous," he sighed as he pushed a few strands of hair away from my face.

"I never thought we'd get here," he murmured before his lips descended again and kissed a trail from my ear to my collarbone that made my entire body tingle. A surprised gasp erupted from his lips as I yanked his shirt from where it'd been loosely tucked into his shorts.

"Let me make you feel good." His breathless plea as he stilled my hands had me pulling his face up so I could look him in the eyes.

"I want to make you feel good, too." One of my hands dropped to his button, and I flicked it open before his hand stopped me and refastened it.

"Not now. Please."

I nodded, and he pushed my shirt up, his hands reaching around to unfasten the clasp on my bra. "I've been thinking about this for months. I want to see you."

Soft lips and tongue swept along the swells of my breasts. His fingers traced my abdomen, teasing me. I moaned as he finally pulled my nipple into his mouth. He laved it with his tongue before a jolt of pleasure ripped through me at the sensation of his teeth lightly tugging.

I arched my back, writhing against his leg as he pulled my shirt over my head. Leaning forward, I shrugged out of my bra and dropped it to the carpet. His hands were warm as they cupped my bare skin, his covered hardness grinding into the soft material of my shorts.

"Mmm..." he hummed into my overheated skin as he sucked and plucked and drove me closer and closer to the edge. The gentle pulses of his hips combined with the voracity of his mouth overwhelmed me to the point of no return. I crashed headlong into an intense climax, pulsing as I rocked against him.

"Oh, my God. What was that?" My voice was breathless as I panted against his cheek. He smiled into my hair as he kissed my ear.

"That was hot. That's what that was."

Wanting him to feel that same pleasure, I reached for his shorts and unfastened the button again before his hand closed around mine. "Later. I'm fine."

"But I..." His head turned, and his lips captured mine in another slow, sensual dance that almost made me forget my name, much less what I'd been trying to do.

Climbing into his lap, I ground myself against him, nipping at his lower lip before he threw his head back and groaned. I could feel him hard beneath me, pushing insistently against me with every swivel of my hips.

It'd been months since I was this intimate with another person, and I desperately wanted to explore this connection with him. I'd made him wait months, and it wasn't like we were strangers.

"Fuck," he groaned as I slid myself against him, his hands clamped on the sides of my hips, encouraging my movements. I could work with this. I could still make him feel good with our clothes on.

Leaning forward, I placed opened-mouthed sensual kisses against the side of his neck, encouraged by the way his hips sprung up as I moved against him.

As I sucked against his pulse point—not hard enough to leave a mark—he groaned and shuddered underneath me.

He panted as I leaned back, sensually rubbing myself against him, arching my back as he held me in place. "Fuck, keep going."

I nodded as I moved faster, bracing my hands on his strong thighs behind me. His eyes were hooded as he watched me, the intense gaze he held me in only briefly flickering down to my exposed chest as he licked his lips.

The way he watched me was turning me on, the smooth fabric covering me sliding against my wetness and pushing me towards another intense release. Despite the clothing separating us, I felt connected to him in a way I'd never expected.

As I looked into his eyes, I felt myself fall apart again, my head thrown back as I convulsed against him. His fingers dug into my hips as he threw his head back and found his release, a loud groan filling the air.

I was terrified to let myself fall for someone again, but I trusted Joel not to lead me astray. That would have to be enough, because the future was never certain.

# Chapter Twenty-four:
## Senior Year
### AUGUST

*Rory: Do you hate me?*

The text message that came through as I wandered around the university bookstore was completely unexpected. Not knowing how to broach the subject of my date with Rory, I hadn't told Joel yet. I wasn't sure if he needed to know. They had been friends since high school, and I didn't want to be the reason they had a falling out.

*Kendall: No.*

*Rory: Not going to talk to me?*

*Kendall: It's been a month. Not sure what to say. A lot has changed.*

*Rory: ...*

*Rory: You put him out of his misery?*

Things over the last few weeks with Joel had been good. We went on dates, and we watched movies. I got to know him better in a different way than when we'd been friends.

He made me laugh, and he was kind. Joel made me feel valued in a way that Dylan hadn't. Despite Kale trying to plant the seed of doubt, Joel told me he hadn't been physical with the girls he'd dated since the one after Gretchen. I found it kind of adorable that he didn't want to rush things between us, so we'd not moved much past the kissing and groping stage.

*Kendall: You make it sound like I killed him.*

*Rory: ...*

It bothered me that I'd pushed Rory to the back of my mind, but I couldn't wait around forever. We'd been on one amazing date, but he had shown no interest past that.

*Rory: Can we talk? I feel like I owe you an explanation.*

*Kendall: ...*

*Rory: I wanted to apologize.*

*Rory: In person.*

Talking to him wouldn't change my mind about Joel, but Rory was my friend. I owed him the chance to clear the air. We couldn't let the events of one day destroy our relationship. He was going to be around if I was seriously dating Joel.

*Kendall: It's not going to change anything.*

I wanted it to be clear to him I had made my decision. For a hot minute, I'd felt connected to him in more than a friendly way, but that moment had passed, and I was moving forward. I didn't feel like my date with him was a mistake, but it was over, and we'd both moved on.

*Rory: ...*

*Rory: I know.*

Rushing around the store to find the rest of my textbooks, I felt simultaneously guilty and curious about what he needed to say.

He looked tired when I sat down across from him in a coffee shop a few doors down from the bookstore.

"Hey." His voice was quiet, and I could tell he felt just as awkward about this as I did.

"Hi."

He stared down at his coffee cup, picking at the paper sleeve, an untouched muffin on a plate next to him.

"Did you just..." I started.

"I'm sorry that..."

Nervous laughter rose out of both of us as we stopped talking over each other.

"Go ahead," he nodded as he took a deep breath and looked at me with a curious expression.

"No, it's okay," I shook my head. "You wanted to talk, you go."

I hadn't even been completely sure what I wanted to say to him. It didn't seem like any of my questions were relevant anymore.

"I..." He scrubbed his hand over the top of his head, making his longer than usual hair stick up on end.

"You don't owe me an explanation," I told him quietly. It'd been over a month since I heard from him last, and things had changed a lot in his absence. He didn't owe me anything.

"Yeah. I do," he sighed. I felt bad that he seemed so withdrawn around me, but he'd created this situation with his silence.

"Here." He unlocked his phone and set it on the table in front of me.

A picture of a tiny little girl in a pink knit cap was on the screen. I recognized Rory's watch on the wrist of the arm supporting her small, little body. "Oh, wow. Is this...?"

"My niece," he smiled, his adoration clear as he looked down at the picture proudly.

"That was the family emergency," I whispered, the reasons for his quick exit from my apartment becoming clearer. I hadn't even known that his sister was pregnant.

"Yeah. I kept meaning to text you or try to call, but she was late and huge. They ended up having to do an emergency c-section."

"Is your sister alright?" I knew women had c-sections all the time, but he fell off the face of the planet. I was worried that maybe something had happened to her to cause his radio silence.

"Yeah. She's fine," he nodded with a small smile. "But her husband had to go back to work after a few days, and I stayed to help."

I looked back down at the little girl in the picture, wrapped in a little polka dot blanket and a pink hat with a little butterfly embroidered on the front.

"She's adorable. Congratulations, Uncle Rory."

The smile he gave me spoke of how much he cared for her already. "Thank you. She will be a handful, but I was glad to help. My sister wasn't allowed to lift her for the first few weeks."

"What's her name?"

"Nathalie," he sighed as he swiped his finger and brought up another picture of him holding her. The radiant smile on his face tugged at my heartstrings. He adored her, and it was clear by how he looked at her. I wanted someone to look at my babies like that in the future.

"Aw, that's cute," I gushed as I glanced up at him. He was smiling at me with a little twinkle in his eye.

"They kinda named her middle name after me."

"Well, don't keep me in suspense," I laughed.

"Nathalie Aurora Fields," he said proudly.

"Oh, my God," I breathed as I looked over at him.

He pointed at me as I giggled at her middle name. "No. Don't even think about it."

"Oh, come on, Aurora," I teased as I observed his cheeks turning a little pink.

"You are NOT allowed to call me Aurora," he said firmly as he picked his phone back up from where I'd placed it on the table between us.

"Then why did you tell me that? I won't be able to help myself," I giggled. I'd missed the teasing banter. It felt familiar, but I knew that I'd have to keep it platonic.

"Stop laughing," he frowned at me as he leaned back in his chair, looking a little less tense, but still guarded around me. I think it was hard for him to know where the boundaries were.

"Nope, it'll be okay." I shook my head as I smirked at him, a little laugh slipping out. "Aurora."

He smiled as I tried to calm my laughter. I was so going to keep this to use against him.

A few weeks ago, I thought he'd dropped off the face of the planet. Now, I felt horrible that I hadn't tried to contact him. His silence wasn't because he wasn't interested. He had more important things going on in his life than some short-term summer romance. Things would never have worked out with us, right?

"I'm sorry I didn't text you. I guess I could have, too," I apologized quietly.

"Yeah, it was kind of bad timing, huh?" he smiled sadly.

Nodding, I swallowed hard. We both just looked at each other for a few moments across the table, a tense silence permeating the air.

"So, Joel?" he asked, his posture straightening up, a wall sliding into place between us.

"Yeah."

He looked back down at his cup at my nod, and I had difficulty reading his face. "He's a good guy."

"He is," I agreed. Now that I'd finally let Joel in, he'd confirmed my assumptions that it'd be easy to fall for him.

"He's my best friend. I'd never want to hurt him," Rory assured me as he pinned me down with a serious look. I wasn't sure if he was referring to me hurting his friend or his attraction to me.

"I know you wouldn't," I nodded. Rory wasn't the type to pursue someone who was taken. We'd both been burned by cheaters before and respected others too much for that.

"I knew he liked you, but nothing ever seemed to happen between the two of you," he mumbled.

"He was giving me space to be ready to date," I nodded. Neither of us had shared the details with anyone about why we weren't together, but on the outside, I could see how Rory would perceive that Joel and I weren't interested in each other.

"That's why he went on those bullshit dates," Rory laughed lightly.

Frowning, I motioned for him to continue. "What are you talking about?"

"He went on one date with those girls and never went on another. I thought he was playing hard to get or something when a few of them asked why he ghosted them, but..." He held his hand out to gesture toward me.

"Oh." I'd thought Joel wanted to go on dates with them to give me space, not because he was trying to fulfill some requirement he perceived I'd set up for him.

"I guess I should have known. He didn't want the guys at the house to talk about you after that shit went down with Dylan." Rory shrugged. "He even told Tyler to stay the hell away from you."

Nervous laughter bubbled out of me. I hadn't realized that Joel had done that.

"I mean, I never liked you with Ty anyway, but..."

"My God, you guys are like a bunch of kids," I rolled my eyes. "I'm not some toy to fight over."

"That's not how it was," he told me sincerely, shaking his head. "He was just trying to protect you."

"Still."

He took a deep breath and ran his hand over the top of his head. "I won't say anything to him."

"Shouldn't I?" I asked quietly. I was still torn about whether I needed to be upfront with Joel about this.

"Kendall, it was one date," Rory sighed. "I mean, it was kinda fucking amazing, but…"

"Yeah," I said lamely, feeling a little hurt at how he was downplaying it. But dwelling on it wouldn't change things.

"I'm not gonna pretend that I didn't develop feelings for you, but if you're with him…"

I waited for him to respond, but he just continued to pick at the cardboard sleeve on his cup.

"Joel doesn't need to know about it. Nothing else happened."

If he hadn't gotten that call, I couldn't promise that things would have stopped at kissing, but it was in the past. Rory was right. It'd just cause unnecessary drama.

"I'm sorry," I whispered. I hated that he seemed a little sad when he looked at me now.

"I'm not trying to make you feel bad, Ken. I just wanted to clear the air," he admitted, and I respected he wanted to put all our cards on the table. "You don't have to worry about me causing problems with Joel."

I slowly reached my hand across the table and covered his. "Thank you."

The timing sucked, and my unresolved feelings for Rory might always be in the back of my mind, but I'd chosen Joel, and I was happy with him. I was determined to give this new relationship a real chance because I was already falling for him. Destroying the trust I'd built with him for something that'd happened before we got together wasn't worth the risk.

# Chapter Twenty-five:
## Senior Year
### NOVEMBER

"Are you sure that they don't mind me coming with you?" Joel asked quietly as he squeezed my denim-covered knee.

"They wouldn't have asked me to invite you if they weren't. You need to calm down." His eyes flitted over to me once more before he looked back to the road. He was so worried about meeting my family. It would be adorable if he didn't get himself so worked up about it.

"Your parents know I'm nothing like Dylan, right?" I cringed at the mention of my ex-boyfriend, but I knew he was nothing like him. My parents had always found Dylan a little arrogant, but they'd known him since he was a little kid. It's hard to see the adult people have turned into when you still remember the child. In his case, he didn't get better with age.

"Dylan is not an issue, trust me. They still won't socialize with his parents. I feel kind of bad, but they knew something was going on with Lisa before we ever broke up." When my mother had told me Dylan's mother confessed to meeting Lisa before I called it off with him, that cemented the end of their friendship.

"Well, I just want them to know how much I care about you," he confessed quietly. I shifted in my seat and hugged his arm, laying my head on his shoulder. He had nothing to worry about.

"Are you sure your parents aren't mad that I stole you away for Thanksgiving?" With how big his tight-knit family was, I'd been worried that his mother would hate me for changing his plans to return home. After his summer of cold showers, he wasn't too keen on spending an extended weekend sharing a bathroom with his younger brother.

"My mom was disappointed, but I think she's got her hands full right now. My nineteen-year-old sister wanted to bring her boyfriend home, so she let me off the hook," he sighed as he briefly leaned his head against mine. "Although she mentioned maybe you need to come to visit over Christmas break."

My heart sped at the thought of meeting his large family. Joel was one of five, the second oldest, and I was intimidated at the thought of meeting his mom and older sister. He talked to them regularly, and Joel had confessed that he had never brought a girl home. Not even in High School. "No pressure or anything."

"It'll be fine. My sister already asks about you when I call. She's eager to meet you."

I cringed as I looked up at him. "Hopefully, it's not a letdown."

"Are you kidding? She's excited to have another adult female around. My younger sister has reached that obnoxious stage where she thinks she knows everything about everything. When Andrea was visiting this summer, I thought the two of them were going to go wrestle in the yard over politics."

"Speaking of... Let's leave that subject elsewhere. Nothing good ever comes from talking politics at family gatherings."

"I couldn't agree more," he smiled as he kissed the top of my head. We still had another hour until we got to my parent's house. I hoped Joel would relax a little once we got there, but he still seemed tense.

"Any other topics that I need to avoid?" he laughed.

I thought about it for a moment. There wasn't much that was off-limits in our house. My parents were both open-minded people.

"Don't ask my sister's boyfriend, Duke, about fishing. You might risk death by boredom. Other than that, I think we're good."

"They won't think I'm an alcoholic for bringing wine, will they?" Joel asked as he pulled out the brown paper bag we'd gotten from the liquor store. We'd just pulled into my parent's driveway and parked beside my sister, Sara's, car.

"You have got to calm down. It's my mom's favorite. She'll probably thank you for bringing it once my sister drinks all of her stash."

"Maybe your family are the alcoholics," he laughed as he pulled my bag out of the trunk, trying to juggle both bags and the wine.

"Maybe," I smirked. The only time they drank was during holidays, but sometimes it was a lot.

"You know I can carry my bag," I teased as I watched Joel struggle to balance everything. He frowned and handed the wine to me as he shifted the bags to one hand. I rolled my eyes that he wouldn't let me carry anything else, but loved how much of a gentleman he was.

"I'm trying to make a good impression here," he laughed nervously as we approached the front door.

Before I could plan a response, my mom was yanking the door open with a bright smile on her face. Her eyes cut to Joel, and they lit up. Uh oh... that was the hugging face. "You guys made great time. I'm so glad you're here!"

"Calm down, Leanne," my dad laughed from behind her, pulling her back out of the doorway and holding open the storm door so we could come into the house.

"Take those bags from him, Gary," she gestured as Joel swung them back slightly. My dad was trying to steal his thunder.

"I, uh, I can carry them, Mrs. Grant, I don't mind. If you'll show me which rooms we're in," Joel stumbled over his words a little as his cheeks turned pink. It was quite the change from the slightly cocky attitude he had at school sometimes.

"Oh, psh, Joel," she dismissed with a wave of her hand. "Sara and Duke are in the guest room. You two can share Kendall's."

That was new. My dad wouldn't even let Dylan stay in my room. I gave him a curious look, and he shrugged his shoulders as he nodded toward the staircase.

"You're a guest here, Joel, at least for this visit. Gary can take those bags up for you. Kendall, why don't you come to introduce your young man to Sara."

Joel shot a panicked look back at me as my dad relieved him of the bags. We'd talked about this a few days ago; I fully expected my parents to put him in the den on the pullout couch. I never in a million years expected my parents to put him in my bedroom. At least they'd traded in the two twin beds for a queen once Sara left for college.

"It'll be fine. Just go with it," I whispered as I tugged him toward the living room at the back of the house. My sister was harmless, and Duke would talk to anyone. I was just happy my dad didn't drag him upstairs to have a 'talk.' He'd never been the 'don't mess with my daughter' type, but he'd also never let a boy sleep in my room.

"Ken! Finally!" my sister exclaimed as she crossed the room, the white wine in her glass sloshing dangerously.

"Hi, Sara," I greeted with a big smile, glancing over at Joel, who was standing slightly behind me. *Sorry, bud. There's no protection from my sister.*

"You must be Joel," she smiled as she sidestepped me and pulled him into a hug. The poor guy looked at me again with a nervous smile, awkwardly patting her back.

"Nice to meet you, Sara," he told her, clearing his throat and holding out his hand when she pulled away. He normally wasn't this awkward around people, but he'd also never done the whole meet the family thing either. She looked down and ignored his hand, grabbing him by the elbow.

"Duke was just about to tell Dad about the bluegill he pulled in on his last boys' trip," she smiled as she looked back to her funny, but weirdly obsessed with fishing, boyfriend.

"Abort, abort," I whispered in his direction and then smiled at my sister. "I think we're going to go get cleaned up and rest a little. We had papers due all week, so we're a little burned out."

I didn't give her a chance to argue as I turned and tugged Joel towards the stairs, hoping my dad was gone. We saw the coward hiding from Duke with my mom as we passed the kitchen.

"Hey, I was just opening a fresh bottle," my mom hollered as she saw us trying to sneak away. She held up a wine bottle and gestured to the empty glasses sitting on the kitchen island.

"Here." I pushed the brown paper bag in my hand into Joel's, and his eyes widened. "Go, peace offering. Might buy us some time."

"I uh... got you a bottle of your favorite, Mrs. Grant, for letting me stay for the holiday," Joel stuttered as he held the bag out towards my mom. She flashed him an extremely large smile and took it from him, her eyes lighting up as she peeked inside.

"Oh, I like you, Joel," she smiled as she placed it on the island and came around the corner, pulling him into a hug. "No more of this Mrs. Grant business, call me Leanne."

He nodded as she pulled back. The poor guy was getting hugged all over the place.

"Mom, we're going to go up to my room for a bit. It's been a long week," I told her as I grabbed Joel's hand and started backing toward the kitchen door.

"Oh, of course," she smiled as she looked between the two of us. "Go get a little rest. We're going to do pizza tonight since we'll all be up early tomorrow."

My dad raised an eyebrow but didn't say anything as we retreated toward the stairs.

"Leave the door open, Kendall," he yelled as we were halfway up, and Joel stopped.

"He's joking," I rolled my eyes as I tugged his hand again.

Then I heard my mom scold him, embarrassingly. "Gary, leave them alone. They're adults, and it's perfectly normal for them to be sharing a bed."

Joel was full out laughing by the time we reached my room, but I was glad my goofy parents had gotten him to loosen up a little.

"Sorry about them," I apologized as I closed the door behind us.

He stepped forward and slipped his arms around my back, kissing my forehead as I looked up at him. "They're fine. Your family is nice, but thanks for the save in there with Duke."

I faked a shudder and cringed. "No one should have to sit through that."

"You up for a nap?" I asked as I stepped backward toward the bed.

"Shouldn't we leave the door open?" he teased as he leaned down and kissed along the side of my neck.

"Nope," I laughed. "Didn't you hear? My mom says we're adults."

Pulling away from him, I pulled down the comforter and kicked off my shoes before I climbed into the bed. Joel was right behind me, pulling me into his chest and tucking my head under his chin as I settled against him.

"I love you, Kendall," he whispered as I fell asleep.

"Mmm, me too," I responded quietly. Despite his nerves, I had a feeling this would be a pleasant break from our studies. Being home for a break always made me feel recharged.

"Wake up," Joel's low voice in my ear roused me from the deep sleep I'd fallen into once we got back to my apartment. The visit to my parent's house had been good, but I think we'd both been exhausted from midterms before our brief break. Add the stress of a formal boyfriend introduction, and we were both on edge.

I was so proud that Joel had opened up and seemed to fit well into my family. My parents loved how attentive he was, and Sara liked his sarcastic humor. After the initial introductions, the awkwardness was gone. The wine and conversation flowed freely on Thanksgiving Day, and the next morning we'd headed back to campus, ready for our last few weeks of classes.

"Mmmm..." I hummed as I rolled over to face him. His hair was sticking up, but he'd gotten redressed since we went to bed. "What's going on?"

He smiled as he leaned down and kissed my forehead. I could barely make out the faint smile on his face with the glow from the streetlamp that streamed through the blinds on my window. "Get up and get dressed. It's snowing."

"What time is it?" I asked with a yawn as I squinted towards the digital clock on my drawing desk. The numbers read 3:05, but it was still dark out. What was he doing in the middle of the night? "Why are you awake?"

"I couldn't sleep. I went to get a drink in the kitchen and noticed it was snowing," he shrugged. Studying his face for a moment, I smiled and nodded, humoring his apparent need to play in the snow in the middle of the night. We'd gotten flurries on the car ride home, but this was the first actual snow of the season. It was still amazing how quiet the campus seemed when it snowed. It was like all the chaos had stopped for that one beautiful moment. Then it all turned to slush the next day.

"Don't you want to try to sleep for a few hours and then go out?" I was still tired, but if he was insistent, he knew I'd go with him.

"Please," he whispered as he leaned forward, his elbows on either side of my head on the pillow, pressing his nose to mine. "I just want to go for a walk."

"No throwing snowballs at me," I warned, pursing my lips. Joel smiled and leaned in, kissing me softly before he leaned back.

"I promise I won't throw any snowballs at you," he assured as he sat up and then leaned down to pull on his boots. "Ten minutes, hurry and put on something warm."

"Ugh, fine. But you owe me breakfast after this," I groaned as I sat up and stretched my arms above my head.

"Of course," he smiled as he kissed my cheek and stood up. "I'll get the coffee going."

"Now you're speaking my love language," I laughed as I rolled myself off the bed, letting out a huge yawn.

Ten minutes later, Joel and I walked hand in hand down the sidewalk toward campus, the light of the streetlamps glowing off the freshly fallen snow. It was still coming down, but the wind had stopped, so it settled softly on the ground, looking quite ethereal.

Joel had been quiet, but I don't think either of us was completely awake, him not having gotten much sleep and me being woken up in the middle of the night.

I knew he had trouble sleeping sometimes, but he typically never woke me. I also slept like a rock once I was out.

As we crossed the side street that led to campus, I looked over to him, watching the snowflakes accumulate on his hair. He still never wore a hat outside, men were just like that sometimes, but I'd given up on teasing him about it. Joel had a soft smile on his face, and I was glad that some of the stress of midterms and the impending end of the semester had melted away for him in the last few days.

For the first time since we'd started dating, I felt secure knowing that I'd made the right decision. We just fit. His sarcasm and caring nature fit in well with my anxiousness and the need to plan for every contingency. He didn't mind that I worried too much or over thought every decision, just patiently waited for me to figure things out. I loved that he never criticized how I handled things, and he always kept his promises. If Joel told you something, he stuck to it, sometimes to a fault.

"Want to sit down?" he asked quietly as we approached the familiar bench where we'd landed on Valentine's Day last year, when I was still questioning my ability to be in a relationship. If I knew how effortless it'd be to fall for him, I might not have dragged my feet so long.

"Do we have an itinerary for this middle-of-the-night excursion, or are you just flying by the seat of your pants here?" I teased as I watched him wipe the planks of the bench clear with his bare hand. His fingers were icy when he grabbed my hand, and I squeezed it as I took my seat.

"I just wanted to enjoy this before classes start again tomorrow," he told me in a quiet voice. He played with my fingers as we watched the snowfall in the beam of the streetlamp across from us, softly covering everything in sight. It'd probably all be gone tomorrow, pushed aside when the groundskeepers cleared the sidewalks in a few hours for the students.

"Alright," I answered softly as I looked over at him. He shoved his other hand into his coat pocket, which was odd for him since he was never really bothered by the cold.

"Do you ever think about the future, after graduation?" he asked quietly after a few moments. I turned and looked over at him, noting his guarded eyes despite the small smile pulling at his lips.

"Me? Think about the future? Never," I joked as I shook my head. "Of course, I do. Have you met me?"

"Do you see me there?" he inquired, his blue eyes searching mine.

Letting out a soft sigh, I squeezed his hand and brought my other to his scruffy cheek, wiping away a few stray flakes that'd landed there. "How could I imagine a future without you in it?"

Tears appeared in my eyes as I watched his entire posture change, his smile widening as he sat up straighter. He pulled his hand out of his pocket and opened his palm, a small gold band with a diamond solitaire sparkling in the dim light.

"Oh," my breath caught as a thrill raced up my spine. We'd talked about marriage in the abstract, but it'd always been something for the future, after graduation. We'd only been together for four and a half months, wasn't it too soon?

"Marry me?" he whispered as he leaned forward and pressed his forehead to mine.

The words caught in my throat as I swallowed hard and stared into his eyes. I was scared, not because I didn't love him, but because I was afraid that things would all disappear like they had the last time. Marriage had been a little tainted for me when things fell apart with Dylan. It meant being vulnerable enough to trust someone to take care of my heart.

"Kendall?" he whispered as he pulled back and looked at me closely.

"Okay," I whispered, my voice thick. A small nod was all I could manage, but I felt the tension in my throat ease as he took a deep breath and picked up my left hand, sliding the solitaire over the tip of my ring finger. This ring was much different from the one Dylan had picked out, but I think that's why I loved it so much, because Joel had picked it for me. I hadn't even realized that he'd been thinking about taking this step.

"Yes?" he asked again as he hesitated halfway, the ring hovering above my knuckle.

"Yes," I breathed, a tear trickling down my cheek as he pushed it firmly into place. Blowing out a shaky breath, I leaned forward and met him halfway, my lips softly melding with his in a kiss.

I hadn't expected this when he'd dragged me out of my apartment in the middle of the night, but this was an amazing way to celebrate the first snow of the winter, just us, watching it fall, knowing our futures would be intertwined.

# Chapter Twenty-six:
## Senior Year

### APRIL

Joel was completely engrossed in his computer screen as I crept up behind him.

"Hey, you." He startled when I placed my hands over his eyes and pushed the lid of the laptop closed.

"Hey." His voice sounded nervous as he placed his hands over the top of mine.

"How's your paper going?" I knew he'd been working hard to get his term paper done for one of his musculature and anatomy classes. Senior-level classes were more difficult for both of us, so we'd been hit-or-miss spending time together between school commitments and wedding planning.

"Oh. I finished it," he sighed as he looked back over his shoulder at me.

"You didn't respond to my text earlier. Did you have time to look at the pictures for the centerpieces?" Joel's fingers pulled mine down, and he spun in his chair, cupping his hands on the backs of my thighs.

"I didn't. I'm sorry. You know you'll just end up picking the one you like, anyway."

He rested his head sideways on my stomach, and I combed my fingers through his hair. It needed to be cut, but he'd been busy studying for finals and papers for the last several weeks.

I'd been busy finalizing all the wedding stuff and making sure everything was on track for the senior Fine Arts exhibit.

After Joel's spontaneous proposal after Thanksgiving, our plans had been put on steroids. And of course, we were insane because we'd jumped on a cancellation opening at a local country club for this summer when we'd looked at venues around campus. My parents had wanted us to wait longer, but Joel didn't want to wait for another year.

"Hey, I let you pick the colors," I teased.

"After I vetoed purple," he laughed as his fingers slipped underneath the hem of my shirt and caressed the skin of my lower back.

"It would've looked nice with the green," I insisted. We still had a few touches of purple in the flower arrangements but had switched gears on the overall color scheme.

"But the navy looks better," he smiled as he looked up at me.

"It is very masculine," I chuckled at the proud look on his face. He hadn't wanted the wedding to look "too girly," so we'd chosen the more neutral sage green and navy blue as the dominant colors. I thought he would look very handsome in his navy-blue suit.

"Just like me." The sarcasm in his voice was strong. I hated it when he put himself down. This seemed to be a common occurrence lately, and I wasn't sure how to comfort him.

"Stop it." I knelt in front of him and cupped his jaw in my palms, forcing him to look at me. He downcast his eyes, and the pain in them sometimes broke my heart.

"You know I love you no matter what, right?" I insisted. I wasn't letting this minor hiccup in our lives define us. I'd committed to him, and I was in this for the long haul.

"I know," he responded quietly, but he still refused to look me in the eye.

"Please talk to me. I don't know how to help you," I pleaded. He had been so down lately, and I wasn't sure how to stop it. With only a few weeks left of school, I was hoping the reduced stress would help, but then with the wedding, the honeymoon, and grad school starting in the fall, it didn't seem like we'd be having a break anytime soon.

"I'm just stressed. All these papers and no sleep are getting to me. I don't know how I'm going to make it to final exams."

My hand ran up the soft material of his athletic pants. I felt a stirring as I reached the apex of his thighs, but his hand stopped mine, nonetheless.

"It might help. Relieve a little stress, and it may clear your head." I pushed up on my knees and drew his head towards mine, nipping at his ear. A frustrated groan rang out, and I knew he was going to shut me out again.

"Please stop. I... I just can't right now."

"I know what you like. Please..." I hated feeling like I begged him all the time. Early in the physical part of our relationship, it became clear that my sex drive was much higher than his. At the time, I hadn't known the cause. After he'd come down with the flu a few weeks before spring break, it'd only gotten progressively worse.

"We can try the gel again. It worked last time," I whispered in his ear as I placed soft kisses behind it.

"Kendall... just..." His fingers loosely grasped my shoulders and pushed me backward.

I sighed, frustrated that he was shutting me out again. "What's wrong?"

"They sent some of my test results over today." Joel had gone home over spring break and had some tests done. He was worried that his condition was affecting our sex life, and it frustrated him when he thought he was letting me down.

He knew I didn't mind when he had problems. He'd never left me unsatisfied with his tongue or his fingers. It was the other part I missed sometimes.

"What did they say?" I could tell it wasn't good news from the look on his face, and I braced myself for the results.

"It wasn't anything I didn't expect. My testosterone levels are low, but not low enough to do the injections," he sighed.

"I thought the gel was working," I asked quietly. He'd had to use testosterone gel to help maintain his arousal lately. The stress and low hormones in his body had made things difficult for him sometimes, and when it happened, his mood just got worse, which made the condition worse. It was like a never-ending cycle of frustration for him, and I just had to sit back and try to be supportive.

"It does, but I know it gave you the rash last time." He'd been practically traumatized when I had to get a steroid cream to help because my skin had reacted to the gel we were using.

"It wasn't that big of a deal. We'll figure this out," I assured. One brief hiccup wouldn't turn me off. This was just something we were going to have to figure out.

He shook his head and avoided eye contact. "You shouldn't have to figure it out, Kendall. We're twenty-two, and I'm broken. Do you think this is going to get better over time? It's only going to get worse."

"Joel, stop. Please. I love you regardless of all this. I fell for you before I knew about this, and that will not change."

"Until we're forty and childless and your husband has a dick that doesn't work."

The shock at the tone of voice caused me to sit back heavily on my heels. "You don't know that."

"Really? Because the doctor says otherwise," he explained, grasping my waist and lifting me off him.

"What? What did he say?" I asked, worried about these mysterious test results that he'd received.

"That I'm probably infertile." My heart started beating faster as he wrenched up the lid on his laptop. "Right here… let's see. It says, 'Low motility. The sample has a low sperm count, and the sperm visible are malformed. Probable cause: 'low testosterone because of congenital disability.'"

Joel had been reluctant to become physical with me at the beginning of our relationship early on, always trying to focus our intimacy on me or start things without getting completely naked. I hadn't thought much of it until he'd finally suggested taking our relationship further.

The reason he'd been reluctant to undress or let me touch him was that he was born with a congenital disability in his genital region. He was missing a testicle. It hadn't been a problem in his younger days, but as he got older, he'd had issues with performance.

"Say something."

My head snapped up, and my eyes widened at the open look of devastation on his face. "We'll"…

"Stop. Just stop. You always say we'll figure this out. This is me. Something is wrong with me. You can't fix this by being supportive," he practically yelled.

"I'm not trying to," I whispered as I tried to process what was going on.

"You've told me you want kids," he said in a quieter voice as he looked at me with so much pain visible on his handsome features. I hated he was struggling like this.

"I do." My voice was just a whisper between us because he knew I'd never lie to him. I wanted kids. He'd said he wanted them, too.

"And what happens if these tests are as good as it gets?" He asked, gesturing to the email pulled up on his laptop.

"We'll just keep trying. God, Joel, we aren't even ready to have kids yet. Isn't this something to worry about in the future?" I asked in a pained voice. For once, being positive wouldn't fix this. "We both have a minimum of two years left of school. You have PT school, and I've got my master's. We don't want a baby right now."

He pushed his chair to the side, and my hands dropped heavily into my lap. "The longer we wait to have kids, the lower my count will probably drop. We might never conceive a kid normally."

His expression changed, and he turned his face away from me. "And that's if I can perform well enough to get it up."

"Stop putting yourself down. It's only happened a few times, and you know I wasn't upset." He usually could after a little coaxing, and we figured out what got him going, but a few times, he hadn't been able to at all. I'd hated how he retreated into himself when it had happened.

"But I was!" The way he pulled at his hair as his head fell forward made me want to just pull him into my arms and comfort him, but I knew he'd push me away right now.

"Joel, they wouldn't have medicine for this if it wasn't a problem for a lot of men," I whispered.

"Yeah, older men. If it was twenty years from now and we had a house full of teenagers, this might be frustrating," he sighed. "Right now, I'm supposed to be in the prime of my life, and I can't fucking get it up half the time. My hot as fuck girlfriend sits on my lap, and I can't even get a twitch sometimes."

A tear made its way down my cheek, and I swallowed hard as I watched him. "I'm your fiancée."

"Fuck," he growled, staring hard at me.

"Joel," I sighed, not liking how he was staring at me. It scared me to think about what might go through his head.

"Yes, you are. But what if this is all a huge mistake?" It felt like a punch to the gut when he said that. It was one thing to be frustrated by this, but asking if our lives and plans were a mistake was just...

"No." I shook my head and wiped my cheeks with the back of my hand. "You don't get to push me away for this. I know the score. I'm not going into this uninformed."

"Am I just supposed to sit around and wait for you to leave me when I can't give you what you want?" His voice broke as he looked at me, and tears flooded my eyes.

Knowing he didn't like to be touched sometimes when he was upset, I cautiously stood up and approached his chair. He didn't push me away when I cupped his cheek, leaning into my hand and closing his eyes.

"I will not leave you," I swore. I wouldn't. When I agreed to be his wife, I signed up to go along with the good and the bad.

"You don't..." he murmured softly, but I interrupted him.

"Despite what you may think, I'm not just in this for what's in your pants," I told him. He was my partner. I wouldn't know what to do without him at this point. He'd been there for me when my life was falling apart, and I was going to be there for him, too.

"Obviously." He choked out a weak laugh, opening his eyes and looking up at me.

"I love you. I agreed to marry you, and we are getting married in two months. We'll get through this."

His arms wrapped around my waist, and he kissed my stomach. "I'm sorry. I just... I'm fucking terrified of what this means for our future."

"This isn't your fault," I told him, but I felt like it was falling on deaf ears. "There's nothing you can do to control this. And I'm here no matter what happens."

He snuggled into my stomach as I slowly combed the strands of blonde hair. I'd imagined little boys running around our backyard someday with light blonde hair and their father's pretty blue eyes.

Would we be okay if that never happened?

### ~ TWO WEEKS LATER ~

I'd started packing up little things, knowing that I only had six weeks left in my apartment. Alison was staying in the apartment we'd shared for the last three years. She was supposed to have a roommate moving in the week after the wedding.

Joel had arranged to have movers come in a few weeks to take my things to our new townhouse on the other side of campus. He'd talked about adopting a dog when we got back from our honeymoon, so he wanted a yard.

"Hey." I spun around and laughed when I saw him leaning against my door frame.

"You scared me," I smiled as I looked up at him. He looked different today. Like some kind of weight had been lifted, but his eyes were still guarded.

"I'm sorry. I was just watching you," he apologized softly.

"That's okay. How long have you been standing there?" He'd looked like he was trying to memorize me. Soon he wouldn't need to steal brief moments to watch me. He'd be with me all the time.

"Just a few minutes."

I frowned at the blank expression on his face. Things had gotten better in the last week, and I felt like we were finally making headway in moving forward with his issues. "You okay?"

He sighed as he shoved his hands into his pockets. "Can we talk?"

"Are you alright?" I stood from where I'd been sitting in front of my dresser, sorting out what I wanted to keep. Things I hadn't worn in years had gotten shoved in there, and it was time to purge.

"Yeah. Is Alison home?" He walked into the room a few steps and sat down on my desk chair.

"No, she's going home for a few weeks since she finished finals. She'll be back the week before the wedding."

His eyes scanned the room, lingering on the small stack of boxes in the corner.

"Did you get the keys today?" I wanted to take some things over during the next few days, so we didn't have to do it simultaneously.

"No." The look in his eyes made me pause, frowning at the slight shake of his head. "Can you sit? I need to tell you something."

Closing the small distance between us, I leaned down to kiss him, and he turned his head, my lips glancing off his cheek.

"What...?"

He sighed as I straightened back up and nodded at my futon. "Kendall, sit. Please."

"I'm not the dog, Joel. You don't have to bark commands at me," I laughed, but he didn't, and he continued to avoid eye contact with me. My hand rose to touch his face, and he caught my wrist loosely before my skin made contact.

"Sit down." There was something in his voice that startled me, and I nodded, stepping backward and sitting down heavily.

"What's going on? You look..."

"Fuck. I don't..." he swore as he leaned forward. "Here..."

He pulled a crinkled envelope out of his back pocket and held it out towards me. My hand was shaking as I grasped the paper. I had a feeling whatever was going on was about to make an enormous impact on my future.

Joel had calmed down since he freaked out about the test results a few weeks ago, but he'd still been a little distant.

"What is this?" I asked as I held the folded paper in my hand, terrified to open it. I had a feeling that this wouldn't be something positive.

"Just read it."

I glanced at the return address. It was from the admissions office for a university on the other side of the country.

Joel's face was completely devoid of expression when I looked up to him, and my palms started to sweat.

I carefully pulled out the paper and unfolded it. "I don't understand."

"It's an acceptance letter," he whispered, but I had already read that part.

"I can see that," I told him as my palms started to sweat. "But I thought you'd decided to stay in the program here."

"I had." He nodded and then looked down at the carpet.

"Then what does..." His voice cut me off, and my mouth snapped shut.

"I'm going."

"What?" I felt like the wind had been knocked out of me. "But what about next year? What about PT school? We're supposed to get married in six weeks. That's not enough time for me to go with you to find a place to live. What am I supposed to do about school next year?"

I was practically hyperventilating as he looked at me with a placid expression. "Is there somewhere close that has an art therapy program I can transfer to next semester?"

The faster my heart pounded, the higher my voice got. I was panicking, and Joel was just sitting there.

"I already have a place to live," he whispered, and I took a shallow breath.

"Wait? What? What does it look like?" Is that why he didn't get the keys for the rental for next year? Had he been planning an alternative for us?

"It's a studio apartment near campus."

"A studio? But what about the dog? I thought we were getting a dog?" He wasn't making any sense. We had all these plans, and he was just changing the script this late in the game.

"It's big enough for what I need." The way he said 'I' made me pause.

"What about what I need?" I whispered. I needed something with a little studio space for my easel and drawing desk.

"You've got what you need right here."

"I..." I sputtered. Here? But... "I don't understand. What are you saying?"

"I'm going," he told me, his voice a little stronger. "It's a good opportunity. Honestly, it was my first choice of physical therapy programs when I applied. I just didn't think I got in. They opened up more space in the program."

"So, you want to get married and then go to schools a thousand miles apart?" None of what he was saying was making sense. If he needed to make this opportunity work, we should have made these decisions together.

"No." He shook his head.

"You don't want to get married, or you don't want to live apart?" My voice was small and vulnerable, and I couldn't believe this conversation was even happening.

He sighed as he sat forward and rested his forearms on his thighs. "I've been thinking about this non-stop for the last several weeks. It wouldn't be fair of me to marry you, knowing that I probably won't be able to give you a child."

"But it's fair of you to break up with me six weeks before our wedding, leaving me homeless and moving across the country?" My voice rose as I realized what he was saying. "Is that what I'm hearing?"

He gave a hesitant nod.

"Are you fucking kidding me?" I cursed as I watched him flinch. Good. This was insane. "We talked about this!"

I wasn't sure who this person sitting in front of me was, but it wasn't the man I'd fallen in love with.

"No. You talked about this. I will not tie you to me out of some sense of obligation." His voice was the most resigned I'd ever heard. He'd boxed me out, and there wasn't anything I could do to get back in.

"I don't get a say in this, do I?" I whispered.

He shook his head slowly as he looked me in the eye. "It's already done."

"But..." Covering my mouth with my hand, I stifled a sob as the tears that had formed started flowing.

"I know this is horrible timing. You're probably going to hate me for a long time," his voice broke as he looked at me, and it was the first sign of emotion I'd seen out of him today. "To be honest, I kind of hate myself right now."

He covered his face with his hand, and I saw a tear streak down his cheek. "A few years from now, you're going to see I did you a favor."

"When are you leaving?" I whispered.

"Right now," his voice responded quietly as he sat with his head in his hands.

"How long have you known about this?" And how had I missed the signs? He was resolved. This wasn't something he decided today.

"Four days." He'd had four days to plan this. Four days to decide my future for me while I naively sat around making fucking wedding plans for a wedding that would never happen.

"You did all this in four days, and you couldn't talk to me?" My voice broke with the betrayal I was feeling.

"When I got that letter. I knew it was a sign."

I couldn't believe that this was it.

"So, what would have happened if this letter hadn't come? Were you going to leave me at the altar or something?" I don't know which thought was more crushing, that he did it now or dragged it out.

"I don't know," he confessed. "We probably still would have gotten married."

"I..." My breath picked up when I thought about a single piece of paper changing my life so dramatically in a matter of days. "I don't even know what to say to that."

He nodded as he just stared at me from his place on the chair. "I know saying I'm sorry doesn't mean much."

The bitter scoff that came out of me made his eyebrows raise.

"This will be better for both of us," he assured me, but I didn't know how he could believe that.

After a few moments, he stood up and crossed to where I was sitting.

I flinched away from him as he placed a gentle kiss on my cheek and turned toward the door. He didn't say a word as he walked away. His steps faltered as he heard me finally break down and begin to cry, but he didn't turn around.

The mechanical noise of the deadbolt on the apartment door engaging was the only sound I heard before I lost it and sobbed into my hands.

I wasn't sure how long I cried before the sobs finally died down, and I looked down at my phone. My shaky fingers scrolled through my contacts and hovered over his name before I hit the button to dial his phone number.

"Kendall?" Rory answered, and I could hear the smile in his voice that was always there for me. It made my heart twist painfully to know that I was about to shatter that.

I didn't know who else to call.

# Chapter Twenty-seven:
## After Graduation
### JULY

"Come on. It's noon," Alison sighed as she peeled back the blankets that covered my head. She'd come back from home early after Joel left. Rory called and told her everything.

Her job started next week, and she had been trying to get me motivated to get out of bed on my own in the mornings. "You've gotta stop doing this to yourself."

A lone tear spilled from the corner of my eye and slid down my cheek. I thought I'd run dry a long time ago, but it still hurt when I thought about how my life had fallen apart.

"I'm sorry," I told her as my lip quivered.

"Hey, I don't blame you for being sad, but school starts soon, and you can't let this affect you like this. You've worked too hard to let him take this from you, too."

I pulled myself up to sit, pushing my limp, dirty hair out of my face.

She was right, but the last few months had been a nightmare. Somehow, in my zombie state, we'd all made it through graduation, but I'd retreated into myself once all my family went back home.

My dad wanted to drive across the country and kill Joel. He'd disappeared, and none of us had heard from him except his mother, who was not telling me anything. His dad had sent a check to cover the money we'd been forced to lose on deposits, but that was the last we'd heard from them. Joel even got a new cell phone number. He had completely cut everyone out of his life, including Rory.

He'd been the biggest collateral damage in this situation. Rory was supposed to be his best man, his oldest friend, someone he had known for much longer than he'd known me.

"I'll take a shower, but I'm not going anywhere," I conceded, knowing that I needed to, not that I wanted to.

"As long as you get out of this bed, I don't care."

That was another problem. I was soon to be homeless. Alison's other roommate was supposed to move in next week, and I still didn't have a place to live.

"I guess I should finish packing," I sighed as I looked over at the boxes stacked in the corner of my room.

"You know I hate this," Alison frowned as she looked down at me. She felt guilty that I had to leave, and I still had nowhere to go. At this point, I'd honestly considered moving home, but then I'd just be getting looks of pity. First Dylan, and now I was left before I even got to the altar.

"I know, but maybe it's time for me to move out on my own." I'd never lived on my own. Alison had always been there. It was going to be a change to be reliant on myself.

"I can ask around in the building and see if anyone else needs a roommate. We might be able to find another apartment for her," she offered. Allie had asked the landlord about any vacancies several weeks ago, but they'd told her they didn't know of any. I wasn't holding out hope.

"Maybe I should go look and see if there's anything left around campus," I sighed. "It's probably too late for me to find something now."

I had called the rental office for the townhouse we'd signed the lease on for next year. Joel had paid the fine to cancel the lease, and it was already rented to someone else. There was no way I could've covered the rent by myself, but now I didn't have any options.

"I can see if anyone at my office or Benji's is looking for a roommate. Maybe someone at the house knows someone?" she offered, but even she looked skeptical. With school starting in a few weeks, everything habitable was probably gone.

"No, I'm not asking any of the guys. It's bad enough I had to call all of them to tell them the wedding was off," I shook my head. Rory had called the ones I didn't know, but I'd been the one who had to tell everyone else. They were all sympathetic, but I hated having to do it. Several of them had already spent money on their suits to be groomsmen and were out of their deposits.

"Not sure what you want me to say here, Ken. He didn't plan any of this out very well. You had all of this dropped in your lap while he just started over," she sighed. She'd been just as shocked by his sudden departure as the rest of us. "I always liked him, but this was crazy. Are you sure you don't want to talk to someone about this?"

She was right. Between my abandonment issues with Tyler, my trust issues with Dylan, and now Joel betraying both, I wasn't sure how to move on from this.

Joel had left because he was afraid we would have a different future than we'd envisioned. I wasn't sure if I could trust a man enough to date any time soon, much less one to have a family with.

Either way, my life fell apart, and he just pretended I never existed.

"And say what? That I'm the worst judge of someone's character ever? Or that I drive men away without even realizing it?" I was beginning to think that the problem lay with me. I seemed to be the common denominator.

"Kale might know someone here," she shrugged. "Doesn't the student health office have counselors?"

They did. It was a work-study experience for the clinical Ph.D. candidates. Yet another way the psychology department gained experience was by using students as labor and for practice. I had to hand it to them. The department knew how to leverage its strengths.

"They do, but I know some of the Ph.D. students. I'm not sure that I could open up to them." It'd just be awkward.

"You know you can always talk to me, but I might be a little biased," she smiled.

"Thank you. I don't know what I'd do without you and Rory. You two are the only thing keeping me together these days."

"Speaking of, didn't Rory move off-campus? Maybe he knows of some places to look," her face brightened. He'd been here for me the first few days afterward, but then I'd felt weird given our history and his relationship with Joel. As time passed, I'd stopped contacting him, and now we were in this place where I was afraid to reach out.

"He might. I just feel weird spending so much time with him."

"Joel doesn't get to claim him. He left him behind without a word, too. Half the guys in the house are pissed at him," she insisted.

"They don't need to be pissed at him. I still don't understand why he did it the way he did, but Joel's fears were legitimate." I understood it was more self-preservation than anything. He wanted to get out before I had the chance to hurt him. If only he hadn't been forced to drop a bomb on our lives to do it.

"I just hate that he pushed you away," she frowned. "You should still contact Rory. He's worried about you but doesn't know what to do to help."

I wasn't sure what would help either. The mysterious 'they' said time healed all wounds, but this one cut deep.

"I need to go to meet Benji. He's hopeless with dressing himself, so he's freaking out about buying work clothes," she rolled her eyes. He started his very own big boy job next week as well. I couldn't imagine the chill guy who hung out in cargo shorts and flip-flops on my couch the last few years wearing dress clothes and ties.

"Go. You don't need to hang around here for me. I'm not going anywhere," I waved her away. She couldn't put her life on hold for me, either. Life was going to go on, eventually.

"Maybe that's the problem. Maybe you should go somewhere. Get some fresh air, go to the movies, do something other than sit in this room all day."

Knowing she was right and doing something about it were two separate things. It was easy for her to tell me to pull myself out of this because she wasn't in the thick of it.

"Go shower," she nodded to the bathroom.

"Okay. I'm going," I sighed.

She wagged her finger at me as she pulled my door closed. I rummaged through the few clothes still left in my dresser and went into my bathroom. I set an Amazon radio station to random and synced my phone with the Bluetooth speaker on the counter.

The hot water felt good as it beat down on my head. I knew I needed to take better care of myself, but the wallowing was just so much easier. My legs were scary as hell as I tried to shave off several weeks' worth of growth. It's not like anyone else was touching them anytime soon.

The message alert on my phone went off several times as I washed and conditioned my hair, turning into the spray to make sure it was all washed out. Once I was finally clean, I turned off the water and wrapped myself in a towel. I wasn't telling Alison, but I felt marginally better. Baby steps.

*Rory: Allie said you're still looking for somewhere to live?*

*Kendall: Yeah... I don't think my car is going to cut it.*

*Rory: I can take you a few places if you're feeling up to it this afternoon.*

*Kendall: I'm fine. You both act like I have some terminal illness.*

*Rory: Don't bullshit a bullshitter.*

*Kendall: Yeah, okay, Walter White.*

Rory sent back a crying laughing emoji. This was why we were friends, he got my strange references, and I got his.

> *Rory: You're feeling better today if you're going to give me a hard time.*

> *Kendall: Debatable.*

> *Rory: I'll be there to pick you up in an hour.*

> *Kendall: I'll be ready.*

> *Rory: I'll throw you over my shoulder and haul you out of there if I must.*

> *Kendall: Promises, promises.*

Looking at myself in the mirror, I realized I'd lost weight in the last month. I also hadn't been outside to exercise since before Joel left. I needed to get back into healthy habits.

Knowing that he was serious about dragging me out of my room, I got dressed and tried to look somewhat presentable. My hair was clean and brushed, so were my teeth, and I even put on a layer of mascara.

"Wow, she has real clothes on," Rory gasped as he leaned against my bedroom door frame.

"God, you've got to stop sneaking up on me," I rolled my eyes as I held my hand over my heart. Hopefully, he showed up after I was completely dressed.

"Where's the fun in that?" he grinned. "You ready to go? We've got an appointment in twenty minutes."

"That was fast."

"There were a few places in the student classifieds that still had openings, not sure if they're shitholes, but it's a place to start," he admitted. I still wasn't holding out hope, but I appreciated that he was helping me.

"I can always figure something out later. I just need something close to campus with my own room." There was no way that I was sharing a bedroom with a stranger. I was too old for that shit.

"Worst-case scenario, I can see if my sister still knows anyone in the dorms. Maybe a Resident Advisor position opened up."

"Aren't those usually undergrads?" I was desperate, so I'd consider it if it were an option, but they usually tried to filter people into grad student housing.

"Sometimes they make exceptions," he shrugged.

"Was your sister an RA?" I don't remember him telling me that before.

"Yeah, I thought you knew that," he said as he tilted his head at me.

"Why would I know that? She's older than us, right?"

"Yeah, but she was Alison's orientation leader freshman year," he frowned. "You met her."

My mouth dropped open as I looked over at him. "That was your sister?"

"Yeah, Alison still talks to her. And she was invited to..." He stopped talking abruptly.

"To what?"

His voice was quiet, and he gave me an apologetic look as he explained. "She was invited to your wedding."

"Oh," I replied softly. "How did I not know this?"

"Well, we don't have the same last name anymore," he said slowly, smirking at me. I was so slow.

"Why would Joel invite her?" I frowned.

"They were friends," he drew out the words, tilting his head at me.

"What?"

"Did you two not talk, ever?" he laughed as he looked at me like I was crazy.

"We talked," I insisted.

"What did he do every summer in high school and over summer break when he went home?"

"He was a lifeguard." I knew this stuff. I wasn't a total idiot, other than my taste in men, apparently.

"With my sister," he said, shaking his head. "For years."

"I thought your sister was named Stefanie." I frowned. I knew I was depressed, but apparently, my brain was not functioning anymore.

"Oh, you *were* paying attention," he teased, and I narrowed my eyes at him.

"You be nice to me," I pouted, knowing that he wouldn't. He was such a great friend like that.

"He seriously never talked about her? They might've even been better friends than he was with me before college."

"He told me about his friend Steve," I shrugged, but I think I would have remembered a Stefanie.

"Not Steve," he laughed as he shook his head at me. "Stevie."

"Wait. Stevie is your sister?"

"We went over this. Yes!" His laughter had reached the hysterical stage now, and I couldn't help joining in.

"I met her and her husband on my birthday," I smiled. I liked her. I was such a moron.

"Yes, you did. She liked you." He continued shaking his head as he looked down at me in amusement. It felt good to laugh, even if it was at my expense.

"You talked to your sister about me?" What was with these men and talking to their sisters about me?

"I was stuck in her house at her beck and call for weeks after Nat was born. Do you know how much infants sleep?"

"You're avoiding the question." I raised an eyebrow. He looked away from me and scratched at the side of his neck. He didn't want to answer me.

"We don't have time for this. Let's go." He loosely grasped my hand and tugged me toward the front door. I grabbed my purse and hit the lock button on the way out.

"Why won't you answer my question?"

He was quiet as he led me down the staircase and out to where his car was parked in the back lot. The look on his face as he opened the passenger door and then closed it after me almost made me want to drop it, but I didn't.

"Rory. Why were you talking to your sister about me?" I wanted to know.

"You aren't ready for me to answer that question," he told me with a pointed look. My heart stopped as I looked at his serious face. I felt like I was crossing a line with him.

"Why?" I asked anyway, because we've established that I'm an idiot.

"I'll tell you. But not today."

The ride across campus was quiet. I stared out the window as he tapped his fingers on the steering wheel. Something told me not to push him. I still didn't understand the need for secrecy, but he didn't owe me an explanation.

We toured the first two apartments, both of which were way too expensive for outdated buildings that didn't even have laundry rooms.

"This place better look amazing inside, because so far, I'm underwhelmed," he sighed loudly as we stood in front of an old stone house with a room for rent. The outside wasn't giving me much hope.

"How much is this place?"

"Too much, but you're running out of options." He frowned at me and shook his head. Today had been a bust so far.

"It's got to be better than living out of my car," I offered hopefully.

It wasn't. It was gross. The owner had five dogs, and the place smelled. It was official. I was going to be a homeless grad student.

"Well, I guess I'm getting a roommate," he sighed as I buckled my seatbelt and looked over at him with a frown.

"What are you talking about?" He hadn't told me about a roommate before.

"You can't live there. If I have to explain that to you, maybe your test scores lied." He'd missed his original GRE test date, so we'd ended up in the same one last fall. It still bothered him that my scores were higher.

"Oh, shut up, you're just mad I scored higher than you," I laughed.

"By four points," he rolled his eyes. "Hardly a huge margin."

"I'm not living with you," I shook my head. That'd just be all kinds of awkward, and he'd said more than once that he wanted to live alone.

"Why not? I have an extra room," he shrugged.

"But..." No. Just no.

"Do you have a better alternative?" he asked as he gestured out the windshield to the house we'd just left.

"No. What are people going to say? Joel and I just broke up. And then I'm moving in with you?" There were still enough people around that we interacted with that would say something. I didn't want to drag Rory down with me.

"Fuck them," he spat. "People can be judgmental if they want to, but I'm not leaving my best friend homeless."

What?

"I'm your best friend?" I whispered.

He looked across the console towards me, and I froze. "Well, yeah, kinda. I mean, Joel left and hasn't talked to me in months. So, yeah. I guess that makes you it by default."

My breath left me in a woosh, both a little offended, and I don't know what. "Oh, wow. What an honor. I'm all that's left over."

"That's not," he sighed as he reached towards me, but his hand froze and dropped back onto his lap.

"No, I get it," I told him as I glanced away, trying to keep myself from crying again.

"I don't think you do." He cautiously reached across the space between us and gently took my hand in his. "I don't have to fake things with you. And you call me on my shit. Sure, I've got other friends, but you're definitely in the top five."

"Five?" I laughed as I looked back toward him.

"Okay, top two," he shrugged.

My eyebrows rose, and he laughed at my expression. "Who's my competition?"

"My brother, Cam," he shrugged. "But he's not here."

"You're in my top two also," I confessed quietly, and I saw a smile twitching at his lips.

"Am I ever going to beat out Alison?" he asked with a little smirk.

"Maybe. You are a parasite, after all. You stick around whether or not I want you to."

His grin widened, and he squeezed my hand, his thumb grazing my knuckles. "I sound so charming when you describe me."

"Super charming," I rolled my eyes. I felt the old spark of attraction that I'd pushed aside flicker as I watched the shy smile form on his face.

"Anyway..." He cleared his throat, and I gently slipped my hand out of his.

His fingers flexed before he returned them to the steering wheel. "Let's go figure out a way to get your boxes over to my place."

He drove us back to my building and hovered behind me awkwardly with his hands shoved in his pockets as I unlocked the door.

"Hey! You're back! I've got good news," Alison poked her head out of the kitchen as we closed the front door behind us.

"Let's hear it," I sighed. Anything had to be better than the morning we'd had so far. At least it wasn't all bad.

"I found somewhere else for Bree to live. The unit upstairs was partially vacant, and I convinced the property manager to knock some money off her rent if she took that place."

"Oh." I glanced over at Rory, and he shrugged.

"What? Did you already find someplace? I hope you didn't sign a lease," she said with a cringe as she looked between us.

"No, no. This is great. Thank you for going to all that trouble." I pulled her into a hug and looked sadly at Rory over her shoulder. He watched the two of us with a faint smile and gave me a thumbs-up behind her back.

"I'm sorry." I mouthed.

He shook his head, mouthing back. "It's fine." But I felt like maybe in my heart it wasn't fine.

# Chapter Twenty-eight:
## First Year of Grad School
### EARLY SEPTEMBER

No matter how many times I walked into this office, my palms started sweating every time I sat down. The waiting before a session was always the worst part.

"You ready to come back?" Taking a deep breath, I nodded as I followed Cortney through the door and down the hallway to her office.

"How have you been since I saw you last?" she asked over her shoulder.

"It's only been a week," I laughed. And my weeks were pretty much all the same now. Go to school, do homework, repeat.

"I know, but a lot can happen in a week," she replied with a shrug, smiling at me. I was well aware of how life could change overnight.

"It's been... good, I guess." Busy.

She sighed as she took the seat behind her desk and motioned toward my usual couch. "You know how this works, Kendall. The more you open up freely, the more we can get into why you're here."

"My classes are all going well so far. It's early on, but I think I've got a pretty good grasp on the work for the semester," I admitted. Despite the funk I'd been in over the summer and early fall, I was able to start my semester with no hiccups.

"And have you given a thought to what I asked you to examine during our last session?"

"About Joel?" I asked as I blew out a breath. This was the only part I didn't like. I needed to delve into the stuff I wanted to avoid to move past this.

"Yes," she nodded as she tapped her pen against her notebook.

"Yes. I'm trying to disconnect myself and see that his decision was made to protect himself." Looking back, it was clear that he saw this as a way out of a situation he didn't want to face.

"We've talked about how sometimes people have trouble seeing outside themselves when they are in a stressful situation."

"I know. But I just feel like I keep picking these men that make decisions that affect me without my input." That was the major source of my frustration. I'd given these men the power to control parts of my life, and I couldn't do anything about how their decisions impacted me.

"You're referring to Tyler as well?"

"Yes. He did the same thing. Something happened for him, and I wasn't even factored into the decision." I hated feeling like an afterthought.

"Do you think that you two would have been able to maintain a long-distance relationship with him in another country?"

"Probably not," I admitted, "but he didn't even try."

"Men don't always process emotions or decisions the same way that women do," she pointed out. We'd talked about this before, about the emotional burden that women took on in relationships that men didn't even realize.

"But he took the decision completely out of my hands," I argued. They both had. They all had. Tyler with his study abroad, Dylan with Lisa, and now Joel with his health issues and the late acceptance letter. All situations I was left out of that affected me.

"Sometimes, we decide something that we know is best for ourselves. If you made your mind up about something that you know wouldn't change, would you want to keep trying to defend your decision, knowing that?"

"No. But I thought partners were supposed to decide together." As time went on, I realized that none of them had been my partner. They never put me first. Even Joel claimed he did this to prevent me from having future heartache.

"That is ideal, but life doesn't always let people's decisions align with one another."

"Tell me about it," I said sarcastically. She raised an eyebrow, but I was serious. I pulled my legs up underneath me in the seat, thinking about how I'd let myself be walked on unintentionally over the last several years.

"So, apply the same knowledge to your relationship with Joel."

"But I was engaged to Joel," I argued. We'd already agreed to be partners. The wedding just made it official.

"Did Joel know the severity of his condition before you two got engaged?"

I shook my head slowly. "No. I mean, we knew he had issues, but we didn't know about possible infertility."

"Would you have said yes if you knew you might never have a child with Joel?"

I didn't know. I wasn't allowed to answer the question. "There's no way for me to know that."

"Would the inability to have children be a deal-breaker in a relationship with you?" She was full of all the fun questions today.

"It might have been." I nodded. It definitely would have made me pause.

"And Joel knew this?"

"That I wanted kids? Yes," I nodded. We had talked about that often. He came from a big family, and he'd wanted kids too.

"So, if this was something you found out after you'd already been married, would this have been an issue you could've worked past? You personally?" she questioned.

I leaned forward and massaged at my temples with my fingers. "There are alternatives. We could have gotten a donor, tried IVF, adopted..."

"And if none of those worked? Would you have resented Joel for his part in that?"

A few tears leaked out of the corner of my eyes, and I swiped them away.

Cortney leaned forward with the tissue box, and I grabbed a few, holding them tightly in my fist.

"I loved him," I confessed sadly.

"That wasn't my question. Would you have resented Joel if you could never have children?"

No matter how much I tried to rationalize it and justify that there were alternatives; I knew my answer with little thought. "Yes. On some level, I would have been devastated if we never had kids."

"Would you have asked him for a divorce if you knew he was the cause?"

I shook my head as I closed my eyes. "I don't know."

"So, it's safe to assume that Joel knew that having kids was a potential subject that could have permanently damaged your relationship?"

"Yes," I nodded sadly.

"And Joel knew that there was not much he could do to change his situation?"

"We don't know if there was something they could have done to help, but it looked that way," I confirmed. He'd kept me out of that part of the discussion. There were hormone therapies and boosting drugs, but he never wanted to talk about it.

"If you had a friend whose husband was in the same situation and came to you for advice. What would you tell her?"

I thought about it for a moment, but I knew the answer. "To have a conversation with her husband."

"So, it comes down to communication," Cortney pointed out, our session having come full circle.

"Yes! I keep getting left out of these important decisions that affect me, too."

"So, with both Joel and Tyler, their communication skills were incompatible with yours?"

"Yeah, I guess they were," I admitted. I hadn't thought of it that way before.

"What about Dylan?" she asked curiously.

"Yeah, he didn't tell me he'd fallen for someone else while we were still dating. I'd say there were some pretty serious communication issues there." I gave a humorless laugh, and she shook her head at me.

"Infertility and long-distance issues aside. Were the gaps in communication in each of those relationships something that you could overlook?"

"People have to develop communication skills," I told her half-heartedly, but I knew she was right.

"They do, but sometimes we aren't compatible with someone on these base levels, and they don't come to light until we're thrown into a stressful situation."

"So, you think I've been choosing partners I'm incompatible with and don't realize it until it's too late?" I asked.

"Maybe," she nodded. "It's something to consider whenever you're ready to date again."

I thought back to that conversation at the Halloween Party with Kale. He said you had to push past the superficial to find someone you're truly compatible with. There was no way I was ready to date again. The wounds were still bleeding.

But when I was...

I would not settle again.

# Chapter Twenty-nine:
## First Year of Grad School
### FEBRUARY

This year was the first Valentine's Day since I started college that I didn't have any plans. I'd come to terms with my singledom, working through some of my trust issues with Cortney over the last six months. She'd helped me see I was projecting my problem-solving and communication skills on others. I'd neglected to see flaws in the partners I'd chosen because I wanted everyone to think and act as I did. I was setting myself up to fail by not advocating my own needs in a relationship.

One of those needs was an open line of communication.

"Are you sure you don't want to come to dinner with us?" Alison offered for the third time in as many hours.

"Yes. I'll be fine," I smiled up at her. "I've got ice cream, pasta, and Netflix. It's just any other night for me."

"Benji said he didn't mind." As much as I appreciated their concern, I didn't want to interfere with their date.

"You two go have some epic romantic dinner. I'm fine here with my imaginary romances."

"Don't get too lovesick over Peter Kavinsky," she teased.

"I make no promises. He is pretty dreamy." Distracting myself with work, I pulled up the outline for a paper due in a few weeks for one of my psychology classes.

We discussed the subject of codependency and how to maintain professional distancing with your patients. That had been another eye-opener for me. There were a lot of traits I saw in myself when they talked about losing oneself in another person and relying on them for your validation. I'd bounced from one relationship to another, using the attention I got from men to give myself worth. If I wasn't loved by someone else, maybe it wasn't worth loving myself.

I was finally getting to the point in my life where I liked who I was and the decisions I made. Everything I'd gone through, every mistake and heartbreak, had helped shape me, flaws and all.

Rory: What's tonight's flavor?

Kendall: I don't eat ice cream every night.

Rory: ...

Kendall: I don't!

Rory: ...

Kendall: Peanut butter fudge.

Rory: You up for sharing?

Kendall: Depends.

Rory: On?

Kendall: What are you bringing to share?

Rory: A hyperactive 1 1/2 yr old.

Kendall: I'm not following.

Rory: I've got Nat for the weekend. Please save me.

I laughed as I imagined Rory with his niece. He'd show me pictures of her sometimes, and so did Alison. She was pretty adorable. But she seemed to have inherited the Chandler naughty streak.

Kendall: You can't handle a small child?

Rory: She never stops.

Kendall: And I'm supposed to know how to help?

I hadn't babysat in years.

Rory: Maybe if there's two of us...

Kendall: You're that desperate?

Rory: I'm asking you for help, aren't I?

Kendall: Ouch.

Rory: I didn't know who else to ask.

Rory: ...

I let him sweat for a few moments.

Rory: I didn't mean it like that.

Kendall: ...

Rory: ...

Rory: Quit doing that.

Kendall: But I can just imagine you squirming.

Rory: You know I didn't want to ask anyone else but you.

Kendall: Aww...

Rory: Don't read too much into it.

Kendall: You love me.

My finger hit send before I even processed what I'd just sent.
*Shit.*

Dropping my phone in my lap, I stared at it anxiously as my pulse went crazy. Had I gone too far with the banter? Was I reading too much into this? We had these moments sometimes, and I daydreamed about the one time he kissed me, but he'd just been a great friend to me for the last seven months.

> Kendall: ...

What was I supposed to say? *I'm sorry for the flippant comment saying you might love me... But sometimes, I imagine feeling that way about you and wonder if I missed my chance.*

> Rory: Sorry. she got into the pantry and found the peanut butter.

> Kendall: Oh no.

He sent a picture of Nat sitting inside the pantry door. Peanut butter smeared all over the door...

And the wall...

In her hair...

It was everywhere, but the little dimpled smile on her face was triumphant.

> Kendall: I love her.

God. There I went again with that word.

> Rory: We are pretty lovable.

Another picture popped up. It was a selfie of Rory holding Nat, her little peanut butter-covered fingers painting his cheek. He looked down at her, trying to be annoyed, but I could tell that he secretly loved it.

> Rory: I need to get her into the tub. You coming over?

I looked down at my sweats and made the split-second decision to change before I headed over there. Rory had seen me looking worse, but holey sweats and my unicorn slippers were decidedly not my best look.

Pulling out a pair of form-fitting leggings and a loose sweater, I slipped them on and put my hair up into a loose bun. I looked into the bathroom and saw my eyeliner sitting on the counter.

"Fuck it."

Not wanting to take too long, I just swiped on some light shimmery shadow and a coat of mascara.

Rory lived off-campus on the opposite end, so I drove over there, swinging through the McDonald's drive-thru for a happy meal. All little kids loved nuggets, right?

The door was unlocked when I got to his apartment. "Rory?"

"Back here." He called out from the direction of the hallway.

Placing the ice cream in the freezer and the happy meal on the counter, I hurried down the hallway to check out the damage. I'd only been in his apartment a handful of times. It was clean and very modern but still had touches of him. It was more adult-looking than I had expected, but I guess we were adults now, at twenty-three.

The sounds of splashing and excited giggles were coming from the open doorway at the end of the hall.

"Hey. Sounds like you guys are having fun in here." It took a great effort to hold in my laughter as he turned towards me.

"Don't. No commentary on this." Rory looked exasperated with the small giggly child in the tub. "It took more soap than I thought it would to get all the peanut butter off."

He had bubbles in his hair, sliding down the side of his face, and Nat was completely covered in them, floating in a sea of bubbles.

"Did you use the entire bottle on her?" I had to cover my mouth with my fist to keep the laughter inside. But even then, you could tell that I was barely holding it together.

"No, but I put more water in the tub, and they just kept coming." The sheer exasperation in his voice was kind of adorable, but I knew I had to help him get this under control. The poor guy needed reinforcements. Who knew that all it took to unsettle this man was a toddler, a jar of peanut butter, and some bubbles?

I stepped around him and pulled the stopper on the tub.

"What are you doing?" he groaned as the layer of bubbles dropped below the edge of the tub.

"You need to rinse her off, or you're never going to get her clean. I can see the soap still in her hair." Given that, there wasn't much of it. But his method of pouring the soap directly on the peanut butter had left a slime on what fair hair she had.

Nat slapped her little chubby hands in the mound of bubbles while her uncle looked on, overwhelmed.

"Why don't you go get cleaned up, and I'll take care of her," I told him as I pulled a towel off the rack and laid it across his shoulder.

"You don't think I can handle bathing a one-and-a half-year-old?" There was a challenge in his voice, but I could tell that he was happy that I was here to help him. Even he knew when to admit defeat at the hands of a one-and-a-half-year-old.

"Isn't that why I'm here? Because you need reinforcements?"

"Well, that's not the only reason." He pushed himself up off the floor. My eyes were drawn to the way the wet material of his T-shirt clung to his stomach, outlining what might lie beneath. He'd tried to get me to go to the gym with him, but I always ended up getting distracted. And the undergraduate guys were relentless. You'd think the student center was a meat market.

"My eyes are up here, Kendall." The smirk on his face told me I'd been caught ogling, but he seemed to enjoy the attention.

"You get out of here. You're a mess," I laughed, using my fingers to wipe some bubbles off his brow to keep them from dripping into his eyes.

"Are you sure you can handle her?" he asked cautiously, giving a wary glance at the smiling toddler who was smacking the pile of bubbles that still surrounded her.

"Look at her." We both watched as she giggled as little tufts of bubbles floating in the air around her. She was loving life.

"Yeah, don't let the cuteness lull you into a false sense of security." He glared at the little toddler, and I smiled as I watched her give him a toothy grin in response. Nat was a force to be reckoned with, just like the rest of the Chandler family.

"Is that how she got it in your hair?" I laughed as I saw the bubbles clinging to the wet hair on the back of his head.

"And inside my ear, and..." He pulled the neckline of his shirt open to show a smear along his collarbone.

"Down your shirt." I laughed at the disgusted look on his face.

"You be good, Natty." He pointed at the little girl, and the look she gave him made me laugh all over again.

"Bubbles! Bub bub bub," she cheered as he shook his head at her and looked back at me.

"Her bag is on my bed. There should be some clean pajamas in there. There's a pack of diapers next to the portable crib." I hadn't put on a diaper in years, I was out of practice, but I could give it the old college try.

"Am I supposed to know what that is?" I hadn't been around kids recently, and all the gear nowadays was overwhelming.

"It's a bed playpen thing. It's set up next to the closet. You can't miss it." He turned to leave but hesitated, reaching forward to touch my fingers. Despite the layer of bubble film on his skin, a thrill still rushed through me at the contact, and I looked up into his eyes. "Thank you. Really. This is harder than I thought it'd be."

"No problem. That's what friends are for, right?" I shrugged lightly, trying not to focus on the way his tongue peeked out between his full lips. Even covered with bubbles, he was the most handsome man I'd probably ever seen.

Something unidentifiable flickered in his eyes before he turned to leave. My eyes tracked him as he stepped through the door frame, and I saw a flash of skin as he peeled off his soaked shirt.

"Alright, naughty girl. It's time to rinse you off," I told Nat as I turned back in her direction. Luckily, she hadn't found anything else to get into while her uncle distracted me. "Let's see what we've got to work with."

Pulling open the bathroom cabinets, I looked for something to use as a cup. Tucked in the back corner, there was a big plastic mug from one of the campus bars. It'd have to do. Nathalie babbled to herself as I turned on the faucet and filled the cup, rinsing as many of the bubbles down the drain as possible.

"You're giving Uncle Rory a hard time today, huh? He doesn't know what to do with you."

"Rory!" She clapped as I wiped the excess bubbles from her hair and carefully scrubbed with my fingers to dislodge the last of the remnants of peanut butter.

"You are pretty adorable," I told her as I turned on the tap and used the mug to rinse her until the bubbles were all down the drain. "Your uncle was kind of adorable, too."

Once I'd finally gotten all the traces of soap removed, I grabbed a towel off the rack and wrapped it around her before lifting her from the tub. "Let's go see if we can find you something to wear."

Judging from what I could see of the crumpled-up clothing in the corner, her clothes from earlier were not salvageable. There were streaks of peanut butter covering them, and they looked like a lost cause.

"Up, up, up," she chanted while she bounced on my hip as I carried her down the hallway. She was heavier than I thought she'd be.

"It's time for PJs," I smiled as we walked into Rory's bedroom. I hadn't ever been past the doorway. We usually hung out in the kitchen or the living room.

"No bed," Nat shook her head as she started throwing herself backward. "No sleepy."

"Not yet," I promised as I tried to keep up with the flailing toddler. "Miss Kenna got you nuggets. And a toy."

"Toy!" Nat cheered as she smacked her wet little hands against my cheeks. At least she wasn't using me as a finger-painting canvas like she had her uncle.

Rory had pulled out some footie pajamas and a diaper for me, leaving them on the edge of his bed. "Look, your pretty PJs have unicorns on them. I like unicorns, too."

"Lunacowns!" She pointed at them and cheered as I laid her down on the bed.

It was like wrestling an alligator, trying to get her to stay still, as I fruitlessly fought to get her diaper on. "You've gotta hold still, silly girl."

I tickled her stomach, and she burst into excited laughter as I finally got the tabs pushed into place. It was far from a perfect diapering job, but hopefully, it'd at least stay on.

"No, no. No cwose," Nat pouted as she tried to roll herself off the side of the bed.

"Yes, clothes. You can't be naked. That'd be silly." Kind of like my voice trying to negotiate with a one-and-a-half-year-old to hold still so I could get her dressed.

I got her arms into the pajamas and one leg, but I'd managed to leave one leg out and wasn't sure how to get it in without taking the whole thing off her. "Bend your leg, Natty bug."

"No!" she laughed as she tried to roll over and crawl across the bed.

"Rory!" I glanced up at her excited cheer, and Rory was leaning against the frame of the bathroom door, running a towel over his head. His sweats hung low on his hips, and he hadn't put a shirt on yet.

Freezing momentarily, my eyes feasted on all the exposed skin before I grabbed Nat's foot to keep her from diving off the side of the bed. "You get back here, you naughty little thing."

"Not as easy as it looks, is it?" he smirked as he watched me. I had no idea how long he'd been watching, but he looked as amused as I was seeing him covered with bubbles earlier.

"I have no idea how to get these things on her." I wasn't afraid to admit defeat. She was exhausting.

"Just let me grab a shirt, and I can help you." Part of me wanted to tell him that wasn't necessary, but I'd already embarrassed myself enough, blatantly staring at his half-clothed body.

"What are you doing, you crazy girl?" Nat was bouncing herself on the bed, the loose pant leg flapping behind her as she jumped.

"I told you she never stops," he sighed as he shook his head at her. "I don't know what Stef has been feeding her, but it has gotta be a cross between human growth hormones and pure sugar. The kid is a beast."

"But she's so cute," I cooed as I watched her tiny little blonde curls bounce with her movements. Now that her hair was drying, she had little ringlets covering the fair skin of her scalp. The big blue eyes were my undoing, too. They were almost the same shade as her uncles and framed by long, dark lashes. She was going to be a heartbreaker... like her uncle.

"I'm pretty sure that's the only reason she's still alive."

Rory's hand settled on my back as he reached around me to grab Nat, tugging her towards us by the front of her open pajamas. "Get over here, crazy."

"Be nice." I scolded him as I looked back over my shoulder. He smelled good, fresh, and clean, not at all like the peanut butter and bubbles concoction from before.

"I know why my sister stays home now. This kid would probably get booted from daycare," he growled as he tried to hold her still. "Wouldn't you? You tiny little heathen."

I held in my laughter as he picked her up and tried to get her leg bent enough to get it into the pajamas. It was harder than it looked. Toddlers were squirmy little creatures.

"Don't worry, Natty. Being cute will get you out of a lot of things in life." I told her as her uncle wrestled with the zipper on the front of the pajamas.

"It's too bad Kendall doesn't know that," he laughed as he bounced the finally clothed little girl in his arms.

"Hey!" He was such an ass.

"What?" he laughed as he reached forward and tried to pinch my side.

"Tickles!" Nathalie cheered as she poked her fingers at his neck.

"Don't tickle me. Let's tickle her, Nat," he told her as he took a step toward me with his fingers wiggling.

"Yay! Tickles!" she laughed as he reached for me, and I bolted around them, running for the door.

"You can run, but you can't hide," he laughed as he bounced a giggling Nathalie on his hip as he pursued me down the hallway.

"Miss Kendall won't share her nuggets if you tickle me," I threatened, grabbing the red and yellow box from the countertop, I thrust it out, and Nathalie tried to grab it as they got closer.

"I think she's trying to bribe us," he whispered into Nat's neck, and it set off another round of hysterical giggles.

"Is it working?" I asked as I guarded that Happy Meal box with my life.

"I don't know, where's the ice cream?" he questioned with narrowed eyes.

Pulling open his freezer, I pointed at the two Oreo McFlurries, and he sighed. "Fine. I guess we can leave her alone, Nat. I'll just have to tickle you."

He dug his fingers into her belly, and she laughed hysterically, squirming against him. After she was finally giggled out, he put her into a highchair that Rory had strapped to one of his kitchen chairs.

"I don't know, Nat, these nuggets look pretty yummy. I don't know if I can share with you," he teased as he pretended to put one into his mouth.

"No, mine!" she yelled as she reached for the box.

He placed some apple slices, a few fries, and some nuggets on the tray, and we watched as she babbled and munched on her food.

"Is she always this happy?" I asked as I watched her little dimpled grin appear as she looked up at us with a mouthful of food.

"Nope. Not even close. She's either happy or pissed. You do not want to be within hearing range when this kid throws a fit about something," he laughed. "I've never seen a child cry on command with actual tears until her."

"Are you a little drama queen like your uncle, Natty?" I laughed, and he reached forward to pinch my side.

Rory narrowed his eyes at me as he turned sideways, facing me as we leaned against the kitchen counter. "I am not a drama queen."

"Yeah, mmhmm," I smirked as I looked at the pout on his mouth. "Sure."

He took a step closer to me, and my heartbeat sped up as his pant leg brushed against mine. "Take it back, Kendall."

Despite the warning in his voice, I wasn't retracting the statement. "Mmm. Nope. It stands."

"Ken. I'm warning you." He looked pretty hot when he was threatening me.

"Oh no, I'm so scared," I teased as I leaned forward. "The big bad drama queen is going to get me."

Before I could back away, he pulled me forward into his chest, pinning me against him with one arm as he dug his fingers into my side.

"No, no, no. Stop!" I shrieked as I wiggled against him.

"Take it back," he growled as he held me against him.

"N-n-n... never!" I laughed even harder as he doubled his efforts. "Oh, my God! Stop!"

His fingers slowed as our chests heaved against each other, his loosely gripping the material of my sweater as he held me stationary. "Are you done now? Going to take it back?"

"I think you just proved my point," I told him breathlessly as I gripped his shirt in my fist.

"I am not a drama queen," he told me seriously as he looked down into my eyes. I hadn't been this close to him in a long time. His chest was warm, and I could feel the frantic beat of his heart against mine.

"Okay, you can be the drama king. I'll even go to Burger King next time to get you one of those little crowns."

His eyes rolled, but I could tell by how he was still smiling that he wasn't upset. Alison was right; we teased each other like some weird kind of foreplay.

"Are you going to be my queen?" he asked quietly as he brought his fingers up to my forehead and pushed my hair back behind my ear.

"Maybe..." I whispered, and his eyes flicked to my mouth.

"You sure you could put up with me? I have quite the flair for dramatics apparently," he rolled his eyes, but the smile was still on his lips.

"I'm sure I could manage," I told him quietly.

The air seemed tense, with some unspoken attraction bouncing between the two of us. He showed no signs of releasing me, and I wasn't arguing. Pressed up against his warm chest, I forgot all the reasons that this was probably a bad idea. And when his tongue slid out of his mouth to wet his lips, and he swallowed hard, I watched with rapt attention.

Things were changing between us. What had been a supportive friendship was morphing into something that blurred all the lines.

"We should get to bed." His voice was low, and my eyes widened as he slowly released his hold on me. "I mean, we should get Nat to bed."

We both looked over at the little girl in the booster seat. She was blinking heavily as she munched on a piece of apple, watching the two of us with curious eyes.

He unstrapped her from the chair and carried her down the hallway. I followed silently behind as he moved around his room, finding her blanket and her stuffed animals, laying her down in the portable crib with a soft caress on the top of her head.

"Come on, let's go get that ice cream." His voice was a low whisper as he turned off the light and closed the door behind him. "Let's hope she falls asleep and doesn't try to hang from the curtains like a monkey while we aren't watching."

"She's probably already falling asleep. All the excitement of Uncle Rory's pantry adventure wore her out," I chuckled.

"I can understand why their house is covered in baby locks now. She sees everything." He shook his head. "I can understand why my sister calls her 'the heathen.'"

"She's a sweetheart," I smiled as I looked up at him. Despite the mischief, I could tell that she had everyone wrapped around her tiny little finger.

"You're just saying that because she isn't yours," he teased as he bumped his shoulder against mine.

"Are you saying that you wouldn't want one of those someday?" I asked, curiosity seeping into my voice. We hadn't talked much about what we wanted besides our career goals in our futures. If I was feeling these emotions resurfacing for him, I needed to know that he wanted the same things I did.

"I didn't say that," he smiled. "She's just a lot of work. I'm not quite ready for that yet."

I wasn't either, but I was someday. If I ever found someone who didn't flee from commitment. Maybe that person was closer to me than I'd thought.

"Hey, no frowning around the ice cream. It's happy time," Rory teased as he took a bit of his own and held the spoon in his mouth.

"You're such a dork." I rolled my eyes and shook my head at him.

"But I'm your dork," he said without skipping a beat, but my heart did.

I wasn't sure what to say to that. I don't think he even realized that he said it. But as time went on, I secretly wanted it to be true.

"Want to put something on Netflix?" he asked, handing me the plastic cup full of ice cream. "We've already got our chill."

"That works for me. Those were my exciting Valentine's Day plans all along."

I followed him to the couch and awkwardly perched myself on the edge of the cushion next to him, aimlessly stirring the soft serve with my spoon.

"Are you thinking of drama? Action? Comedy?" he questioned as he pulled up the menu. "One of those cheesy girly movies you like?"

"It doesn't matter." My voice was quiet as I glanced over at him. His posture was relaxed as he leaned against the cushions.

"Since you'll probably fall asleep in the first twenty minutes, anyway?" He bumped his arm against mine, and my breath caught. It was getting harder and harder to maintain the friendly boundaries we'd put in place. After that day in the coffee shop, our one date and those kisses that almost led to something else were never mentioned again.

When I was with Joel, that was a good thing. But now I couldn't stop thinking about it.

"You're quiet." He set his empty cup on the table as the opening intro flashed across the screen for whatever he'd put on started. I was too busy stuck in my head to notice.

"Sorry. I've just got a lot on my mind," I admitted as I put a small bite of ice cream in my mouth.

"Like?" he asked, his gaze openly curious.

"Just stuff," I sighed, *like possibly falling for one of my best friends despite my best efforts to stay detached.*

He put his arm around my shoulder and pulled me towards his chest. My hand rested over his heart, and I could feel it thumping steadily under my palm. "I'm here to listen if you need me."

"I don't think you can help with this." My voice was quiet but tinged with a bit of melancholy. Lately, as my feelings grew, I'd wondered what my life would look like now if Stefanie hadn't gone into labor when she had.

"I know I'm not the most serious person sometimes." I tried to hold in my snort, but it wasn't successful. "But you know I'll always be here if you need me."

"I know. That's one reason I..." Not knowing if he could handle the truth about my feelings for him, I trailed off as my fingers traced the material of his shirt.

"One reason you what?"

I tilted my head up to look at him, wondering if we were going to be permanently stuck in this friend zone or if he returned even a fraction of my developing feelings. The open acceptance of his gaze made it hard for me to stay quiet, but I was terrified.

"One reason what? Finish what you were saying." The low, pleading quality of his voice stopped me short.

"One reason I l...like you so much."

I'm not sure which one of us moved first, but an overwhelming heat spread through my body as his hand wove into the hair at the back of my head, and his lips touched mine urgently.

This kiss felt different from the ones we'd shared before. It was harder, more desperate. I was panting against Rory's mouth as he tilted his head and pulled me back toward him. Neither of us said anything as we pulled away, we just looked at each other. My lips were burning as I tried to gauge his expression but failed.

Not knowing if kissing him again would be either the most foolish or the bravest thing I'd ever done, I threw caution to the wind, sitting up slightly and throwing my leg over his lap. His hands settled on my hips as we stared at each other, my hands resting flat on his chest.

"This is..." I trailed off as I shifted and felt him press hard and hot between my legs.

He was waiting for me. I knew he was. He didn't want to push things, but I could tell he wanted me just as much as I wanted him.

"Please don't say crazy," he whispered as the open look on his face morphed into one of hesitation.

"No," I sighed. The faint smile on his face fell, and I moved my hand to his cheek, rubbing my thumb over his cheekbone. "This is right. God, is this right."

Our lips crashed into each other again, desperately pulling at each other as our fingers gripped onto each other's clothes. My hips rocked in his lap, and Rory groaned into my mouth as he pushed back against me. Lost in each other and the feelings that had steadily been growing between the two of us for months, I finally surrendered to the pull of my attraction to him.

# Chapter Thirty:
## First Year of Grad School
### APRIL

"Have you given any thought about what your living situation might be like next year?" Rory asked quietly, as he scooted closer to me and pulled me back into his chest. We'd finally had a break in our studies after mid-term papers were due and had a weekend to relax before studying for final exams would take up all our free time.

I'd spent the night at his apartment, both of us deciding we needed some alone time together. Things had been good between us, but I could still feel myself holding back a little. Being with Rory was so effortless that it scared me. We'd both been burned before, so being cautious was just how it was going to have to be for a while.

"Alison and I renewed our lease again for next year in January," I told him quietly as I shifted on my pillow and snuggled back into his powerful arms. His bed was so comfortable. It made me realize I was getting too old to sleep on a futon mattress.

"She doesn't want to live with Benji?" he asked, shifting the hair away from my neck and kissing my shoulder. Our feet tangled together under the covers, and I was enjoying our brief escape from adult reality.

"His parents are super religious. I don't think they want him to live with a woman until he's married." Alison had talked about it a little, but none of it seemed to bother her. They spent enough time together, and I don't think she was in a rush to get down the aisle with her career still finding its footing.

"Doesn't he stay at your apartment most of the time, anyway?" My eyes closed as his warm breath fanned over the side of my face. He was being inquisitive this morning.

"Yeah, but they still help him out with rent, so they'd find out if he moved in with us. They don't want things to get messy with his parents."

"Hmm," he hummed quietly. "Speaking of parents..."

My heartbeat picked up as my eyes popped open. "Uh-huh?"

"Mine want to meet you. They overheard me talking to Stefanie about you during spring break."

His arms tightened around me as I felt a lump catch in my throat. Not that I didn't want to meet his family; it was that I was terrified of including other people in our relationship. My parents were still gun shy after Joel, I'd told them I was dating again, but they didn't know it was Rory or semi-serious. I was afraid to admit that it was this serious.

"Kendall," he sighed as he pulled on my shoulder and turned me to face him. I tucked my face into the soft cotton of his t-shirt and gripped the material covering his shoulder tightly in my hand. "It doesn't have to be some big thing, but I see you here, in my future. I need to know you want that, too."

Taking in a shaky breath, I tried to tamp down the urge to cry. I was scared. Admitting that I saw Rory in my future made this too real, too scary. I didn't want to jinx things and have it all fall apart. I'd been there and done that, and you could only mend a heart so many times.

"I guess asking you to move in with me next year is off the table then," he laughed. My wide eyes shot up to his, and his expression sobered as I looked at him in a panic.

"What?"

"Don't look so terrified. You're here a lot, anyway. I mean, if Alison hadn't been so damned efficient, you'd have been here already," he chuckled as he ran his fingers through my hair. "Kendall, you know I love you. I have for quite a while. I want you here."

My breaths were shaky as tears pooled in my eyes. I hated that I'd put that disappointed look on his face, but I wasn't jumping into this without looking first. It was too soon.

"I...." We'd said the words, but I still had a hard time trusting myself. My judgment had burned me before, and the feelings I had for him worried me. They were more intense than before, more all-encompassing than the warm feelings I'd had for Joel. If Rory left me, I would be left beyond repair. He was one of my closest friends and now my partner. Taking a chance on him meant a tremendous leap of faith on my part, and I was just not ready yet.

"We're going to have to address this eventually," he sighed as he cupped my jaw and kissed me lightly. "I don't want to scare you away, but I need to know you are as serious about this as I am."

Averting my eyes, I stared at the faded letters stretched across his chest. I knew how I felt about him, and I was secure in that most of the time, but these old fears held me back from really letting myself trust anyone. He was as close as I would allow anyone to get to my heart, but I knew that sometimes it wasn't enough for him. My counseling sessions had prepared me for a relationship in theory, but once feelings were involved, I felt myself slipping back into that defensive mindset.

"Do you love me?" he asked in a quiet voice as he tucked his scruffy cheek next to mine. I hated making him doubt me.

"I do," I replied in a rough voice, trying to hold back the tears as I shifted and met his gaze. "I do love you, but you scare me."

He gave me a sad nod and pulled back a little, wiping the tears that had leaked out from my cheeks. "I don't know how to prove to you I won't hurt you."

My chin quivered as I fought to keep my composure, but as he leaned in to kiss my forehead, a sob pushed its way out. He pulled me in closer, pressing my forehead to his shoulder and just holding me as I let it out. I hated crying around him, but sometimes I just couldn't keep the emotions inside anymore. My wounds from Joel had been given a year to heal, but I still felt them.

"Maybe you need to talk to Cortney about this," he whispered as my breathing settled. His long fingers combed through the hair on the back of my head as I clung to him. He was right. I needed to talk to someone about this if this was my reaction to meeting his parents and wanting me to move in.

"I know," I sniffled as I nodded my head against his shirt. "I'm sorry."

"Don't apologize for this," he sighed, squeezing me tighter. "I just don't want to make you cry every time I try to mention our future together."

He was right. This wasn't a healthy reaction for him wanting to take the next natural step in our relationship. I couldn't keep avoiding my fears.

"So, you called me here for a reason," Cortney sighed as she pulled open her notebook and sat back in her chair, looking at me with a blank expression. She had to be the hardest person I'd ever met to read. "We weren't scheduled to meet until next week."

"I did," I sighed as I pulled my legs up onto the couch and hugged my knees. I knew this was my defensive stance, but I just felt better, literally holding myself together. I was afraid that all the progress I'd made during the fall was slipping. "Rory wants me to meet his family."

She pursed her lips, and a faint smile crossed her lips. "That's a big step. You two must be serious for that kind of invitation."

A shaky nod was all I could manage. "We are, I mean, we decided to be exclusive, and we've said we loved each other, but... I don't know why this is freaking me out so much."

"Have you talked to him about your fears?"

I wasn't sure how to answer that. I had talked to him about how I still felt worried about letting down all my walls around him, but I didn't want to give away too much and have him pull away. He didn't know that sometimes I woke up with panic attacks at the thought of him leaving me. I could understand where Joel was coming from now. The irrational fear that your partner may decide you're not enough or not worth the effort was terrifying.

"I'm going to take your silence as a no," she observed as she jotted something in her notebook.

"We've talked about my fears of letting someone in, but I don't think he realizes how often I worry about it." I did all the time. I loved him so much already, but I just couldn't manage to take down the walls I'd constructed to protect myself.

"You told me that open communication was something necessary for you. If you're not sharing your fears with him, you are actively pushing him away. Has he done something to make you question your trust for him?"

I shook my head, chewing at my lip as I looked up at her. She was right. I was pushing him away, and I hated that I still felt like this.

"Do you feel like he'd judge you if he knew you were feeling this way?"

Did I? I wasn't sure. Self-preservation seemed to be the motivation I'd identified myself, but maybe I was secretly scared he'd judge me for feeling like I did sometimes. "I don't know. He's been supportive, but I just can't get past this wall."

She nodded as she tapped her pen against the paper lying on her desk. "Self-preservation is a strong instinct sometimes, but you need to think about how your actions may impact others. You may not intentionally be hiding your feelings from him, but it sounds like that's what is happening."

"I don't know how to stop," I confessed. I didn't even realize I was consciously doing it sometimes.

"Alright, here is what I want you to do," she started as she sat up a little straighter. "I want you to sit down and write down what you are afraid of. In life in general, in your relationship with Rory, in your professional life, anything that may give you anxiety or fear, I want you to write down."

"Okay," I agreed, knowing that it'd helped to journal the last time around. "What do you want me to do with this?"

"That's up to you," she shrugged. "Burn it, tear it up, flush it down the toilet, show it to Rory or someone else you trust. Whatever you need to do to get these emotions out so you can start processing them. Owning your fears will take their power away. You're putting too much emphasis on what could go wrong that you are taking away from all the good things."

I nodded as I took a deep breath and let it out slowly. I could do that. I would confess my deepest fears to Rory so I could move past them, then they wouldn't cripple me anymore.

*Rory: You coming to mine tonight, or am I coming to you?*

*Kendall: I can come to you. I need to show you something.*

*Rory: Something sexy?*

I laughed as I read his message and finished packing up the things I needed to bring home with me from my desk. I shared a small office space with a few other Fine Arts grad students, and we were all burning the candle at both ends, helping to grade final projects and getting ready for exams. I felt like I saw my office mates more than Rory or Alison lately.

*Kendall: Sexy can wait for later.*

I was finally going to show him the letters I'd written at Cortney's instruction. He hadn't mentioned meeting his family again, but I knew it was only a matter of time with summer break coming up. He was planning to go back home for a few weeks to visit, and I knew he wanted me to come for at least part of that time.

*Rory: No, it can't. I haven't seen you enough this week. I'm lonely.*

> **Kendall: You saw me Wednesday.**

> *Rory: You fell asleep after 20 minutes.*

> *Rory: I miss you.*

Shoving the last file folder in my bag, I pulled the strap of my bag over my shoulder and locked up the office behind me. I'd walked today since the weather had cooperated, so I took off at a brisk walk across campus, glad that Rory's apartment was closer to the Fine Arts building than mine.

"Hey." He smiled as he opened the door, bracing his hands against the top of the doorframe, a sliver of his toned pale skin showing at the edge of his T-shirt.

"Hi." I stepped forward and wrapped my arms around him, laying my head against his heart as he pulled me into his embrace.

"You alright?" he asked as he stepped back through the doorway and pushed the door closed.

"Yeah," I told him quietly, not quite knowing how he was going to take my confessions this evening.

"You sure?" he asked again as he pushed me back lightly by the shoulders and lowered his face to look into my eyes.

"I'm sure," I smiled as I cupped his cheek and leaned in to give him a soft kiss. He looked worried. His arms wrapped back around me, and he lifted me into his arms as he tilted his head and deepened the kiss. His tongue desperately slipped between my lips, and he kissed me passionately until I had to pull back to breathe.

"What did you want to show me?" he asked as he slipped my hand into his and tugged me toward his couch. I pulled my bag off and laid it down on the coffee table. He sat down and pulled me to his side, kissing the top of my head. I could hear his heart beating faster than normal and felt guilty that I made him nervous.

I sat up and turned myself toward him, biting my lip before I leaned over and opened the flap on my messenger bag, pulling out the envelope I'd stuffed the letters into the night before.

"What is this?" he asked as his expression sobered. I could see why he was nervous. It felt eerily similar to how things had gone down with Joel.

"I've been talking to Cortney weekly for the last few weeks... after...," I trailed off.

"After I suggested you meet my family," he sighed. I nodded and pushed the envelope into his hand.

"Just read these. She suggested writing down what was scaring me and letting someone I trusted read them." He looked down at the envelope in his hand and back up to me, placing it on the couch cushion between us.

"Can you tell me what's in there before I open it?" He was looking at the envelope like it was going to bite him. "If things have changed for you, please just tell me. I don't want to read it. I want you to talk to me."

"Hopefully, this doesn't change things," I smiled as I reached down and opened the envelope, unfolding the pages and handing them to him. "There's a lot. It'll be easier to understand if you read it."

Whenever I tried to articulate my feelings in person, I got choked up or felt like I needed to edit things. When I sat down and finally wrote it all down, I didn't censor myself.

"Promise?" he asked as he gripped my wrist.

"I promise. I think this will help." He blew out a breath as he finally took the papers, turning them and leaning back into the cushion behind him.

---

*Dear Rory,*

*I know that I've been pushing you away lately, and I'm sorry. It's nothing you've done. I'm just scared of letting myself love you fully. Hopefully, these letters will help you understand things from my perspective.*

*Cortney helped me process and move past my abandonment issues when I was in counseling last fall, but some of my old fears started creeping in when we started dating. I don't want you to doubt my love for you, so, at her urging, I'm writing it all down. You've been so patient with me, and I haven't been fair with keeping my hesitations from you. I'm tired of feeling scared, so this is my way of taking back the power from my fears.*

*First, my feelings are my own, and nothing you've done has caused them. If anything, I feel more guilty about them with how supportive you have been. You have shown me you are fully invested in this relationship, and this is my attempt to return that. I want to trust you as much as you trust me.*

*Joel will always be the elephant in the room, but I want you to know that my feelings for you are separate from those I used to have for him. I won't hold you accountable for his mistakes because he betrayed both of us. Never question that my love for you is solid, and even if he were to come back into our lives, I would always choose you.*

*I'm scared sometimes of how calm things are between us, and it isn't fair of me to be afraid of waiting for the shoe to drop. You've always shown me genuine love and respect. I want to be strong enough to return that to you.*

*Meeting your family doesn't scare me. Getting attached and losing you and them scares me. I don't want them to judge me about my past mistakes or what happened with Joel. I still feel embarrassed at how everything ended, and I don't want them to get the impression that I was the reason for the wedding not happening. I also don't want them to question that what I feel for you is real. You are not a rebound, and I do not see you as a temporary part of my life. When I think about the future, I see you in it. I see myself building a life and a family with you, which scares me.*

*I know your feelings are genuine, but I still find myself afraid of them fading or disappearing. Dylan and Joel both made me question if I was loveable as a person. It's been hard for me to let you in because I haven't wanted to give another person power like that regarding my self-worth again.*

*That is also why I'm so hesitant to move in with you. After Joel almost left me homeless, I knew I wanted to control my home and not rely on another person to provide one for me. As much as I want to take that leap for us and trust that things will work out this time, I need to be in control of my living situation. If and when we move in together, I want a permanent relationship established with you.*

*I know that right now, neither of us is ready to talk about marriage because it's too soon, but I need you to know that when that happens, it will be for good. I want you to be in this relationship one hundred percent because I only intend to get married once. I'm done playing around with the idea and choosing the wrong people to commit myself to. If we remain in this relationship, I want it to be serious, and both be on the same page.*

*I know this is a lot to process, but writing it down has helped tremendously. It's hard to look at you and formulate the words, but I want you to know what is in my heart.*

*Love,*

*Kendall*

"Wow," he breathed as he leaned forward and placed the first letter on the coffee table. When he looked up into my eyes, I felt a few tears leak out, and he was quick to lean forward to wipe them away. "I'm sorry. I never asked how you were feeling about all this."

"No," I shook my head as I gripped his wrist. "This isn't anything you did or didn't do. You don't need to feel guilty about this."

"But I," he blew out a shaky breath and pulled me forward into his lap, hugging me to his chest as he buried his face into my hair. "Maybe we weren't ready. I never wanted to pressure you. I tried to be patient, but…"

"Stop," I leaned back and cupped his cheeks, forcing him to look at me. "I am ready. You didn't pressure me. My feelings are just as strong as yours, but I needed to be honest with you about my fears."

He nodded and leaned forward, slowly caressing my lips with his, urging me closer to his body with his hands braced against my back. "I love you so much. Thank you for sharing this with me."

"I always want to be honest with you. I want you to know the good and the bad. I felt horrible for keeping this from you, but I wasn't sure how you'd react," I confessed, staring into Rory's eyes.

"I get it, trust me. I've been afraid that maybe you hadn't taken this as seriously as I had. I didn't want to scare you away, but my mom had asked, and I want you to meet them."

"Can we promise always to tell each other the truth?" I asked quietly, my voice catching with my returning nerves. "I don't want to keep secrets from you anymore."

"I promise," he nodded as he pulled me forward by the back of my neck, tucking my face against his chest. I hugged him tightly, listening to the steady beat of his heart, knowing that we were on the same page and that we both wanted this. That was all that mattered; fears be damned.

# Chapter Thirty-one:
## Summary After First Year of Grad School
### JULY

*Rory: I'm bored.*

I rolled my eyes as I pushed down the notification. He shouldn't be bored since he was supposed to work today. I was in the studio prepping materials for the fall. I would be teaching a curriculum class for the Art Therapy undergrad students that helped plan real-life lessons for their future clients or students.

*Rory: Wanna play hooky?*

I'd pretty much wrapped up my work for the day so that I could leave a little early, but Rory usually worked until five-thirty most days. He was working in an entry-level position for the company he hoped to stay at after finishing his MBA.

He'd almost been scouted for a job several hours away, but with finishing grad school and my position as a graduate TA with the university, he'd turned it down. I'd been worried that his parents would think I influenced his decision, but he hadn't wanted to be even further away from them, either.

In May, after finals, I'd finally accompanied him home. It'd been a little awkward at first because they all knew my past, but his sister had been amazing. Nat had gotten even bigger in the few months since I'd seen her last, and she was a pleasant distraction for us all to keep things light.

His mom had cornered me after lunch and given me the 'what are your intentions?' interrogation about her son, but she'd relaxed after I'd assured her that my feelings for him were real. I knew she was just concerned about him because of how things had turned out with Bridgette.

*Rory: Yes? No?*

*Kendall: Aren't you supposed to be working?*

*Rory: Half day. The servers are down. IT is supposed to have it fixed tomorrow.*

Looking at my watch, I saw it was after two and wondered how long he'd been done.

*Kendall: Where are you?*

*Rory: Where are you?*

I finished packing up and headed out into the hallway, noticing a familiar head of hair sticking up over the top of the bench outside the doors to the building.

"Why didn't you just come in to find me?" A smile lit up his face as I appeared at the end of the bench, and he patted the space next to him.

"The doors were locked, and it's nice out today," he shrugged as I sat down next to him and leaned against his side. He'd changed out of his work clothes and wore athletic shorts with a fitted compression shirt. He'd been hitting the gym in his apartment building most mornings before work and it showed.

Sometimes, he'd even coaxed me out of bed, but I just walked to work on campus most days. I was still logging some hours in the psychology labs, but Kale had moved on, pursuing his P.h.D. at another university.

"So, what's the plan?" I asked as he leaned down and kissed the top of my head. We were in a great place lately. My sessions with Cortney had slowed down, and I'd finally been able to open up to Rory more about my feelings. He was patient with me, but I know he was finally opening up to me as well.

While his days with regular counseling had ended, he'd told me it'd helped him deal with his feelings of rejection after Bridgette broke up with him.

He'd confessed that between Joel and me getting together and him leaving, he'd dated a little, but he was afraid to open up at all. I didn't ask if he'd been celibate the whole time, but I knew he was always safe, so it didn't bother me because it'd happened before we got together.

"We don't have anything going on tonight, do we?" he questioned as he turned toward me. I sat up and pulled my knee up to face him, and it made my heart warm to see the content smile on his face.

"No," I shook my head. "Alison and Benji are going out of town this weekend, so I'm assuming she'll be packing tonight."

"You up for something fun?"

I squinted as I looked over at his mischievous smile. Sometimes his idea of fun was borderline criminal. "We won't get arrested for this, will we?"

He rolled his eyes and pulled my hands into his lap. "No, what kind of amateur do you take me for?"

"Do I need to change?" I looked down at my khaki shorts and blouse, my attire not matching up to his.

"I've got some things for you in the back of the car," he nodded to where he'd parked down the street.

"And where do you plan on having me change into these things?" I laughed as he eyed my chest.

"I'll cover you," he promised with a lifted eyebrow. "I promise I won't peek... much."

I swatted at him and laughed lightly. "Oh, like you haven't seen it all already."

"That I have." He gave me a once over, and I felt my cheeks turn pink at the heat in his eyes. The fact that he still looked at me like he did five months later made me feel desired.

"Alright, perv, let's see what ridiculous outfit you've brought for me."

It didn't turn out to be anything bad. Luckily, I had a tank top on underneath my blouse, so I only had to do some creative wiggling in the back seat to change into some athletic shorts as he watched me in the rearview mirror.

"See," he smiled as I rejoined him in the front. "Nobody got arrested."

"Yet," I laughed, giving him a saucy wink.

He shook his head at me and took my hand, intertwining our fingers on the center console as he started driving toward town.

"Where are you taking me?" I asked, as he kept driving once we got to the downtown area.

"You'll see," he smiled as he made a few turns, and my eyes lit up as a familiar sight came into view. The large wheel wasn't lit up yet, but I had a special fondness for Ferris wheels.

"Really?" I asked as I bounced in my seat a little. Despite it being a weekday, the traffic backed up a few blocks away from the fairgrounds. I couldn't believe he brought me back to the county fair. Last year I'd still been in zombie land when it was in town. Having fun was the last thing on my mind for most of that summer; I was trying to stay afloat.

"It's here for a few more days, but I knew I wanted to come to get you to go once they let us out of work today," he smiled as he looked over at me.

I squeezed his hand as we waited in the long line of cars waiting to find their parking spaces in the big open field nearby. "I'm glad I can look back on that day now and see part of our beginning, not a regret."

"I'm not sure I could ride a Ferris wheel again and not think of that kiss." I laughed out loud at the accompanying suggestive wiggle of his eyebrows.

"It was a memorable first date. If only someone hadn't run off and ghosted me at the end," I teased, but I saw a flash of something serious on his features before he turned to face me.

"Trust me. I can't tell you how many times I've cursed my sister for having the absolute worst timing to go into labor." I was right there with him. While I was completely committed to my relationship with Joel after that, I often wondered what would have happened had Rory not been called away that night.

I know that I would have slept with him, but I wasn't sure what would have happened afterward. Would it have just been a short-lived fling, or would it have worked out? Would we be engaged or married by now?

"Hey," he squeezed my hand as he pulled into a parking space and turned off the car. "Stay with me, okay? I know we've both got some regrets, but I'm happy with where we're at. Let's make some new memories today."

"Sorry, I..." *overthink everything.*

"I get it, I do. That day changed my life, too. I'm just thankful we found our way back to each other."

Nodding, I let out a deep breath and let go of his hand, opening my car door and meeting him around the front. He grasped my hand and led us toward the fairgrounds. We wandered through the animal barns until our stomachs protested, then we ate until we were too full. He didn't make fun of me for molesting a corn dog this time, but he gave me some knowing glances when I couldn't hold in the moans as we shared a freshly fried elephant ear.

"What do you want to ride first?" he asked, tugging me excitedly toward the flashing lights of the midway as the sun was setting past the clouds.

"Nothing too crazy. I'm still full. We already established puking was a hard pass in our relationship."

"Ferris wheel?" he asked quietly, his eyes looking serious as he tugged me along.

"Sounds perfect."

We were quiet as we waited in the line, his arms wrapped tightly around me as I leaned back into his broad chest. One perk of having a freakishly tall boyfriend; he always made me feel small and wanted.

As we boarded the small metal car, I had flashes of that summer two years ago, when I felt like something significant was developing between us.

"What're you thinking so hard about?" he asked as he pulled me to his side and whispered in my ear. The same chills he always gave me in close proximity made me shudder, and his smile widened.

"Just stuff," I said nervously as I chewed on my bottom lip. The air was tense with something I couldn't identify. It felt like maybe we were in the middle of another significant moment.

"Hmm..." he hummed as he turned my face toward his. "If I recall correctly, from the last time we were on here, it's quite the head rush to make out at the top."

"Oh, you think I'm going to kiss you up here?" I teased as the car approached the top of the wheel, rocking a little as it slowed to a stop.

"I love you," he whispered as he cupped my jaw and slowly drew my face toward him. His warm lips parted mine as he coaxed me into another intense kiss at the top of the Ferris wheel. Neither of us noticed as the wheel started moving again, the sparks from the kiss enough to sufficiently distract us from the lights flashing past our eyelids.

"You up for one more stop?" he asked after we'd come down and ridden as many rides as our tickets allowed. I was tired, but still a little wound up from all the adrenaline the rides had caused.

"Well, you haven't gotten me arrested yet. Why not?"

He opened the car door for me, tucking me into my seat with a scorching kiss that made me melt into the leather upholstery.

As he pulled his car into a visitor space along the side of one of the engineering buildings on campus, I wondered what he was up to. His apartment was only a few blocks away.

"Come on," he urged as he opened my door and pulled me out of the car.

The campus was quiet as he pulled me between the old brick buildings, the sound of rushing water faint as we stepped onto the sidewalk at the far side of the engineering quad.

The colored lights in the fountain were flashing as he pulled me towards it, a boyish grin on his face. I hoped he wasn't about to strip down and run naked through the fountain as his brother had. Bailing him out of jail for public indecency wasn't on my to-do list for the evening.

"Wait," I pulled his arm and got him to stop as we approached the stone benches that bordered the jets of the fountain.

"Live a little, Special K," he teased as he tried to pull me into the spray with him, that naughty smirk pulled across his lips.

"Aren't we a little old to be running through the fountain?" I laughed as I watched him lean down to pull off his shoes.

"We're never too old to have fun," he smiled as he knelt in front of me and pulled off my sneakers.

"If we get yelled at by campus police..." I warned as he stood back up and gave me a soft kiss, placing our shoes up on the bench.

"It'll be fine," he laughed as he took both my hands and started leading me towards the water jets. "Trust me?"

I tilted my head and gave him a jerky nod. "Always."

"Let's go," he laughed as he dragged me into the spray, and we got blasted by the closest jet of water.

I had to admit. It felt good just to let go and have fun with him, carting in and out of the stone pillars, splashing each other, and acting carefree as the water soaked us. I was a little distracted by how his t-shirt clung to his muscled chest, half wanting to go home to get him out of his wet clothes.

"Show me what ya got," he taunted as he pointed to the jet in the middle, "Think you can still do ten push-ups?"

"Pfft," I laughed as I rolled my eyes at him. "You first."

"Alright," he nodded, a cocky grin on his face. "Count me off."

Water was dripping from the both of us as I followed him toward the center jets and watched him drop into an almost perfect push-up. Mine would never be that graceful, but it was quite enjoyable to watch him.

I counted as he got into a rhythm, and then he showed off, clapping at the top of the push-up and splashing water up at me.

"Show off," I laughed as he sat up on his knees and cupped his hands, so the water sprayed directly at me. I tried to shield myself, shrieking as the cold water assaulted me.

When the jet went back down, Rory was still kneeling, staring at me with an expectant look on his face. I swiped a hand across my eyes to clear the excess water and stepped closer, a surprised gasp escaping me. "What?"

"What do you think?" he laughed as he held his hand out toward me, a sparkling diamond ring held up between his fingers. "Want to be stuck with me forever?"

My right hand came up to cover my mouth as I took a few steps forward, nodding my head.

He reached out and grabbed the left one, slipping the ring onto my finger. "Yeah?"

"Yes!" I shouted as the water jets bubbled at our feet.

Rory hopped up and pulled me into his arms, spinning me around as the jets started again, soaking us both. I laughed into his neck as he turned, completely surprised by the events of the evening.

He'd given me no sign that he was about to propose, but the way he pulled it off was perfect. I knew he'd take care of my heart and never fail to make me laugh. I couldn't imagine a better man to commit myself to for the long haul.

# Chapter Thirty-two:
## The Wedding
### PRESENT DAY

"**D**on't let go," I murmured, clinging tightly to my father's arm.

"Don't worry. I've got you." He smiled down at me as he patted my hand.

Words would never be enough to thank him for all that he'd done for me in the past few months. He had been a shoulder to lean on when I'd had hiccups with my final exams. When I wasn't sure whether to continue with my school after I graduated, we'd come a long way from the father who once gave me a lecture on my future and being a responsible adult.

"Just breathe," he encouraged. I took a deep breath and let it out. "And try not to trip."

"Don't jinx me," I laughed as we stepped over the threshold of the sanctuary doors.

My eyes connected with the man at the end of the aisle, and it was crystal clear I'd finally made the right decision.

"Looks like you win. I see tears," my dad whispered as he leaned in close.

"Quit," I smiled as I gripped his arm a little tighter.

He was right, though. My normally stoic groom was staring at me with a look of awe I wasn't sure that I deserved, but I was going to revel in, nonetheless.

When my father took the last few steps down the long aisle and placed my hand inside my groom's larger one, I could see the unshed tears pooled in the corners of his bright blue eyes.

"You look beautiful." He mouthed, and I couldn't even attempt to hide the blush that stained my cheeks. Even after the things we'd been through in the last few years, he still had a profound effect on me every time he looked at me.

I'd almost forgotten there were other people in the room when the pastor began talking about love and faithfulness. That was something that both our pasts had shaken, but we'd found in each other.

As my sister read a passage from EE Cummings, I clung to my beloved's hand, knowing that the words she was reading applied to how I felt about him.

*"I carry your heart with me, I carry it in my heart. I am never without it."*

He reached his free hand up to his chest and tapped the fabric of his lapel that laid over his heart.

"I love you." I mouthed as he smiled at me and mouthed it back.

*"I fear no fate, for you are my fate, my sweet. I want no world, for beautiful you are my world, my true."*

"You're my fate." He mouthed, and I smiled as we listened to her read through the last few lines.

The pastor gave his sermon on fidelity and the sanctity of marriage. I'd always known that I'd be committing myself to someone someday, but it'd always been some far-off concept.

"Today, I bring together this couple in the eyes of God. May He bless their union."

When he said those words, it sunk in that this was it for me. I'd finally found the elusive one. That person who would always have my back. We'd talked about writing our vows, but I knew I'd never make it through them without blubbering like a baby as I talked about how special this man was to me.

He'd seen me at rock bottom and helped me find my way back, silently guiding me to the place I stood today. This day meant more than just a second, third, or even fourth chance at love. It symbolized the bond that had brought us together.

He'd been worried when the only date available for our venue had been two days after the date of my previously canceled nuptials, but I took it as a sign. We were rebuilding something out of the ashes that was much stronger than it'd been originally. He'd been instrumental in my rebirth after heartbreak.

He'd proven to me that his friendship was the foundation of our relationship, and it couldn't be broken. He'd been patient with me when I was reluctant to trust him. He'd been compassionate when I'd faltered.

As he repeated his vows after the pastor, tears trickling down his face, I knew that he'd always be by my side.

Then, it was my turn.

"Will you please repeat this vow, saying after me..."

"I, Kendall, take you, *Rory*, to be my husband, to have and to hold from this day forward, for better or for worse, in sickness and in health. I promise to love and cherish you."

The smile on my handsome groom's face was unshakable as the pastor continued.

"Do we have the rings?"

We looked over at Rory's older brother and best man, Cam, who dutifully played his part while he pretended to have misplaced them.

"Oh, my bad. Here they are," he teased as he reached inside his interior coat pocket and pulled out the two white gold wedding bands.

"Always the funny guy," Rory teased back as Cam dropped the two bands into his palm.

"Someone in this family has to be." My newly appointed brother winked at me as his brother rolled his eyes, causing laughter to sound out from the pews.

Of course, they couldn't behave themselves during a wedding ceremony.

Rory handed me his band, and we followed along as the pastor talked about the exchange of rings.

"Rory, will you please take this ring and place it upon the third finger of Kendall's left hand, and, holding her hand in yours, please repeat this promise to her, saying after me."

"With this ring, I seal my promise to be your faithful and loving husband, as God is my witness." He looked into my eyes as he carefully slipped the band onto my finger.

"Kendall, will you please take this ring and place it upon the third finger of Rory's left hand, and, holding his hand in yours, please repeat this promise to him, saying after me."

"With this ring, I seal my promise to be your faithful and loving wife, as God is my witness."

He continued with the ceremony, but I had a hard time paying attention as Rory ran his thumb over my ring, staring at me with more love than I ever thought I'd find.

"Ladies and gentlemen, it is my privilege to introduce to you for the first time, Mr. and Mrs. Chandler." He smiled widely as he held his hands out towards us. "You may now kiss the..."

Rory didn't even let him finish as he cupped the sides of my face and kissed me soundly to the cheers of our friends and family.

When I met him six years ago, this moment was the furthest thing from my mind. Knowing now what I didn't realize back then, I could see that every decision I'd made starting that day led me to him.

"I love you," he whispered, cradling me against his chest and kissing my forehead before pulling back and clasping my hand tightly in his.

"I love you, too."

We turned to face the crowd hand in hand, bright smiles on our faces.

Every screw-up, misunderstanding, and heartache along the way had all been a part of our story, and now the future was ours to write together.

# Chapter Thirty-Three:
## The Wedding Reception
### PRESENT DAY

The fading sunlight cascaded in the wall of windows and threw shadows across the floor as I sat quietly on the narrow couch that faced the gardens beyond. We'd chosen to have our wedding reception at a botanical garden. The guests were all out at a cocktail reception in a tent on the lawn while Rory and I tried to finish our wedding pictures.

We'd finished the group shots after the ceremony was over, both at the church and here. I was sure our wedding party was probably off causing mischief somewhere while we tried to get these pictures.

"Alright, Rory, stand behind her with your hand on her shoulder. Both of you look out the window. Try to keep your head at the same angle as hers," the photographer instructed. "Nice. Hold on, let me adjust the back light."

We'd been all over the grounds, taking pictures for over an hour. I hoped the photographer was done soon because I was starving.

"Kendall, stand up and move closer to the window. Rory, stand behind her with your hand on her waist. Tuck your face in next to her neck like you're telling her a secret."

I felt his warm breath fan over my shoulder and sighed as his muscular chest pressed against my back. "I'm about to go rogue if he doesn't finish soon. You in?"

Biting my lip to keep from laughing, I whispered my consent and leaned back into him.

"Alright, last shot. Let's make it count. Kendall, turn and face Rory. Left hand on his shoulder, make sure the rings are visible," he coached as he pointed at us expectantly. "Rory, hands on her waist and pull her flush with you. Look into each other's eyes."

Slowly shifting in his hold, I got into place and stared up at Rory as he looked down at me. I still had a hard time believing that he was mine now.

"You're glowing," he whispered, and my face flushed as he stared down at me with open admiration.

"I like what she did with your hair. You look very handsome today," I complimented. He looked very sophisticated.

"Are you saying I don't look that way every day?" That cocky smirk of his was in full effect. He knew I thought he was attractive. He was fishing for compliments.

"You don't wear a tux every day."

"This dress is..." he trailed off as he pressed his hips forward slightly. Someone was feeling a little frisky.

"Rory! Geez. Is that all you ever think about?" I laughed, pushing my hips back away from him.

"Not all, but it's your fault," he insisted.

"Hmm. It must be all those leggings I wear at home. I didn't realize that grad student chic did it for you."

I felt his thumb slip between the lace and my skin along my lower back, softly caressing me. "I don't care what you're wearing. It's you that does it for me."

"Well, we've still got a few hours left, and then you can do whatever you want with me," I whispered.

The photographer called out a few more directions, and Rory tucked his face into my neck as I stood up on my tiptoes with my arms draped over his shoulders. "I'm going to hold you to that."

"I'd rather you just held me to you," I told him honestly. We hadn't had a moment alone with each other since our little stolen rendezvous in his kitchen the other day.

Now that I could finally call him my husband, I was aching to touch him. To show him how I felt about him.

"We don't need to go to the reception, right?" he whispered, the husky quality of his voice giving away his arousal.

"I'm pretty sure our parents would kill us. And Nat. You promised her a dance," I reminded him. She would give him hell if he backed out on her.

"So, we go eat dinner, dance a little, sneak away, and then I eat you for dessert."

"No wedding cake?" I scoffed as I looked at him with wide eyes. The smirk pulled across his lips showed he knew I was teasing him.

"I'm sure you're sweeter," he murmured as he lightly kissed along my neck. The photographer was about to get a show if he didn't finish soon.

"Okay. I think we've got enough for now. I'll let you guys take a break." Speak of the Devil. He started packing up his equipment and slipped out of the hallway as Rory continued to kiss along my neck and shoulder.

"Finally," he breathed into my skin as he banded his arms around me and pressed me into the frame of the window beside us.

"It's not exactly private here," I laughed, which then turned into a moan as he sucked on my sensitive skin. "Stop it. You're going to leave a mark."

"Maybe I want to."

I shook my head and pushed his shoulders half-heartedly. "We need to go out there. They'll start looking for us soon."

His posture deflated as he hugged me to him, humming against my skin.

"As much as I want to sneak away with you. We've got plenty of time for that later," I assured. We had all the alone time we wanted on our upcoming honeymoon.

"There's never enough time for that," he said, still pouting. I closed my eyes and clung to him as he swayed back and forth. It was almost like we were dancing.

"Would you two quit humping and get out here," Alison startled us as she walked into the entryway. "People are getting restless, and they're going to need food for all the alcohol they're slugging down."

"Go away, Allie," Rory growled into my neck, causing me to giggle.

I turned my head toward my best friend and laughed at how she held her hands on her hips. "There's gotta be a hose around here somewhere that I can turn on the two of you."

"Fine. We're coming... we're coming," I sighed as she gave me an unimpressed look. I would remember to cock block her when it was her turn.

"Well, not now, we're not," Rory whispered, and I giggled as he nipped at my ear.

"You've got five minutes until I let Nat loose in here to drag you out, and she's been shot gunning full-sugar Capri suns and skittles all afternoon."

"Okay, okay, we'll be right out," I groaned as Rory continued to kiss my neck.

She slipped back around the corner, and Rory straightened up, cupping my jaw in his large palms and gently kissing my lips. "We can still run. We're already married. They saw the important part."

My finger traced along his hairline as I gazed up at him. "She's right. We should enjoy the party. We're only going to do this once."

"Hmm. I don't remember that part. Maybe you should remind me," he teased.

"You're stuck with me until death do us part."

"Oh, that part. I guess I'm on board with that," Rory sighed dramatically.

"You better be. Too late now."

"Will you still love me when I'm bald, and there's hair on my back?" he asked with wide eyes.

I laughed as he kissed my cheek again, his nose nuzzling against my ear. "I guess. As long as you love me when I'm bald with hair on my back, too."

"Ehhh..." he groaned and pulled back, making a face and shaking his head a little.

Pinching his side, I pulled his face back towards me and kissed him. Soft, tentative pecks at first that quickly escalated into something more. The fire that'd been there in our first kiss just kept intensifying with every one after it.

"Let's go before the tiny cockblock comes to find us," he whispered.

"Be nice. You love Natty."

"I was talking about Cam," he laughed loudly and took my hand, leading me back toward the rest of our annoying family.

It'd been a whirlwind from the moment we'd stepped into the tent, watching our siblings give speeches, our dads getting sentimental during theirs. I spent half of dinner with Nat on my lap, talking excitedly about everything that'd happened today.

"I can take her." Stef's husband, Porter, stood behind my chair, watching his daughter curled up against my chest with an amused smile.

"She's going to sleep hard tonight." I smiled at him as I gave the warm little ball on my chest another hug.

"I'm not tired," she yawned as she rubbed one of her little fists against her eye.

"Why don't we go find mommy and see if she wants to dance with us," Porter suggested, and her little head popped up.

"Where's Uncle Rory? He's a better dancer than you." Knowing my husband's less-than-stellar dance moves, that was an insult coming from a preschooler.

"Ouch," I stifled my laughter in her hair and shifted over so he could pull the sleepy little girl from my lap.

I couldn't believe she was only three. It was easy to forget with how tall she was and her talkative nature. Looking at her always made me wonder what my children would look like when the time came.

As I looked out at the dance floor, I watched as Rory twirled his dance partner out and then spun her back in. When I'd first met his mother, she'd been highly skeptical of our relationship once she discovered I'd been the bride that Joel had left jilted at the altar.

She'd slowly come around as she spent more time with us and once she saw me with Nat. The little girl had claimed me as her own and followed me around whenever we visited.

"Today turned out nice." My sister took the seat next to me and picked up her forgotten champagne flute, downing the contents.

"It did. I'm glad the weather cooperated."

"I'm sure it would've been great even if it was downpouring," she smiled.

"But we would dance in a mud puddle if it did," I laughed, glad that the day had been perfect.

"I don't think it would matter. The two of you would still manage to make it fun."

I reached over and grabbed her hand, smiling. We'd never been super close, but I hoped that'd change now that we were a little older.

"He's a good fit for you." She nodded to Rory, who had swapped partners and was dancing with Nat, twirling the little girl, blonde braids flying out behind her.

"I think so, too," I agreed. It may have taken me longer than I expected to find the person who fit, but he did. So well.

"I know I wasn't there for you when Joel left," she apologized, "but I'm glad that Rory was."

"It's kind of hard when we live so far apart, but I want to be a better sister, too," I nodded. She lived several hours away and traveled for her job a lot. We only saw each other on holidays. I always felt like I was following in her shadow throughout my childhood, so I hadn't tried to keep in touch when she moved away after college.

She'd been upset that I had gotten engaged to Joel before her long-time boyfriend proposed, so they'd eloped in Vegas and not invited any family. Our poor mother had been beside herself between my wedding being called off and Sara's slight.

"I've been thinking about moving back. Duke can work from anywhere, so if I found something back here, it'd be kinda nice to have family close whenever we decide to have kids." I eyed the champagne glass in her hand. "Not soon or anything, but we've been talking about it."

"I'd love to be Aunt Kendall," I smiled.

"You are pretty good at it. I see you with Nat and don't want my kids to miss out on that."

"It'd be nice to have Aunt Sara around when the time comes," I admitted. I wanted my kids to have lots of family close by.

"Have you guys...?" she asked curiously as her eyes flitted over my shoulder to Rory.

"No, no." I shook my head. Rory was still getting established in his office as a consultant, and I'd decided to work for the university in the Fine Arts department. They were hiring more part-time faculty for the Art Therapy major, and I could slowly work towards a P.h.D. "That's still a few years away, but someday."

Rory and I talked about everything. His insecurities about people not taking him seriously. My fears of abandonment and not being communicated with openly. We'd decided that when we started dating that if it was going to work between us, that complete transparency was non-negotiable.

Alison thought it was weird that we told each other everything, but I'd never been more comfortable with a partner. I knew he truly respected me, and I returned it. The mistakes of our youth had taught us both that we were worth investing the time into.

"Well, I'll let you know what we decide to do. I think you're being summoned."

My eyes followed her line of sight, and I saw my goofy husband standing in the middle of the dance floor, tie askew, jacket missing, and sleeves rolled up, giving me a sexy smirk while crooking a finger in my direction.

"Thank you for standing up with me today. It meant a lot," I told her sincerely as I squeezed her hand. "Love you."

"Of course. Don't keep him waiting," Sara laughed at whatever he was doing behind me.

Knowing that he'd just come to drag me out there if I didn't hurry, I rushed around the tables and took his outstretched hand as a song with a slow, romantic beat started. "Have we put in enough time yet?"

His hands drew me into his chest further as I placed my arms over his shoulders and dug one of my hands into the hair on the back of his head. "Hmm, maybe. Are you tired?"

"No, definitely not tired," he whispered as his hand pressed low on my back, his hips grinding into me. The whole day had been one elongated test of both of our patience, and I was ready to be alone with him.

"Hmm..." I hummed as I leaned in closer and kissed the side of his neck. "You think they'd be mad if we just snuck out? It's going to take forever to say goodbye to everyone."

"It's our wedding night. We can do whatever we want," he whispered.

The distant clinking of silverware on glass made us both glance toward the guest tables. Alison and Benji were being obnoxious again and clinking their forks on their champagne flutes.

"It's so going to be payback at their wedding in a few months," I told him as I narrowed my eyes at my best friend.

"You know they'll love it," he laughed.

I pushed up onto my toes and kissed him gently, slowly pulling back and running my hand down the side of his hair. "Let's get out of here."

"I thought you'd never ask," he smirked, and then we plotted our escape plan.

"Oh, my God, you're going to drop me." I tried to stifle my laughter, but I couldn't help it. Thankfully, the lot next to us was still vacant, and the neighbors next door hadn't moved in yet.

"I won't drop you. Quit squirming. This satin is slippery," Rory scolded.

Instead of the traditional method of carrying your wife across the threshold bridal style, my groom had scooped me out of the back of the limo and thrown me over his shoulder in a fireman's carry.

"What's wrong with bridal style?" I giggled as he strode up the front walk.

"This skirt is so poofy that I'd never be able to see over the top of it. Then, I'd drop you."

"Watch out." My fingers tightly gripped the back of his shirt as my head narrowly missed the post on the front porch.

"You're fine. I've got you," he told me. I could just imagine him rolling his eyes.

"If you knock me out on the door frame, you're not getting laid," I teased.

"I'm not going to whack you into the doorframe. Would you just let me be romantic for once?" he asked, exasperated.

"Should I be pretending you're a hot fireman here to extinguish the fire in my loins?" I giggled. Maybe I had indulged in a bit too much champagne.

"If you've got burning in your loins, we've got bigger problems than hitting your head on the door frame," he laughed.

Thankfully, the limo driver had driven us to our new home. The champagne had been freely flowing all night, and we were both a little tipsy.

"Did you remember the key?" I asked as we were paused at the door.

"They installed the deadbolt with the code on it this morning."

"Do you remember the code?"

He scoffed. "No. We're just going to camp out on the front porch."

"Sounds romantic," I laughed.

"Yup. I threw down a moving pad and everything," he said in his serious, but not completely serious, voice. "Perfect wedding night accommodations."

"Of course, I know the code. It's your birthday." I couldn't help the shriek I let out as he transferred his grip on me to one hand and punched the code in the door with the other.

"Isn't that kind of dangerous? What if people look up my birthday and rob us?"

"We can change it later. We've got more important matters to attend to right now," he told me, his voice impatient.

"Hmm. Wonder what those could be."

"It's a mystery," he laughed as he pushed the door open and turned so he could fit inside the door without giving his new bride a concussion.

The first floor looked like it had a few days ago when I finally made it back over here, with one illuminating exception.

"When did you do this?" I breathed in wonder, looking at all the twinkle lights draped across the mantle and electric candles clustered in the corners and up the staircase. He gently sat me on the corner of the kitchen island, my full skirt falling around my legs.

"This morning," he smiled shyly. "The contractor turned everything on when they finished up today."

Rory moved in closer to me, resting his hands on my waist as I reached for him. Brushing my fingers down the side of his cheek, he leaned into my touch, and his eyes slipped closed. "This is beautiful."

"I'm glad you like it. I know I said before I wished they were further along so I could bring you back to a proper home on our wedding night."

"This is still our home," I insisted. "I don't care if there aren't appliances or furniture. Those aren't what make this home to me."

"You're home to me, too. I didn't think I'd ever feel like this about someone. I was afraid we'd missed our chance for so long," he told me, his voice full of emotion.

"I'm sorry. If I would have known…" A single tear slipped out of my eye. I could have missed this.

"Hey." He placed his palms on my cheeks and looked into my eyes. "We made our way back to each other."

I nodded, and he leaned forward, kissing me softly. My hands fisted in the material of his vest as I kissed him back, spreading my legs wider so I could pull him closer to me. He laughed against my lips as he couldn't quite get close enough to press against me, the layers of tulle in my dress getting in the way.

"Take me to bed," I breathed in his ear as I kissed along the side of his face. My eyes widened as I looked at our mostly empty living room. "Wait. Do we have a bed?"

"Yes, we have a bed," he smiled.

"We do?" We'd picked one out, but all the deliveries were scheduled for weeks from now.

"Cam and my dad made sure the furniture store delivered it this morning." He looked so proud of himself, and I couldn't believe he'd pulled it off without me knowing.

"You're just full of all kinds of surprises."

"Gotta keep you interested," he smirked as he ducked his head a little. He was so thoughtful sometimes.

"I don't think you'll have a problem with that. I'm very, very interested." The muscles in his abdomen flexed through his shirt as I trailed my hand lower and released the button on his dress pants.

"Don't get too far ahead of yourself. We have to get you out of this dress first. I don't think I could find you through this mess," Rory laughed as he bunched up the layers of the dress and pretended to look under my skirt.

"Help me down."

"You want a ride?" he winked. Placing my hands on his shoulders, he lifted me off the island and helped me settle onto my feet.

"Not up the stairs," I shook my head. "Then we'd both end up with a concussion. Going to the ER for stitches isn't my idea of a romantic wedding night."

He grasped my hand, and I followed him closely up the staircase, my heels clicking on the subfloor since they hadn't installed the carpet on them yet. My eyes scanned the changes they'd made in the last few days. The builders had installed the wood floor in the hallways, the light fixtures, and the plastic was off the windows in the rooms they'd painted. It was looking like an actual home, and soon enough, the rooms would be filled with our possessions.

I'd thought he was crazy when he suggested building a house when we still hadn't finished our degrees, but it'd just made this whole adventure more real. We weren't just going through the motions. We were truly building a life together, both physically and metaphorically.

The battery-powered tea lights followed us from the living room downstairs to the master bedroom. When I'd been here a few days ago, the room had been painted but was still bare. Now, the wood floor gleamed in the lights, and someone had set up a large four-poster bed on the wall we'd decided it belonged.

"My mom picked up all the linens that were on the registry, but if you don't like how it looks, we can…"

Deciding I'd had enough waiting, I yanked on his hand and pulled Rory towards me, plunging my tongue into his mouth while I gripped his hair tightly.

"Please get this off me," I begged as his hands roamed my back, searching for the top of the zipper. My hands frantically pulled at the lace sleeves as I tried to free myself from them.

"You've been wearing this all day?" The growly quality of his voice made my heart beat faster as he helped me peel the dress down until it fell to the floor in a whoosh. Alison and I had picked out a strapless lace bustier for me to wear under the dress.

"Would you rather I have been naked?"

My laughter rang out as his large hands cupped the cleavage that pushed out the top, and he buried his face into my chest. "No, this is sexy as hell. But I would like you naked now."

His long fingers nimbly released the set of clasps that ran down the front, and he peeled the lace back, tossing the garment to the floor. Warm hands cupped the backs of my thighs, and he lifted me out of the fabric pooled around me, wrapping my legs around his waist as he took the few steps towards the bed.

"I feel like I'm at a disadvantage here," I laughed as I gripped his hair while he kissed along all the newly exposed skin.

My flesh pebbled as his stubble scraped along my abdomen. Leaning back on my elbows, I watched with rapt attention as he peeled the rest of the fabric covering both of us away, his pale skin glowing in the faux candlelight. It was still hard for me to believe sometimes that this tall, leanly muscled, eternally goofy man was my husband.

"I've been waiting for this all day." His voice was low and rough as he climbed onto the bed, backing me into the pillows as his warm skin covered mine. My body was vibrating with anticipation as he rocked his hips into mine, using his fingers to push the loose curls out of my face. "Today was like a dream. I know that's impossibly cheesy, but it was worth all the months, and months, and months of waiting to call you mine finally."

"I didn't keep you waiting that long."

He smiled as he kissed the corner of my mouth. "Years. Plural. I waited for years."

"Well, it's not my fault you're so spoiled for attention you can't make the first move," I teased.

"Not anymore," he shook his head with an amused smile. "You make me do the chasing, and you've tested my patience. But it's been worth it."

"Where would the fun be in making this easy?"

"Being with you is the easiest thing I've ever done," he told me quietly, the look in his eyes shifting from playful to tender. My hips squirmed against his restlessly. I loved that he was sweet, but I just wanted to feel him.

"I love you..." I sighed, and he leaned in to kiss me softly.

"I..."

"Shh..." Placing my finger over his lips, I wrapped my legs around the backs of his thighs. "I'm gonna need my husband to stop talking now and fuck me already."

"And you call me the bossy one," he chuckled as he tucked his face into my neck and lifted his hips slightly.

"Ohh." My cry was almost breathless as he guided himself into me, and I thrust my hips forward, pulling him in further. The only talking he was doing was whispering breathless oaths of devotion into my skin as he drove himself into me over and over. My back arched, and my thighs shook, yet still, he pushed me higher and higher until I snapped... shaking against him while my hoarse voice cried out into the room. "Yes."

I watched through glassy eyes as he rose to his knees, tilted my hips, and pressed his powerful hands into the backs of my thighs. Pleasure I didn't know was possible rocked through my body until I was keening, desperately grasping the sheets between my knuckles as he drove into me.

"Fuck, I'm close. God..." he moaned as he threw his head back and snapped his hips forward, holding me to him as he pulsed inside of me. My hand gently touched his stomach as he sat back, chest heaving, smiling down on me. "That enough of a performance for you?"

"I may need an encore," I smiled as I looked up at him.

"You're going to have to give me a bit. I'm an old man," he groaned as he pulled out and flopped onto his stomach, his face turned towards me on the pillow next to mine.

"Because twenty-four is ancient."

"I'm going to need a nap first. Maybe a snack..." he mused as I rolled my eyes at him.

"Wasn't I supposed to have you for dessert?" His voice was teasing as he flung his arm across my stomach and pretended to chew on my shoulder.

"You're so weird."

"But you love it," he smirked.

"I do."

"That was your line earlier today," he teased as he looked over at me with a contented smile.

"You think you're so clever."

"I am clever," he told me proudly.

"I just let you believe that. Wouldn't want to bruise that big ego of yours."

"Oh, I'll show you a big...*ego*," he growled as he pulled me into his chest and then rolled on top of me. Laughter rang out in the room around us as he tickled my sides, rubbing his stubble into my collarbone.

Despite his stating the contrary, it didn't take him long to recover. When he slipped inside me for a second time, it was everything I'd expected to experience on my wedding night. Rory used his body to show me things I knew neither of us could find the words to express. It was unhurried and passionate, soft caresses and breath-stealing kisses.

As we both eventually drifted off to sleep, his arms wrapped tightly around my waist, heart slowly thumping against my back, I knew that I'd finally found the love I'd always been waiting for.

# Epilogue:
## The Honeymoon
### PRESENT DAY

Faint sunlight streamed in the small gap where the curtains met, and I rolled over to try to escape from it.

"Are you awake this time, or am I going to get smacked for talking to you?"

My naked back arched against the soft sheets as I stretched. I had no idea what time it was, but Rory had been awake for a while.

As I rolled over to curl into his side, I saw the remnants of a cup of coffee on the nightstand next to him. "How long have you been awake?"

"Not long," he confessed. "I had some emails I needed to go through."

He laughed as I groaned and burrowed further into his side. His long fingers combed through my hair as he put his arm around me. "You promised you wouldn't work this week."

"You were asleep, and it's not like we have anything better to do today. It's been pouring since last night," he nodded toward the window where the sky was still an ominous shade of gray.

"We're on our honeymoon. I'm sure that we can come up with something to do..." My fingers trailed against the soft material of his cotton boxer briefs, the hard muscles in his thigh flexing as my hand lingered.

"Hmm, you might be right about that."

"Might be," I laughed as he placed his small laptop on the table and slipped back underneath the covers with me. "You know just how to make a girl feel sexy."

"You don't need me to point out how sexy you are. I know you're well aware of the effect you have on me." He grasped my hand and flattened it against him, flexing into my fingers and showing me exactly how much I affected him and certain parts of his anatomy.

"I'm not sure. You might need to show me."

"I think I can im-press upon you what my thoughts are on the matter," he joked with that cheesy grin of his.

"You're so corny sometimes," I rolled my eyes at him, but his grin only widened.

"But I'm horny all the time." He leaned in and nuzzled into my neck, biting and kissing as his hand dipped between my legs. I writhed against him as I tried to push his boxers down.

"Fuck," he groaned into my mouth as I grasped him loosely in my fist, pressing his hips into my movements. Rory's lips found mine, and he possessed my mouth, thrusting his tongue hotly as he leaned me back into the pillows.

Over the last few days, we'd been all over each other, but I truly couldn't—and didn't want to—keep my hands off him. Every time I saw that metal band on his finger, it just did things to me.

"Oh God..." I moaned as my neck craned back against the pillow. He was doing this thing with his teeth that drove me insane. After being together for over a year and a half, you'd think we'd have learned all each other's tricks, but it wasn't like that with us. Every time was exciting. Every time I lost myself in the feeling of his touch... his lips... his long fingers doing things to me I couldn't even put into words. "Ohh..."

The smile I could see him holding against my chest as he continued his onslaught of attention made me want to laugh. He loved the way I responded to him... and I loved the way he never stopped trying to explore new things.

As the hand between my legs pushed me over the edge in earnest, I cried out and convulsed on his fingers. "Oh, fuck."

My skin tingled as I lay there panting, simultaneously surprised and not that he could get me to the edge so quickly. Being in this romantic location with him, with no distractions, no commitments to balance, was amazing.

"Mmm, someone was wound up this morning. Didn't take you long to..." His wiggling eyebrows made my heart warm. I loved that he could go from playful to intensely sexy and back without even trying.

"I think it's time I returned the favor." Pushing him onto his back, I climbed on top of him and quickly guided him inside of me, rocking slowly.

"I am all about reciprocity, but I don't think we'll be even after this one." His thumb pressed against where we were joined, and I moaned as I leaned forward, bracing my hands on the pillow next to his head.

"Are you complaining?" I panted as I swiveled my hips against his.

"No. Oh, definitely not..." His voice was strained as I rocked, grinding into him once he was fully inside and making us both groan into each other's mouths.

"Fuck. I love you," I moaned as I slid along his length.

"Oh, God, yes. I love you, too..."

Using the bed for leverage, I forced myself onto him, my skin slapping against his with every backward movement.

"Just keep... going... God..." Sometimes he was talkative during sex; I hadn't had that before, but it was so hot how he vocalized his pleasure.

Words were forgotten as I sat up and bounced in his lap, one hand braced against the headboard and one hand gripping his thigh behind me. It didn't take long until I was collapsing against his chest, frantic heartbeats racing as we pulsed against each other.

"Mmm. I think I'm going to keep you," he hummed into my hair as one of his large hands spanned the width of my back. I pressed my cheek against his shoulder, my body spent.

"That's a relief," I huffed into his neck as my eyes closed.

"Hey, no sleeping," he teased as he pinched my ass.

I squirmed against him and yawned again, earning another pinch. "M'not."

"Liar... let's get up and take a shower. I'm hungry for more than jus..." A hand grabbed hold of my ass and gripped it firmly as his hips pushed up into me. I snorted into his skin, and he slowly rolled us until he was hovering over me. "I mean, I could have a few more servings of that today, but I need some protein to refuel."

I couldn't hold in my laughter at the way he said protein; making me think of other kinds of 'protein.' We were suited well with each other because we were both hopelessly perverted.

"Bacon... dirty girl. I need bacon. Probably shouldn't say sausage too because then you'll just start snickering like a twelve-year-old boy again." he scolded, but we both knew he wasn't serious.

"But I know how much you love sausage." He shook his head and stood up from the bed, walking to the bathroom completely nude as I giggled.

"Are you coming?" He paused at the threshold of the bathroom door and turned towards me, an amused smile on his face.

"Not yet," I smiled as I leaned up onto my elbow.

His eyes rolled visibly, but I could tell he found me amusing. "Then get in here, and we can do something about that."

An hour later, we were strolling down a covered walkway, listening to the sounds of the wildlife in the trees. The rain had finally stopped, but the leaves in the trees were still dripping.

"Maybe we'll get to go to the beach today after all," I mused as I saw the sun peeking through the clouds.

"It's going to be hot. The humidity is already coming back," Rory nodded as his hand tightened on mine.

"Well, we are on a tropical island, so it's going to be humid wherever we go."

"Oh, I'm not complaining. I'm quite enjoying the suitcase full of bikinis you packed. Which one will it be today?" he mused as he shot me a playful smirk. "The purple floral one... no... maybe the navy blue one."

"You're enjoying those, huh?" I smiled as I laid my head against his arm. When I'd first met him, I'd judged the book by the cover. He was good-looking and athletic, and he had girls like Gretchen crawling all over him.

Back then, I'd thought he was this cocky jerk who preened himself in the mirror. As we got closer, it'd been a shock that while he was a cocky jerk, he was also thoughtful and considerate. He loved to shower me with affection and be goofy sometimes. His humor and open playfulness drew me in more than the chiseled jaw or the sculpted chest. Don't get me wrong; those were nice additions to the package, but who he was as a person was what I fell in love with. And I'd fallen hard.

"It's too bad the university has a dress code. Although, I'm not sure I'd want your students to see you like that. Nope. It's turtlenecks and long skirts for you. Don't need any horny coeds ogling my wife."

"I'll save the bikinis for vacations then," I assured him. I loved his reaction to them.

"Hmm. You planning on me taking you on all sorts of vacations?"

"I thought that was part of the package," I fluttered my eyelashes at him and tried to look innocent.

"What happens when we have kids? You going to be that hot mom making all the other dads drool on the beach?" he teased.

"Yeah, because I don't already have problems with you turning all the thirsty wives' heads in your direction when you take off your shirt," I replied with an eye roll as I pinched his side. He'd gotten quite a few looks so far this week, but I secretly loved it because I was the one he took back to his bed.

"I don't know what you're talking about," he smiled innocently.

We'd gone on a catamaran boat trip to go snorkeling on our second day here. The highlight of Rory's trip had been when an older woman had grabbed his ass on the boat. Her husband hadn't even been mad, laughing hysterically at his drunk wife's antics while I tried to defend Rory's honor by hiding him out of reach. She was frisky for an elderly lady, ogling the deckhands while downing rum punches.

"Yeah, let's just hope we don't see that lady again." He was my man, and no sugar mama was going to tempt him away.

"Is someone jealous?"

I reached down and grabbed a fistful of the back of his pants, squeezing as he tried to jump away from me, laughing. "No, but if anyone gets free gropes of this, it's me. Old lady can find her own hunk."

Rory reached across me and playfully cupped my chest. "As long as I get to return the favor."

Laughing, he leaned down to kiss me, tenderly nipping at my lips as his hand cupped my cheek.

"There's no one I'd rather get random spankings and boob grabs from," I laughed against his lips.

"Well, I'd hope so," he teased. "And same. I don't get spanked nearly enough."

This was what I loved about his personality; he always made me smile. "I'll see if I can work on that."

The sun was coming from behind the clouds as we finally sat down next to the windows that overlooked part of the beach. Sunlight sparkled on the crystal-clear waters, and I knew I never wanted to leave. The last few days had been like a dream. No responsibilities. No relatives or friends were hounding us for things. Just us, a beach, amazing restaurants, a giant king-sized bed, and amazing sex—lots and lots of amazing sex.

"You're doing it again," he teased as he raised an eyebrow in my direction.

"Hmm?" I turned toward him as I pulled the spoon that I'd been using to eat my yogurt from my mouth.

"You're molesting the cutlery again."

"I am not." The blush was already rising in my cheeks as he stared across the table at me with an eyebrow raised.

"What are you thinking about?" he asked in a whisper as he reached across the table and took my hand in his, running his fingers along my palm.

"Well, that's not helping." Shifting in my seat, I watched as his smile widened. The cocky jerk knew exactly what I was thinking about.

"If I had known about this side of you, I would have hip-checked Tyler out of the way during orientation," he laughed as he continued to caress my hand softly.

"You were too busy with Gretchen trying to climb you like a tree."

"God, we were idiots," he laughed as he shook his head.

"We eventually figured it out," I shrugged as I pulled my hand back and took another bite of my yogurt, and slowly licked the spoon.

"Do you think about it? What might have happened if life didn't get in the way?"

I nodded and glanced out the window. This subject always made me a little melancholy. "I used to. All the time. When we were in that weird place after Joel left."

"I wish I had told you in that coffee shop how I felt about you then." I thought about that, too, what I might have done if he had pursued me instead of stepping back.

"But I don't know what good it would have done. I was already dating him. Things didn't change until after we got engaged. I was happy," I confessed. Rory pushing the issue back then may have ruined our friendship. I'd never have wanted to risk that.

"I know you were. That's why I gave you the out. I didn't know that the medical stuff with him had gotten that bad. He never talked to me about it."

"He barely wanted to talk to me about it," I smiled sadly.

"I know we agreed not to open that email, but I still worry about him sometimes. It killed me when he left," he whispered, looking down at the tablecloth. "You were this broken, vulnerable mess, my best friend..."

He squeezed my hand...

"I know what you mean," I nodded. Joel was an important part of both our lives.

"My... he left. Part of me wanted to murder him, and you know I still feel that way sometimes. But the other part just wanted to help him."

"Do you...?" I trailed off as I studied his face.

"Do I what?" he asked, a small crease forming between his eyebrows.

"Do you think we should read it?"

"We're solid, right?" He still had these moments of insecurity, and I hated that the demons of his past caused them.

"Yes, we're solid. Nothing he could say to me would ever change my feelings about you and this life we've built together," I assured him sincerely. "That's part of why I never opened it. That part of my life is over."

"Do you want to do it now? Or wait until we get home?" His knee tapped against mine underneath the table. I could tell talking about this was making him anxious. I didn't want this to be the elephant in the room because we never dealt with it. "Should we just delete it and be done with it?"

"Let's go for a walk on the beach, and then we can go back and check my email on your laptop before lunch."

We finished our food and left the restaurant, heading out along the beachfront toward our building. Rory held our sandals by the straps in one hand while he gripped one of mine tightly in his other.

"You know that nothing in that email will change things, right?" I asked as I looked up at the side of his face. He sighed as his steps halted, and he turned towards me. I cupped his cheek in my hand and hated that he looked unsure of himself. "I love you, and I married you. Nothing from our pasts can shake that."

His large hand covered mine, and he leaned into my touch, staring down at me. "I know, it's just... I felt like I lost you to him once. The thought of that happening again freaks me out."

Pulling my hand from inside of his, I turned it around and held my rings up in his face. "These mean something to me. I'm not giving them up without a fight. You're my future, and I won't let him diminish what we have by planting doubt in your head."

"Baby, I don't doubt you. I guess I still have a hard time remembering how you two were together. It's different than we are."

"Of course, it's different," I murmured as I pushed up onto my toes to kiss him softly. "You're my partner. I don't feel like I have to keep things from you, and I know you don't keep things from me. You're the first man I've trusted to put my needs above your own. I don't take that lightly."

"I love you." He cupped my cheeks and kissed me as the water lapped at my heels. I could never and would never take him for granted. I knew what it was like to have your opinion discarded in a relationship.

"I love you, too. No doubts, okay?" He nodded as I stared into his eyes. "Because I have absolutely no doubts about you."

Rory reached down to pick up our shoes, and we continued the rest of our walk in a less tense silence. Facing down the ghosts of your past was scary, but with him by my side, the contents of that email were irrelevant.

"Well, shit…"

We'd avoided the elephant in the laptop after we'd walked the rest of the way back to our room.

Rory had been frantically pulling off my sundress the moment we walked in the door. I don't know if that's what he needed to convince himself that I was his, but I wasn't arguing as he pushed me onto the bed and fucked any doubts out of his mind while pinning my hands above my head.

"What? What's wrong? Is the internet being weird again?"

He was propped up against the padded headboard, bare chest on display, a faint pink blush staining his pecs the only remnants of our tryst. He'd pulled his boxers back on and grabbed the laptop when I'd gone to get myself cleaned up in the bathroom.

"No…" He patted the space next to him on the bed. "He sent me one, too."

"Joel sent you an email?" I frowned. We went almost two years with nothing, and suddenly he was reaching out to both of us.

"Yeah… just… here. Read this." I tried to gauge his expression but couldn't get a read on him. I pulled my cotton sundress over my head and crawled up next to him. He placed the laptop on my legs, and I scrolled back to the top of the message, starting from the beginning.

> *Rory -*
>
> *I know that I'm probably the last person you want to hear from, but I felt like I needed to apologize to you as well. I don't know if Kendall read the email I sent her, but I was just as horrible to you.*
>
> *Let me start by telling you I'm sorry. I didn't trust you as a friend enough to let you in when I struggled. You knew I had some health problems, but I never told you what was going on because I didn't want you to judge me. You've always been the life of the party, and I felt like I never measured up to you growing up.*
>
> *You were taller, more athletic, never had trouble talking to anyone, and I was the quieter, smaller sidekick who tried to step out of your shadow. I never resented you as much as I wanted to, but I also couldn't bring myself to trust you fully. You didn't deserve that. You were my friend, and I should have told you what was happening. I thought that when I left, you'd be better off without me, too.*
>
> *I'll admit. When I heard about your wedding, I was angry. But then I thought about it; it made sense, the two of you. You two always had an ease in*

*your friendship that complimented each other. While I know I can never make
up for what I did to both of you, I wanted to give you and myself some closure.*

*I've been in counseling for the last few years, and I have come to terms with
my illness and what it means for my future. While she didn't agree with me
at the time, I know you can give Kendall the future that she deserves. I trust
you to take care of her and be the man I couldn't be.*

*Congratulations and take care, man.*

*Joel*

Softly pushing the lid on the laptop closed, I wiped an errant tear and leaned my head against Rory's shoulder. He slipped his hand inside of mine and interlocked our fingers, turning to kiss the top of my head.

"Does it make me a horrible person if I still want to be mad at him?" he whispered, his hand squeezing mine.

"No. I do, too. But I'm a little heartbroken for him as well."

"He sounds...okay." Rory's voice was a little unsure.

"He does," I agreed. "I don't know what I was expecting, but not that."

"Do you want to read yours?"

I did, just purely to satisfy my curiosity. "Is that okay?"

"Now that I know he's not trying to steal back my wife," He laughed as he pulled up the screen again and nodded to me. "Go ahead. Might as well see it."

Closing out his email client, I pulled up Chrome and logged in to my Gmail, scrolling past all the messages that'd piled up since before the wedding and stopped next to the one with the subject line 'Please Read Me.' My finger hovered over the laptop button, and I looked up at Rory before I pressed it.

"Just open it. I can remind you who you belong to after if you're that worried about it," he teased.

"Belong to, huh?"

"Hey, you claimed ownership of my ass earlier." He leaned forward and kissed me softly, using one of his fingers to press mine down, opening the email. "The sooner you read it, the sooner we can put this part of our lives in the past, where it belongs."

My eyes scanned the first few lines, it was like Rory's email, but when I got to the third paragraph, I knew he put effort into writing this for me.

*I know I deserve nothing from you, but please don't let my mistakes keep you
from living a happy life. I was young, and I had to let go of something I cared
a great deal about. Holding you back from the future you wanted would have*

*crushed both of us. Enough time has passed that I can see clearly that we would never have worked out long term. I know we loved each other, but optimism only gets you so far in life. Not every love story is meant to have a happy ending.*

*You showed me it was okay to open myself up to people, be vulnerable, and lean on them for support. I desperately wanted you to be the person I married, but I wasn't ready. Rory will love you like you deserve to be loved. He will be the partner that I failed to be. Please don't hold my mistakes against him. He's a good guy under that cocky exterior.*

Rory laughed, and I smiled up at him.

*Please don't carry my ghost on your wedding day. I know that makes me sound like an arrogant ass, but I know I hurt you. Go into this new part of your life with peace and an open heart. All I ever wanted was for you to be happy.*
*Joel*

It felt like a weight had finally been lifted. It seemed like Joel had gotten to a better place in his life between both emails. While both of us had dealt with our feelings for Joel a long time ago, this helped put away the subject for good.

"That was a little anticlimactic," Rory laughed as he pulled the laptop from my legs.

"Expecting some long, drawn-out dramatic thing?" I honestly wasn't sure what to expect when it'd shown up almost a week ago. It was easier just to ignore it at the time.

"No, but I was expecting to have to defend my woman."

"You're such a caveman," I rolled my eyes.

"I still don't know why he tried calling you. The email was enough," he frowned.

"Who knows, but now we can both let him go." Pushing up to my knees, I straddled his lap and laid my head on his chest. "You okay?"

"Yeah. I'm good." I felt him nod against the side of my head. "You?"

"Mmhmm," I hummed. "Am I still number two?"

He squeezed me tightly to him and tucked his face next to mine.

"Feeling needy, are we?" He laughed as he kissed my cheek.

"Just checking."

"You knocked Cam out of the running the first time you climbed into my lap." I laughed into the side of his neck as I held him close to me. "What about Allie?"

"Well, she doesn't normally climb into my lap since that's the criteria, but I'm sure she could... mmm..." I hummed as he held the sides of my head and kissed me thoroughly, plunging his tongue into my mouth and effectively shutting me up.

"She doesn't kiss like you do, either." My voice was breathless as he pulled back and released me.

"You two have kissed?" His eyebrows were up in his hairline.

"Well, there was this one time..." I smacked him on the shoulder as I saw his pupils dilate. "No, you perv. Of course, you're my new BFF. You locked this shit down. Your balls are chained."

"Sounds kinky," he laughed as he pushed me backward onto the bed and climbed on top of me.

We spent the rest of our honeymoon enjoying the sun, sand, sex, and endless snacks. At the end of the week, I wasn't ready to head back to reality, but I knew I'd be okay with Rory there by my side to keep me sane.

"Has my sister started bombarding you with texts yet?" he asked, his hands gripping the steering wheel.

"No. Why? Is she supposed to?" After we landed, I checked my phone while Rory got our bags into the car. We still had an hour's drive home from the airport.

"About that..." he trailed off guiltily, and my head swiveled towards him.

"What did you do?"

"Um, you know how she was supposed to go to Cabo with Porter for their anniversary?"

I nodded. "Yeah, your parents were going to take Nat for the week."

"About that..." he cringed as his eyes stared straight ahead on the road.

"Would you quit saying that, you dork?" I smacked him on the arm, and he shot me a smirk, shaking his head at me. "What did you do?"

"Dad planned a trip with mom and didn't tell her. He booked the cabin for the same week that they're gone."

"So, they're taking Nat with them?"

The cringe on his face spoke volumes. "Porter said he'd buy the bed in the guest bedroom for us as a housewarming present if we do this."

"You're lucky I love you," I laughed as I reached across the console and patted the top of his hand.

"Oh, thank God," he breathed out as he grasped my hand with his.

"You know I love Nat," I assured him. She was my niece now, too.

"I'm sure it'll be fine. How much damage can one three-year-old do?"

It turned out that one three-year-old was exhausting. Both physically and mentally. Nat showed up at our barely finished house like a tiny tornado and showed us that while we were at a good place in our relationship, we were okay waiting a few more years for kids.

"I was wrong. So... so... wrong." Rory flopped back onto the bed after we'd finally wrangled the cranky toddler into bed. Nathalie was one of those kids who acted like a little angel for approximately thirty minutes after dinner. If you didn't get her through her bedtime routine in that amount of time, you were screwed. "How can someone that small be so strong?"

Tonight's episode of 'Naughty Nat loses her shit' featured running around the house at top speeds, completely naked with a cup full of bathwater. We'd both gotten soaked by the little crazy person after we'd finally cornered her in the laundry room, and I snuck up on her with a towel.

"I'm kind of impressed your sister hasn't lost her mind yet," I laughed as I looked over at him.

"Pretty sure she self-medicates with wine and trashy romance novels," he smirked as he turned toward me.

"Well, I know why they haven't tried for a second one yet."

"Porter said they were in negotiations," he confessed as he shook his head.

I laughed as I climbed onto our bed and snuggled into his chest. "You know, Nat's kinda how we got together."

"She's not the only reason," he sighed.

"Hmm. Valentine's peanut butter bandit will always have a fondness in my heart," I confessed. That night, I finally let him know how I was feeling. Despite the few hiccups we'd had after that, I never regretted that decision.

"That was a good night. I was just happy she didn't scare you off."

"Were you ever going to make a move?" I asked curiously.

"I'd been contemplating it," he told me quietly as he hugged me tightly.

"Why didn't you?" I had never asked why he hadn't pursued me.

"I was afraid that my feelings were one-sided. That I'd built you up in my head, and we might've been better off as friends."

"I kept waiting for you to tell me you'd met someone," I confessed. I thought about it a lot in those awkward months where we were friends, but I felt so much more.

He turned and looked down into my eyes, running his fingers through my hair. "After he left, I knew I didn't want anyone else."

"What if I would have met someone while you were sitting around, not telling me things?"

"I would have scared him off," he told me in that cocky voice he used when he felt uncertain. I'd learned that it was one of his coping mechanisms.

"I didn't want anyone else, either," I told him sincerely as I continued to look up at him. A part of me had fallen for him before I was ready for it to happen, but I'd never regret my feelings for him.

Despite our exhaustion from wrangling Nat, it didn't take either of us very long to disrobe the other. We fell into the soft sheets—chest to chest, mouth to mouth, heart to heart—and I knew without a doubt that I had met the right man at the altar.

## THE END

# Also By
## E.L. KOSLO

### THE DIRTY WORDS SERIES

### Foreplay on Words (Amazon)

Book One of The Dirty Words Series
Evan and Chase
Preview of Foreplay on Words: https://BookHip.com/WCJHJGA

### Mark my Words (Amazon)

Book Two of The Dirty Words Series
Sam and Kristine
Preview of Mark my Words: https://BookHip.com/QHWGXTZ

### Bound by Words (Amazon)

Book Three of The Dirty Words Series
Nathan and Kelly
Preview of Bound by Words: https://BookHip.com/NRRHRBN

.
.
.

# More Than Words (Amazon)

Book Four of The Dirty Words Series
Adrian and Isobel
Preview of More Than Words: https://BookHip.com/TARMSTL

.

.

.

## MASKED MEN OF SAGE SPRINGS

# Accidental Abduction (Amazon)

Book One in the Masked Men of Sage Springs Series
Hudson and Charley
Preview of Accidental Abduction: https://bookhip.com/CDPWXAB
Coming to audio soon!

# Illicit Illustration (Amazon)

Book Two in the Masked Men of Sage Springs Series
Reid and Hazel
Preview of Illicit Illustration: https://bookhip.com/CDPWXAB

# Smokin' Situation (Amazon)

Book Three in the Masked Men of Sage Springs Series
Annie and Tristan
Preview of Smokin' Situation: https://bookhip.com/FCDAKTZ

.

.

.

## Standalones

## The Midnight Voyeur (Amazon)

Now available in Duet audio featuring Branden Davis-Butler, Cole Eubanks and
Troy Duran: https://books2read.com/themidnightvoyeur
(Wide at all audio retailers)
Spicy, taboo, reverse age-gap, stand-alone – Ginny
Preview The Midnight Voyeur: https://BookHip.com/SZXGKKQ

## The Mystery Correspondent (Amazon)

Steamy Christmas novella, stand-alone – Ryder and Stella
Preview of The Mystery Correspondent: https://BookHip.com/XPBVAMB

## Meet Him at the Altar

New Adult coming of age, written like a romcom/mystery
Kendall & The Groom
Preview of Meet Him at the Altar available on ELKoslo.com

# Social Media

**Website:** ELKoslo.com

**Instagram:** @elkoslo_writes
**Threads:** @elkoslo_writes
**TikTok:** @elkoslowrites & @elkosloauthor

**Facebook:** E.L. Koslo
**Page:** EL Koslo Romance Writer
**Private Reader Group:** E.L. Koslo's Dirty Words Brigade

**Pinterest:** @elkoslo

**X:** @ELKoslo
**BlueSky:** https://bsky.app/profile/elkoslowrites.bsky.social

**Amazon:** amazon.com/author/e.l.koslo

**Linktree:** linktr.ee.Elkoslo

**Newsletter:** https://elkoslo.beehiiv.com/

# Acknowledgments

This book definitely holds a special place in my heart. While there are parts of myself in Kendall, and some of the men in this book were inspired by ones I've long put behind me, the storyline took on a life of its own and I'm so proud of how it turned out. Love is messy. LIFE is messy. But above all, finding a way to stay true to yourself is the most important lesson you can hold onto. Circumstances beyond your control may make your life veer off onto a different path than you expected, but sometimes the journey through the hard parts can define and shape the best parts of yourself.

Thank you so much to my readers, you are the reason I am still here over ten books later and still telling stories. Thank you to my team of alpha readers, you keep me sane and motivated in ways you don't even know. ARC readers, you are the best hype team a girl could ask for, and you make me cry on a regular basis with your love (or in some cases extreme dislike) of my characters.

Thank you to Nicole from Naughty Nook PR. I love navigating the chaos of the book world with you and your endless support.

And I can't even express the gratitude I have for my husband, who may have been a large inspiration for our groom. Thank you for making me believe in love again after heartbreak. The last two decades have been far from easy, but I wouldn't trade our life for anything.

Until next time,

E.L. Koslo

# About

## E.L. KOSLO

**FIND THE FUNNY IN YOUR LIFE.**

E.L. writes spicy romantic comedies with a variety of cinnamon roll heroes and strong heroines. She grew up in the midwest US, married her college sweetheart, now lives in one of those flyover states with her four spirited children and emotional support/writing companion Bernedoodle, Quinn. Banter and second-hand embarrassment are her jam, so be prepared to laugh with or at her characters.

Her novels combine her love of steamy romance, awkward but loveable leading males, and headstrong heroines with a dash of humor and a little bit of kink.